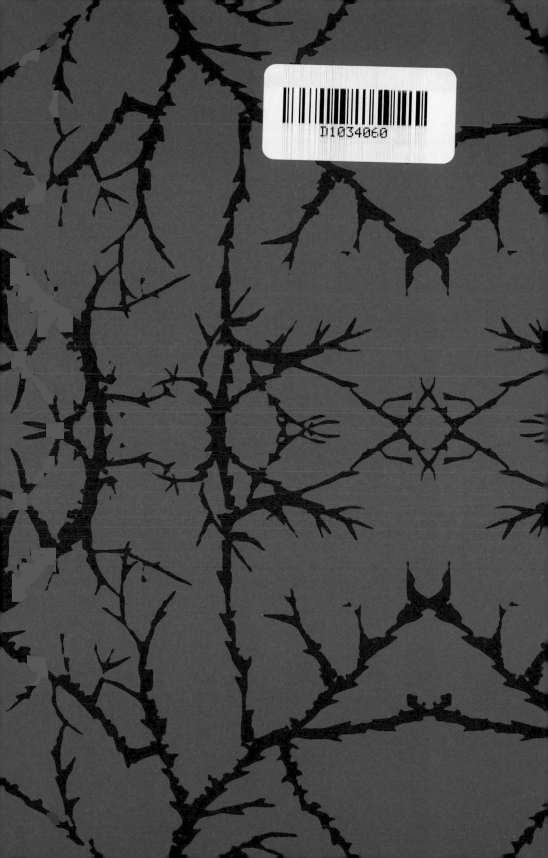

GONE TO THE WOLVES

FARRAR, STRAUS AND GIROUX

NEW YORK

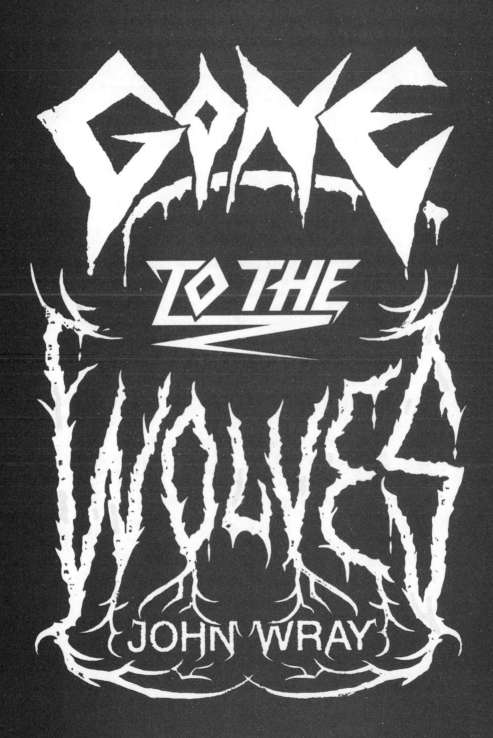

GONE TO THE WOLVES

JOHN WRAY

Farrar, Straus and Giroux
120 Broadway, New York 10271

Endpaper design and hand lettering on title page and part title pages
by Thomas Colligan.

Library of Congress Cataloging-in-Publication Data
Names: Wray, John, 1971– author.
Title: Gone to the wolves / John Wray.
Description: First edition. | New York : Farrar, Straus and Giroux, 2023.
Identifiers: LCCN 2022055063 | ISBN 9780374603335 (hardcover)
Subjects: LCGFT: Novels.
Classification: LCC PS3573.R365 G66 2023 | DDC 813/.54—dc23/
    eng/20221114
LC record available at https://lccn.loc.gov/2022055063

Designed by Gretchen Achilles

Our books may be purchased in bulk for promotional,
educational, or business use. Please contact your local bookseller
or the Macmillan Corporate and Premium Sales Department
at 1-800-221-7945, extension 5442, or by email at
MacmillanSpecialMarkets@macmillan.com.

www.fsgbooks.com
www.twitter.com/fsgbooks • www.facebook.com/fsgbooks

1 3 5 7 9 10 8 6 4 2

For JDC

In life, things never happen like they should. In rock, things always happen like they should. That's why it's fascist.

—LESTER BANGS

BERLIN 1991

She was gone before Cannibal Corpse took the stage. The faithful had mustered in full force that night, hundreds of German headbangers sardine-canned into a Kreuzberg club that would have been claustrophobic at eighty—but Kip knew Kira was leaving, doing just as she'd promised, taking advantage of the crush and confusion to make her escape. He felt it as an itching in his brain.

He had his back to the stage when the first roar went up, searching that sea of open mouths for anything out of place, any contrary current, someone small but determined pushing out through the crowd. Already the itching had given way to dumb animal fear. Kira had stood pressed against him for hours, resting her head on his shoulder, sometimes even taking his hand in both of hers—and now she was nowhere. He needed to find her. He stood groping for handholds in the smoke-heavy air, desperate to lever himself upward, to levitate for a fraction of a second above the beer-slick floor. He was stoned but just barely. A voice said something to him in German, politely but firmly, and he told it in German to go fuck itself.

The houselights went dim and the roar seemed to thicken, going heavy and anxious, the way it always did before the first riff dropped. Kip caught sight of something—a silver-blond head between two hulking bouncers, one of whom looked to be wearing a genuine spiked helmet from World War I. The air started strobing, fluttering against his eardrums, like it does in a car with the back windows cracked. This was Kira's favorite moment: before the first riff, when every possible outcome is conceivable, when the show that you've imagined is the only show there is.

Something drifted across his field of vision: a Viking face, flat-nosed and bearded, its grinning teeth already slick with blood. By that point he could barely draw a breath. The crush was the law now. The German voice came again, less politely this time. He paid no attention. Someone punched him in the stomach and the room went bright and still.

Kira beside him, rapt with listening, craning her scrawny body up to see the stage. Kira six days earlier, in her first-ever snowfall, biting her lip to keep from looking happy. Kira the year before, asleep on a bus seat, her hair dyed some shade of greenish blue he didn't have a name for, her small skull warm and certain in his lap. Kira smoking a cigarette that someone had thrown out of a limo on West Sunset. Kira smoking a menthol. Kira smoking a philly. Kira the night they'd gotten busted at the hot springs, floating facedown in the steaming dark, pretending to be dead.

When he came back to life the Corpse was in full glory. The Corpse of his youth, of his Florida childhood, shrieking and hammering, calling down air strikes, giving that dog-faced crowd the only thing it wanted. He'd forgotten how beautiful the transaction was: how uninhibited, how generous, how pure. He would never have fought the undertow on any other night, never have been such an idiot as to try to resist—but he had to see Kira make her great escape. He needed to see her go with his own eyes.

He summoned his last reserves of strength and willed his body upward. He saw a fire door pushed open, a pale-haired silhouette, the yellow of a traffic light, the purple of the street. It was snowing again. She wasn't alone: at least two men were with her, maybe three.

That was all Kip saw. He sank back into the current like a fishing weight with his arms against his sides. Every other head in that basement was facing the opposite way. The urge to surrender was even more massive than the riffs behind him—and suddenly he did surrender. He'd seen more than enough. She was leaving him, leaving everything she'd been, stepping with a group of strangers out into the snow. Something inside him shifted, painfully but inevitably, as if his organs were returning to their natural positions. He shut his eyes and clenched his teeth and let relief run through him. He didn't hate her, not now. In some sense he was grateful. She'd made a clean break. Kira always knew what she was doing.

A year would pass before he learned that she'd been taken.

I

1

Leslie Z had three strikes against him already: he was Black, he was bi, and he liked Hanoi Rocks.

That third strike especially was borderline suicidal on the Gulf Coast of Florida in the late 1980s, where even teasing your hair up was enough to get you stomped into applesauce by the bikers, or the skinheads, or some zit-faced banger in a Carnivore shirt. Having sex with boys, or wanting to, was a minor misdemeanor in comparison. Glam was out, death was in. But Kip Norvald had no idea about these mortal ruptures in the metal scene when he first met Leslie Z. He barely even knew what metal was.

Their paths crossed on the day the Furberold kid, Lindsey Grace, was officially listed as missing, which was also Kip's first day at Venice High. Leslie was sitting at the back of the class, his spindly legs stretching into the next row, carving something into his desktop with a bullet from his belt. The homeroom teacher—whose name, GLADYS KRUPS, took up most of the blackboard—was introducing Kip to the class in an opiated mumble, mispronouncing his name, and he could feel himself starting to panic. What he wanted more than anything, that particular fall, was to be introduced to no one. He could barely meet his own eyes in the mirror. Now he sensed an out-of-body experience coming on, and his eyes went automatically to the classroom's farthest nook: there they encountered Leslie Z, messing around with what Kip somehow knew, in his gut, was an actual bullet. Any farther from Gladys Krups and he'd have been in the next room.

Leslie looked creepy, unsavory, accustomed to violence—which was probably his secret to survival, because he also looked ridiculous. He was too tall for his desk and way too skinny for his clothes. His studded black leather jacket might have looked cool on someone else, but Leslie wore it draped over his shoulders like a cape. His T-shirt said MY OTHER T SHIRT IS THE SKIN OF MY DEFENSELESS VICTIM. His jeans were cut to ribbons just below the knee, where they disappeared into a battered pair of yellow rubber boots. Kip's grandmother had boots like that: she used them for gardening. It cost him considerable mental effort to make sense of them on a six-foot-plus ectomorph in eyeliner and a tasseled paisley scarf. By any reasonable standard—by any *Florida* standard— Leslie Z should not have been alive. The sight of him made Kip momentarily forget who he was, and where he was, and the sequence of simple but nightmarish events that had gotten him there. For a count of ten he didn't want to die.

Leslie Z had no clue about any of this, of course, and Kip would have eaten glass before he told him. He was a quarter of the way through his senior year when he washed up on the Central Gulf Coast, three weeks shy of seventeen, and he already had a long list of things that he hoped never to have to talk or even think about again. His goal for the year was to keep his mouth shut. His new classmates were dead ringers for kids who'd beaten him up in seven municipalities and counting: fidgety and slow-brained, corn-fed and sullen, impatient for the next bad thing to happen. Venice was a way station, a holding facility. His own survival strategy was simple—to render himself invisible until the second week of June.

It took ten days for Kip's master plan to tank. He was tooling around his grandmother's gated community two Saturdays later, on a banana-seat Schwinn he'd found in her garage, when the gods of fate saw fit to intervene.

It happened in seconds: he took a corner a little too hard, got a case of the wobbles, managed not to wipe out, then practically ran over Leslie Z. A man in a Confederate cap had him backed up against a Coke machine behind the public restrooms. The man cursed under his breath; Leslie stammered out *hey* in the voice of a five-year-old girl. Alarms went off in Kip's bewildered brain. He braced his right foot lightly on the curb.

"Leslie, right?"

The least possible nod. "Leslie Z."

"I sit next to you in homeroom. Not next to you, really. More like off to the side."

"Fuck off, fag," said the redneck.

"I'm Kip Norvald."

"I stand corrected," said the redneck. "Fuck off, Kip."

"I know who you are," mumbled Leslie.

"Cool," Kip heard himself answer. "What's going on here, if you don't mind my asking?"

Slowly, mechanically, the redneck's head revolved to face him.

"We *do* mind you asking."

The redneck said this in a thoughtful tone, as though Kip's question had a certain merit. He had a red neck in the most literal sense, sun-blistered and tatted, and a ruby stud in one of his front teeth.

Kip got off the Schwinn. Things were taking a distinctly dreamlike turn. Mrs. Rathmore, one of his grandmother's neighbors, glided by on her scooter and wished him a good morning. It was already late afternoon.

"I'm going to have to ask you to stop what you're doing," Kip said to the redneck.

"Is that right."

"That's right. Or I call the police."

"With what?" said the man. "Has your bike got a phone?"

Leslie let out a breath. "Maybe we could all just kind of—"

Kip was still trying to figure out what to say when he punched past the redneck, barely missing his face, and slammed his fist into the Coke machine. Its front wasn't glass but it shattered like glass. Cold air snaked up his arm. His vision had gone blank—white with flickering geometric patterns, like the screen of a busted TV—the way it always did when he had one of his *episodes*. Things went silent and white, then dim, then inky black, then back to normal. All in less than a second. He felt no pain at all.

"Shit on this," said the redneck. "I'm gone."

He pushed away from Leslie, made a lazy lunge at Kip, then crossed the little parking lot and ducked into the bushes. There was a cutoff in there—a narrow dirt track, always slightly muddy, that Kip had thought he was the only one to know about. He was shaking now, which usually happened afterward, and beginning to feel things again. Mostly what he felt was fear. He pictured the redneck coming back from somewhere with a gun.

"Wow," said Leslie.

"I guess."

"Kind of fucked up, aren't you, son. Or maybe you're just stupid."

"You're welcome," Kip said, pulling his bike up off the pavement.

"Your hand is bleeding."

"Yeah," Kip said, willing himself to stop shaking. "That happens sometimes."

"Excuse me?"

Kip didn't answer. It was too much to explain. Leslie sat down on the curb and closed his eyes.

"How about you, man? You okay down there?"

Leslie passed a hand gingerly over his face. There were tiny purple crosses on his fingernails. "You want the truth, Norvald? I've had better days."

"I believe it."

"He *believes* it," said Leslie.

"What was that all about?"

"That was Harley Boy Ray. He was selling me weed."

"Oh," said Kip.

"Now he gets it. Now he starts to understand."

"I don't actually," said Kip. He'd bought marijuana himself—half a dozen times, maybe—and it had never involved being assaulted behind a public restroom by a man with a rhinestone in his teeth. But he asked no more questions, not then, because the icy wave of shame that had dogged him every waking moment since he could remember, waiting for him to make the slightest miscalculation, the least social misstep, had already come thundering down.

"Shit. Sorry about that. It's just—it kind of looked as if—"

"Ray does beat me up sometimes, if you want to know the truth." Leslie looked past him now, across the parking lot. "It's situational."

Kip had no idea how to reply. A breeze stirred the treetops. Mrs. Rathmore scootered by again.

"Norvald," Leslie said, apparently to himself. "Kip Norvald."

"That's me."

"What kind of name is that?"

"Nothing." He reminded himself to breathe. "It's a nickname."

Leslie nodded for a while, squinting down at his shoes, as though Kip had told him something unexpected. Kip expected him to ask what his given name was but he did no such thing. He just sat on the curb. Kip pretended to inspect the back tire of his Schwinn.

"Got a smoke, Norvald?"

"What?" The wave hit him again. "No, man. I wish."

"I wouldn't mind taking a spin on that bike you've got there."

Kip couldn't tell whether Leslie was being sarcastic or not—a problem he'd soon be having with him on an hourly basis. "Seriously? On this piece of crap?"

"That's the one."

"Be my guest."

He found the Schwinn an hour later, lying on its side in the carport of a mud-colored bungalow on Madrugada Drive. Leslie himself was standing in the bungalow's picture window, wearing some kind of housecoat, staring thoughtfully out at the burnt-looking lawn. He opened the front door just as Kip was reaching for the bell.

"Hey there, Norvald."

"What the fuck, Leslie?"

"Z," said Leslie, stifling a yawn.

"I don't even—"

"What the fuck, Leslie Z."

He yawned again and shuffled back inside. Kip lingered on the threshold, an old habit, trying to get a read on what kind of domestic situation he was about to step into. The house smelled like pot smoke and marinara sauce and cloves—and also, in some way he couldn't put his finger on, like the past. It was musty and dark. He felt a sudden urge, standing there with the sun on his back, to turn around and grab his bike and go. That forgotten-seeming bungalow, with its motionless air and mottled carpeting and peeling paisley wallpaper, was quite possibly the most melancholy place that he had ever been.

He found Leslie in the bungalow's tiki-themed kitchen, making himself a peanut-butter-and-banana sandwich. No one else was home, apparently. Leslie offered him a can of Dr. Pepper in an absentminded way, as if his being there were the most natural thing in the world. Years later, once Kip knew Leslie Aaron Vogler the way you can only know someone you've seen die and come back to life on the floor of your bathroom, he would realize that stealing the bike had just been Leslie's way of inviting him over. He was as solitary as Kip was, maybe even as lonely, and he wanted someone to bear witness to the high point of his day: the hour and a half—never more, never less—when he played records on his parents' stereo.

The system was a mid-seventies Marantz 1060, hands down the most beautiful object in the house, with one pair of speakers behind the magenta-and-turquoise sectional in the sunken den and a second down the hall in Leslie's bedroom. This meant that he had to cross the entire house to flip his LPs, but he didn't seem to mind. The setup spoke well of Leslie's parents, it seemed to Kip—of their permissiveness, not to mention their income—and he fought back a pang of resentment. He pictured them as kindly, even-keeled progressives who just so happened, judging by the prominence of Liberace and Lawrence Welk in their record collection, to have slightly campy taste in music. As Leslie fiddled with the EQ, Kip found himself wondering where the two of them were, and what they did for a living, and why their spacious home was so neglected-looking. The longer he thought about it, the more baffling it seemed. He couldn't make the pieces fit together.

"Good to go!" Leslie sang out, jumping up and bobbing ahead of Kip down the hallway like some kind of flightless bird. Kip had never seen him move so fast before. They made it to the bedroom just in time for the opening lick.

"What is this?" Kip shouted.

Leslie shot him a wild leer and passed him the sleeve. Five men in lipstick and wedding-cake hair, tarted up in heels and scarves and bangles, any one of them hotter than the best that Venice High School had to offer. The platinum blond in the middle, who was obviously the singer, made Kip uncomfortable in a way he didn't want to think about. He set the sleeve down gingerly on the bedside table, sure by now that he was getting in over his head. It was time to go home.

The feeling ebbed, however, as the song built toward its chorus. Something was definitely happening. The music didn't do much for him, not yet, but it clearly did something for Leslie. His eyes had rolled back in his head and his torso was twitching. He looked like someone walking on hot coals. Watching him get off on those tinny riffs and plastic vocals, sappy though they were, made Kip's throat go tight with envy. He'd never seen anyone enjoy anything that much, not even drugs. He hadn't known that kind of joy existed.

"Hanoi fucking *Rocks*," Leslie said once the needle had lifted.

"Hell yes!"

Leslie regarded him coldly. "You didn't dig it."

"What? I haven't even—"

"Spare me the song and dance, Norvald. It's not like I'm surprised."

"You're not?"

He shook his head. "You've got no sense of beauty."

Leslie strolled back down the hall, in no particular hurry now, and put on the A side. The first song kicked in soon after—three descending chords, manic and bitchy, with a moderate frosting of distortion—but Leslie was nowhere in sight. Kip sat cross-legged on the floor with his head against the side of Leslie's bed, feeling the minutes slip by, doing his best to get his brain back up to speed. There was plenty to process. He let his eyes wander, barely listening to the music, and tried to pretend that the bedroom was his: the blood-colored walls, the slasher movie stills taped to the door, the tiny gymnastics trophy on the desk in the corner—HON MENTION GRADE 6—and the closet full of rumpled, extravagant clothes. He picked up the sleeve again and studied the band: if there was one thing the men in that photograph showed no trace of, it was the desire to disappear. He came to understand, somewhere between "I Want You" and "Kill City Kills," that he desired everything that photograph represented, everything that Leslie's room contained—the gypsy scarves, the eyeliner, the shamelessness, the self-indulgence. He wanted to live in that bedroom. He wanted to have already lived there for years.

Halfway through the second guitar solo on the sixth track, Kip heard Leslie's world-weary falsetto in his ear. "'Self Destruction Blues,' kid. It's right there in the name."

"Where have you been?"

"I've got to be alone when I listen to 'Love's an Injection.' It's kind of my ritual."

Kip nodded without opening his eyes. He was trying hard, in that moment, to feel the thing Leslie was feeling. Loud though they were, the guitars somehow sounded like toys. Not a bad thing, necessarily. Track five had something to do with blowjobs, which was cool.

"These guys ever come to Florida?"

"Never." Leslie let out a sigh. "Their drummer died two years back. His car flipped on a beer run with one of the dudes from Mötley Crüe. You know the Crüe?"

"Obviously," Kip said, relieved to hear a name he recognized. "They kick ass."

"They *suck* ass," said Leslie. "Nikki Sixx is a junkie. Vince Neil can't sing for shit. They spend more time on their *bangs* than they do on their songs."

The same thing could be said of Hanoi Rocks, it seemed to Kip. But he kept his mouth shut.

"Listen to that freaking drum fill, Norvald. *Puh puh puh puh puh.*"

"I don't know much about metal, to be honest."

"No shit."

"I'm into classic stuff, mostly. Like Creedence Clearwater—"

Leslie made a violent retching sound.

"Come on, Leslie. You can't possibly be saying that the record we just heard is better than—"

Kip got in exactly sixteen words in the next twenty minutes. Leslie's reaction to his heresy went far beyond simple righteous fervor; it was almost Pentecostal. He was passionately devoted to the boys in the band—especially their Keith Richards lookalike guitarist, Nasty Suicide—but he was just as obsessed with the guitars that they played, the pedals they humped, even the offset printing process used to make the album's sleeve. That made Kip feel like he'd stepped into the wrong house again. But he also felt grateful, at that touch-and-go stage in their mutual courtship, to have discovered what the magic topic was.

"Hear that high-end fuzz, Norvald? That's an Aria Saber run through a Cry Baby wah, with an Ibanez Tube Screamer at the finish. It's all Nasty plays now. Shut up and listen. Hear that sticky sustain? That's the Aria trademark. They're one of Asia's top-rated producers, the best of the best, and the Saber is their Mustang, their Testarossa, their DeLorean X. Chamfered cutaways, Norvald. Seymour Duncan pickups. Crystal shaping. Are you hearing what I'm hearing?"

"What I'm hearing is—"

"Listen to Nasty bend at the end of this riff. Right *there*. Are you even listening? That's a semi-recessed Floyd Rose whammy. Nasty keeps a lit cigarette tucked into his headstock. Never even smokes it, kid. Just lets it fucking burn."

Leslie chattered all the way through, barely pausing for breath, like a golf announcer at the U.S. Open. He knew every lyric, every key change, every drum fill, every solo. By the time the side was over Kip was starting not to hate it. He opened his eyes to find Leslie standing in front of a pentagram-shaped mirror on the far side of the room, staring forlornly at his kinky hair.

"I need a straightener," he murmured. "The Guardians won't let me."

"The who?"

"The *Guardians*, Norvald. You're not paying attention. The legal entities whose property this is."

Kip deployed his trademark noncommittal nod. Leslie made a monster-movie face at his reflection.

"Do you ever listen to any non-metal stuff?" Kip heard himself ask.

"What are you even talking about?"

"I'm talking about other kinds of music, that's all." Kip could feel himself wilting. "Like Prince, maybe, or—"

"Or who, exactly? Stevie Wonder? The Sugarhill Gang? LL Cool J?" Leslie's voice had gone tight. "What exactly are you getting at, Kip? What's the subtext here? Should my musical taste maybe be a bit more ghetto?"

"What does the Z stand for?" Kip said, desperate to change the subject. He'd noticed, coming in, that it said VOGLER on the mailbox.

"It stands for *me*, Norvald. Because it's my name."

"Just the letter *Z*? That's it?"

"Let's talk about you for a while. What the fuck is your deal?"

"I don't know what you mean," Kip sputtered as the wave came crashing down. "I just came because my bike—"

"You live with your grandmother?"

He nodded.

"What's up with your folks?"

"Cool cover," said Kip, pointing at an LP on the windowsill.

It was actually the ugliest cover he had ever seen: a crudely airbrushed rendering of a zombie in a purple robe, one eye dangling from its socket, with a look on its face that could best be described as befuddled. The band's logo was unreadable to Kip's untrained eye, but the title was printed in generic block letters: SCREAM BLOODY GORE. There was nothing even remotely appealing about that cover, nothing sexy, nothing cool. It looked like a *Tales from the Crypt* illustration copied by a seventh grader. Leslie smiled and shook his head. "Forget it, kid."

"Let's put it on."

"Seriously, Norvald. You're wasting your time."

"What is it?"

"That's Chuck's record. Chuck Schuldiner. His mom goes to our church."

That explained everything. The album was the vanity project of some local bowlcut, recorded on a boombox and put out with money scrimped and saved from mowing lawns. But Kip was nonetheless impressed that a record—*any* record—had been made by someone who knew someone that he knew. Things like that just didn't happen, at least not to him. He grabbed the LP and passed it to Leslie.

"I'm giving you a public service announcement, Norvald. This one is above your pay grade. This one hurts."

But the look on Kip's face must have swayed him, because he went down the hall without another word and put the record on. Kip sat back and closed his eyes and listened to Leslie's bare feet on the runner. This time there was no warning, no preamble, no preliminary crackle. Leslie dropped the needle with studied accuracy onto the first bar of the third track on side A: "Denial of Life." Kip was officially on his own now. He'd been kicked into the deep end of the pool.

It hit him too fast to make sense of at first: a pelting hail of hammered notes, a low-end hiss, an epileptic bass line. His body reacted before his brain did, shifting reflexively into fight-or-flight mode, legs and arms and spinal column clenching. The sound was massive, domineering, relentless. This music was to Hanoi Rocks as an aircraft carrier is to a rubber ducky. He felt physically sick.

Then the shrieking kicked in. It sounded like someone trying to sing a nursery rhyme while being burned at the stake. The singer could have been angry, or ecstatic, or in excruciating pain—there was no way to know, because the lyrics were impossible to decipher. Horror films were

Kip's only point of reference, and not just because of the airbrushed zombie on the record's sleeve. He was being offered the same purifying fear, the same catharsis, the same revelation midnight slasher movies gave: that everything wasn't going to be all right. Not now and not ever. And that made perfect sense to him.

Once the needle had lifted, Kip sat back and waited. Leslie came waltzing in with a grin on his face, obviously expecting to find a charred and smoking carcass—but Kip met his eyes calmly. He felt nauseated but his mind was clear.

"My father's in prison."

"Prison?" said Leslie, bobbing his head to cover his confusion. "What for?"

"For hurting my mother."

Leslie opened his mouth and closed it. "Right," he said finally. "Okay."

Kip had already told him more than he'd told anyone else except the Greater Tallahassee Police Department and the case worker he'd been assigned, but he could see that he'd have to keep going. What surprised him most was that he didn't mind.

"I got sent here, you know—here to Venice, I mean. It wasn't optional."

"Me too."

Kip looked at him. He wasn't getting it.

"I don't know what you've heard, Leslie, but it wasn't because of bad grades or skipping school or selling pot or anything." Kip took in a breath. "My grandmother said she'd take me. She went to the hearings and filled out the paperwork and did the interviews. I still have a call every Tuesday at six."

Leslie just stood there.

"You remember what happened," Kip said. "Back there with your dealer or whatever."

"Kind of hard to forget."

"There's this thing that—" Kip bit down on his tongue for a few seconds. "That hits me sometimes. It just comes out of nowhere. My dad has it too." He tried to speak slowly. "It happens when things get— I don't know. Fucked up somehow. Like back there. With the Coke machine and all that."

"I'm listening."

"I was six the first time. Everything just goes white. White and empty. Like a blank piece of paper. I don't—" He shook his head and tried again. "It's more like—I don't know. Like the lights all come on, all at once. It's too much. So I can't even see." He was breathing hard now. "It's not something I *do*—that's not what it feels like. It's something that happens to me."

"Right," said Leslie. He didn't sound as if he was agreeing.

"Then things go back to normal. *I* don't even know what I'm going to find, most of the time." Kip let his eyes close. "But I always find something."

"Something bad," Leslie said. "Something crazy."

Kip didn't answer. His head felt enormous and light.

"How often does this happen? Is it like narcolepsy, or—"

"Not every day or anything." Kip kept his eyes shut. "Maybe like once a month."

"Holy shit."

"It started when things kind of went—off at my house, I guess you could say. When they got sort of stressful."

"With your parents, you mean? Did they—"

"It was just something inside my head then, or inside my chest. Nobody noticed. But I was always—I don't know. Waiting for it to happen. I even had a name for it."

"A name?"

Kip nodded. "I called it the White Room."

"The White Room," Leslie repeated.

"The funny thing is, I'm more scared of it than anybody. Especially now."

"I'll bet," said Leslie. "You're basically telling me you're a homicide waiting to happen. A multiple homicide. The next Bernie Goetz."

That made Kip look up. Leslie's face was unreadable.

"Bernie who?"

"Remind me never to go to the post office with you. Or on a bus. Or anywhere, basically."

"Listen to me, man. I'm just—"

"When you're ready to blow up the school, I'd appreciate a heads-up. I'm not ready to die yet. The Guardians just got me my own VCR."

Kip passed a hand slowly over his face. "You're making a joke out of this. Okay."

"I don't have any problem with domestic terrorism—I want that on the record. I'm just asking for a little advance notice. A couple of hours."

He stared hard at Leslie for what must have been a minute. Leslie never cracked a smile.

"I wouldn't mind blowing it up, to be honest," Kip said.

"And you've only been here for a week and a half, Norvald. Imagine how *I* feel."

That was a good moment. Kip felt all right about having mentioned the White Room. He felt almost proud. It lasted until the next thing Leslie said.

"There's a rumor going around about you."

"A rumor?" Kip murmured. He knew what was coming.

"I guess that's what you'd call it. About why you got sent here." Leslie hesitated. "What I heard was, your father—"

"This Schuldiner kid," Kip said, pointing at the zombie. "He goes to your church?"

Leslie blinked at him. "His mom does. Chuck lives up near Orlando."

"What's the name of his band?"

"Death."

"Excuse me?"

"That's the name." He sat down next to Kip and picked up the LP and pursed his lips. A subtle humming carried to them from the hallway. The stereo, Kip decided. Behind it he seemed to hear the sound of voices. Leslie was less freaked out by the White Room than Kip would have expected—a lot less. Maybe he still didn't understand.

"You liked this one, huh?" Leslie squinted at him. "Don't bother answering. You've got that look on your face like you just took a dump."

"I don't even know what just happened."

Leslie touched a finger lightly to his temple, like a mentalist trying to read someone's mind. "Chuck plays a B.C. Rich Intruder run through a Boss DS-1 into a Marshall Valvestate with a built-in chorus feature. That's how he gets that gnarly high end."

"I don't care how he gets it."

Leslie gave one of his congested-sounding chuckles. "Fry my nuts in acid, kid. You *liked* it."

Leslie's parents turned out to be as ancient as their stereo. They were sitting on the living room sofa when Kip and Leslie came out, contentedly watching the turntable turn. Kip wasn't sure who they were at first: they were old and pale and dainty, and they were dressed much too warmly for Venice. They were dressed for Minneapolis–Saint Paul.

"This is Kip," announced Leslie, sliding *Scream Bloody Gore* back into its sleeve. "He's Mrs. Cartwright's grandson."

Mrs. Vogler told Kip that it was delightful to make his acquaintance. Mr. Vogler nodded dreamily, still smiling at the stereo. That was their entire interaction.

"So you're adopted?" Kip said once they'd gotten outside. For some reason Leslie was walking him back to his house—he was even pushing the Schwinn.

"What makes you say that, Norvald? My mahogany skin tone? My rich singing voice?"

"I can take my bike back whenever you're ready."

"Your confusion's only natural. I'm the first non-pasty person you've seen in your life. You thought us brown folks were the stuff of legend."

Kip went red in the face and stared down at the pavement. It had only just occurred to him that Leslie was, in fact, the only Black person he'd laid eyes on since getting off the Greyhound. He thought about the redneck again, and about Leslie's lily-white record collection. He thought about the Voglers sitting quietly in their house where time stood still. It was all so improbable. In that respect Leslie was perfectly right—the cognitive dissonance made his head spin.

"They still fuck," said Leslie. "I hear them."

"What?"

"Nate and Rachel. The Guardians."

Kip put his hands over his ears. "I can't even—"

"They just didn't want to add to the, you know. Global over-population."

"Jesus Christ."

They walked in silence for a while. "They're playing at the youth center next Friday," Leslie said eventually.

"What? Who?"

"Death, obviously. If you wanted to go."

Kip felt himself nodding.

"All right, then. Catch you Monday."

"Cool."

"One more thing, Norvald," Leslie said, turning back toward his house.

"What?"

"Don't ever wear that U2 shirt again."

2

Christopher Chanticleer Norvald arrived at the East Venice Avenue bus station on October 22, 1987, clutching a bag of dirty laundry, a Walkman, and a seven-page letter—written all in caps, in pencil—to his grandma Oona from his mom. You couldn't get any older or any whiter than downtown Venice on a weekday afternoon. It was cataclysmically tranquil. People moved there to die, comfortably and quietly, and if you had other plans then you were in the way.

To the north lay Tampa, sprawling and soulless; to the south, a no-man's-land of half-drained swamps and gridded subdivisions. Inland was a crazy quilt of meth labs, migrant workers' shacks, and citrus farms gone bust. The Gulf itself was always there, lazily brining the sunlight, but there's only so much time you can spend floating in lukewarm brackish water on your back. At times the boredom grew so punishing that the more sensitive Venice residents went quietly out of their minds: people took drugs at random and gave their life savings to megachurches and drove head-on into interstate dividers. The month Kip got to town, one of his grandmother's neighbors dug a hole in his backyard, as wide and as deep as the property line allowed, and tried to start charging admission.

The snowbirds reclining in their deck chairs by the shuffleboard courts down on State Street, needless to say, couldn't have cared less about these occasional eruptions of swamp fever. They wanted anyone under sixty out of their line of sight—except when their lawns needed mowing, or their Winnebagos needed an oil change, or they wanted a cone of soft-serve on the beach. Sometimes Kip actually found it hard to breathe in Venice: the air felt thin, secondhand, oxygen-poor. The undead had triumphed over the living in Sarasota County sometime back in the seventies, and the victory was total. You could feel it on your skin.

Less than a week after their first hangout, from one day to the next, Leslie Z was gone from Venice High. The Powers That Be intended it as a temporary suspension, no more than a slap on the wrist—but he took it to heart, to Kip's astonishment, and never went back. As Leslie told it, Principal Sennheiser's motives were "crypto-political"; according to everyone else, he'd shown up to morning assembly in a pair of assless chaps. Kip couldn't help but wonder how the Voglers had reacted to the news. He pictured them smiling up at their son from that psychedelic sofa of theirs, holding hands like college sweethearts, assuring him that all was for the best. But it was just as likely that he never told them.

He dropped by Kip's house the day of his suspension, dressed normally again—normally for Leslie, at least—in green jeans and a Morbid Angel T-shirt. Nothing about him indicated what had just gone down. Kip's social anxiety kicked in instantly: he was terrified that Leslie would suddenly start picking Oona's brain about the family, or that he'd criticize her baking—or that he'd somehow scandalize her just by being Leslie—but the two of them hit it off from word one. Leslie ate three hefty slices of her trademark key lime crumble, rolling his eyes in delight, and told her about his brand-new plan of working as a chef. He'd been kicked out of high school that morning, he explained, and an experience like that was liable to make a young man think about his future. Oona laughed what Kip liked to call her "dirty granny" laugh and lit another Camel. She was having the time of her life. Leslie asked if he could bum a smoke, and she winked and pushed the pack across the table.

Kip added that to his mental list of things that only Leslie Z could get away with.

There was no way he was going to let Leslie see his bedroom—with its NASCAR sheets, its Huey Lewis and the News poster, and its general air of defeat—so they hung out in the den, barely talking at all, watching reruns of *Fat Albert* and *The Rockford Files*. The house was a far cry from the Voglers' expansive split-level, and Oona's trashy Swiss chalet aesthetic made the rooms feel even smaller. It was like watching TV inside a cuckoo clock. His grandmother sat with them for a while, making no attempt to conceal her satisfaction at seeing him with a flesh-and-blood companion, then returned to her mysterious old-lady business.

"That crumble," Leslie said softly, watching her go.

"What about it?"

"It was awful."

Things went quiet after that. Kip had never felt his shyness or his poorness more acutely. Leslie was still an enigma to him, a borderline-supernatural being, a visitor from the stars who spoke in riddles. Kip kept thinking that he was about to confess, to explain why he'd committed academic suicide that morning—but all that came out was the occasional half-grunted word. Watching reruns on Kip's sofa was preferable, apparently, to digging a hole in his backyard and charging admission. But not by much.

"Leslie."

"Present."

"I guess I'm still wondering. About today at school."

Leslie let out a yawn.

"Seriously, though. When will they let you come back, do you think?"

"I don't."

Kip hesitated. "You don't what?"

"Care," Leslie said, sticking out his tongue at the TV.

Finally, for want of any other option, Kip deployed the magic topic. It worked instantly. Leslie picked up the conversation exactly where they'd paused it on the walk back from the Voglers', as if he'd been wait-ing all week for the secret password. He became a completely different person when he was talking about metal. Kip understood him less but liked him better.

"Electric guitar is the greatest instrument in the world, Norvald—that's been proven by science—and heavy metal is the music that pro-ceeds from that reality. What else is there—piano? Synthesizer? Give me a fucking break. We've finally got the guitar where it belongs: up on the throne, on the altar, even higher than the singer. We've got electronics to shape the output now, to make the Word flesh, to boost the signal and to have it do our bidding. I'm talking about transistor-driven ana-log effects. I'm talking about the greatest musical instrument known to *humanity* put in the service of medieval knowledge: the infamous tri-tone, Norvald. The forbidden interval. The unholy trinity—*diabolus in musica*—not that I actually know what that means. Monks were burned alive for using it in their compositions—and that's when they were playing it on *lutes*. But we've got the goods now. We've got the heavy artillery. We've got the electric guitar."

"If you say so."

"Look me in the eyes, Norvald. This is important. These lines have been converging for centuries—since the Dark Ages, basically—and they finally met in *our* lifetime. It's just dumb luck that we're alive to see it. It's one in a billion. Are you listening to me?"

"I'm right here."

"Sometimes I think about how easily I could have been born in a completely different era. I could have missed the eighties altogether. That unsettles me, Norvald. That gives me the chills."

"I guess I never thought much about it," Kip managed to get in. He was starting to wonder, in some dusty crawl space of his conscious mind, whether hanging out with Leslie might not be the best idea.

"It's more than just a *sound*, of course. It's more than an aesthetic. It's the road less taken, Norvald. It's the fucking left-hand path. It's a complete shadow culture, with its own laws, its own myths, its own scripture. You could call it a whole *Weltanschauung*. If you were a Nazi."

"Hold on, Leslie. You're going a little too fast—"

"Take shredding, for example. Killer guitar licks are a fundamental feature of the heavy metal code. Unlike your standard punk riff—which can pretty much be played by a bonobo—this is music that demands OCD-level commitment. Think Yngwie Malmsteen, Norvald. Think Eddie Van. Think Randy Rhoads. These guys are basically neurotics. This is music that was technically impossible when our parents were our age. Guitars didn't even have *amplifiers* when my father was a kid. Can you grok what that *means*?"

He went on like that for ages, from *The Rockford Files* to *The Facts of Life* to *Remington Steele*, and Kip sat back and watched him like a movie. Maybe the weight of what had happened that morning was catching up with him, or maybe he was as giddy with freedom as he claimed to be; whatever the reason, Leslie Z was in the grip of ecstasy. None of the inhibitions and anxieties Kip suffered from existed for him—at least not at the moment. He was high, obviously, but it wasn't just that. He was operating on a conceptual level Kip could only dream of.

"I've had a gun to my head three times," he was saying now, apropos of nothing. "One time it was Harley Boy. Twice it was the cops."

"*Three* times?" Kip said, more than a little dubious. "What were you doing?"

Leslie sighed. "Get a clue, Norvald. I wasn't doing shit."

"I'm just saying, to pull that much heat—"

"Jesus Christ. Pull heat? Where did you hear that one, *Starsky and Hutch*?"

"People don't get guns pointed at them by policemen for nothing, that's all. Not in my experience."

All at once Leslie looked brittle and tired. "We must have had different experiences with law enforcement," he said. "I wonder why that is."

"Come on, Z. You're a rich kid. Or not rich, exactly, but definitely—"

"You're so hung up on the money thing. There's worse problems, Norvald—at least around here. You think the good people of Venice see me walking down the street and stop to consider the Voglers' fucking *equity*?"

Kip squinted at the TV for a while.

"Three separate times?" he said finally. "You're not making this up?"

"The last time was Thursday." Leslie was cheerful again. "I'd been hanging at the Perkins out on the 41 bypass with Rozz—Chris 'Flamer' Rozz, you don't know him yet—and he was driving me home in this car that he's got. You've maybe seen it around school—he deals out of it sometimes. A brown Isuzu Gemini. You've smelled it, probably. He keeps it full of garbage. Keeps the po-po away."

"I *have* smelled that car, now that you mention it."

"So we're rolling up the Tamiami with the windows cracked, listening to the new Amon demo—barely even flamed—when Greenwood pulls us over. You know Greenwood, right? Sheriff Greenwood? Usually he's parked out by the mall."

Kip shook his head.

"*You ladies got any idea how fast you were going?* Greenwood says to Rozz, shining this dinky little pen-flashlight into the back seat. He doesn't say a word about the garbage. It's possible he has no sense of smell."

"Go on."

"By this point Rozz is pretty much wetting the bed. He's mumbling something about his speedometer being busted, about a family emergency, about having to go to the bathroom. Greenwood is just standing there grinning. Then he reaches in and opens the driver's door, unbuckles Rozz's seat belt, and says in the silkiest damn voice you've ever heard in your life: *You were moving at an average speed of sixteen miles per hour.* That's when I knew we were roadkill."

Kip was having his doubts again. "Wait. So he pulled you over for—"

"They don't need a reason, Norvald. This *place* is the reason."

That shut him up again. Leslie yawned and slid a hand between the cushions of the couch. Eventually he came out with a quarter.

"That Amon tape is lethal, by the way. It caved my pointy head in."

The Death show at the youth center was two days away.

3

Kip woke up that Friday to rain against the bug screens—lukewarm, greasy Gulf Coast drizzle—and zero desire to get out of bed. It was the low-grade depression returning, settling over him like a soft, translucent blanket, and the panic this triggered was so intense that he forgot what day it was. He worked himself into a sitting position eventually, against his better instincts, and took up the ritual he'd followed every morning since Leslie had entered his life: sifting through his bleak array of pleated slacks and polo shirts to find the least un-metal combination.

Oona was sitting in the breakfast nook when he finally came out, studying the Sarasota County police blotter and nursing her first Camel of the day. It was something to do, a way to pass the time on uneventful mornings—meaning every morning that she didn't go to church. Kip had spent six whole summers with his grandmother back in the good time, when she'd lived at 33 West Lincoln Street in Slack Falls, Minnesota, and he'd always been enraptured by the cat-and-mouse game she played with her first cigarette of the day. She liked to stub it out from time to time—gingerly, so as not to break the paper—then watch it not burn for a wildly unpredictable interval, playing absentmindedly with her lighter, only to light it again with an elegant show of reluctance. Her standing record with a single smoke, from June 12, 1985, was just over three quarters of an hour.

"A middle-aged male, Caucasian, broke into a home in Palmdale, shattered a glass-topped coffee table, and did his business on the floor of the TV room. Then he ate the contents of the vacuum cleaner. The *vacuum* cleaner, Christopher. Can you imagine?"

"Do I have to?"

"Palmdale's always been a little—well. Those inland towns. You know."

Kip kissed her on the forehead, waited for her grunt of acknowledgment, then went and cracked two eggs into the skillet. She made no mention of the fact that he was already fifteen minutes late for school.

"That friend of yours, Christopher."

"Leslie."

"Is that the one?"

"He's the only friend I have, Oona. So definitely."

"He's just—beautiful. Don't you think?"

Kip tried to interpret the look on her face. It took him a while.

"I'm not gay, if that's what you're asking."

"Oh, thank goodness."

"I'm not adopted, either. And I haven't been kicked out of school yet. I'll probably be president one day."

"There's no call for you to take that tone." She smoothed the blotter out across the countertop. "A nice young person, anyhow. Good manners. Bit skinny."

"He mostly eats Oreos."

"I'm sure he'll do very well in the restaurant business."

"Oona, what's this about?"

"I got a letter from your mother. She asked me to tell you."

Kip lowered the flame on the burner. "Tell me what?"

"Just that. To tell you she'd written."

"That's it?"

His grandmother didn't answer.

"Okay." Kip focused his attention on the skillet. He caught sight of his face in the window above the stovetop and adjusted his expression before he turned around.

"So where is she?"

"She's doing well, Christopher. She wanted me to tell you. She's been working for a dentist—taking calls and such." She paused again. "That's what she said."

"A dentist."

"A *Jewish* dentist," said his grandmother, with what might have been pride.

"Where is she, Oona? Did she give you a rough sense? A state? A time zone?"

"Kip—"

"Did she ask you for money?"

"She's in Indiana. Indianapolis, I think. The return address was general delivery."

"How much did she ask for?"

Oona closed her mouth and let her eyes glaze over. It was a gift she had: the ability to disconnect whenever the conversation turned unpleasant. There was no reaching her then and it drove Kip half crazy. It made him feel nonexistent. He gripped the handle of the skillet with his bare hand for as long as he could stand to. He marveled, as he always did, at his mother's power to cause misery from a thousand miles away.

"There's no dentist, Oona. No dentist, no desk job. You know that much, don't you?"

He regretted the words even as they left his mouth. Oona's whole face shut down. His grandmother was not one of those seniors who sat in government-issue deck chairs on the esplanade, eating provolone sandwiches and waiting to be hoovered up into the clouds. She was squarely on the side of life, however much she tried to hide it. She wasn't prepared to give up on her daughter.

In that respect Kip was way ahead of her.

School, when Kip finally got there, was even more soul-flattening than usual. He steered his body forward by remote control, eyes fixed on the space Leslie might have occupied if he'd still been around, rolling with the insults, the rabbit punches, the monotony, the unasked-for erections. He could practically *hear* the chemicals sloshing around inside him: the sex hormones and the anxiety hormones and whatever hormone makes you want to fake your own death, churning and frothing, acting and reacting, refusing to remain at equilibrium. Past experience told him it was only a matter of time before something terrible happened. He spent the day telling himself None of This Matters, reciting it under his breath like a mantra or a medical diagnosis. None of This Matters. None of This Matters. It worked because he knew that it was true.

It didn't work that particular Friday, however, because something was different. He could see it in his classmates' blotchy faces, as a kind of flickering behind their blank expressions, and he could feel it in the sticky Gulf Coast air. The usual boredom had been replaced by something that looked almost exactly like boredom but wasn't. It was possible that he was starting to see the strangeness under the skin of things that Leslie sometimes hinted at; it was also possible that he was projecting. Because he'd finally realized what day it was.

Death was playing in six hours at the youth center downtown.

Kip barely knew more about them than he'd learned that first day at Leslie's: there was no fan club, no archive, no database that he could access. All he had to go on was a name, Chuck Schuldiner, and a few garbled rumors, and a logo he'd seen scrawled in ballpoint pen on someone's locker. No mailing list, no lyric sheets, no photos of the band. None of which mattered to him, not really, because he could see Death with his eyes closed every time their record played. They were huge and dark and bearded. They had razor blades for teeth.

As soon as school was done that day he rode straight to the Voglers'. His bookbag weighed as much as his bike did, and he was dying for a shower, but he was afraid that if he went home he'd find Oona exactly as he'd left her, still fidgeting with the same cigarette, waiting for him in the breakfast nook to talk about his mother. The outfit he had on—madras boating shorts, jogging shoes, and a polo shirt emblazoned with the name of a nonexistent surf club—was impossible, unthinkable; but the rest of his wardrobe was worse. By the time he rang the Voglers' doorbell his self-consciousness was so severe that he could barely form a sentence, but he needn't have worried. The first thing Leslie said was that he needed a new look.

Kip approached Leslie's closet with caution. It was a zone he'd kept clear of so far—not because it didn't interest him, but because some vestigial, pre-Venice Kip Norvald suspected that having entered its enchanted twilight he might never come back out. It took Leslie himself to break the spell: he pulled the closet door open casually, in a bored sort of way, then drifted down the hall to put a record on.

Glam might still have reigned supreme in Leslie's wardrobe, but since he'd dropped out of school, Kip couldn't help but notice, his taste in metal was inclining toward the brutal. The LP he put on was *Seasons in the Abyss*, by a West Coast band called Slayer that Kip had never heard before: lyrics about pandemics and demons and serial killers, screamed by what sounded like somebody's gun-toting uncle. This music would have caused him acute distress just two weeks earlier; now it simply seemed appropriate. He reached into the dark and pulled a shirt out at random. He wasn't sure what to make of its pattern—ankhs against a field of midnight blue, interlaced with spiky leaves that might potentially be pot—but by that point he'd have tried on anything. It was made of something silky that was probably not silk.

"This isn't going to be that kind of show."

"What do you mean?"

"That blouse belongs to my mother. Rachel Veronika Vogler. That's what I mean."

"Do you think she would mind?"

"It's not her I'd be worried about, Norvald. Like I said—it's not that kind of show."

Leslie's voice gave Kip pause. At the venue, among their own kind, he'd assumed they'd be safe. But the bangers hated queers as much as the bikers and the jocks did, at least from what little he'd seen. It was possible that no place was safe for Leslie.

"What about you?" Kip asked. "What are you going to wear?"

"Just what I have on."

He was lying on his bed as he said this, left arm propping up his head, like Bowie on the cover of *The Man Who Sold the World*. He had on a crepe turquoise blouse, fingerless yellow driving gloves, and champagne-colored paisley spandex tights. He looked about as metal as Susan Sarandon.

"Jesus Christ, Z."

"Something to say?"

"If *I'm* going to get my ass kicked, what the hell is going to happen to you?"

"It's different for me." He let out a sigh. "I get around, Norvald. I'm a known quantity."

Leslie's answer was coherent, more or less, but it made no sense to Kip. "I guess so," he muttered.

"You don't look satisfied."

"In the beginning, though." Kip groped for the right words. "Before you were a quantity or whatever. There must have been a time when people saw you and just—"

"I said that shit about the blouse because it's ugly, if you want to know the truth."

"I got it from your closet!"

Leslie blew him a kiss. "I mean ugly on you."

Kip must have made some sort of face—hurt, even despairing—because Leslie nudged him aside, not unkindly, and slid past him into the gloom. "Don't take it personally, Norvald. It's a skin-tone thing." He handed Kip a lemon-yellow tuxedo shirt, complete with frills.

"How is *this* any better?"

"Solid colors. Less girly."

"I don't think I can wear this."

"Deep breaths, Norvald. It's a process." He passed Kip a shirt that said CHICKS DIG SCRAWNY PALE GUYS and another that said BONIN' THE CARBARIAN.

"What does that even mean?"

"Put it on."

"I don't know about this, Leslie."

"You don't know about this, Leslie Z."

"Are you listening? I can't pull this off. I'm not you."

That drew Leslie back out. He was close to Kip now, easily a head taller, both palms resting lightly on his shoulders. The look on his face was familiar—excruciatingly so—but it took Kip a moment to place it. He'd seen it on the cover of the Hanoi Rocks album, in the eyes of the singer whose perfect face had made him so uneasy. He felt that way now. Leslie was about to say something—he'd taken in a breath to say it—but he stopped himself. A few seconds' hesitation. A tingling hush. Kip felt his grip tighten.

"Not me," Leslie said thickly.

Kip kept perfectly still.

"Of course not. Who is?" He stepped away and turned back to the closet.

Over the next two hours Kip came to understand that Leslie's excitement about the show, intense though it was, wasn't nearly as intense as his excitement about picking out their clothes. The Venom and Exodus and Repulsion songs making the bungalow quake were just barely aggressive enough to disguise the truth: that the two of them were playing dress-up. Kip wore frosted white jeans. He wore leopard-print leggings. He wore silk scarves and mod boots and faux-leather chaps. He tried on things he didn't have the words for and could never have afforded. Leslie put on LP after LP after LP: *Back to Mystery City* and *Fear of Tomorrow* and *Master of Puppets* and *Hell Awaits* and *Bonded by Blood* and *The Ultimate Sin*. At times Kip forgot what they were doing there in the dark, what exactly were the terms of their engagement, Leslie hissing and cooing and singing his praises, him letting Leslie dress him and pose him and boss him around. For minutes on end he was free of himself. He felt lighter than air. Then suddenly he was back in his body, at the edge of the bed, and Leslie was saying it was time for them to go.

He caught sight of himself in the mirror as he got to his feet. He was wearing the shorts he'd arrived in, a Mötley Crüe cap, a fake shark's-tooth necklace, and a Poison shirt, faded and frayed, that Leslie had turned inside out and cut the letters *D-E-A-T-H* into with a pair of toe-nail scissors from the bathroom. He was halfway up the hall before he realized he was moving. The Voglers were in the living room again, close together on the sofa, watching *The MacNeil/Lehrer NewsHour*. They wished the boys a very pleasant evening.

The youth center was more or less as Kip had pictured it: a blacked-out storefront with a scattering of kids outside, keyed up and impatient, eyeing everyone who walked by as though bracing for a fight. Fifty kids, maybe a hundred. They had a haunted look, it seemed to Kip. He followed Leslie like a dachshund. He saw nobody he knew.

"Where are all these kids from?"

Leslie shrugged. "Lots of out-of-towners. I know some of them from Tampa. I used to live there."

"I feel like we're the only locals."

"Lots of these kids are from Venice. You're not seeing them, that's all."

Kip looked around. "Not recognizing them, you mean?"

"That's right, Norvald. And they're not recognizing you."

Kip caught sight of Pete Frantz while Leslie was talking—a bony, bleach-blond burnout who sat next to him in History. Frantz had something like war paint on his face: three thick smears across each cheekbone, like football blacking put on in a hurry. Behind him skulked a chunky kid that Kip knew from the lunch line, Billy something-or-other, who was always asking younger kids if he could have their milk. He was wearing a plastic top hat. Sweat was pouring down his blotchy face already.

"Weird crowd," Kip mumbled.

Leslie made a face. "Tragic, you mean."

"Some kids are—in costume, I guess—but most just look normal."

"Most kids pick their scabs. Most kids jerk off into tube socks. Most kids have zero flair for reinvention."

"Maybe they don't want to reinvent themselves," Kip heard himself mutter.

Leslie spun around at that, practically knocking Kip over, his brown eyes fiercer than he'd ever seen them. "*Show* me," he hissed.

"Huh? I don't—"

"Show me one kid in this crowd—just one—who loves his life and wouldn't change it for the world. Where's that kid hiding, Norvald? Do you see him around?" He stepped closer still, closer even than they'd been in his bedroom, and jabbed Kip hard in the ribs. A ring of rubberneckers closed around them.

"Go ahead and be sad little Kip Norvald forever—I don't give a fuck. You'll do fine in this place. You match the wallpaper. But that's not an option for me, shit-for-brains, in case you haven't noticed."

By the time Kip stammered out an answer Leslie had left him to the questionable mercy of the crowd. These were kids from outside Venice, from inland, where things got weirder and more fucked up in a hurry. They reminded him of other kids in other towns, other states—places he'd spent time in with his mom. Their fathers had been her landlords, or her boyfriends, or her dealers, or some combination of the three. He'd been at the center of circles like this one before.

"Are those shark teeth for real?"

Kip cleared his throat. "What?"

"That necklace. All due respect, son. It's wicked."

The individual speaking these words was heavyset and pigeon-toed and wearing a shirt emblazoned with the logo Kip had first seen on the sleeve of *Scream Bloody Gore*. It dawned on him, after an empty-headed moment, that they both had on Death shirts.

"Absolutely real," he said finally. "A hundred percent."

"Death, am I right?"

"Death," Kip agreed.

"Evil Chuck is the raddest."

"No contest."

"You heard about Cutter?"

This from a glassy-eyed bruiser with a gap in his teeth. Kip realized, to his own amazement, that he *had* heard about Cutter.

"Chuck kicked him out of the band, right? Then let him back in? Then kicked him out again?"

"It came down to shredding," the gap-toothed kid said. "He was brutal—no doubt. But not brutal enough."

"Not for Chuck. Chuck is driven."

"*Beyond* driven."

"It was a brutality issue."

"Chuck's not a people person," said the heavyset kid, with what seemed to be sarcasm.

"I'm not even sure he's a person at all," Kip put in. "Am I right?"

The silence this triggered was so total that he felt his guts clench. He'd surprised them somehow. They both stared at him blankly.

"Right," the gap-toothed kid answered. He said it slowly, meditatively, as if he'd have to give the matter further thought.

"Cool shirt," said the heavyset kid, turning away with a nod. "But lose the cap. We usually stomp on glammers, as a rule."

Kip drifted rudderlessly through the crowd after that, not sure whether he wanted to run into Leslie or not, finding himself pushed over and over—mysteriously, centrifugally—out to the curb. The scene had identified him as foreign and reacted accordingly, like a healthy young body ejecting a splinter. Without Leslie beside him he felt like a fool.

If Kip had nursed any lingering doubts as to where the teenage population stood in Sarasota County's hierarchy of values, the interior of the Greater Venice Youth Center would have dispelled them for him nicely. Apart from a sagging Ping-Pong table jammed into the far left corner, there was nothing in the place but the walls and the stage: no curtains, no proscenium, no lighting to speak of. If not for the way the kids in front of him had arranged themselves, and some leftover Halloween decorations tacked to the walls—glitter-smeared cardboard stalactites and cotton cobwebs—the stage itself might have escaped him. This was a venue without a budget for a demographic without pull. The front third of the room was packed; the back was almost empty. He saw no one over twenty-five, no one he felt like talking to, and not a single girl.

First up was a local kid named Jared—no last name given, almost certainly for reasons of self-preservation—who made up for what he lacked in metal credibility with sheer batshit bravado. Jared sported an old man's seersucker slacks held up by hot pink suspenders, a Zippy the Pinhead T-shirt, and hair the color of Oona's key lime crumble. He came onstage dragging a battered guitar by the neck, shouting *"Death metal hell! Death metal hell!"* over and over, then plugged the guitar in and left it feeding back against somebody's amp. He told nonsensical jokes, barely intelligible over the feedback, punctuated by petulant kicks to the back of the guitar: the crowd couldn't seem to figure out whether he was a band, or a stand-up comedian, or just some lunatic with a death wish who'd wandered in off the street.

At some point the unfathomable Jared was shanghaied offstage and Kip snapped out of it and went to look for Leslie. Impatience and irritation seemed to be sharpening the energy in that stifling drop-ceilinged space, making it somehow serrated—but Kip was feeling bolder now himself. His camouflage was working. No one cared that DEATH had been cut into his shirt with cuticle scissors. If anything it seemed to boost his cred.

Eventually he ended up back at the entrance. A kid with a rattail haircut who couldn't have been a day past fifteen was working the door, drawing pentagrams on everyone's wrist with a Sharpie. Kip watched for a while. He saw no sign of Leslie.

He was leaning against the blacked-out storefront window, wondering where to put himself, when a girl came out of nowhere and kicked Rattail in the balls.

He'd been expecting a fight to break out at some point—it had seemed preordained—but not one like this. Rattail went down and stayed down. His attacker stood motionless above him, feet set wide apart in dirty low-top Chuck Taylors, waiting for him to look up at her. She was lost to the world, hunched and blank-eyed with fury—which meant that Kip could gawk at her in safety. Chipped green nails, long-sleeved Iron Maiden shirt, hair the dull metallic red that a black dye job turns after weeks in the sun. Acid-wash jeans with a hole in one knee. A cheap studded choker. A pink puckered scar running along her hairline from her widow's peak to the lobe of her left ear. She stood there rocking lightly on her heels, opening and closing her fists. She was willing to wait. She wanted the kid on the floor to get up, Kip realized, so that she could kick him again.

Just then about sixteen things happened at once: the lights dimmed, a power chord rang out, the girl elbowed angrily past him, and the whole room seemed to slide in the direction of the stage. This band wasn't Death—not by half—but at least they were loud. From what Kip could make out through the sudden crush of gangly bodies there were four people performing, all about his own age, with greasy dyed-black hair and matching sleeveless T-shirts.

"Venice—we are *HMGHHKGDSSGMMMMSSS*!"

"What did he say?" Kip shouted into the ear of the nearest available banger.

"Name of band."

"Who are they?"

The banger shrugged. "Sounded maybe like Homeostasis."

The learning curve for Kip that night was steep.

Homeostasis—if that was their name—introduced Kip to three phenomena of the scene that he'd soon come to know all too well: kids in the mosh pit whipping hair into one another's eyes, band members unabashedly wearing their own merch, and the queasy, in-and-out-of-phase sound of a drummer struggling to keep up with a riff. They sucked, in other words, but Kip didn't mind. He'd never heard overdriven, down-tuned guitars before—not like this, not live, cranked so loud that he could feel it in his lungs. If he'd been offered nothing else that night, nothing more than that idiot crunch, he'd have staggered home amazed and gratified.

He went outside to piss at some point, and it was there that he finally found Leslie, standing in a clump of unfamiliar silhouettes between two idling cars and smoking what looked, from a distance, to be a slightly bent Virginia Slim. Kip approached slowly, not sure what to expect. The first face he recognized belonged to Harley Boy Ray. The second belonged to the girl.

"Norvald! You remember Ray, don't you? Come here and shake hands. French-kiss and make up. Peace in the Middle East."

Leslie was swaying in place, renegotiating his relationship to the ground on an ongoing basis, bobbing and tilting like someone floating on invisible pontoons. Ray cocked his head at Kip, squinting a little, as though he might be a trick of the light. The girl was facing away from them now, talking to someone in one of the cars. She was leaning lightly, almost imperceptibly, against Harley Boy's back.

"What did you think of that Halitosis set?"

It took Kip a few seconds to process what Leslie was saying. "Is that what they're called?"

Leslie laughed. "Hear that, Ray? Norvald here didn't even catch the name. I'm kind of jealous, honestly."

"You seem unsure about what's going on here, Kip," Harley Boy said softly. "Maybe you should call the police."

"I want to apologize about that."

"He wants to *apologize*," repeated Harley Boy.

"Who is this kid, Ray?"

It was the girl, turning her head to give Kip the once-over. If not for the hole in the knee of her jeans and the fact that she was literally the only girl he'd seen all night he might not have recognized her. The rage was gone completely and she looked sleepy and serene.

"This here is Kip Norvald, pumpkin. Metal maniac. Professional shit-kicker. Proud owner of a banana-top Schwinn roadster, with a phone."

"I don't really—"

"Shut your mouth, cocksucker."

Kip shut his mouth. The girl considered him in a dreamy sort of way.

Of course she was the girlfriend of a thirtysomething dealer with a spider neck tattoo. Of course she was. She held out her hand and he took it. It felt weightless and cool.

"Kip Norvald," she said, as if trying out the words.

He nodded.

"K-I-P," she said. "N-O-R-V-A-L-D."

"That's me."

"I like to spell things so I don't forget."

She let go of his hand and took her lower lip between her teeth. They were spaced slightly farther apart than normal, he noticed. They looked feral and sharp. The ruby in her right incisor matched the one in Harley Boy's.

"Kip," she said one more time.

"It's short for Christopher."

"That's got to be the most un-metal name I've ever heard."

She said the words gently, almost sadly, like some jaded older sister. Harley Boy let out a cackle. Leslie held up a hand.

"I think 'Norvald' sounds metal as hell, personally. It's got a Viking ring to it. *Woods of the north* or some such."

"'Kipper,' on the other hand," said Harley Boy. "I'm pretty sure a kipper is a fish."

"I'm kind of surprised that you know that," Kip found himself answering.

"What?"

"I'm just saying," he continued, seeing himself speak the words as if from above, a genuine out-of-body experience, watching Leslie and the girl watching him. "You look kind of ignorant."

Harley Boy's face seemed to flatten. "You did not just say that."

"It's the Viking coming out," Leslie whispered. "I *knew* it."

"My name is Christopher," Kip said, feeling righteous and wild. "Christopher Chanticleer Norvald."

"Scion of kings!" shouted Leslie.

Harley Boy passed a hand over his eyes, as though rousing himself from a nap, and Kip took the opportunity to steal a quick glance at the girl. She was about to say something. He was still waiting to hear it when he realized that he was facedown in the dirt.

"Okay, Ray. That's enough. Mission accomplished."

The girl's voice, Kip thought, or possibly Leslie's. Something was wrong with his hearing. He lifted his head and the sidewalk tipped sideways. He held his breath to keep from being sick.

"Are they starting? It sounds like they're starting. I'll catch up with you guys."

Definitely Leslie's voice this time. Kip pushed his forehead into the gravel and listened to the footsteps moving past him. Everything was being run through a distortion pedal now.

"All right, Chanticleer. Up we go. He got you good but not that good."

"Ughh."

"I told him not to hit you in the face. So you'd still have your beauty."

Kip counted down from five and sat upright. Leslie was squatting beside him, stoned eyes open wide, visibly struggling to come down to earth. He passed an arm around Kip's waist and hoisted him smoothly up onto his feet. He seemed possessed of otherworldly strength.

"Upsy-daisy."

"I'm all right now. I'm good."

"Of course you are. The blood of Vikings."

"Where exactly did he hit me?"

"In the face."

"Fucking fag-bashing cracker."

"Our boy's dealing with some issues. They bubble up sometimes."

Kip bent over, feeling nauseated again.

"Come on, Norvald. They're starting."

"Is *that* Death?" In spite of everything he could feel himself grinning. "I can feel it in my *teeth*, man. And we're not even in the building."

"Shut up and move."

They walked for what felt like a couple of miles. "What happened back there?" Leslie said finally. "I thought you were supposed to be some sort of psycho killer."

"It's not like that."

"I was hoping to see—"

"I don't want to talk about this right now."

Leslie sighed and said nothing. Kip felt inexplicably guilty.

"I was trying to score points with his girlfriend," he mumbled. "How stupid is that?"

All at once he found himself alone at the door to the center, staring into the spooked blue eyes of the kid with the rattail. He turned around to find Leslie doubled over.

"What's so funny now?"

"You could have saved yourself a split lip, Norvald. That trailer trash peanut isn't Harley Boy's *girlfriend*. That's crazy Kira Carson. She's his cousin."

Kip would never be able to say, looking back, how much his experience of that next hour was colored by the fact that he'd just taken a blow to the skull. Leslie breezed blithely past Rattail and insinuated himself into the mob, seeking the crannies and negative spaces, while Kip trailed dazed and punch-drunk in his wake. The ringing in his ears blended so seamlessly with the bottom-end mudflow submerging the room that he couldn't say for certain where his body ended and the noise began. He brought a hand to his lips and found to his horror that they seemed to be made out of something like wax.

With his hearing shot he focused on the visible. He and Leslie were close to the stage now, within spitting distance, and through the undulating screen of hair he caught his first glimpse of the band. In place of the razor-toothed ogres of his imagination he found three baby-faced kids, not much older than he was, concentrating so hard on what they were playing that they barely seemed to know the crowd was there. He craned his neck to see Evil Chuck himself: a medium-sized banger in a gray muscle shirt, too pretty to be intimidating, squinting down at the neck of his guitar like an engineer trying to take its square root.

At some point the ringing in Kip's head receded and he found himself back in consensus time, in the throbbing synesthetic soup of it, watching snarls of wire rise gleaming from the auditory sludge. He was seeing crystal bridges, fractal arabesques, obsidian lagoons. The world shrank to a pinprick. There was nothing but the signal and the space it occupied.

Then the speed of it hit him. It felt like an airlock being opened on a spaceship. It sucked Kip back into himself: he was aware of his surroundings again, of his body's relationship in space to other bodies. The glare of the tube lights, the blood down his shirtfront. Kids to every side were being raptured up to heaven. He got as close as he could to the bass player's amp and let its woofer shake the air inside him. The fillings in his teeth were slowly working themselves loose. He saw the girl straight ahead of him, then six feet to his left, then almost too far back for him to see. It was his own body that was moving, not the girl's. The whole room turned around her. She was its focus, its fulcrum, standing absolutely still.

4

The next time he saw her was seven days later, at a bonfire out in the Grids.

"The Grids" was what people called Ponceville, which was only hypothetically a place. Just fifteen minutes south of Venice, Ponceville was Florida's fifth-largest city by square mileage, but nobody lived there at all. The gold rush had swept Sarasota County a decade before—an especially nasty strain of bug-eyed land fever—and an area bigger than Tampa had been dredged and drained and divvied up by speculators, every one of whom had disappeared by the time the bill came due. The result was an uninhabited no-man's-land, development for development's sake, but it was also strangely beautiful: crossword puzzle blocks with nameless signposts at the corners, graded roads enclosing nothing, drainage ditches running spirit-level-straight into the woods. There were treasures hidden in the Grids if you knew where to look: mildew-dappled McMansions at two-thirds completion, some of them even furnished, where kids went to drink and blast their boomboxes and set furniture on fire. "The Grids belong to nobody," Leslie gushed as they rode out to Ponceville in the back of Chris Rozz's Isuzu. "That's what makes them the best place. No human beings, Norvald. No what-you-call *social context.* You can be whoever you want out in these fucking bogs. They exist outside of space and time."

That sounded good to Kip. "Who are you going to be tonight, Z?"

Leslie's eyes took on a faraway look. "I'm trying to decide between Martina Navratilova and Val Kilmer."

Kip saw her from the car before Chris Rozz had even parked it. She was kneeling in the red dirt at the bonfire's perimeter, as close as you could get without actual pain, tearing cardboard packing boxes into strips. Fire was the key to the Grids, the hub around which all the action turned, and this one was the size of a small house. A shed of some kind had fallen in, collapsed under a storm-downed king cypress, and its roof was burning gloriously from the inside out. Kids were throwing on pressure-treated fence posts, vinyl siding—anything they could lift—and green and blue and yellow sparks were shooting straight up through the trees. Kira didn't seem to notice. Kip went and stood a few feet off, waiting for her to look at him. It took forever.

"Norvald," she said thoughtfully. "N-O-R-V-A-L-D."

"That's still my name."

She nodded. "I heard you passed out."

"What?"

"At the show. In the mosh pit. That's what Leslie Z said."

"I got pretty into it," he answered, trying his best to sound bored. The heat was so intense that he could feel his pant legs steaming. "I might have fallen over."

"Word is you fainted."

"Also your piece-of-human-garbage cousin punched me in the mouth."

"Go ahead," she said. "Shit on Ray. Everyone else does."

A minute went by—more than a minute, possibly. The scar at her hairline was livid in the firelight. She seemed to have forgotten he was there.

"What are you grinning about?"

"I'm just remembering when Ray clocked you. You weren't even *looking* at him."

"That's true," he said. "I wasn't. I was looking at you."

He could see he'd surprised her. The smile left her face. "I've been thinking about that."

"What about it, exactly?"

She picked up a box and tore a strip from it—slowly, a finger's width at a time. "I was thinking it was bullshit. I was thinking you were putting on a show."

He'd had the advantage of surprise and then lost it. He'd lost it so quickly. He sat down next to her on the baking ground, as close as he dared, slightly more than an arm's length away. She was lining the strips up in a careful row.

"What are you doing?"

"You've never built a fire, I guess. Not like us pieces of human garbage."

"There's a fire right behind you. It's about a thousand feet tall."

"That's not my fire," she said simply.

He sat back and watched as she pulled a plastic shopping bag from Wojack's Fish & Game Supply out of the back pocket of her jeans and filled it with the strips she'd made. When it was full she got to her feet and picked up an even more precisely ordered stack of splintwood cinched together with a belt. In that coppery glow, with her hair hanging down and the wood on her back, she looked like a daguerreotype of some lone pioneer, or a statue in a graveyard, or the old man on the cover of *Led Zeppelin IV*. Every other person at the bonfire was wearing some kind of band shirt, but Kira had on a plain white V-neck, like an octogenarian's undershirt, that someone had drawn on with a silver marker: a decrepit, empty cottage in the middle of the woods. It reminded Kip of an illustration in a book of Russian fairy tales he'd had as a child—a witch's cabin, standing on two gigantic hen's feet in an enchanted birchwood forest. He'd stared at that illustration for hours on end, imagining he lived there. He tried to remember the name of the witch. At the moment he was having trouble thinking.

"They're called tits, Norvald. Most women have them."

"That drawing," Kip mumbled. He didn't even feel embarrassed.

"What about it?"

"It's messing with my head."

"What's that supposed to be—flattery?"

It took him a few seconds to answer. "You *drew* that?"

"I draw things. So what." All at once she seemed flustered.

"It's—incredible. Like something out of a kids' book. And you drew it on a shirt."

"I ran out of paper," she said abruptly, turning to go. Kip scrambled to his feet and stumbled after her, gathering sticks here and there as he went. His feet were soaked before he'd gone a dozen steps. Suddenly the name came back to him.

"Baba Yaga."

"Ooga booga."

"Sorry. It's a name that I was trying to remember."

"The name of a band?" She pulled a branch aside for him to pass. "Sounds about as metal as 'Kip Norvald.'"

"It's the name of a witch. Is that metal enough?"

"Maybe. Maybe not."

"Picture it with umlauts over all of the *A*s."

She almost smiled. "A witch, huh?"

"The creepiest kind. A *Russian* witch."

"I bet she wouldn't last an hour in these woods."

"What's so bad about these woods? They're a little damp, maybe—"

"Kids disappear out here all the time. Little girls mostly. You heard about Lindsey Furberold?"

"Shit. That was here?"

"Close enough. And don't forget the Lobster Boy murders."

"The what?"

She shot him a look of genuine surprise. "L-O-B-S—"

"I know how to spell it."

She shrugged and kept walking.

"You're not going to tell me? Seriously?"

"Fifty miles up the coast there's a place called Gibsonton. You know how Venice is Barnum and Bailey's winter HQ? Yeah? Well, Gibsonton was founded by the freaks. *Real* freaks, Norvald—not fire-eaters or jug-glers or fat men in dresses. There's a bar there that's run by an honest-to-god giant." She stopped. "You've got that brain-dead look again."

"I've heard of Gibsonton, all right? Tell me the story."

"You asked for it." She set the kindling down and held up both hands, fingers bunched into Vs like the Vulcan salute. "Grady Stiles is this kid whose hands and feet came out looking like flippers when he was born. A genetic disorder. He's sixth generation—his family's been on the sideshow circuit since before the Civil War. Only Grady comes out different. It isn't just his body. Something's wrong inside his head."

"I'm listening."

"They bill him as 'Grady the Lobster Boy,' and he's a hit from the start. A big hit. He takes to the stage like a natural—does a spooky lit-tle bit about the limits of science, about the secrets of swamp country, that charms all the suckers—but offstage he hardly ever talks. He just watches. He can't walk at all, he pretty much just flops around, but he grows up and gets stronger and learns how to drag himself forward with his big burly arms. He starts going off by himself, for whole days at a time—into the forest." She shot Kip a significant look. "Into the swamps."

"He dragged himself all the way down here—is that what you're saying? All the way from Gibsonton?"

"Of course not. He was no good on land—useless, pretty much. He was better in the water."

She knelt on the cool ground and untied the bundle. Kip glanced re-flexively over his shoulder. He could still see the ghost of the fire through the pines. She waited to go on until he'd come and knelt beside her.

"In the summers Grady toured the country as part of the World Famous Underwater Family. He was the worst case—the most severely deformed—which also meant he was the star. He sat on a special cush-ioned armchair to make it less painful. Between shows he drank. He could cross a whole bar on his hands before some asshole's insult had even come out of his mouth and rip him down off his bar stool and just go to town. Mostly he was a choker."

"How do you know all this?"

She didn't seem to hear.

"Kira. Hey." He'd never said her name out loud before.

"Just old family gossip." She shook her head. "Probably Ray or somebody."

"But why would Ray—"

"Eventually, god knows how, Grady got himself a wife—a regular person, what freaks call a 'passer'—and had two baby daughters: one with the family gift, one without. Having children did something to him. He hated Doddy, his firstborn—the one with the flippers. He wanted to kill her. But he loved his other daughter. She was tiny and snow-white and perfect."

Kip just stood there and waited for her to keep talking, cradling a rotting two-by-four in his arms like an infant. She started arranging the kindling.

"Grady's wife, Mary Pearl, started waking up in the middle of the night in their double-wide just outside Gibsonton to find him sitting on her chest in the dark with the pincer of his left hand around her neck. The left one was bigger, just like on a crab. He'd lean down with his boozy breath and tell her he was finally going to do it. He was finally going to do it and then he'd deal with that bitch Doddy too, and he and little K were going to disappear. *Get your affairs in order, honey*, he would say to Mary Pearl. *It won't be long now.*"

Kip kept quiet for as long as he could stand it. "What did she say to that?"

"She didn't say a single word. She paid her nephew Raymond eight hundred and fifty dollars to blow her husband's face off with a Colt pump-action shotgun. He used the money to get a little ruby for his right front tooth."

Kip tipped his head backward to look at the sky. He could still hear the hissing and popping of the bonfire they'd left, the revving of engines, the occasional muffled peal of shitfaced laughter. Apparently that was the end of the story. Kira was building a little pyramid out of twigs.

"Bullshit," he said.

"Fess up, though. I had you going for a while."

"I've only ever seen you with shoes on. You could have flippers or something under there."

"Good point." She dug out a crumpled little book of paper matches and lit one and held it underneath the pyramid. "You've never seen my feet."

"Now is probably as good a time as any," Kip heard himself answer.

"What's that?"

"I said that now would be as good a time as any."

Kira finished with the kindling, waited a moment to make sure the fire caught, then stood and brushed the needles off her jeans. She barely seemed to move but she was suddenly beside him. She looked full into his eyes, her expression polite but impassive, as though she had no stake in what she might discover. As though whatever happened next was predetermined.

"As good a time as any for what?" she said. She was close enough that he could feel each word against his skin. "To show you my feet?"

"What I meant was—"

"Should I just maybe suck your cock instead?"

His mouth hung dumbly open. Behind Kira's playfulness was genuine hostility, and behind that in turn was something he could not have put a name to. He'd caught a glimpse, however fleeting, of something that he had no business seeing. He'd seen her put some part of herself to sleep. To his amazement he found himself shaking his head.

"No?" she said, coming out from behind her eyes again. "Your loss, Norvald of the North."

"It's not that I don't—"

"Let's get this fire going."

He got down on all fours next to the pyramid and fanned it with a scrap of pine bark, glad for the reprieve. "Listen," he said.

"Do I have a choice?"

"What I want is for us, both of us, to—"

"Yes?"

He had no idea what he wanted. "To communicate, I guess. To understand each other."

She brought a hand lightly down onto his shoulder. It thrilled him in some way that was categorically new.

"You don't like girls," she said. "I get it."

"What?"

"I ought to have known it as soon as Ray decked you. He only beats up boys he wants to fuck."

The blood rushed to Kip's head. "Are you saying that your cousin—that he's—"

"There's that look again. Like your brain is in a ziplock bag somewhere."

Gradually his jumbled thoughts and sense impressions settled into a pattern he could understand and handle. He had a different take on Harley Boy now, needless to say. But that didn't mean he liked him any better.

"Get that ziplock open, Norvald. You can do it. Pinch and pull."

"Why does he always have that stupid hat on? Is he going bald or something?"

Kira closed her eyes and sank gracefully backward. "We're *all* going bald, Norvald," she said, coming lightly to rest on the needle-thick ground. "Some of us before we're dead, some of us after. Does it make that much difference?"

By the time the pyramid had burned away he knew slightly more about her. She'd gone to Venice High, which was how she knew Leslie, and would have graduated already—last year at the latest—if her father hadn't lost his mind and yanked her out of school. She was being homeschooled now, she said. Which meant she'd never graduate at all.

"You'll graduate."

"Shows how much you know."

"You still do homework, don't you? You read books and take tests and all that?"

"I feed the dogs and clean the guns and read the fucking Bible. Not exactly the fastest way to get your GED."

"Oh."

"Don't feel bad for me, Norvald. I learned how to turn a kerosene lantern into a lethal weapon the other day. It's easy." She smiled up at the treetops. "The hard part is deciding who burns first."

"I don't get it."

"Do you ever?"

His face went hot. "I only just moved to this piece-of-shit town. I can't be expected to know everything about you."

"But *I* know about *you*, Christopher Chanticleer Norvald."

He was on his guard instantly. "There's nothing to know."

"You moved here from Gainesville the end of October. You came by yourself on the Greyhound. You live with your grandma. Your mom gave you up."

Kip fixed his attention on feeding the fire. The shame he felt whenever his mother was mentioned flared up as always, filling his throat with sawdust—but that was to be expected. What was strange was that he also felt elated. To know that much about him she had to have asked.

"That's some pretty deep intel."

"My sources are solid."

He stoked the fire. "Leslie."

"Not even. My mother. She goes to your church."

"Just your mom?"

"Not me, if that's what you're asking. I'd spontaneously combust."

"Kira, listen." He lay down beside her. "I think I want to—"

A branch snapped behind them, the classic slasher-flick segue, and he jerked back as if he'd been tasered. Kira already knew who it was.

"Hey, Z."

"What's up, Carson."

Leslie stepped out of the pines and stood above them. Kira prodded the embers with the heel of her boot. No one spoke for a moment.

"Executioner split up," she said. "You hear about that?"

"They didn't split up," Leslie told her. "They just changed their name."

"Is that right? What to?"

"Xecutioner."

She squinted at him. "Are you high?"

"It sounds the same but it's not. There's some hardcore band in Boston called Executioner, so they're spelling it different. With a capital X."

That was the first time Kip heard Kira's laugh: a sharp, girlish giggle, nothing like he'd expected. It was almost a whinny.

"With a capital X? What difference does *that* make?"

"You don't seem to get it. They can't have the same name as a bunch of hardcore dicks from Massachusetts."

"But they *do* have the same name."

"Lowercase x," said Leslie. He was making a great show of patience.

"I don't care what their name is," Kip told them. "They're fucking amazing. That main kid, John Hardy—"

"Tardy," said Leslie.

"—his voice is insane. It sounds as if he's coughing up a kidney."

Kira was grinning at him now. "That's *exactly* what it sounds like."

"Where the hell did you go, Kip?" said Leslie.

"Here, obviously," Kip said, feeling guilty again without quite knowing why. "What kind of a question is that?"

"You could have said something." Leslie was staring past him at Kira. "Flamer was worried sick."

"Ignore this jackass," Kira said. "He's stoned."

Leslie didn't seem stoned. He seemed hurt and disgusted.

"Sit down with us, Z. Let us partake of your wisdom. Tell us the difference between a Gibson SG Premium and a Gibson Flying V."

On any other night this would have set Leslie off for hours. He shook his head mechanically. "I ought to be getting back to Ray."

"Cute," said Kira.

"Fuck you, bitch."

"Where's he at, anyway?"

"He's swamping."

Her expression changed completely. "Who with?" she said, already on her feet.

"A couple of mouth-breathers from Tampa."

"Don't tell me. He's wasted."

"I can neither confirm nor deny."

By then she was running. Leslie didn't bother to hide his satisfaction as he watched her disappear.

"Perfect timing," Kip said bitterly.

"You don't know how perfect."

"Excuse me?"

"Consider that blocked cock a public service, Norvald. Terms of my parole."

"You're jealous," Kip said, blinking at him in a kind of wonder.

Leslie heaved an extravagant sigh. "Kira Beth Carson, born June 1969, legal residence Port Charlotte. Subject puts out for domestic-abuser types, preferably alcoholic, preferably with an underbite. Gun racks a definite pussy lubricator." He fished a pack of Parliament Lights out of his back pocket. "She wants to hate whatever dude she's with. It *relaxes* her. She told me so herself."

"I don't have to listen to this. It's pathetic, Leslie."

"Fair enough." He lit a cigarette and took a deep, unhurried drag. "She offer to suck your dick yet?"

Kip cursed under his breath and started walking.

"Not that I don't appreciate her, for the record—I appreciate women, you know. But that girl has an actual death wish. She'll take you places you don't want to go."

"Fuck off."

"You can thank me later, Norvald."

Legend had it that swamping had been invented by Carnivore's original drummer, Tyler Christie, whose other claim to fame was getting busted for breaking into a Waffle House in Orlando at four in the morning, butt naked, and trying to fix himself breakfast. All you needed was a car and a swamp, and even the swamp was optional. You got up on the roof of somebody's pickup or hatchback—four-wheel-drive preferred— then went straight off the road. The one and only rule was that you had to keep upright. At some point Tyler had refined his technique by attaching a single water ski to the roof, usually with duct tape, to extend the ride and boost the m.p.h. It wasn't quite as suicidal as it sounded, at least not in the Grids. Cars tended to bog down before anyone got snapped in half.

They found Harley Boy on top of a Jeep Wagoneer, face and shirt-front slick with lager, trying to strap one of his feet into the ski. Leslie kept his distance—the occupants of the Wagoneer had on backward Dolphins caps and camo jackets and didn't look like fans of Hanoi Rocks. A silent crowd was gathering, coming out of the woods like an army of zombies, attracted by the possibility of disaster. Harley Boy was having trouble. He looked up when Kira called his name, craning his neck to see who she was with.

"Is that Kip the *Kipper*? Come up here, you sweet bitch. Let me give you a pinch."

Kira threw a bottle at him as hard as she could. It broke against the truck. "Get down from there, asshole."

"That sounds like the voice of my hot-as-shit cousin."

"Whose car is this?" She shaded her eyes to look in through the windshield. "Is that Gunner Burton in there?"

"Yo, Kira."

"Get him down off of there, Gunner. He's already pissed through his jeans."

"My hairy ass!" crowed Harley Boy. "That's beer."

It wasn't until Kira turned to Leslie that Kip could see how terrified she was. "You're letting him do this? You can't be letting him do this. Remember what happened to Tyler."

"What happened to Tyler?" said Kip.

"*Flapjacked*," someone whispered.

That meant nothing to Kip but it didn't sound good. The kid named Gunner was out in the open now, frowning drunkenly at Leslie. He turned to Kira in slow motion.

"What's this jungle bunny doing here?"

"Not a thing," mumbled Leslie, fading back into the crowd. The social context had caught up with him at last. Kira slapped Gunner's cheek, but only lightly—more to get his attention than anything else. Kip was starting to get a seasick sort of feeling.

"*Go go go go go*," shouted Harley Boy. "Thrusters engage!"

The Wagoneer's radio was playing "Separate Ways" by Journey, a song that Kip had always hated. He tried to settle on the proper course of action, some way to distinguish himself. He took a step forward and felt a hand come down on his shoulder, where Kira had touched him ten minutes before—but this hand belonged to someone with a crew cut and a handlebar mustache.

"*Excelsior*," shouted Harley Boy, banging three times on the roof.

Gunner climbed into the Jeep and hit the gas. Harley Boy gave a kind of battle cry as the front wheels spun out, spraying gravel in the face of a girl who was lying asleep by the side of the road. The cheer that went up was oddly halfhearted, as though the crowd had already stopped paying attention. Kip turned to say something to Kira and saw that she was sprinting after the Wagoneer as fast as her boots would allow.

The Jeep left the road at the very first bend. It was a massive machine, with a jacked-up suspension and monster truck tires, and it actually seemed to accelerate when it hit the chaparral. Kip was running now too. All he could make out ahead of him was Kira's silhouette—her long straight hair whipping from side to side as she ran—and the sand of the roadway beneath his own feet. Then the dark swallowed Kira and he was alone. He followed the noise of the Wagoneer into the scrub, throwing himself forward blindly. For the space of a breath, just before he went down, he seemed to hear the sound of someone singing.

He'd had the wind knocked out of him before—more times than he could remember—and he knew from experience to lie back and wait. He'd been running through waist-high sawgrass, rough as chickenwire against his clothes, and now it arched over his body like an awning. He felt calm there, sequestered, temporarily excused from duty. The stars were low and steady and exquisitely arrayed. The singing returned, much clearer than before, and he realized that he recognized the voice. It was Harley Boy Ray. Then an engine revved somewhere nearby and drowned the singing out.

Eventually he compelled himself upright and made for the sound of the engine. After a dozen steps he caught sight of a glow through the pines—a warm amber glimmering, not unlike firelight—and soon after that he reached the clearing. The Wagoneer sat idling on a hummock, hazards blinking serenely, to all appearances in perfect working order. He recognized Kira first, her head and shoulders shining in the brake lights, crouched low in the grass with a fist to her mouth. The kid named Gunner knelt next to a log on the ground, which would have been straightforward enough, not confusing at all, except that the log on the ground was a body. A second kid stood up when he saw Kip and started screaming.

In time the kid's screaming resolved into speech. Kip was aware of himself nodding and saying that he understood. The thing on the ground wasn't singing, he knew that, but what it was actually doing was beyond his comprehension. Someone was repeating the same phrase over and over and Kip was listening and bobbing his head in agreement. Kira was there somewhere but he didn't look at her. He knew now what was being asked of him. He gave the kid a thumbs-up, like an astronaut on a spacewalk. Then he started running back out to the road.

It was none other than Flamer Rozz himself who gave Kip a lift to the South Ponceville Precinct—Rozz had happened to be driving by, as if by divine intervention, when he'd stumbled out of the woods—but by the time Kip came back out, in the company of Sheriff Thomas Hartley Greenwood, the fabled brown Isuzu Gemini was nowhere to be seen. The sheriff said next to nothing on the drive out to the Grids, his manner unaccountably tense, cracking the knuckles of his right hand rhythmically against the steering wheel. He was handsome and smelled pleasantly of sunscreen. The nameless not-quite-streets seemed interchangeable at night, at least to Kip—but Greenwood knew where he was going. It wasn't hard to make out where the Jeep had left the road.

There was barely anybody left in the clearing—all the kids who weren't too blitzed had long since headed for the hills. Ray hadn't moved at all, as far as Kip could tell, but Gunner had bolted. Stupid Gunner. Kira was lying in the grass now, running the tips of her fingers through her cousin's blood-caked hair. She didn't get up, didn't acknowledge their presence in any way, even when Greenwood shone his Maglite in her face. She just lay there, on her side in the trampled grass, whispering to Ray.

"Kira," Greenwood said again. "Kira, honey. Get on up."

"Is the ambulance here?"

"Any minute."

She stayed where she was. Greenwood didn't insist. Kip got the impression that they knew each other well. They were probably cousins. Everyone in Sarasota County was related to everyone else, as far as he could tell. Except for him and Leslie Z.

He spotted Leslie a moment later, just a few yards away, sitting against an old pine with his arms around his knees. Kip had never seen him look so small.

"That you, Norvald? I figured you'd split."

"I came back," said Kip. "With your pal Sheriff Greenwood."

"You're a good little white boy. Did he let you turn the siren on and off?"

Kip sat down next to him and put an arm around his shoulder. He could hear sirens now, faint but approaching, as though Leslie's pitiful half joke had called them into being.

"It's not like I'm in love with him, you know. We just smoke weed and fuck."

"You're still here, though."

"What's *that* supposed to mean? So are you."

Kip nodded. "Maybe you should go over there. See how he's doing."

"I can't go over there, dipshit. I've told you about me and Greenwood."

As he said this an ambulance stopped on the road. Two EMTs appeared soon after with a stretcher, looking young and self-conscious, like extras or civilian volunteers. Kip helped Leslie to his feet and walked him over. The EMTs were lifting Ray onto the stretcher. Greenwood was talking quietly to Kira—Kip was vaguely surprised that he wasn't arresting anybody. He'd thought making arrests was what policemen did.

"Sheriff Greenwood?" he said.

Greenwood turned with a start, as though someone had kicked him. "What do you want?"

Kip looked past him at Kira. In the flickering dark her tear-stained face was luminous and strange.

"Are you hearing me, son? I asked what you wanted."

"Yes, sir. I just thought, if you needed someone to explain what happened—"

"You had the whole damn ride to tell me, Mr. Norvald. I'm speaking with this young lady here, in case you hadn't noticed."

"That was you, Kip?" he heard Kira murmur. "You're the one that went and got him?"

"Sit down and don't touch anything," said Greenwood. "I'll get to you in a minute."

"Yes, sir. I think you need to know—"

"What the *fuck*," Greenwood spat out, pushing past him.

Kira's pupils seemed to darken as her bleary eyes went wide. Kip followed her line of sight to find Leslie skipping back from the stretcher, both arms raised to show that he hadn't touched anything.

"Every time I turn around," Greenwood was saying in a kind of singsong. "Every time I turn around, Vogler. Every last goddamn time."

Leslie's mouth opened soundlessly. Kip had misunderstood his gesture. He'd raised his arms because he expected to be hit.

"What are you doing here, Vogler? Answer me. Is this your vehicle?"

"I just—" Leslie seemed to be gasping for air. "I just wanted—"

"Are you interfering with the work of these two men?"

It was then, watching Leslie fold in on himself without a word of protest, that Kip realized he'd never seen him frightened.

"Is this your vehicle, Vogler?"

"You know it's not, sir."

"What the hell did you just say?"

By the time Greenwood reached him his eyes had gone blank. "I said it isn't, sir. It's not my car."

"If it's not your car, Vogler, then you've got no reason to be here. Or am I missing something?"

Leslie's mouth gave a twitch. It was ugly to see.

"I've busted you and Ray Carson before. You're homeboys, is that it? Blood brothers? Is that why you figured you had a right to distract these men from their important work?"

Leslie made a sound that could have had any meaning at all.

"Did you touch him, Vogler?" Greenwood turned to the nearest paramedic. "Did he touch him?"

The EMT said something without looking up. It was Greenwood who was bothering them now, not Leslie. This was an emotional event for him in some way that Kip could not decode. Seeing Leslie next to Ray had thrown some sort of mental switch.

"I'm going to ask you one last time. I want you to *think* for me, Vogler. Give me one good reason why I shouldn't—"

"Tommy," came a voice.

Of course it was Kira. She was standing up straight now, her right arm braced against the Wagoneer's hood, her thin wet face shining. All she said was his name. Greenwood's whole posture changed as he turned toward her, away from Ray, away from Leslie, and there was no mistaking his expression. It was one of relief.

Kira's punishment for interfering was being kept out of the ambulance. Greenwood offered her a ride home and she didn't even answer. Kip could see that it hurt him. They were neighbors, or they were relatives, or they had some other kind of understanding. He didn't want to think about it anymore.

Eventually Kira walked out to the road and Kip and Leslie did the same. The three of them stood together, more or less, staring back into the trees. There was nothing to see. Leslie mumbled something in a tired voice and Kira nodded and put an arm around his shoulders. Behind them Kip noticed a faint wash of red: the bonfire was still burning. It had been burning all that time, and it would keep on after they'd gone, with no one to watch it or feed it, until it finally burned itself away to ashes.

The thought of that followed Kip all the way home.

5

Harley Boy didn't die. He'd broken his jaw against the trunk of a scrub oak, cracked the top three vertebrae of his back, fractured his pelvis, and snapped the fibula and tibia of the leg he'd attempted to strap to the ski—but in spite of it all he pulled through. He'd forgotten to finish buckling the straps, apparently, which the EMTs believed had saved his life.

The owner of the Jeep—the kid Kira called Gunner—was actually named Winston Presley Burton. He was sentenced to six months for reckless endangerment, driving while intoxicated, and leaving the scene of an accident (automotive), to be served at the Volusia Regional Juvenile Detention Center, just north of Orlando; apparently you could see the Epcot Center from the roof. Ray himself would be spending sixteen weeks in the care of his mother, Sheriff Thomas Hartley Greenwood's second cousin by marriage, in a full pelvic cast and something referred to as a "halo device." A halo device, it turned out, was that cyborg-looking neck brace with the screws that go into your skull.

Most of this Kip got secondhand from Leslie, who'd somehow bamboozled his way into visiting privileges with Ray's white supremacist mom; the rest he got from Kira. The three of them had walked back to town after the accident, which took most of the night, and they'd been what Leslie liked to call a "unit" ever since. They went to shows

at the youth center and hung out at the twenty-four-hour Perkins on
State Street and stared out at the water from Caspersen Beach and got
high and talked about bands. They talked about bands so much, in fact,
that they hardly ever talked about themselves. That seemed to be what
everybody wanted.

Evil Chuck had fired his whole lineup again, and Chris Reifert,
Death's drummer, had moved to California to start his own band, and
Xecutioner was called Obituary now, which even Leslie had to admit
was slightly better. Amon had changed their name to Deicide and gotten
a new bass player named Glen Benton, rumored to be an escapee from a
mental asylum in West Tallahassee, who liked to brand an upside-down
crucifix into his forehead right before he stepped onstage. Kip and Leslie
both considered that ridiculous; Kira had decided it was cool.

It was cool, she explained to them patiently, because it was the clos-
est anything they saw onstage had ever come to being *real*: an actual
human being doing something with consequences, not some underage
glue-sniffer striking a pose. Leslie rolled his eyes at that, his standard
reaction to Kira's pronouncements, but he knew better than to argue.
Kira was the genuine article, a metal *mujahid*, a wild-eyed true believer,
and the scorn she felt for music—for anything, really—that was soft or
safe or tentative was too ferocious to resist. She never discussed whether
a riff or a song or an LP was heavy, or dark, or brutal; all she ever talked
about was whether it felt true. But what Kira Carson considered "true,"
Kip quickly came to understand, was pretty much as brutal as it got.

The three of them did occasionally talk about other topics, at odd,
unguarded moments—at the tail end of a night of aimless driving, for
example, in the pause between the end of one tape and the opening
hiss of the next. They talked about drugs, and food, and the sinister
enigma of old people, and whether Reagan really had Alzheimer's, and
who in the scene was having sex, and what kind of sex, and who with—
anything, basically, but parents or school. Sometimes they even talked,
in a cautious, superstitious sort of way, about the future.

Leslie was always front and center then. He was the only one of
them confident enough, or naïve enough, to have given the question

systematic thought. He was headed to Los Angeles the day his bank balance hit eight hundred dollars—he'd arrived at that sum by means of some mystical calculation that he refused to disclose, and the figure never wavered. He was going to live in a studio apartment on the Sunset Strip and cook in a steakhouse or a Chinese restaurant and work the door on weekends at a club. The bands out in Hollywood had a lot more in common with Hanoi Rocks than they did with Deicide; but for Leslie—as opposed to Kira—the two sides of the great divide seemed to coexist in peace. He was a pluralist by nature, an equal-opportunity banger, whereas Kira was a purist to the core. Kip was in Leslie's corner, temperamentally speaking; but lately he'd found himself leaning toward Kira. He was leaning more with every passing day.

His life had a clear structure: after school he made a beeline for the Voglers', where Leslie spent his days in a pair of his father's ancient silk pajamas, smoking marijuana out of apples and working his way through *Mastering the Art of French Cooking* one red wine reduction at a time. They'd play two or three records, depending on how impatient Kip was, then go pick up Kira. She lived with her folks on the outskirts of town, on the edge of the Grids, which would have posed a problem under normal circumstances. But everything was different now, because they had a ride.

Oona had offered Kip her decrepit Suburban, right after Ray's accident, in a frantic Hail Mary to keep him in school. Kip had no intention of dropping out—he was too naturally cautious for self-sabotage, too distrustful of the future—but he'd kept that minor detail to himself. Leslie had christened their new chariot Kthulu—either after the H. P. Lovecraft monster or the Metallica tune, he never specified which—and they put more miles on it in six weeks than Oona had in half a decade. The timing was perfect. They saw Obituary at a goth club in Largo and Morbid Angel at some kind of kiosk in Five Points Park in Gainesville and Possessed at a converted loading dock in downtown Ybor City. Leslie had always insisted that they were lucky to be alive at that particular instant in history, and he turned out to be absolutely right. They saw Autopsy and Terrorizer and Atheist and even—on their first-ever pilgrimage south from the Rust Belt—the incomparable Cannibal Corpse.

The night of the Corpse show was one Kip would always remember. Leslie was up in Tampa, on some typically covert Leslie business, so Kip drove out to get Kira on his own. Her house was so far back from the road that he'd never actually seen it—her mother ran something called the Nordic Breeze Academy and Boarding Kennel, which Kip had always pictured as some sort of right-wing paramilitary training camp for dogs. Kira was usually waiting by a peeling roadside sign that read VERY BEST FOR BABY. SHOW DOG STYLING. HOUR RATES but on that night she was nowhere to be seen. He parked at the turnoff, watching uneasily for some sign of life, more than a little reluctant to head up that long gravel drive. Kira met him at the roadside for a reason. He could more or less imagine what it was.

The Carson house was hidden by a stand of sagos and Brazilian nut trees that seemed a remnant of some wilder, more primordial Gulf Coast. All that Kip could make out was a green chain-link fence and the slant of a buckling tarpaper roof. He sat idling in Kthulu for a good twenty minutes, feeling more like a coward with each passing second, visualizing Kira watching from some hidden upstairs window. Finally he stepped off the brake and let the automatic transmission inch him forward.

There were two kinds of homes on the outskirts of Venice in the eighties: starter-kit McMansions—generally in unfinished developments with names like Plantation Commons or Buckingham Dells—and houses like the one at the end of that drive. What at some point had been a standard double-wide trailer had long since metastasized in every direction, tarps over tarpaper over particleboard over plywood, the whole lunatic assemblage sloping sadly toward the driveway on the pilings of a weather-ravaged porch. Kip knew that he was poor—Oona's shabby little bungalow was daily proof of that—but Kira's place was in another category. People who lived in houses like Kira's were the reason gated communities in Florida had gates.

He stayed in Kthulu for another eternity, keeping the engine running, then sat up and forced himself out of the car. The sun hadn't quite set, but the space under that enormous sagging porch was enclosed in a permanent hillbilly dusk. The truck parked out front was barely bigger than the Voglers' Lexus, with standard-gauge wheels and a homemade plywood shed on the back that said N O R D I C across it in childish block letters. A neglected-looking carport stood off to one side—beyond it was nothing but pine scrub and swamp. Where the show dogs were boarded he had no idea.

As he passed the little pickup his eye was drawn to an insignia he hadn't noticed from the car: a crucifix, with branches or possibly antlers sprouting from its crown, floating over the silhouette of Sarasota County. All manner of cryptic hieroglyphics could be found on the backsides of Florida trucks, most of them more or less Christian—but this one held Kip's interest. It was beautifully painted, first of all: nothing like the clumsy stenciled letters. And it reminded him of something.

"Saint Eustace's cross."

A bearded man stood in the shade of the porch, bracing himself against the heavy railing. The man had spoken softly, as if to somebody behind him. But his watery close-set eyes were fixed on Kip.

"Beg your pardon, sir. I don't know what that is."

"Ever had a shot of Jägermeister?"

The question was meant sincerely, as far as Kip could tell. "You bet," he said.

"That's the cross on the bottle. Eustace was a sportsman and a soldier of the Lord. Christ's cross appeared to him when he was hunting in the woods—he saw it glowing between the antlers of a stag. A fourteen-pointer. He spared the animal and received God's grace."

Kip smiled up at him. "I'm guessing that wasn't in Florida."

"What's that, now?"

"I'm just saying—hunters hereabouts—" He cleared his throat and tried again. "Not that I know anything about it—"

"Of *course* you don't know anything about it. The only people seeing Saint Eustace's cross these days are frat boys and indigents." He spat into the grass. "You either of those?"

"I'm not, Mr. Carson."

"I'm not, Father."

"Excuse me?"

"Call me Father, Christopher. It's the one thing that I'm proud of."

"Sure thing. Okay."

"Okay what?"

"Okay, Father."

"Come on in."

Kip followed him into a surprisingly spare and tidy room with a sofa at one end and a wood-burning stove at the other. Carson had an odd way of moving—a slow, cautious shamble, just shy of a limp. He reached for the back of an armchair and braced himself against it, the way he'd done out on the porch. He gestured to the sofa and watched Kip sit down.

"Christopher Norvald."

Kip nodded.

"You're not from around here."

"I've lived all around the state, sir. I was born in Oklahoma."

"You're an *Okie*."

No one had ever called Kip that before. It had an antiquated, Dust Bowl feel to it. Carson wasn't smiling.

"Yes, sir. I guess that I am."

"What did I say about calling me sir?"

Kip blinked at him. "You said to call you Father."

"Not in a religious way, you understand. In a family-type way."

"Okay."

"Are you laying with my daughter?"

"Absolutely not, Mr. Carson. Not at all."

"That's hard to believe, Christopher. That's a steep bill of sale." Carson chewed on his beard. "However. I'll accept your answer in the spirit in which it was given."

"Thank you," Kip managed to stammer.

"My daughter is in the WC, in case you're wondering. The water closet. Putting her face on."

"Okay."

"She'll be coming out soon."

"Sure thing."

"Then you two lovebirds can flutter away."

In the silence that fell Kip gradually became aware of certain sounds: faraway barking, the muffled clatter of dishes, water running somewhere overhead. He and Carson seemed to be at the core of the house, in the original double-wide. The walls bowed subtly inward. Something fell to the floor in the next room—a spoon, or possibly a saucer—and Kip gave a slight start. Carson stayed as he was. He was like no adult Kip had ever met before. For one thing he seemed not to blink.

"My wife," he said hoarsely.

"Sorry?"

Carson brought up a fist, thumb extended, to point at the wall past the sofa. "Clumsy."

"My grandmother's like that," Kip told him, if only to say something. "Does your wife—excuse me, I mean Mrs. Carson—"

"She's got two left feet." He was grinning now. "My wife. Or maybe I ought to call them two left hooves."

Kip began to wonder what the hell was keeping Kira.

"Not like my daughter," said Carson, as though reading his mind. "She's learned all the graces. Etiquette. Housework. Comportment."

Kip didn't answer.

"That mural you were admiring? Saint Eustace's cross? My little one painted that all by herself. The week before her thirteenth birthday."

"It's beautiful."

He nodded. "I've imparted all my values to that child."

"I think she could—with as much talent as your daughter has, I mean—that she could really—"

"All my values," Carson repeated. "Which is why I believe you, Christopher, when you say you two aren't screwing."

"Mr. Carson, sir, we haven't even—"

"Speak of the devil," said Carson.

Kip looked up to see Kira in the doorway, wearing a T-shirt and jeans and no makeup at all. Whatever she'd been doing, it hadn't been putting her face on.

"Let's go," she said, in the most lifeless voice that Kip had ever heard.

The person on the other side of the wall said something then, presumably to Kira, but she paid no attention. Somehow Kip got himself up from the sofa. The voice came again. It was halting and garbled.

"Let's go, Norvald," Kira repeated.

"Pleasure chatting with you, Christopher." Carson shuffled over and held out a hand. His grip was strong but somehow awkward, and Kip glanced down to see why. Carson's fingers were fused into two thickened digits, irregular and mottled, like the pincer of a crab.

6

You must wait in line to enter the arena, along with the faithful.

The lobby, when at last you reach it, hums with activity. The action is centered around the concession stands, where T-shirts, programs, and other items bearing the logos of Anthrax or Metallica are being sold. The young "metalheads" (as they call themselves; they are also known as "headbangers," or "bangers") press forward anxiously, awaiting their chance to purchase one or more of the tokens on display.

Young folk are filing in gradually, in groups of two to six individuals, and taking their seats. It is evident that these metalheads have come to exalt not only the performers and their music but volume itself—sheer volume. "Heavy (expletive) metal!" a beer-swilling, mesomorphic young man of about twenty years of age shouts out periodically. One girl walks down the aisle wearing a dress better suited to prom night than to a heavy metal concert. Others wear clothes that are not only suggestive but frankly obscene—a brunette passes you in the lobby in a blue spandex top, with no brassiere of any kind. But not all the girls are dressed in this neo-prostitute style. Many are dressed like the boys, in the trademark "metalhead" style of denim jeans, a black "concert" shirt bearing the logo of a heavy metal band, and a leather or—slightly less frequently—a denim jacket.

The first band to take the stage is Anthrax, named after the prominent cattle disease. The crowd roars in greeting. The lead singer of the band shouts a greeting in return—"All right, (expletive) Orlando!"—and the concert commences.

In its essence, death metal can be reduced to the following characteristics:

- Incomprehensible, growling vocals;
- Down-tuned, damaged-sounding guitars;
- Relentless, rapid drumming—the so-called blast beat—featuring use of a double kick drum;
- Tortuous song compositions, with numerous breaks, stops, and tempo changes;
- Lyrics about death, gore, horror, and personal dissatisfaction.

The volume of the sound that follows is stunning, even for those who are prepared for it. On occasion you can feel your rib cage vibrating. Melody and harmony are virtually absent. All you can hear is the beat being pounded out by the drums and the bass guitar, and the singer's voice, screeching something unintelligible, over and over and over.

Whatever an unbeliever might think of this music, the "heads" appear to be enjoying themselves thoroughly. Often they sing along at the chorus, indicating their prior familiarity with the song. When they are not singing, many of them have a mesmerized look—eyes half-closed, mouths open. The fans on the floor of the arena have cleared out the chairs to form a dancing "pit" about twenty-five feet in diameter. In it there are bodies crashing into one another—and the more you watch, the more it becomes apparent that they are doing so deliberately. This is what metalheads call "moshing" or "slam-dancing." After one especially forceful collision, you see a boy put a hand to his head as he struggles to rise from the floor. He appears to be bleeding—but he is giggling, in a pained, bewildered way.

Is he smiling in spite of, or because of, his injury?

The Anthrax group performs with great gusto, the drummer assaulting his kit with simulated violence, the guitar players and singer *jumping, running, twisting, writhing in what appears to be discomfort. The crowd loves it all. The customary barrier between adolescents' private profanity (with their friends) and their public restraint (with adults) has been thoroughly dispensed with. Vulgarity is made public and celebrated. You can easily see how the term "headbanger" originated: Many of those in attendance "bang" their heads up and down to the rhythm of the songs, hands raised in the "devil horn" salute. The drummer throws his sticks to the crowd, and the metalheads reach and scramble for them, the way medieval peasants might have fought to grasp a reputed fragment of the cross that Jesus bore.*

"Well! That pretty much (expletive) sums it up," Kip said when Kira had finished. They were headed north on I-75 to meet Leslie at the show in Sarasota. Kthulu's speedometer flatlined at 58 mph, so that was officially how fast they were going. The light rain made the car seem warm and private. The blacktop shimmered in the headlights.

"What does *mesomorphic* mean?" she asked him.

It seemed like a word Kip should have known—the version of himself that Kira liked, at least, which was the version he was constantly trying to be. He did his best to think of something funny.

"Cool name for a band," he got out finally.

"It probably means ignorant." Kira frowned down at the pamphlet in her lap—*Youth Subcultures: Heavy Metalists*—then tossed it over her shoulder. "Like a caveman or something."

"Where did that thing even come from?"

"My dad sent away for it. It's a guide for cops, if you can believe it. He's marked some of the bits with a highlighter. *Beer-swilling. Headbanger.*" She grinned at him. *"Cattle disease."*

"The holy trinity."

"He's trying to understand my (expletive) alienation."

"That seems more like a mom thing."

Her expression changed subtly. "My mom doesn't read."

Kip wanted to ask what she meant—whether her mom didn't like to read, or couldn't read, or was actually *prohibited* from reading—but he couldn't come up with any way of posing the question that wasn't wildly offensive. He decided to keep his mouth shut for a change.

"Anthrax isn't even death metal," he said finally. "Anthrax is thrash."

"No shit."

He looked at her. "Hey, Kira." He turned down the volume on Kthulu's battered stereo. "Listen."

"I'm trying to."

He hesitated. "I'm not going to get in your business."

"Much appreciated."

"Right. But if you ever wanted to talk about—you know, whatever's going on at your house—"

She stared at him as if he'd started talking backward.

"For fuck's sake, Kira. You know what I'm trying to say. If your dad or whoever—"

"Ever close your eyes when you're driving?" Kira sat forward and put her left hand lightly over his. "On purpose, I mean. Just to find out how long you can stand it?"

He gripped the wheel harder. "Literally not once ever."

"That's what I admire about you, Norvald." She sat back with a sigh. "You're basically the opposite of me."

As so often with Kira—and with Leslie too, come to think of it—Kip didn't know whether to feel affirmed or devastated. It was raining harder now and he could barely see the road.

"I didn't even know you had a driver's license," he mumbled.

"They don't issue *licenses* for driving with your eyes shut. That's kind of the point." Her own eyes were closed and she looked peaceful in the green glow of the dash. Kip had that feeling he sometimes got around Kira—that she'd forgotten he was with her—but tonight he didn't mind. It meant she trusted him completely. Nothing anyone could do or say could change the fact that she was in his car.

"It's better at night," she said under her breath.

"What?"

"It doesn't matter how fast you're going. But the road should be straight." She nodded to herself. "Gravel shoulders, so that you can hear the wheels. In case you start to drift."

"What about other cars?"

Kira didn't answer. She seemed almost asleep. He might have been asleep himself for all the attention he was paying to the road. The sudden crunch of gravel jolted him out of his trance, exactly the way she'd described. He hauled Kthulu back onto the highway.

"How high did you count?" she said, opening her eyes.

"I didn't count."

"Why not?"

"Because I don't have a boner for head-on collisions."

She grinned. "The highest I ever got was twenty-four."

"Excuse me if I don't believe you."

She shrugged.

"What car were you supposedly driving? Your dad's?"

"Greenwood let me drive his cruiser."

He looked at her. "I never know when you're fucking with me and when you're telling me the truth."

The grin left her face. "That's because you don't know me."

"Don't say that."

"Telling the truth is the one thing I care about. Seeing things like they are. Not pretending they're better." She stared out at the blacktop. "That's what metal is for. It's a flamethrower, Norvald. It burns all the bullshit away."

"That's how you use it, maybe."

"That's what it *is*."

"Come on, Kira. A lot of it is fantasy. Horror movies. Black magic. Look at someone like Leslie."

"I was enjoying not talking about Leslie for once."

They drove in silence for a while.

"He warned me about you," Kip found himself saying. "That night at the Grids. He told me you had a death wish."

"Sweet of him."

"He said you'd take me places that I didn't—"

"Pull over."

"Huh?"

Her voice went shrill. "Pull over, god damn it. Right now!"

Against his better instincts he stepped on the brake. Kira was capable of walking all the way to Tampa in the rain.

"Right here," she said, more gently now. "Watch out for the fence."

They lurched to a halt in the mud of the shoulder. Kthulu's headlights strafed the guardrail and a sloping field of grass. Just past the hood a concrete marker read MILE 25. In the flickering dark beyond it stood what might have been a cow.

"Have you got a flashlight?"

It took him a few seconds to answer. "I think Oona keeps one in the glove compartment."

"Good old Oona. Plastic bag?"

"Plastic bag," he repeated.

"No? Doesn't matter. We can use our jackets."

"For the rain? I think there's probably a windbreaker—"

"Grab it." She opened her door and disappeared into the mist.

"Where are we going?" he called after her.

"We're not going anywhere, stupid. We're already here."

She was on the far side of a livestock fence already, the flashlight bobbing and weaving like a firefly. Kip found the spot where she'd wriggled under and did his best to follow suit, tearing the hood of Oona's cherished L.L.Bean windbreaker on a snarl of rusted wire. By the time he'd reached the spot where Kira was crouching, waiting for him with obvious impatience, he'd stepped in seven cowflaps and his sneakers felt like cannonballs. Kira looked even wetter than he was.

"Hold this," she said, passing him the light. "I can't do two things at once."

"I don't know where to point it."

"City slicker." She caught him by the sleeve and pulled him toward her. "At the ground."

Kira always had reasons for the things she did, and—unlike Leslie—they were reasons Kip could usually, with a certain amount of effort, comprehend. This time was no different.

"Holy shit."

"Give me some more light, would you? I'm trying to get this knife open."

Sprouting in discrete bunches out of the manure, somehow both feminine and phallic, a dozen thumb-sized toadstools steamed and glistened in the light. Kip would learn their scientific name later—from Leslie, of course—but he understood what he was seeing right away. He'd been around enough would-be psychonauts by then, in Oklahoma and Florida and points in between, to know that magic mushrooms grew in pastures; he'd even tripped once, or close enough, with a sad-eyed stoner in a park in Pensacola. But the papery debris he'd dutifully chewed that day was worlds removed from the iridescent glory at his feet.

"Should we eat them now?"

"We'll let them dry for a few days. They taste nasty when they're fresh." She smiled up at him. "I just wanted to show you this place."

He muttered something appropriately mush-mouthed and did his best to keep the flashlight steady. Rain was running down Kira's hair into the grass. As he watched her extracting the mushrooms, with obvious skill, from the reeking black muck, the book of Russian fairy tales crept back into Kip's mind: Baba Yaga at midnight, dank hair covering her face, gathering newts and toadstools for her witch's brew. He felt better in that moment, mud-spattered and shivering though he was, than he would ever have believed someone could safely feel. The witch had been hideous, of course, as witches always are in children's books. But the trees and stars and firelight had often formed the backdrop to his dreams.

The rain stopped as they hit Sarasota. Leslie was waiting for them outside the Stardust Lanes & Roller Rink, smoking a cigarette that looked too small for him and talking to a dough-faced kid who claimed to be some sort of roadie. Kip got a suspicious vibe right from the start—he asked the kid which band he roadied for, specifically, and didn't get an answer. Leslie told him not to be a buzzkill. Obviously the kid had something Leslie wanted: drugs, maybe, or information. It made no difference to Kip. He was perfectly content to sit down on the curb and wait there for his soggy clothes to dry. Kira had gone off to buy Marlboro Reds. He rested his forehead on his knees and imagined the conversation going on behind him as an old-time radio play.

ROADIE: Deicide's brutal. The sickest. I'm telling you, brother— they'll sandblast your brain.
LESLIE: That's the intel I'm getting.
ROADIE: You remember their old shows? Back when they were called Amon? The new shit is sicker.
LESLIE: Sicker how, exactly?
ROADIE: I can't tell you that. They made me sign a waiver.
LESLIE: A what?
ROADIE: (*silence*)
LESLIE: All right. I get it. What else can you give me?
ROADIE: Just, you know, rumors. Man-on-the-street type of stuff.
LESLIE: Such as?
ROADIE: (*pause*) Xecutioner's called Obituary now.
LESLIE: My mother knows that. And she's seventy-three.
ROADIE: (*longer pause*) You know Glen Benton, right?
LESLIE: What about him?
ROADIE: He's getting plastic surgery to look like a goat.

The next time Kip raised his head Leslie was off somewhere, making his ceremonial rounds, and the sidewalk behind him was packed to the curb. He scanned the crowd sleepily—it was more heterogenous than usual, more like any other rock show. He saw glammers and skaters and burnouts and jocks. Girls in camouflage tank tops. The occasional parent. The scene was expanding.

Kira had come back with her smokes and was playing a game with the roadie, who didn't seem—as far as Kip could tell—to have a single other friend. They were trying to come up with the most horrible name of an existing metal band. Kip closed his eyes again and waited for the kid to go away.

"Krank."

"Horslips."

"Abominog."

"Chinchilla."

"Helloween."

"Chemikill."

"Volitile Zylog."

"Sad Iron."

"Inkubus Sukkubus."

"Détente."

"Faster Pussycat."

"Wadge."

"Secretion."

"San Antonio Slayer."

"Sapphic Ode."

"Onanism."

"Rites of the Degringolade."

"W.A.S.P."

"Recalcitrance."

"Diktht."

"Sieg Heil."

"Arsetronaut."

"Lucifer's Friend."

"Sarcasm."

That appeared to clinch the duel in Kira's favor. The roadie called her bluff, a little peevishly, and she informed him that Sarcasm were a four-piece from Kranj, Slovenia, who'd opened for Anal Cunt on their Suffer Fools tour the previous summer. The roadie seemed personally offended by the depth of Kira's knowledge. Kip allowed himself to hope the kid might slink off somewhere to sulk, but he wasn't going anywhere. He was hopelessly in love.

Kip decided to take a walk around the block.

The crowd had thinned out by the time he got back, which meant the venue doors had opened. Leslie and Kira and the little roadie were conferring in whispers. The muscles of Kip's jaw were starting to cramp. Grow up, asshole, he ordered himself. You can't go to a show and expect all the douchebags to leave you alone. Not if you're hanging out with Kira Carson.

"Norvald! *There* you are, you creeper. Time to mobilize."

Leslie's voice always went up an octave when he was trying to hide his excitement. Kira and the roadie were already in motion, giggling and cooing, away from the crowd and the Stardust's marquee. She had her arm curled through his now, Kip noticed, as if she needed his protection. It made him want to lie down in the middle of the street.

The roadie took them around the side of the rink to a half-closed metal shutter labeled LOAD IN / EXIT SERVICE. He pushed up the shutter and ushered them inside as if he owned the place. Kip hated him by then, but he couldn't blame Leslie for kissing his ass. He couldn't even blame Kira. This kid was for real.

He'd expected it to be dark inside, the way backstage areas always are in movies, but the corridor they stepped into was clean and starkly lit. They passed a door marked UTILITY, a door marked ELECTRIC, and another, smaller door marked VIP. Leslie let out a cackle. None of them had ever been VIP to anything in their lives.

"What's behind that door?" Kip couldn't help asking.

The kid checked his watch—which, Kip noted with a mixture of envy and disgust, was an honest-to-god pocket watch, complete with fob. "Behind *that* door, brother, is Cannibal Corpse."

Kira sucked in a breath. Cannibal Corpse had put out their first demo just a few months before, but they were already being talked about in the tape-trading demimonde as the Next Sick Thing. Kip had had no idea they were even on tour, let alone on tour with Deicide. Leslie looked back at him over the kid's head—just a casual glance, but Kip got the message. They were backstage, for free, at the show of the summer.

"We hear good things about the Corpse," Leslie squeaked. He sounded as if he'd been sucking on a helium balloon.

"The Corpse is the *sickest*. They'll sandblast your brain."

"You said the same thing about Deicide," said Kira, licking her pinkie and sticking it in the kid's ear. He let out a delighted little chirp.

"No way. Did I really?"

"Fifteen minutes ago," said Kip. "Literally those exact words."

The kid laughed. "Doesn't make it not true."

"Technically it *does*, though," said Kira. "They can't both be the sickest."

"Keep your finger in my ear," the kid told her. "I like it."

They climbed a low flight of concrete steps to another corridor, turned left, turned right, went down a second flight of steps, down yet another corridor, then past the door marked VIP again. It was a different door, the kid assured them, and this time Deicide were behind it—but by then Kip was starting to doubt him again. He'd done nothing to prove that he was in any way affiliated with the bands or the venue, after all, other than raising a shutter.

Leslie was entertaining a similar notion—Kip could see it on his face—but by that point it didn't much matter. Someone close by was running a check of their gear, stomping in a businesslike way through a series of distortion settings, and even that by-the-numbers soundcheck was crushingly heavy. They hadn't been busted for trespassing yet, or even asked who they were, which was probably the most important thing. But it also seemed significant, the more Kip thought about it, that the roadie and Kira were now holding hands.

"Where's the stage from here?" Kira asked, in a whisper that Kip could hear perfectly. "Are we close now? It *sounds* like we're close."

"Close enough," said the kid. "That's Maurice, in case you're wondering. Guitar tech for the Corpse. His last name's Baalzebub."

Leslie squinted at him. "Beelzebub, you mean?"

"*Baalzebub*, actually. With two *A*s."

"Hold up a second. We've been wandering these halls for the past half an hour. We must have circled the whole rink by now."

"I don't see the hurry," the kid said, making goo-goo eyes at Kira.

"What kind of guitar does Suzuki play?"

"Say huh?"

"Jack 'Bloodfingers' Suzuki. Lead and occasional rhythm guitarist for the Good Time Family Cannibalistic Corpse Revue."

"Your friend's sort of weird," the kid murmured to Kira.

"Answer the goddamn question."

"Some kind of Gibson," the kid said, avoiding his stare.

"I didn't quite hear that."

"A Gibson, I said. A vintage SG."

"Would that be the SG Special, with the P90 pickups? Or the Standard, maybe, with the buckers?"

"I don't know, man. It's got strings on it. It's black."

Leslie was right behind the two of them, practically on the kid's back, looming over him like some gothic stick insect. "You've got to know about the amps, at least. I'm assuming Marshall custom."

"Sure," the kid said, speeding up.

"I'm having trouble hearing you, brother. Stop mumbling."

"What's up with your bro?" the kid whined, looking Kip in the eyes for the first time. Leslie was in front of them now, risen to full freakshow height. Even Kira seemed impressed.

"Lend me a moment of your undivided attention," he said in an amiable voice.

"I don't know their damn *amp* specs, okay? What the hell is your deal?"

"If you're going to lead us around in circles with your hand down my friend's pants, little man, the absolute *minimum* we expect is reliable intelligence," Leslie hissed. "There's no one named 'Bloodfingers' Suzuki in Cannibal Corpse."

"Forget this kid," Kip cut in, ignoring the death rays that Kira was sending his way. "I'm pretty sure the door we just passed—"

As if on cue the door creaked slowly open, like a bedroom closet in a midnight movie, and the ogres of Kip's metal fever dreams emerged. They looked sullen and hungry. It took him a long, empty moment to recover from his shock, and another to realize that he was in their way.

"Glen!" the roadie warbled. "Help a brother out real quick."

The first of the three, the one who best approximated the razor-toothed demons of Kip's imagination, made a sound of displeasure somewhere deep in his throat. He wasn't as tall as Leslie was, not quite—but he could have eaten three Leslies and still had room for a coconut cream pie at Perkins. He had long greasy hair and a forked black goatee. As he lumbered toward the kid, squinting down at him as if he were too insignificant to see, his face caught the glow of an EXIT sign just down the hall. A crucifix had been burned into his forehead.

"Glen, man, I brought these personal friends of mine inside the perimeter—"

"Like I told you never to do."

The kid chirped again. That was his laugh, apparently. "Like you told me never to do, exactly, and the thing is, now they're—"

"He wants you to tell us who he is," Kira said cheerfully. "Could you do that for us, Glen?"

The ogre's heavy head turned toward her. Kira gave him her best smile. There was a slight but unmistakable distance between her and the kid now, although his hand was still in her back pocket. His little mouselike eyes were wet with fear.

"Who he is," growled the ogre.

"Who or what," Kira answered.

"I'll tell you *what* he is. That's easy." The ogre grinned and pinched the roadie's cheek. "He's meat."

Cannibal Corpse were up first. The Stardust's stage, such as it was, had been set up on a little oblong island in the middle of the rink where disco dance-offs had been held in bygone times. They climbed onstage without fanfare, plugged their instruments in, and matter-of-factly proceeded to kill. Five hundred bodies pitched themselves forward, overcompensating for their shock, and Kip watched the kids in the front row go fish-eyed when their bellies hit the stage. He and Kira and Leslie were sitting wedged between the bass rig and the peeling plywood backdrop, dizzy with amazement at their idiot luck. The Corpse dressed like men who still lived with their parents—the light was low, but Kip was pretty sure the singer had on sweatpants. Make a note of that, Norvald, he said to himself. That's what confidence looks like. As he was having this thought the singer shuffled over to the mic, blew a chaste kiss at Kira, then let out a roar that sounded like the death throes of a mammoth.

The front row went apeshit. Spit flew and teeth gnashed and eyeballs rolled back in their sockets. Everything wasn't going to be all right, you could hear it and see it, and it scared the hell out of Kip in the way he most desired and deserved. Like Death at the youth center, the Corpse appeared lost to the world, locked in battle with the monstrous difficulty of the music they were playing, and the violence of that battle was the only thing that counted as the low end sucked him under—the ugliest, most perverted, most transcendent noise on earth.

Between sets Leslie dropped out of sight as usual, pursuing his unknowable agenda. The roadie came and went, humping gear as advertised; Kira ignored him. Kip told himself that she'd let the roadie touch her to get them backstage, and he knew it was true, but the knowledge somehow failed to reassure him. She sat within arm's reach, legs crossed at the ankles, looking more relaxed than Kip had ever seen her. The thing to do now was to leave it alone.

"I guess you don't mind having some random shithead's hand in your back pocket."

"Excuse me?"

"You like being the only girl at every show. The power it gives you. Am I wrong?"

He watched her make a conscious decision not to take the bait. "You don't seem to mind what it gets us," she said, patting the floor of the stage. "At least not tonight."

"That's not what I asked you."

"I'm ignoring your question."

He felt worse with each word but he couldn't stop talking. "What would you have done, though? I'm just curious. If he'd tried something, I mean."

"He did try something."

"Something else."

She gave his question due consideration.

"Hand job, I guess."

"Hand job?" Kip repeated. He felt like a passenger on a jumbo jet whose engines had been cut.

"Yep. That's my limit."

"What do you mean?"

She made a vague gesture. "For people like him."

Leslie found them there a few minutes later—Kira sleepy and thoughtful, Kip gray-faced and grim. He ignored the bad vibes, being Leslie.

"Consider me entertained, friends. This damn show is *scrunty*! I didn't even feel the need to spark a bowl."

"But you did anyway," said Kira.

"Smoke 'em if you got 'em, darlin.'"

No one argued with that. Kip felt a sudden desire to get pissingly drunk.

"Glen fucking Benton," he muttered. "Did you see that scar?"

Leslie was midway through a weed-fueled disquisition on self-mutilation throughout human history when Kip suddenly noticed the smell. It was impossible to ignore—the sweet pong of decay, like in a supermarket basement, or on the wet floor of a butcher shop, or at the bottom of a dumpster on an August afternoon. Kira quickly pinpointed its source: a spattered black trash bag being dragged across the stage by their favorite roadie, out of which a much more fearsome roadie was pulling football-sized pieces of overripe meat. It was only once they'd been arranged on a row of traffic cones that Kip could see the hunks of meat for what they were: the skinned and blood-encrusted heads of some kind of livestock, milky blue eyes staring placidly at nothing.

By this point the Stardust was jammed with more metalheads than Kip had seen in one place ever. The crowd was rippling and heaving and folding over onto itself, breaking into lavalike fissures whenever someone lost their footing on the beer-soaked wooden floor. The lights dropped without warning, as if a fuse had blown, and in the glow of the amps Kip saw four stooping figures take up their positions. In place of the usual band shirts and sneakers they wore long-sleeved black tunics, military jackboots, and what looked in that dim light like actual armor. This was worlds removed from Cannibal Corpse's leisurewear approach to performance—this was metal as Satanic vaudeville. The silhouette standing center stage, which could only have belonged to Glen Benton, leaned into the mic just as the lights came up.

"This song is called 'Sacrificial Suicide,'" he barked out. "It's about thinking what you want to think, doing what you want to do, and being exactly who you want to be."

An hour later they were back in Kthulu, depleted and rattled, rolling in punch-drunk silence down I-75. Usually they put on a tape of what Leslie referred to as "comedown music" after a show—something classic and mellow, like Mercyful Fate—but this time, by unspoken consensus, the tape deck stayed off. Kira was in trance mode, playing with an unlit cigarette. Kip was fully focused on the roadway. Leslie was in the back seat picking meat out of his hair.

"I've seen sick shows before. Lots of them. But this time I might need to see a doctor."

"That felt genuinely evil," Kip said quietly.

"Deicide," Leslie mumbled. "Those perverted sons of bitches."

"Mind equals blown."

"A for effort," said Kira. "I guess."

Kip wasn't sure he'd heard correctly. "What did you say?"

"I'm just expressing my opinion."

Leslie kicked Kira's seat in disgust. "Bullshit, Carson. I saw you during the Corpse's set. You were practically in tears."

"Yeah," she said, yawning. "For a while there—I don't know. They almost seemed like the real deal."

"Jesus *Christ*," Leslie croaked. Kira stared out the window. Kip had never felt annoyed by her before, not even a little, but now he found himself wishing he and Leslie were alone. What he wanted was to come down as gently as possible, to bring Kthulu home safely, and to bask in the afterglow of that perfect show until he fell asleep.

"I'm trying to figure out what you mean," he heard himself saying. "About that not being real enough."

"Eyes on the road, Kip."

"Because I was pretty damn convinced when those pig heads exploded. That kind of put to rest any lingering doubts."

"That was just carny stuff," Kira said tiredly. "Smoke bombs and colored lights. Grown men playing dress-up. You can buy a pig's head for ten bucks at the Piggly Wiggly."

"I'm going to sleep," announced Leslie.

Kip was still watching Kira. "I can't believe I'm hearing this. We're covered in blood. Glen Benton burned a fucking *cross* into his *forehead*."

"Scars fade, Kip. Trust me."

"What would satisfy you, Kira? Someone getting burned alive?"

"Admit it," she said softly. "That would be a thing to see."

"Not going to sleep, actually," mumbled Leslie. "Going to throw up."

Kip pulled over and helped Leslie roll down his window. Leslie slithered out headfirst, making noises that Glen Benton would have envied, and disappeared into a clump of Spanish ferns. Kip and Kira sat and waited, listening to Leslie's extravagant retching, staring out at the pines through the bug-spattered windshield. Kip was furious now. Something was being taken from him that he didn't have a name for. It was tiny but it mattered.

"I'm sorry, Kip."

"You should be."

"It's not Glen Benton's fault. It's not your fault. It's nobody's."

"What isn't?"

"Never mind."

"Want to tell me what the hell we're talking about right now?"

She drummed her chipped black nails against the dash.

"The feeling I get," she said. "The unreality. Like a plexiglass sheet between me and the world. Like I'm looking backwards through a telescope."

"What does that have to do with—"

"I've had it for years. Since things went bad at my house. Sometimes I even think that's *why* I have it. Does that even make sense?"

Kip thought hard for a while.

"It protects you," he said finally. "I think that's what it's for."

The smile she gave him then was so unguarded, so grateful, that Kip's mind went momentarily blank. He'd never seen her smile like that at anyone.

"Maybe," she said. "But other times I think I've always been this way. That it's the opposite—my being this way is *why* the bad things happen. I know that sounds crazy."

Kip shifted in his seat. "What kinds of bad things?"

"Thanks for hearing me out, Kip. I should have known you'd understand."

"Why?"

She took his hand in both of hers. "Because you're the *understander*."

He waited for the rest of her answer, something definite, an explanation he could get his head around; but Kira was done talking. His feelings toward her then were complicated to a degree that was completely new to him. There was the willingness to take a bullet for Kira, to kill for her if he had to; and pride in that willingness, run through with something that felt almost like shame. Underneath was a sense of unease, even foreboding—and also amazement that so many conflicting pressure systems could exist in his body at one and the same moment, each of them in some way justified.

"I've felt that way myself," he said. "The checking out, I mean. When something fucked up is happening. There's a word for it, actually—a medical word. Before I moved here, I got sent to a state-mandated psychiatrist, and he told me—"

"Dissociation."

They turned to find Leslie right next to the car. Kira got over her surprise first. "Dissociation?"

"That's the clinical term."

She leaned out the window and pulled him back in. "I thought maybe you meant the grindcore band from Finland."

Leslie was out cold again by the time they got to Venice. Kip and Kira had barely spoken since the pit stop: she'd put on a low-key doom tape— *Day of Reckoning* by Cathedral—and set off for the astral plane again. She was second-guessing herself already, Kip could tell. She was thinking she'd told him too much. But as he turned into her driveway, past the VERY BEST FOR BABY sign, she sat up straight and looked him in the eye.

"Christopher."

No one called him that except his grandmother. He lifted his foot off the gas. "Present."

"What are you scared of?"

He gave it some thought. "Zombies, mostly," he said. "Maybe the undead in general."

"Are you scared of my dad?"

He held on to the steering wheel and counted down from ten. He was sober enough to guess the answer she expected him to give. And he also knew the answer that she wanted.

"Not at all. Fuck that dude."

"Come on, then."

According to the glow-in-the-dark clock in the dash it was past two a.m., not much shy of two thirty, and the Carson house looked hulking and abandoned. Kip parked Kthulu halfway up the drive and they walked from there, keeping to the grass to make less noise. Kira didn't tell him what the situation was and he didn't need to ask. They were almost to the front steps when a light went on somewhere behind the house.

"Two nineteen," came a voice from the dark of the porch.

Kip thought she might reach for his hand but she did no such thing. She pushed away from him and climbed the steps without a word. She wanted him with her, but not for protection. She wanted him there as a witness.

The problem was he couldn't see her. He heard a sharp crack, like an old floorboard breaking, then the sound of something landing on the floor. He fell over in his hurry to get up the steps. The house was even blacker than it had looked from the car—everything had gone flat, as if a blanket had been dropped over his head. He heard no shouting, no weeping, no sounds of distress. He stumbled again as the screen door creaked open. A hand came down and closed around his wrist.

"Mr. Norvald."

"What's going on? Where's Kira?"

"You're intoxicated."

"I just want to see Kira."

"She's gone on inside."

Kip hunched over, still unsure of his balance, and watched as things around him took on form. The hand on his wrist neither loosened nor tightened. He felt oddly thankful for its steady grip.

"Mr. Carson?"

Carson said nothing.

"Mr. Carson, I'm trying to understand what just happened."

"Me too, son. Sit with me a minute."

"I'm not drunk," Kip said.

"Compared to what?"

No answer came to him. Carson let out a grunt that could have meant anything at all and steered him toward a couch that stank of mildew. There was no one else on the porch now, Kip was sure of that much. The creaking must have been Kira going inside.

"You're still standing, son."

"I want to know if she's all right." He was trembling now and wondered if Carson could feel it. Most likely he could.

"What exactly are you asking me, Christopher?"

"I'm asking you whether you hit her."

He heard a low sigh, or an intake of breath. Carson's face was in shadow. "Sit down here and I'll tell you. One man to another."

Kip let himself be guided downward. His head felt weightless and round, like a weather balloon. What was the word Leslie had used? Dissociation.

"That's better." Carson hummed under his breath for a while, some vaguely martial melody. "Here's what just transpired. I hit that calculating bitch as hard as I could with the heel of my palm. Old infantry trick. Drop anyone that way, pretty much, if you catch them right under the chin." He let go of Kip's wrist. "You probably noticed that she took it quiet."

Kip felt himself nodding. He couldn't control it. "So where is she now?"

"I told you that already. She's gone in."

Neither of them spoke for what seemed a long time. Carson said nothing, Kip could only assume, because he was savoring the moment; Kip said nothing because something was shifting inside him. He kept his body still and let it happen. Everything seemed to slow down, very subtly at first, like a record when you bring a finger lightly to its edge. He was experiencing what certain people mean—firemen, for example, or veterans of combat—when they describe themselves as moving beyond fear.

"Mr. Carson?"

"Yes, son."

"I'd like to tell you something about myself, if you don't mind. You have a right to know."

"Why is that?"

"Because I'm going to marry your daughter."

A slight delay in answering was the only sign that Carson was surprised. "I'd be interested to hear it, son," he said.

"You've probably heard things about me. Rumors and such. About me and my family."

"I place no stock in rumors. I hold with the truth."

Kip kept quiet a moment, composing his thoughts. "People say that I snitched on my dad—that I got him arrested. But that's not how it was."

"No?"

"My parents had—" He stopped himself. "Disagreements, I guess you could say. Differences of opinion. It started when I was eight years old, after my dad got his release. He'd been in the penitentiary in Gainesville on an armed robbery charge, Mr. Carson, even though he was just the guy who waited in the car. He got sentenced the week he turned eighteen, which is a pretty good example of what my mother used to call the Luck of the Norvalds. My dad didn't think that was funny." He took in a breath. "Am I boring you with this?"

Carson gave a quick shake of the head. "Not at all."

"Okay." Kip looked down at his hands. "I'd always been the stay-at-home sort of kid, only child, pretty close to his mom. I knew better than anyone that she could be mean—her temper was worse than my dad's, most of the time—but I didn't like it when those disagreements happened. I couldn't get used to them, Mr. Carson. I'd have done anything to keep the two of them from fighting, or even what my mother used to call 'exchanging words.' You're probably wondering where I'm going with all this."

Carson just sat there. Kip could see his face now. He was paying attention.

"That went on for years. It got more—physical, I guess. There was nothing I could do, not one thing, and my dad made sure I knew it. I was a kid, after all, and he was a man in his thirties."

"Go on, son."

"Here's the part you might find interesting." He paused very briefly. "There's a thing that happens to me sometimes—a place that I go to. In my head, Mr. Carson. When that happens, I do things—or watch myself do them." He looked at his hands again. "I've had a name for that place ever since I was little. It's called the White Room."

"The White Room," Carson repeated.

"That's right, sir."

"I'm not sure I—"

"After we moved to Orlando my mom started working as a dental technician, and one weekend she went off to some sort of conference. It was the day before Easter Sunday, if there's a name for that. She left for the airport at four fifteen, I remember, and my dad came home from wherever he'd been two hours after. I made us some flank steak and brought him his handle of Canadian Club. He'd been buzzed when he came home, which was par for the course for a Saturday, but by the time dinner was over he needed my help to get up. He took a swing at me as I walked him to the bedroom, and he kicked me in the ribs when I was getting him out of his boots—but eventually I got him into bed. I wasn't sure what to do next, Mr. Carson. I just stood there watching him do whatever drunks do instead of sleep. After a while I leaned over and slapped his face—with my open hand, kind of like you were talking about—and all he did was give a sort of sigh.

"I watched my dad a while longer, trying to picture the next day, and the one after that, and the rest of my life. Then I stopped thinking anything. I went and got two leather belts from the closet—one from the closet, actually, and one from the floor—and tied his ankles to the bedposts. He had exactly two ties in his dresser—ugly ones in pastel colors that he'd worn to some job interviews—and I used one for each of his wrists." Kip felt himself nodding. "I left him like that, and in the morning I went to the hardware store around the corner and bought four rolls of vinyl electrician's tape and reinforced what I'd done, to make sure it held. He'd pissed his boxers sometime in the night—normally that would have been the kind of thing I'd have been reluctant to mention to him, Mr. Carson. But I told him right away when he woke up."

Carson sat stiffly forward. "Listen here, Christopher. I don't know what kind of—"

"He tried to get loose, of course. He cussed me out until he lost his voice. But he never once shouted for help, which I still think is strange. He didn't ask me for anything, or apologize either, though he knew exactly why he was lying there spread-eagled, taped to that ugly brass bed. That was all fine by me, Mr. Carson. I wasn't interested in an apology. I was interested in him never laying a hand on my mother again."

He thought Carson might be about to say something else, and he gave him the chance—but Carson kept his mouth shut. He was waiting to be told what happened next. He was eager to hear it. Kip lifted his hands and looked them over for a while, palms upward, the way he'd seen murderers and rapists do in movies.

"I poured some of the Canadian Club into his mouth—I'm not sure why I did that, to be honest—then stuffed one of his socks between his teeth. He'd been ignoring me before, or pretending to, but now he was watching me like I was the most fascinating thing in the world. I sat down on the edge of the bed, against his left side, and opened up my mother's bedside table. He'd gone quiet by then—the same way you've gone quiet, Mr. Carson. My guess is he knew what was going to happen. He just kind of went soft.

"Under the tampons and the skin-care pads and the stubbed-out smokes I found my mother's leather beauty kit—tweezers, clippers, nail file, all that stuff. I got out a pair of toenail scissors, the kind with the curved tip, and tested them by trimming the nail of my father's big toe. It sounds funny when I hear myself say it, Mr. Carson, but that's what I did. It came out uneven the first time, so I trimmed it again. Still no good. I tried it a third time, all the way down to the skin underneath, then a fourth time, right into the meat. Through the balled-up sock and the electrical tape I heard him start to laugh. He wasn't laughing, I knew that, but that's what I imagined. I wiped the scissors on the sheets and closed them and worked them in under his toenail until I hit bone."

"Jesus Christ," gargled Carson. That was all he got out. Kip brought a hand down lightly on his shoulder.

"I was starting on the next one when I realized I wasn't thinking straight—it was his hands that were the trouble, not his feet. Over the next day and a half I pulled out all his nails, one every couple of hours, taping the fingers up after because of the bleeding. I got sort of obsessed, if you want the real truth. It was like drinking, I guess—hard to stop once you've got a buzz on. I was working on his teeth when my mother came through the front door."

Carson was done talking. Kip got up from the couch. He took his time about it.

"I'll take out your eyes if you touch her again, Mr. Carson. I'll take them right out of your head. Thanks for listening."

He went calmly and measuredly down the porch steps. There was some truth to what he'd just told Carson—more than he'd have admitted to, if anyone had asked. But most of it was lifted from his current favorite song: "Bedrest," by a three-piece from Detroit called Primordial Sin.

7

The rest of that school year was borderline perfect. Kira and Leslie were actively plotting escape—she had a cousin going to some art school in Texas; he was as focused on the Sunset Strip as ever—but Kip, for his part, wanted to be exactly where he was. Florida was the heaviest place on the planet that year, which meant the best place, and the three of them had box seats to the show. The gigs they saw that spring—Death, Obituary, Carnivore, Suffocation, Autopsy, Deicide, Exodus, Celtic Frost, Sepultura, Nuclear Assault, Trouble, Morbid Angel, Dark Angel, Death Angel, and at least three other bands with *Angel* in their names—were downright life-affirming in their bleakness. In between they went to garage sales and smoked Cuban weed and spent whole weekends at the far end of Caspersen Beach, at the tip of the sandbar, where the cops were too lazy to follow. Kip did the absolute minimum amount of schoolwork to keep Oona off his back and somehow graduated with honors regardless, which says something about the caliber of the Venice High School class of '88. It all felt effortless, inevitable, like the fulfillment of some ancient prophecy. That was how Kira described it, at least—and Kip would have been a fool to disagree.

Things had changed between the two of them. They never discussed what had happened between Kip and her father, or whether what he'd said had made the slightest difference; but since then he seemed to have become more believable to her, more clearly in focus, more real. She wasn't distant toward him anymore, or dismissive—and sometimes, to Kip's amazement, she seemed very slightly shy. Leslie teased him about it ruthlessly when she wasn't around, which Kip pretended not to enjoy. He couldn't gauge how Leslie felt about it—not exactly—but at least he didn't seem upset. *He's got no reason to be upset*, Kip reminded himself a dozen times a day, *because nothing is happening*. But of course something was happening. If nothing had been happening he wouldn't have felt so stupefied with joy.

As the weeks went by, Leslie's and Kira's exit strategies gradually converged—Los Angeles prevailing over Lubbock, for obvious reasons—while Kip tried his damnedest to dig in his heels. His argument was always some variant of: Things are already awesome. Bands from Los Angeles, from New York, from Oakland, from *Copenhagen* were moving to Tampa, to Sarasota, even to Venice. It made no sense but it was beautiful. Gulf Coast Florida was suddenly the center of the world.

A note of desperation must have been audible in Kip's voice even then, a minor third of foreboding, because Kira and Leslie dismissed his arguments completely. Of course everything was going to be different when they made it out of Florida—that was the whole point of leaving. Things were going to be wildly, radically, unrecognizably different. They were going to be better.

The music was everywhere now, seeping out into daylight, hidden in plain view of the straight world like a network of radical cells. CHUCK IS GOD—or, nearly as often, FUCK CHUCK—started popping up all over if you knew where to look, spelled out in Sharpie on bookbags and in blood-colored spray paint on interstate on-ramps. The band shirts the kids wore were nothing less than a triumph of DIY cryptography: an exchange of intelligence, not to mention a show of tribal solidarity, that the squares couldn't hope to decipher. Every sound, word, and symbol had more than one meaning. Leslie compared it to the French resistance, which was typical Z. But it did feel like an insurgency that spring.

Leslie had started referring to Kira and Kip as his "nuclear family," without specifying who the child was; Kira liked to call them the world's smallest cult. Kip saw no point in defining what they were. The music defined them. They parsed each new record like a cuneiform tablet, submitting it to Sunday school exegesis in Leslie's red bedroom, adding to and subtracting from the canon of the greats. They celebrated black mass and Walpurgisnacht and the Dying of the Light. They didn't have a crumb of musical ability among them—except maybe Leslie, who could carry a tune, more or less—but they'd been blessed with something even more sublime: the gift of true devotion.

Their role in the insurgency ended, as the pagan gods would have it, at the stroke of midnight on the summer solstice. It had been another immaculate day: the beach in the morning, Belgian waffles at Perkins, a long, aimless drive in Kthulu, Dark Angel at the youth center. Years later, it would still seem to Kip to have possessed a full-circle quality, a sense of closure that was almost too perfect—a lazy, golden victory lap past everything they loved.

It was an afternoon show—billed, for some reason, as a "deathgrind matinee"—and the sun was still up when they staggered back out. The usual assortment of stoned sloths stood milling around, waiting for something good or bad to happen. Kip recognized people he hadn't seen since Harley Boy's accident, which made him uneasy. He was getting a déjà vu kind of feeling. Sure enough, the word came whispered down the line: bonfire out at the Grids.

"Let's get out of here," Kip said.

Leslie was still show-high. He yawned into his armpit. "Out of here *where*?"

"Anywhere but the Grids."

"We've kind of exhausted our other possibilities, Norvald. It's our own damn fault. We had too much fun today."

"Do what you want. I'm not going out there."

"What's up your ass tonight? Let's stick around. It's looking like a fight."

Kip surveyed the crowd. "Not from where I'm standing."

"Then let's get one started."

"I've got a better idea," said Kira.

"What's that?"

"Let's go to the Fountain."

The Fountain was a perfectly round, basketball-court-sized opening in the earth—the word *pond* didn't do it justice, somehow—filled with brown, faintly sulfurous water, as warm as a retiree's bathtub. It was accepted as historical fact in Sarasota County that it was no less than the mythical fountain of youth, the one that had lured the great Ponce de Léon to his death. Nobody knew how far down it went; the bottom was assumed to be littered with Portuguese doubloons, Seminole mummies, and the detritus of coke deals gone wrong. Its official name was Warm Mineral Springs Park, but that didn't fool the hordes of Russian pensioners who packed the pool like spawning catfish every afternoon. They knew very well that the Fountain was a place of ancient mysteries, a source of spectral energy, one of the seven navels of the mystic world.

It was also, for these reasons and others, an excellent place to trip balls.

They pulled up in Kthulu at eight, twenty minutes before sunset and an hour after the gates had been locked for the night. The park was eerie enough in the full light of day, with its manicured lawn, its crumbling murals of prehistoric Florida, and the art deco clock set like a headstone at the far end of the pool—but at dusk, with blue tendrils of steam coming up off the water, it looked nothing short of otherworldly. This was Leslie's favorite place on earth, but the three of them didn't sneak in too often, though it was only a short drive down the Tamiami Trail. Going to the Fountain was like eating magic mushrooms, or drawing a pentagram on the floor of your bedroom, or telling someone you loved them. Casual use could drain it of its power.

Kira led the way, fearless as ever, tossing her Wojack's Fish & Game Supply bag over the chain-link fence and climbing nimbly after. They

crossed the lawn barefoot, more out of respect for the high cosmic volt-
age than any particular need for caution. There was nobody around.
The clock sat on a kind of pediment, a pleasantly sunwarmed slab of
poured concrete, and they unrolled their towels there and got out of
their clothes. Kip had seen Kira's body often enough—they went swimming nearly every day—but the sight of her at the Fountain that night,
with the stars coming up through the oaks and the steam hanging silent
and ghostlike behind her, was the image that would soon eclipse all others. Leslie was watching her just as intently. Every movement she made
seemed somehow consequential.

Kira with her faintly freckled shoulders, dark hair hiding her features, reaching down to pick up something from the grass.

They'd eaten the mushrooms on the drive out from Ponceville,
washing them down with lukewarm Pepsi to cover the tang of manure. Kip knew without asking that they were the ones he and Kira had
picked back in April. She'd been keeping them in a palm-sized ziplock
bag, its plastic crinkled from long weeks in the back pocket of her jeans,
with a strip of apple peel to keep the contents moist. Leslie had been
surprised when she'd first pulled them out, and had asked where they'd
come from, but for some reason she hadn't told him. For once he didn't
press the issue.

They were lying on their backs now, watching the moon drawing
up through the oaks, basking in its light like snowbirds working on
their tans. Kip wasn't feeling the effects yet, or at least not the ones he'd
expected; with everything else that he was feeling it was hard to know
for sure. Leslie had a lock of Kip's hair between his fingers and was playing with it in an absentminded way, pretending the sandy unwashed
mess was his.

"Here we go," he said after a while.

Kira arched her back. "Uh-huh."

Kip stared hard at the sky. "I'm not feeling it yet."

"Maybe you're just always tripping, Norvald. Maybe we're finally
seeing the world through your eyes."

"How does it look?"

Leslie heaved a sigh. "You lucky bastard."

They fell quiet again. A smell like sweet bourbon came up off the water.

"The moon," said Kira.

"I *know*," said Leslie.

"I'm not feeling it."

"Norvald—"

"We'll wait for you," said Kira. "On that ninth orange cloud to the left."

"The tenth one," said Leslie. "The ninth one looks crowded."

Suddenly there were ducks on the water. They had definitely not been there before.

"Ducks," said Kip.

"Ducks," Kira echoed. "Those look pretty real."

The droning of long-haul trucks carried faintly through the trees, all the way from the interstate out by the coast. Kip caught himself wishing that Leslie would go off somewhere. He didn't even feel guilty for once.

"Oh!" he heard himself saying. "*That* moon."

"Greetings, cosmonaut," said Leslie. "Don't pee in your spacesuit."

"I'm pretty sure it's not supposed to be those colors."

"Which ones do you mean?" Kira murmured.

"Any of them."

She laughed—that twelve-year-old squeak that always seemed so incongruous—and took Kip's ear and pinched it. He caught her by the wrist. For the space of a breath no one moved.

"Do as thou wilt shall be the whole of the law," Leslie said, getting up.

"Where are you going?"

"My sources tell me there's a portal to the underworld over there," he said, gesturing across the artificial-looking lawn.

"Those are the bathrooms," Kira called after him.

"Portals come in many forms."

He'd wished Leslie away and now Leslie was gone. Kira rose to her feet. He tried to follow her, then lay back down and shut his eyes to catch his mental breath. When he opened them again she was easing herself gracefully into the pool. Its surface didn't even ripple. The constellations were in motion, visibly aligning, predestined and cold. Kira was wading out into the water. It was up to her knees, to her hips, to the small of her back. The dome of the sky was close now, almost low enough to touch. He was naked but he didn't feel naked. He felt clothed in moonlight.

"Come on in," came Kira's voice. "The water's nice and smelly."

"Right behind you."

She was swimming now, moving languidly, not looking back. He found her waiting for him at the Fountain's silent center: a backlit pair of shoulders with the mossy oaks behind her. The water ended at her collarbones, where a ball gown might, and that was what he saw—Kira wearing the entire pool she floated in. She pulled him to her in the stillness and the gown enclosed them both.

"I'm tripping hard," she whispered. "Can you feel how hard I'm tripping?"

"I can hear it in your voice." His own voice sounded dull to him, insignificant and distant, as though it might belong to someone on the far side of the trees.

"Tell me you can feel it," she said, pressing both his hands against her ribs. She stopped swimming completely and let herself go slack. She was looking straight at him, as far as he could tell, or possibly through him. He was becoming translucent, ethereal, decomposing into steam. The thoughts that came to him as he held her, struggling not to imagine the vast lightless caverns below, would have triggered a complex relay of self-protective shutdown protocols in his non-psychedelicized brain; tonight they were harmless. All electrical and neurochemical agents of embarrassment had been flushed out of his skull. He was floating with Kira in the fountain of youth.

"I love you."

"I love *everything*," she said to him. "And also we're not dead."

"We're the opposite of dead. We're as not-dead as you can get."

"Those are the options. It's so fucking obvious. Love something or die."

He pulled her closer and kissed her, marveling from some alternate dimension at his psilocybin self. Kira seemed taken aback for an instant, even slightly bewildered. She'd forgotten that she occupied a body. Then she remembered.

The moon had cleared the oaks now and he saw her so precisely. The steam went right through her. They were down among the dinosaur bones and bags of coke and treasure chests and also they were high up in the air.

"Let's not get cold," Kira murmured. "Not ever."

"Of course not."

"It's too much." She was shivering. "I can see into the future."

"What's it like?"

"It's cold there, Kip. It's *winter*. Please don't ever leave me there."

He was telling her he never would when all the lights came on.

They were cheerful lights, hot pink and turquoise and fuchsia, and he might have thought Leslie had switched them on if not for all the shouting. The stars disappeared and the moon was crushed flat and the oaks all around turned to plastic. The movie was over. Lights up and roll credits. A shot rang out, or something like a shot, and then another. In his confusion Kip sucked in a mouthful of water. He pressed his fists into his eye sockets, kicking and retching, disgusted at how beautiful everything was. He couldn't seem to make the beauty stop. He felt the urge to sink straight down until he touched the bottom. He could swim all the way home, or anywhere he wanted, from one cave system to another. He looked around for Kira and found no trace of her. She must be waiting somewhere in the dark.

He broke the surface again at the slippery, algae-furred base of the clock, hiding in its shadow from the shouting. He found his pants and shirt and struggled into them. The action was across the water, back toward the entrance, where the voices and the lights seemed to converge. He hesitated longer than he should have, longer than he could afford to, trying to decide which way to run. He saw candy-colored comet tails each time he moved his head.

The decision was made for him by Leslie's voice. It carried across the water with exaggerated clarity—with perfect, crystalline fidelity—on account of the acoustics of the Fountain, or the psilocybin, or the barometric pressure of the air. Leslie was making sounds Kip had never heard before: frantic mechanical squeakings, metallic and shrill, like a squirrel he'd once discovered in a spring trap meant for rats. He pulled on his sneakers and started to run.

He found Leslie facedown on the gift shop patio, arms limp at his sides, a towel thrown over his ass and lower back as if he were already dead. It hurt Kip's eyes to look at him. He was weeping onto the pavement, a puddle of spit at his mouth, surrounded by more members of the police force than Kip had ever seen outside of a parade. It crossed his mind quietly, with no particular urgency, that what was happening was the worst thing that could possibly happen to someone under the influence of hallucinogens. He stepped out of the dark and tried to speak.

"Pardon me, officers."

No reaction. They were all so intent on their theater of operations that everything outside the frame was disregarded. In that millisecond-long glitch in the videotape Kip searched the circle of light for Kira and found no trace of her. Thank god, he thought. Thank god for that. Then his arms were forced behind him and his face was in the grass.

"Pardon me, officers."

"Who's this?" said a high-pitched voice. "The boyfriend?"

"Actually I'm—"

"Best shut up now," came a lower voice. Lower but closer. It sounded concerned.

Kip did as instructed. The worst thing was happening and it was happening in a way he couldn't get his head around. So obvious. So cornball. It was possible that the whole operation was being staged for some as-yet-unseen audience—there was a slight but significant chance that the redneck cops to every side were playing "redneck cops," and that if he kept quiet the scene would simply run its course. A spirited conversation was taking place above him, some form of debate, but he'd already stopped paying attention. He lay there slack and unprotesting with his hands on the back of his neck, grateful to have soft grass underneath him. He didn't even want to speculate about what Leslie might be feeling. His gaze came to rest on a knee-high bronze plaque affixed to a boulder not far from his face. Twisting his neck slightly, he read:

PREHISTORIC MAN LIVED HERE

MORE THAN 10,000 YEARS AGO PREHISTORIC MAN, SABER-TOOTH CATS, GIANT SLOTHS, MAMMOTHS AND MASTODONS INHABITED THIS AREA OF WEST FLORIDA WHICH LATER BECAME PART OF LOVELY SARASOTA COUNTY. CARBON DATING OF HUMAN AND ANIMAL SKELE-TAL REMAINS, AS WELL AS WOODEN ARTIFACTS FOUND IN THESE WA-TERS BY UNDERWATER ARCHAEOLOGISTS, HAS DETERMINED THEIR ANTIQUITY. THESE EXPLORATIONS AND SCIENTIFIC STUDIES HAVE RESULTED IN MUCH LEARNED ATTENTION BEING GIVEN TO THESE SPRINGS. RESPECT YOUR PATRIMONY!

"Get this faggot up," said Cracker Cop Number One. He was talking as if his mouth were full of hominy grits, playing to the cheap seats, milking every line for laughs. Even Leslie was overacting now, twitching and mewling in a bizarre, kittenish voice that Kip had never heard him use. The cop who'd been kneeling between Kip's shoulder blades jerked him upright by his shirt.

"What's your name, boy?"

"Christopher C. Norvald, officer."

The second voice offered a guess as to what the C might stand for. The laughter this occasioned sounded kindly and sincere.

"And what are you strapping young fellows doing out here in the dark, Christopher C. Norvald, that you couldn't do by daylight?"

"Beers," Kip said, not looking at Leslie.

"Since when do you need to get stark naked to drink beers, boy?"

"I'm not naked."

"Your butt-buddy is, though. Over there on the ground."

"He jumped in with his clothes on, sir. He took them off right after."

"With his clothes on?"

"Yes, sir."

"What the hell for?"

"He does that sometimes when he's feeling free."

Someone chuckled at that, which Kip took as a positive sign. Fewer of their flashlights were pointed at him now and he could see their faces better. Some of them were enjoying the proceedings, others had their reservations. Number One belonged to the first group. He had a flattop and a sunburn and a gap in his teeth. He might as well have been chewing on a dirty piece of straw.

"What if I was to call bullshit on that explanation, Mr. Norvald," he said comfortably. "What if I was to say you boys were out here snorting crank and playing doctor."

"No, sir."

"What's your little friend's name? He's been trying to tell us. Damn if any of us can understand him."

"Leslie."

"Leslie what? Kareem Abdul Jabbar?"

Louder chuckles this time. The worried cops looked more worried. Number One took out his service revolver and pointed it at the back of Leslie's head.

"Vogler," Kip got out. "Leslie Aaron Vogler. He's president of our class at Venice High."

"Venice, huh." The officer pursed his lips. "Makes sense. Circus town. They'll take anybody."

"Yes, sir."

"Even monkeys in makeup."

"Yes, sir."

"But that's the thing these days, isn't it. Grown men in spandex. Make the young girls go goofy."

"Yes, sir."

Number One smiled at something far away. The color wheel kept spinning.

"I'm going to ask you one more time, Mr. Norvald. What were you boys up to out here, on private property in the middle of the night, running around like a couple of bare-assed babies?"

"We were swimming, officer. Just swimming. I swear to god."

"Swimming," Number One said thoughtfully. "Going for a moonlight dip."

Kip did his best to nod, staring at the ground between his shoes. The grass was moving under them like seaweed in a current.

"Are those your bikes outside?"

"Bikes, sir?"

"The ones locked up by the gate."

This time he answered instantly. "Yes, sir. Absolutely."

For a geologic era no one said a word. Number One looked down at him expressionlessly, blandly, the tropical night air whistling through the gap in his teeth. Kip had never heard a louder sound in all his life.

"Touch your nose with the index finger of your right hand."

He focused the last of his psychic energy into a grain of hard white light and did as he was told.

"You're excused, Mr. Norvald. Get your bike and go home."

He took a few uncertain steps. The ground had gone gelatinous. "Thank you, officer."

"Get walking."

"Thank you, officer. What about my friend?"

"Your friend will be partying with the North Port sheriff's office this evening. He fits a description."

The idea of Leslie fitting any description but his own was preposterous, beyond belief, even in Kip's current condition. He cleared his throat. "I'm having a hard time understanding—"

"You've got exactly eighteen seconds to make yourself not-here, Mr. Norvald. And I've just used ten of them up."

Kip forced himself to turn and look at Leslie, who was still lying facedown on the concrete patio. His left hand gave what might have been a wave.

"All right, Leslie," Kip said, raising his voice so everyone could hear. "We'll be back first thing in the morning. I'll be bringing my uncle."

He started walking without waiting for an answer. By some miracle the lawn underneath him supported his weight.

"Who's your uncle, boy?" someone called out.

"Sheriff Thomas Hartley Greenwood," Kip replied.

He'd half expected Kthulu to be gone—swallowed by a sinkhole, maybe, or towed away by the police—but it was right where he'd left it, more or less in plain sight, fifty feet up the road from the gate. He found Kira in the back seat with a towel over her head, tripping harder than ever, still whispering to herself about the cold. They pulled out with the headlights off and kept them off for the first few miles, driving by the light of the moon. Eventually they hung a left onto a nameless gravel side road and sat in the dark, barely talking at all, just holding hands and waiting for the fireworks to fade. They tried to sleep for a while, then gave up on sleeping and drove around North Port and Port Charlotte until a diner finally opened. Seven cups of coffee later they went back to pick up Leslie.

The cops released him right away, as though they couldn't wait to see the last of him. He looked more dead than alive. Kip had to lead him outside by the elbow. The only thing they could get out of him for the first few hours was that nobody had hurt him. Eventually they learned that he'd spent the whole night tripping in a floodlit one-man cell.

"I'm so sorry, Leslie."

"That's all right. Nobody hurt me."

"We shouldn't have left you alone, man."

Leslie gave a dim little smile and shook his head. "That was a good one, though. About Greenwood. Credit where credit is due."

"Do you think it helped?"

"Not even a little."

They drove east for a while with no clear destination—just due east and inland, the rising sun full in their faces. Leslie sat slumped against the window, humming to himself and watching the scrub pines whip by. Kip's head ached from the coffee and his stomach felt strange. Kira was in the back seat, out of his field of vision, still not saying much. For the first time in his life he understood the urge to close his eyes and see how far the car could make it on its own. She sat forward then, as if she'd guessed what he was thinking, and put her hands on Leslie's shoulders.

"What was it you were saying yesterday, Kip? About this being the best place to live in the world?"

That same night they started packing for L.A.

"

L.A.
GLAM

1

Glam had officially been pronounced dead back in Venice by the summer of '88—but no one, as far as Kip could tell, had bothered to inform the Sunset Strip. The regulars peacocking around Gazzarri's or the Whisky or the Odeon any night of the week were enough to make Leslie's most egregious lapses of judgment look genteel. Spandex and mascara were the rule, not the exception. You were more likely to get hassled for wearing sneakers and sweatpants than you were for wearing lipstick and high heels. What might have been cool back in Florida counted for nothing out here. The Strip on a Saturday night was a cavalcade of feather boas and press-on eyelashes and fishnet gloves and assless leather chaps. It was dominated by men in full-on drag, especially on stage. And the weirdest thing about it was that everyone was straight.

"They *think* they're straight," said Leslie. "I arrived here just in time."

Kira giggled at that—her witch's cackle, a new laugh she was working on. But something about the scene put Kip on edge. It all seemed too good to be true.

They spent their first weeks in town living out of Kthulu: contrary to everybody's expectations, including his own, Kip had finished the school year, and Oona had proven as good as her word. They found a parking space at the end of a cul-de-sac off North Highland Avenue, three blocks away from the Hollywood Bowl, and waited there for destiny to find them. The buddies Leslie had claimed to have in Santa Monica had evaporated, and so—to absolutely no one's surprise—had their only other contact, Flamer Rozz's second cousin. Kip began each day by hiking downhill to the 7-Eleven on Franklin, still sweating from the sunlight through Kthulu's windshield, to buy a jar of peanut butter and a bag of English muffins. They spread the peanut butter on the muffins with a membership card from the American Automobile Association that Leslie carried around in his wallet, made out to ANDREW EDWARD KAUFMANN, DDS. Kip never asked who Andrew Kaufmann was and Leslie never told him.

The precariousness of those weeks would have felt adult and consequential—even exciting, in a desperate, dues-paying sort of way—if not for the fights. Most mornings, coming back from the 7-Eleven, Kip would hear Kira and Leslie shouting before he'd even turned the corner. Leslie had got it into his head that Kira had left him for dead that last night at the Fountain, and in a sense he was right; but that was never what they fought about. They fought about Hanoi Rocks and Tipper Gore and the war in Afghanistan and Ozzy Osbourne's hideous frosted hairdo, which was actually a lot like Tipper Gore's. They fought about money and food and whose turn it was to sleep in the back seat. Nothing that Kip said or did could stop them. It made him want to clip Kthulu's parking brake and watch them roll downhill.

Things had almost reached the breaking point when Kira found a job. She got hired more or less spontaneously, seemingly without the slightest effort, as a weekday hostess at the Rainbow Room. Leslie kissed her full on the lips when she told him the news. It felt like divine intervention. The Rainbow was the place everyone went after their gigs at Gazzarri's or the Roxy—a former burlesque club with cracked pleather booths and pictures of vanished starlets on the graffiti-blackened walls. Everything in there was red and dark and sleazy and alive. Lemmy from Mötörhead hung out at the outdoor bar in the afternoons, drinking Jack and Cokes and playing computer poker. Kip could hardly believe it. Kira was going to be serving Lemmy Jack and Cokes for forty bucks a night.

They moved into a Santa Monica flophouse on Kira's first paycheck—

a mud-colored Tudor that everyone in the scene called the Needle Exchange—then into an honest-to-god one-bedroom on the first of the month. The real estate agent, who'd made a big deal about the fact that the stovetop had six burners instead of four, had leered at Kira openly, but Kip had made an executive decision not to care. Six burners. A refrigerator. Something called a "quarter bath" in what the agent insisted on referring to as the "WC." It felt like a dream.

They celebrated Kira's nineteenth birthday in a derelict house that Leslie had discovered on one of his stoned walkabouts: a chinoiserie mansion at the end of what the locals grandiosely called a "canyon," somehow magically fastened to the mountainside, reachable only by a flight of concrete steps. Green pagoda-like gables, Victorian dormers, scalloped tiles on the roof like the scales of a carp. Kira had christened it Xanadu—not after the Olivia Newton-John song—and even Leslie had to admit the name was fitting. A middle-aged tweaker named Horace squatted there, but he seemed friendly enough, and he usually disappeared after dark. The front porch smelled like cat piss and the back porch smelled like sage. The cliff just past the railing, over which Horace tossed his cigarette butts and beer cans, dropped straight down into a side lot of the Bowl.

Someone major was playing that night, judging by the turnout, and the three of them sat on the porch with a twelve-pack of Coors Light and waited to hear who it was. Kip was next to Kira, and she leaned into him from time to time—but when she came back from her third trip to the bushes she sat down with Leslie. She seemed drunker than four beers could justify.

"It's starting," said Leslie.

They sat up and listened. The music carried up the cliff to them in greasy plumes of sound.

"That doesn't sound like anything," Kira said, kicking the railing. Leslie reached out lazily and caught her by the shirt.

"Let go of me, Z. I'm a grown fucking woman. I'm old enough to join the army."

"The army doesn't take alcoholics," said Kip.

"Both of you shut up," said Leslie. "I know this damn song."

Kip wasn't interested. He finished his Coors. Kira made a face at him and his chest went tight with joy.

"Men without hats," announced Leslie.

"Huh?"

"Men Without Hats. The band."

Kip lobbed his empty can over the railing. "Jesus, Kira. On your birthday no less."

"Shhhhh," hissed Leslie. "I'm listening."

Kira rolled her eyes. "Mind your manners, Norvald. Leslie paid good money for these seats."

"Do not trifle with me, bitch."

"Rich boy," Kira said, pretending to gag. "Sophisticated tastes."

"Come now, children," Kip singsonged, already back in pacification mode. "Let's not spoil a lovely evening."

"*Shhhhhhhh.*"

"Don't you *shush* me, asshole," Kira said, flicking her cigarette at Leslie's face. "Today is my—"

"I don't care what goddamn day it is," Leslie bellowed, lurching to his feet. "If you say one more fucking word—"

"Watch this," Kip said casually. He stepped to the railing, turned around to face the two of them, and flipped his body backward off the porch.

He was lying flat on his back on a little sloping bluff fifteen feet down the cliff, gazing dreamily upward at Xanadu's gables, his left arm oddly folded underneath him. Far below, if he craned his neck, he could make out a pyramid of yellow sand on the hood of a Chevy Caprice.

"Kip," Kira seemed to be saying. "Jesus Christ. Look at me. Can you get yourself up?"

"I am up," he answered.

"Fucking hell, Leslie. Look at his face."

"What's wrong with my face?"

"It's like—I don't know. Dead-baby white."

Leslie came into view now, impossibly tall. "Dead-*white*-baby white."

He threw up down his shirtfront, mumbled an apology, then threw up again when Kira tried to shift him. There was no pain to speak of. His arm was the problem.

"My arm."

"Let's get him upright," said Leslie. "Hold on—I need a better grip. Hold *on*, damn it. I'll tell you when."

He'd thought he might be sick again when they took him by the shoulders but he blacked out instead. When he woke up he was shaking and he couldn't feel his arm. That bothered him in a far-off sort of way. Kira was kneeling beside him, staring into his face. Her eyes were enormous.

"Why would you *do* that, Kip?"

"Third-party intervention." His voice sounded like a message on an answering machine. "Preserving the unit."

"What the hell does that mean?"

"Preserving the unit," he repeated. He knew he was babbling. "Peace-keeping mission. Afghanistan. Lebanon."

They made it back up to the porch and eased him down as gently as they could. The tweaker was there, reclining on an expensive-looking deck chair that was covered in soot. Kip tried to recall whether either the chair or the tweaker had been there before. The pain was rolling in now and it wouldn't let him think.

"Shoulder," Horace said, to no one in particular.

"No shit," said Kira.

"Partial orbital dislocation." Horace's pale gray eyes were less bugged-out than usual. Most days he looked panicked even when he was asleep.

"No bleeding," said Leslie. "That's a good sign. Am I right?"

Horace shook his head regretfully. "There wouldn't be blood."

"How the fuck would you know?" said Kira.

"I've seen my share of these." He shrugged. "I used to be an obstetrician."

No one spoke for a moment.

"I think you mean orthopedist," Leslie said finally.

"I know what I am."

Nobody stopped him as he brushed himself off with a professional air and crouched at Kip's side. "Right," he said, taking hold of Kip's left hand as if to shake it. "What was your name again?"

"Christopher."

"Nice to meet you, Christopher. Can you spell that for me?"

"Shit," said Leslie. "Shit shit shit shit."

Kip kept his eyes on Horace. "C-H-R-I—"

He'd just gotten to *S* when Horace gave a kind of convulsion, as if he'd been hit with a taser, and all of Kip's pain seemed to contract into a single point in space. Leslie was shouting something unintelligible and a cold white light shone down on all of them and Horace himself fell away, both hands up in the air, as if to protest his innocence before some higher judge. Then the moment was past and Kip was sitting upright and the pain he'd felt had simply stopped existing.

"Kira?"

"Right here." Her small voice was tender and close to his ear. He kept still for a long time, afraid the blessed spell of painlessness would end, but when he raised his left arm nothing happened—his shoulder tingled with an angry warmth and that was all. Kira was standing between him and the railing, looking as sober as he'd ever seen her. She seemed to think that he might try again.

"Are you actually okay now, Kip? You look okay."

"I feel pretty good. I feel normal."

"Really? Because if you're telling the truth—if you're really all right—then I need to sit down for a second."

All Kip cared about was that the fight was over. The roar of the crowd carried up from the Bowl, brighter and less muffled than before. He let his eyes close and pictured himself in the spotlight on that big clamshell stage, not doing anything in particular, not singing or playing—maybe telling a joke. He imagined that the roaring was for him.

"Where's Leslie?"

"Leslie went inside. He couldn't take it."

"How about Horace?"

"It's just you and me, partner."

"Kiss me."

He heard the weight of her body shift but that was all. A trill of synthesizer reached his ears—the distance or the acoustics or the weather made for something like distortion, raw and angry and hopeless. It could almost have been metal.

"You don't want to," he said finally.

"Not right now. Is that all right?"

The sadness washing over him felt somehow meditative. "Of course it's all right. But you should tell me why."

"Oh god," she said quietly.

"I just almost died, Kira."

"Is that why you did that stupid fucking thing? To have this conversation?"

She didn't expect an answer and he didn't give her one. He watched her and waited.

"I'll tell you if you want. But you won't like it."

"I wasn't expecting to like it."

Kira took a breath and held it for what felt like half an hour. The roar of the crowd was continuous now. It occurred to Kip, as he lay there looking up at her, that he ought to be afraid of what was coming.

"So I thought that I could do this," she said finally. "Get away, I mean. From Venice and everything else. My family. Ponceville. The last bunch of years. I was dumb enough to think I could get in a car and come out here and be some other person."

"Kira," he said. "Let's forget it, all right? It's your birthday. We don't have to talk about this."

She ignored him. "The problem is that it's inside me. Like bugs in a tree stump. It goes all the way through."

"That's not true." He could feel his voice rising. "That's not true at all. You can trust me on that."

"No," she said.

"Kira, god damn it—"

"That place was a *year* to you, Kip—a single year. That's all." She made a fist. "To me it's my entire fucking life."

He ground his teeth to keep from saying something stupid. Leslie would have known what to do, how to fix things, how to make her see reason. But he wasn't Leslie.

"Is that what you were hoping to hear?" Kira gave a dull laugh. "I guess not."

"I can handle it."

"You want to know the funny part?"

He bit down on this tongue.

"I actually do want to fuck you. You're beautiful to me in some way I can't seem to figure out. It makes my head hurt."

"Then why—"

"Because every time I hear you talk I'm right back in the swamps."

Kip rolled his head from side to side, breathing carefully, feeling the cool damp sand conforming to his skull. "That makes no sense," he said.

"I know that, Kip. I'm sorry."

"Explain to me what all this means."

She took a while to answer. "Just that I'm going to be doing my own thing."

"If this is about art school, about making that happen, you know I support you one hundred percent."

"This isn't about art school."

He sat up again to see her better. She turned away, but not quickly enough.

"You're bailing. I can't believe this."

"School takes money, Norvald," she said tiredly. "Unless you get a scholarship. And I'm not good enough for that."

"For fuck's sake, Kira. How many times have we talked about—"

"Too many times."

Down in the Bowl the show looked to be letting out—which didn't add up, unless he'd been knocked out for an hour. Maybe it was inter-mission. That seemed like the kind of pretentious move a new wave band would pull. His eyes fell shut again.

"You might want to tell Leslie."

"Tell me what?" said Leslie, stepping out onto the porch.

"Leslie knows," Kira said.

In the silence that followed—quietly at first, like a tree branch tap-ping on a windowpane—Kip gradually grew aware of the White Room. This was how it always started: a sense of its closeness, of its presence at the margins of his thought.

"You think you could get up, Kip? You're freaking me out a little, to be honest."

"No," he said, lying back down in the sand.

"Stubborn bastard," someone muttered. He couldn't place the voice and didn't care. He was busy picturing Kira telling Leslie, discreetly and in confidence, what she'd only just told him. He couldn't help but won-der when and where. At the Rainbow, most likely, or at the apartment, or on one of the long walks they'd been taking together lately. Kira asking for advice and Leslie giving it. A decision made regretfully. The best for all concerned.

He forced his eyes back open. She was bent over him now, a faceless outline, her long straight hair brushing his cheek. He clenched his jaw and willed the Room away.

"Screw it," Kira said, digging something out of her back pocket. "I was saving this for an emergency, but tonight's close enough."

"Whoa," Kip heard Leslie murmur. He looked up to find Kira smooth-ing out what looked like a cellophane candy wrapper on her thigh. He knew what it was right away. Just the idea of it made him wake up.

Leslie gave a low whistle. "Is that what I think it is, woman?"

"The wind is coming up. Let's go inside."

No one argued with her. Kip managed to get up without Leslie's help, which was lucky, because Leslie was already in the kitchen. By the time Kip got there Kira had dumped the little bag's contents onto a piece of broken windowpane and was cutting lines with the same card they'd used to spread peanut butter on their English muffins back when they were living in Kthulu. The bag was already sealed and tucked away.

"Where did you get this from?"

"Gift horses, Norvald," cautioned Leslie. "Let's all try to focus on the *now*."

"A friend from work," said Kira, spackling and chopping.

"A friend," Kip repeated. "From work."

"That's what the lady said, Norvald. Now get your nose holes open."

They rolled up a receipt from an In-N-Out Burger—Leslie had heard a rumor that all the dollar bills in the city were contaminated with some sort of flesh-eating virus—and did one bump each. Kira made a point of insisting that Kip and Leslie go first, which fooled exactly nobody. "You've been doing toots all night," Leslie said, narrowing his eyes at her like a TV detective. "That's what was happening out in those bushes."

She tittered at that—another laugh Kip didn't recognize. "No comment at this time."

"Cunning," said Leslie. "Devious. I respect that. Let's have us another."

She got the bag out again and they went through the whole ritual. Kip braced his arms against the counter, feeling luxurious and queasy. All receptors were flooded. His jump was a distant memory now, Kira's revelation only hearsay. What she'd said to him was not to be taken personally. It was a point-of-view issue. A question of perspective. It was really no concern of his at all.

He left the kitchen with its broken glass and suspiciously stained linoleum and moved deeper into the house. The loose panes in the windows facing the Bowl had started to vibrate, if his senses could be trusted, in what was probably a significant seismic event. The air seemed to darken. He stopped in the middle of the living room and sank to the floor. The vibrations were music, he realized. Some insipid endless chorus in a grating minor key.

What Kira had been trying to communicate to him was that his company, which had seemed comparatively non-hick back in Venice, now felt more hick to her than anyone else's in the state of California. It was a question of context. What she was saying, in a nutshell, was that he was the last person she wanted to live with, or sleep with, or have anything to do with at all. She'd meant the cocaine as a distraction but if anything it had sharpened his attention, especially now that he was starting to come down. He saw everything so clearly.

The chorus kicked in for what felt like the seventeenth time: sticky, sluggish, depraved. Things had taken a bad turn. He felt the floor buckling. Xanadu was about to slide over the cliff.

He reached down to push himself up from the floor and his fingers closed around a stiffened piece of cloth. He picked it up gingerly, like a coroner at a crime scene. A rag of some kind. It was still in his hand when he stepped out of the house: a sleeveless turquoise T-shirt with NEW WAVE SUCKS printed across the front in acid-yellow letters. A woman's garment, elastic and tapered. Its neck and hem were brittle with dried blood.

2

Leprosy, Death's hotly anticipated follow-up to *Scream Bloody Gore*, came out at the end of that summer, and Kip bought a copy at the Tower Records on Sunset and brought it straight to Leslie. The balcony had an unobstructed view of the 405 freeway and they hung out there on two trash-picked beanbags, admiring the gridlock, passing a forty of St. Ides back and forth while Evil Chuck spat lightning bolts behind them. This record was even heavier and more terrifying than the last one had been, a flat-out masterpiece, and they attempted to dredge up the requisite awe. But somehow Death already felt like ancient history.

Kira was out somewhere, as she always seemed to be these days. Kip had no idea what sort of system of smoke signals she and Leslie had worked out, what protocol they followed, but he had to admire its effectiveness. Leslie was always home when he dropped by and Kira had always just left. Both of which were equally impressive, from a practical standpoint, because the apartment didn't even have a phone.

"Brutal," said Leslie when side B was over.

"Brutal," Kip echoed, with what he hoped was adequate conviction. It occurred to him that he'd heard *Scream Bloody Gore* for the first time almost exactly one year before, in Leslie's magical blood-colored bedroom. For some reason this made him unbearably sad.

"How are things back at the Needle Exchange?" Leslie said after a while.

"Don't even." Kip shook his head. "They've basically got me living in the boiler."

Leslie laughed. "The boiler *room*, I think you mean."

"I'm pretty sure I mean the fucking boiler."

"What—like, inside it? They made a little door for you?"

"Let's talk about you instead. You're the glamorous half of this unit."

Even the word *unit* made Kip melancholy now. It had the same effect on Leslie, apparently, because his reply, when he finally gave it, had the rattle of false cheer.

"I met somebody, actually."

"No shit! What's his name?"

"It could be a lady, you know. Don't pigeonhole me, Norvald. I appreciate the ladies."

"So you always say. Who is he?"

Leslie sucked in an excited breath. "I thought you'd never ask. His name is Percy."

"Percy?" Kip studied him closely. "Are we talking about Percy Blackwood, the bass player for WhiteOut?"

Leslie nodded.

"I didn't know he liked guys."

"Come on, Norvald. He's the only dude on the Strip who parts his hair on the side."

"Their singer does too. What's his name again—that surfer-looking kid with the permanent grin? The one who thinks *quesadilla* means 'what's the deal' in Spanish?"

"Dusty," Leslie said unsmilingly. "Dusty Sinclair."

Kip looked out over the freeway, processing Leslie's new defensiveness. "How far has it gone with you two?"

Leslie seemed not to hear. "Let's play side A again."

"Do you even like this kind of music anymore?"

"You'll have to explain what that's supposed to mean."

"You've been spending all your time at the Whisky, that's what. At the Whisky and Gazzarri's and the Troubadour. You've been going to see bands with names like Revlon Red."

"Your point being?"

For a moment Kip was speechless. "That it isn't good music, Leslie. That's what I'm trying to say. It's not music of quality."

"I go for the same reason the girls do, Norvald. Young men in tight pants."

"The girls," Kip said through his teeth.

Leslie gave a cluck of satisfaction. "*Now* we're getting down to it."

"How's the Queen of the Strip?"

"I couldn't be better."

"Answer the question."

Leslie rose to his feet slowly but gracefully, like an elderly lord, and flipped the record over. "She's about the same as ever."

"Meaning what?"

"Meaning not as perfect as you think she is."

"I used to hate it when you talked shit about her." Kip took a swig of St. Ides. "Come to think of it, I still hate it."

"You don't have to come over."

Kip nodded. "Have you noticed the light out here? In this city, I mean. How it makes everything look artificial? Like we're living inside a TV?"

Leslie rolled his eyes. "We're in *Los Angeles*, Norvald."

"Okay, but I've just thought of something. Lend me your brain for a second."

"No can do. Brain busy."

"We grew up watching stuff that was shot on studio lots and movie ranches in this town. The light out here is movie light *by definition*. It's not a coincidence. We've been brainwashed to think that California looks like the movies, because California is where the product gets *produced*."

"Kind of disturbing, when you put it that way."

"You still haven't told me anything about Kira."

"Maybe that's because I've been sworn to secrecy."

"In other words she has a boyfriend."

Leslie puckered his lips. "Come with me to the WhiteOut gig this Wednesday."

"Won't you be there with Percy?"

"Percy will be present, obviously. Seeing as how it's his band."

"So why not go with him?"

Leslie opened his mouth and closed it. Something told Kip not to press the issue.

"You're asking a lot of me, Z. That singer sings like someone who can't spell."

"He might be out of the band by then. Percy and Dusty hate each other's guts."

"They must be jealous of each other's non-superstar status."

"Don't compare them, Kip. There's no comparison."

"I'm just saying. The other guy's lack of a record deal always seems a little sweeter."

Leslie looked genuinely hurt. "WhiteOut's had some A and R guys hanging around lately. The real deal, Norvald. Warner Brothers. Combat. Elektra."

"Probably just office interns. Someone sent them out for liquid paper."

"Fuck you."

"I love you too, baby."

Leslie brought his hands together in an attitude of prayer. "I mainly need you to give me a ride to the after-party. It's way out in Burbank, at a place called the Palace. Just come for ten minutes. You can sulk in the corner."

"All right." Kip shook his head. "But you'll owe me a debt that can be repaid only in blood."

"Ten minutes—that's all I ask. Then you can vanish in a puff of brimstone."

3

The Palace turned out to be a band house, the kind of prefab split-level that dirty movies are shot in, tucked away at the top of a garbage-strewn alley. It had been Aerosmith's HQ years before, according to legend—then Ratt's, then London's. A clear downward progression. The houses to either side looked derelict and empty, which was probably for the best.

The nearest parking spot was seven blocks away, outrageous even by L.A. standards, but Kip was in no hurry to arrive. Leslie had dressed him in pipe-cleaner jeans and a hot-pink mesh vest and bright purple Doc Martens. He looked like a parody of something—like everyone else Leslie hung out with these days, in other words. He couldn't shake the feeling that all it would take to bring the whole scene crashing down would be for someone, just one random person, to look around and start laughing.

"I guess I brought my makeup kit along for nothing," Leslie said as they walked up the hill. "I guess some people cherish their virginity."

"I look like a Bulgarian mail-order bride when I wear eyeliner. You said so yourself."

"What rock have you been living under, Norvald?" Leslie stopped and unzipped his kit with an elaborate flourish. "Bulgarians are hot. That's common knowledge."

"I miss the days of sweatpants and Air Jordans."

"Hold still, damn it."

"I'm holding."

"You miss white trash bumfuck F-L-A, is what you mean."

"Every day," Kip confessed.

"Heresy! Blasphemy!" Leslie stepped back to appraise his handiwork. "There you go. You look more like Mick Mars than Tommy Lee, but we can only work with what we're given."

Most of the houses Kip had been to in California had no basement to speak of, but the Palace had a fully loaded bachelor's cave, complete with Budweiser mirrors and wall-to-wall shag and a fiberglass minibar in the shape of an orca. It was packed with Valley girls and Strip kittens and men in their twenties who described themselves as "industry professionals," all jockeying for position near two turquoise vinyl sofas. People were passing around half-gallon handles of Chivas Regal and posing for imaginary pictures and catching their hair on the drop-panel ceiling. Kip went straight to the orca and took shelter there.

"People will try to tell you that a motorcycle flips when it hits a car straight on—that's what happens in the movies—but this one just crumpled. It shot me straight at the driver and I bounced off the windshield and from there I was airborne. This was a rip-in-the-fabric-of-space-time type of deal. My spirit left my body before I'd even touched the ground."

Kip would have recognized Percy Blackwood by his mushmouthed drawl alone. He sat slouched center-sofa, in pride of place as usual, with one arm around WhiteOut's drummer and the other around a woman with the most perfect breasts that Kip had ever seen. They were perfect in a mathematical sense: architecturally crafted, the product of complex calculations, like propane tanks or cupolas on a cathedral. The woman gazed through narrowed eyes at Percy, fabulously unimpressed. Kip caught sight of Leslie just behind her, leaning to one side to keep from hitting the ceiling, shifting eagerly from foot to foot, waiting like all the rest of them for a spot at the feet of the king.

"So I just kind of hung out up there, looking down at myself, and I thought: Here lies a poor pathetic son of a bitch who never even *tried* to shoot the moon. Who never bet the pot. Who never dared. And if I go back *in* there—if there's a sequel to this movie—then the hell with all that. I'm going to reinvent myself. I'm going to play my own damn songs. I'm going to be a slightly better person."

"What happened to the driver?" said the woman.

"Who?"

"The driver. The guy in the car."

"He was fine," Percy said, after the slightest perceptible pause. "Some old dude."

"We're glad you *made* it, baby!" Leslie chirped. It hurt Kip a little to hear it. Percy arched his back and glanced over his shoulder.

"Hey there, Z. That's tight, man. I'm glad that you're glad."

Soon afterward a girl wearing some kind of headdress got up to go to the bathroom and Leslie swooped in like a falcon. No one else stood a chance. Percy was talking in a low, urgent voice to the woman beside him. Even the most tarted-up glammers were straight, as a rule, but Blackwood was hard to pin down—what turned him on seemed to be affirmation, whatever the source. He wasn't getting it from her, at least not at the moment, which meant she had his absolute attention. Sitting wedged in the far corner, visibly straining to hear them, Leslie looked almost petite.

"Come on, Vanessa," Percy said suddenly, raising his voice. "Inquiring minds want to know. What was it like?"

"I'm not sure I follow."

"Bullshit. Working with Leon 'Chester' Alvarez. The Donkey King himself."

"I thought we were talking about you, Percy. About you and your oneness with all of creation."

"We were. You seemed bored."

"And how do I seem to you now?"

That got a laugh out of the drummer. Percy's face remained blank. He turned to address the clutch of underage fangirls on the other couch.

"The Donkey King's dick was what you might call a conversation piece. It had a curvature to it, if I remember correctly. Kind of up and to the left." He glanced back at the woman. "Do I remember correctly?"

"Fuck off, Percy."

"I'll never forget the first time I saw it. It had a starring role in *Star Crack II: The Wrath of Dong*—shot right down the road here at Shangri-La Studios, in beautiful downtown Burbank. I grew up in this town, did you know that, Vanessa? You might say I've got porn in my blood."

"You might just say," the drummer muttered.

"The great Tawny Kitaen was in *Wrath* too, but she was a big star already, so she didn't have to do a scene with Alvarez. I'm guessing it was written into her contract." He grinned. "Now she goes out with the dude from Whitesnake."

"Sign of good representation," said Leslie, over the nervous giggling of the girls. They'd have giggled at anything. The woman called Vanessa looked over her shoulder, directly at Kip, and motioned to him for a drink.

"Kitaen didn't do it—didn't *have* to do it—but Vanessa sure did. She acquitted herself very nicely." He patted her knee. "I've been a fan of her work ever since."

Kip poured whatever he could find behind the orca into a Dixie cup and stirred it with his thumb and brought it over. WhiteOut hadn't been signed yet, as far as he knew, but for some reason everyone in the scene behaved as though they were already selling out stadiums. He'd never seen a woman—he'd never seen *anyone*—not give Percy Blackwood what he wanted.

"Thanks, babe," she said, taking the cup in both hands, as if its contents were too valuable to spill. "You're a gent."

Kip's face went hot instantly. "Don't mention it."

"Sweet Mary mother of God," Percy yelped. "What is *that*?"

"It's vodka, mostly. I mixed it with—"

"Not the *drink*, dipshit. You look like a transvestite." Percy shook his head slowly. "A transvestite that has lost the will to live."

"*Defeated*," Leslie chimed in, in a voice Kip barely recognized. "Just somehow disappointed by the world."

Kip adjusted his body to look down at Leslie. He was less angry or hurt than simply taken by surprise. Leslie was staring at Percy and chewing his lip, which he only ever did when he was anxious. If he'd been a comic-strip character he'd have had beads of sweat on his forehead.

"I guess I made some bad choices," Kip said.

"I guess so," said Leslie, avoiding his look.

Percy let out a chuckle. "Seriously, friend—you might want to talk to your personal stylist. You look like the love child of Liberace and a badger."

"Careful, Percy," said Vanessa.

"Why the hell should I be careful?"

"Because this is the guy who signed Faster Pussycat to Elektra."

What happened next was a thing of complex beauty. The Percy Blackwood with whom Kip was familiar seemed to turn himself inside out. Even his posture improved. "No shit," he said silkily, rising slightly off the sofa. "I didn't catch your name."

"Cody Vogler," Kip said, taking Blackwood's hand and shaking it. He seemed to hear Leslie give a muted gargle.

"Cool," Percy murmured, still gripping his hand. "Very cool. I guess it's a New York Dolls kind of tribute? The outfit, I mean. A so-fucked-up-it's-sexy type of deal?"

"Something like that."

"We've been popping black beauties, Cody. You want one?"

"I'm good."

"Excellent." Percy squinted at him. "I'm trying to remember. Did I see you at the show?"

"Front and center."

"I thought so. That's tight, man." He let go of Kip's hand. "What did you think of the glitter cannon? It's a recent investment." He waited a few seconds. "All, you know, suggestions welcome."

Leslie gargled again. "Percy—"

"I do have some feedback," said Kip. "If you're asking my professional opinion."

Percy's face lit up like a marquee. "Definitely, Cody. Definitely. I'd love to hear your take."

"Two thoughts," Kip said, smiling past him at Vanessa. "Whoever your band mom is—whoever actually pays the rent on this place—marry her while she still gives a shit. And whatever else you do, don't quit your day job restocking the salad bar at Applebee's. You're going to be needing that paycheck, Mr. Blackwood."

The dumbstruck silence behind him as he headed upstairs was the sweetest sound Kip had heard since coming west.

He was on his way outside when he saw Kira. She was sitting on the back steps of the Palace, leaning against the screen door, shelling peanuts and feeding them to Dusty Sinclair.

A porchlight was on, spotlighting the two of them tastefully. The tiara holding back Dusty's expensive-looking dreadlocks was one that Kira had bought back in Venice. Kip could still see the garage sale in his mind's eye—on the lawn of a bungalow just past the Voglers'—and hear her joking with the lady of the house, asking if she'd won the tiara at a pageant. It looked good on Dusty, he had to admit. Beside him Kira seemed almost plain: your garden-variety hometown beauty, a recent arrival, duly grateful for his stoner-god indulgence.

Kip took a small step backward, an involuntary reflex, and caught sight of his reflection in the window: bugged-out raccoon eyes, scorched-looking hair, a dusting of glitter on his forehead that must have fallen from the basement ceiling. The vision held him spellbound. He looked worse than he could possibly have imagined. He was seeing himself as Dusty Sinclair was going to see him—as Kira was going to see him—as soon as they ran out of nuts.

No sooner had he had this thought than he was stumbling down the smoke-filled hallway toward the bathroom. The people in his way were scenery to him, random obstructions, clumps of seaweed in a tidal pool. Everyone was talking about how famous they were going to be by Christmas. They came and went like voices in a dream.

Son of a bitch. Let him talk. In six months he'll be cleaning my Jacuzzi. The moment you doubt it is the moment you lose it.

Everybody's looking the other way right now, is all. We just have to stay here until someone turns around.

Every voice was the same voice. Every dark head was Kira's.

By some miracle the bathroom door was open. His legs began to buckle as he pulled it shut behind him. Everybody was going to make it but Christopher Norvald. Christopher Norvald was going to be sick.

Afterward he took a fistful of toilet paper and wiped at his eyes, ignoring the steady banging on the door. He worked a sliver of hard green soap into a lather, scrubbing and rinsing and scrubbing again, until his reflection began to look vaguely familiar. He drank from the tap and felt queasy again. He studied the face in the mirror, making his peace with it, thinking about killing Dusty, about poisoning him or choking him or running him down in the street. Someone was actually pissing against the door now, he could hear it and smell it, and suddenly he was certain it was Leslie. The face in the mirror was a given, a necessary precondition. It was this face or nothing. He jerked the door open and someone who definitely wasn't Leslie staggered backward with a grunt.

"About time, you glitter-haired fruit."

The person who'd said this was at the wrong party: filthy jean jacket, Mötörhead shirt, muttonchops, lank brown hair nearly down to his ass. He smelled like malt liquor and piss and Dutch Masters. Behind him skulked a kid with a face like a barracuda, grinning mindlessly and brandishing a pool cue. They looked like they'd been airlifted straight in from Tampa. It cheered Kip up right away.

"Check this out," said Muttonchops. "He's blushing."

"I'm not blushing, you moron."

"How's that?" said the one with the pool cue, practically licking his lips.

"You're not going to get much satisfaction out of me, boys. I've just spent the last ten minutes scraping makeup off my face and puking. Whatever you did to me would probably be a kindness."

"We came here to stomp on some hair queers," Muttonchops told him proudly.

"Be my guest."

"You a hair queer?"

"Whatever gets your dick hard," Kip answered.

That shut them up briefly. Pool Cue Boy squinted at him. "Maiden or Halen?"

"Maiden."

"Megadeth or Mötley?"

"Megadeth."

"W.A.S.P. or Slayer?"

Kip let out a yawn. "*Reign in Blood*, motherfuckers."

Muttonchops looked disappointed. "All right, asshole. Here's a word of advice." He gestured behind him to indicate the phalanx of greasy-haired goons in biker jackets forcing its way into the house. "Best to vacate the premises. It's going to get thrashy."

Kip had known that there was a thrash metal scene in Los Angeles, of course, but so far he'd seen little sign of it. If he'd been told, in that moment, that he was looking at the entirety of the SoCal thrash under-ground, he'd have believed it. There must have been a hundred of them. This was not a social visit. They were making no pretense of being there for any reason other than destruction of property and bodily harm.

"I've got a buddy downstairs," he said. "Big Slayer fan. Can I get him out first?"

"Fuck that, brother. It's *on*."

The kitchen was easy enough to get to—he was carried there on a wave of panicked glammers—but the basement was hopeless. He ought to have been worried, panicked even, but instead he just felt tired. A minute or two later, as if by peristalsis, he found himself deposited out in the yard. He looked around for Leslie. People were shouting and shoving and jumping fences in every direction. All the thrashers had pool cues. Someone's hair was on fire. He saw the girl with the headdress actually climb into a trash can and pull the lid closed behind her. He saw a kid in a Ratt shirt get thrown down the steps. The kitchen's picture window exploded outward as he watched, refracting the light, and a Frisbee-sized shard of glass hit the lawn at his feet.

"You took your face off," someone said.

It was Vanessa from the basement, Percy Blackwood's Vanessa, grinning as though she'd caught him with his pants down. It surprised Kip that she could be smiling so serenely in the middle of a full-on rumble—and also that she was physically able to smile. A bleeding glammer in fishnets stumbled into them and she caught him by the sleeve.

"Kind of looks as though this party's over, Cody."

"You don't seem too worried."

"About what—this?" She shrugged her thin shoulders. "This happens every so often. The righteous survive, more or less."

He looked back toward the house. "My friend's still in the basement."

"If he's with Percy he's fine. Nothing bad ever happens to Percy." She seemed to be waiting for Kip to say something. "*Is* your friend with him?"

"He sure thinks he is."

"By now he probably knows, one way or the other." She considered him a moment. "You look almost normal."

"Don't believe it, lady. I'm a freak."

She laughed at that. "He drove me here," she said. "Percy, I mean."

Someone jumped or was thrown through the rectangle of empty night air where the window had been.

"I've got a car," Kip surprised himself by saying.

"I figured you might."

"My grandmother's Chevy." He tipped an imaginary hat. "Probably not what you're used to."

She laughed again—a wistful laugh, mossy and dark—and slipped a graceful spray-tanned arm through his. "I'll tell you what, Cody. Let's not even go into what I'm used to."

4

The first revelation about Vanessa Bordeaux was that she wasn't much older than Kip was himself; the second was that she lived in an efficiency apartment above a Jiffy Lube in downtown Burbank. "Loft living," she announced as she unlocked the door, and he wasn't completely sure that she was joking. Every time he started to get comfortable with her, or with his *idea* of her, she wrong-footed him somehow. But he was getting the feeling, from the fumbling way she tried to make conversation as she showed him around, that Vanessa was as jittery as he was. She wasn't used to having strange men spend the night, he realized. That came as revelation number three.

She took his jacket with mock formality and hung it on a peg and told him brightly—almost squeakily—that she'd be back in two shakes of a lamb's tail. Kip sat down on a leather sectional and tried to get a grip. He spent most of the next fifteen minutes—even after she'd reappeared and started rummaging around in the kitchenette in search of the fixings for vodka martinis—running through the series of actions required to get himself outside and into his car and back over the Hollywood Hills to his pathetic little room.

Her given name was Stefanie Markovits and she'd had an enviable childhood, the way she chose to tell it, in a gated community outside Tallahassee. Kip had just enough sense not to ask what had happened.

The Florida connection struck him as significant, even decisive, and he clung to it like a tiny life raft as she fixed him his martini. She was talkative now, as if the mere smell of vodka was enough to boost her confidence, and he sank into the sectional and watched her. The only light came from a cracked lava lamp on the floor by the couch, so ancient that the whitish goo inside was turning brown; in its beer-colored glow her skin looked less synthetic. The vodka tickled Kip's brain with its icy blue spikes and he came to understand, gradually and without any conscious effort, that he didn't want to go home anymore.

Vanessa was smart, for one thing—much sharper than Kip was, or at least more articulate—and she seemed to expect nothing from him. She talked and he listened. She'd been watching a lot of cable news lately—she described herself as a hopeless C-SPAN junkie—and she'd been following the recent unrest in the Soviet bloc, especially in Hungary and Poland. The Cold War, she explained, was essentially over. Apparently everyone knew this but Kip. He couldn't have found Hungary on a map but he was grateful for the briefing. It felt good not to be talking about metal.

By his second martini he felt pleasantly useless. Vanessa had seemed like an extraterrestrial back at the Palace, and more than a little disconcerting when she'd cornered him in the backyard—but she was coming into focus now, almost a known quantity: someone hazily recalled from summer camp, maybe, or sophomore year. It was obvious that she came from money—she had that prep-school vocabulary, that slight touch of arrogance, the wealthy kid's noblesse oblige—but to a lesser degree so did Leslie. There were worse things in the world.

Kip had just reached this conclusion, and was feeling pretty good about himself, when he realized why he felt as though he knew her. The memory was visceral, a shiver down the spine, a tightening of the bowels. He sat up to make sure. Five years younger, maybe more. Straighter hair and much darker. Thinner lips. Smaller breasts. Everything else exactly the same.

He'd seen her on a tape that his mother's boyfriend—the last one, the worst one—had made a habit of forgetting in the family VCR.

"There it is," she said. "The light of recognition."

He kept his face composed. "The light of what?"

"You're staring at me like I'm your long-lost babysitter."

"The thing is," he began, then decided to start over. "The thing is, I—"

She set her empty glass aside. "Or maybe like there's no one here at all."

Any answer he gave would likely have been fatal. He felt naked and helpless. Her enormous green eyes had gone dim.

"It's been nice talking to you, Cody."

He managed a nod.

"Am I going to have to ask you to leave?"

"I'll be honest with you." Kip looked down at his legs. "I'm not sure that I could."

That river-bottom laugh again. "You're a sweet boy, Cody. I like you. But I don't like that look."

"You're from Florida," he blurted out. "So am I."

"And that matters why?"

He reached for her then, as much to keep himself steady as anything else. "Maybe that's why it feels good to be here."

"Or maybe you're drunk."

He leaned forward and kissed her. "Don't ask me to leave."

She shook her head—a little grudgingly, he thought—and ran two smoke-stained fingers through his hair. He could see he'd surprised her.

"A shy one," she murmured. "But less than I thought."

"I'm not shy at all."

"Fair enough." She slid smoothly down from the sofa.

It took him longer than it should have done to figure out what was happening.

He got up early the next morning—shockingly early, considering how awful he felt—and fried up some eggs that he found in the fridge. He brought them to bed with a piece of toast on a blood-colored plate, the kind the snowbirds bought and sold at yard sales back in Venice. The brand name came to him unbidden: Fiestaware. He'd never been able to make up his mind whether it was hideous or pretty and he still couldn't make up his mind. He wondered whether the plate had come along from Tallahassee. He wondered whether Stefanie Markovits had owned it.

He found her lying facedown with her head under a pillow. He was fully prepared for her to open her eyes and stare at him in confusion, but she sat up as soon as he spoke, as though she'd already been awake, and received his tribute graciously. She ate in absolute silence, which was all right by Kip. He was trying to hide how shell-shocked he was feeling.

Eventually she glanced at him. "This is actually good."

"I'm a one-trick pony. It's fried eggs or nothing."

"Hmm." She took a bite of toast and chewed it as slowly as he'd ever seen anyone chew anything.

"Could you pass me that mug on your side of the bed?" she said, her mouth still half-full. "Should be by your left foot."

"Sure thing."

"I'll tell you a secret. I can't seem to dredge up your name. I'm sitting here hoping that you never told me."

"You were calling me Cody," he said, passing her the mug.

She took it and drank. "That sounds like something I might do."

"I mostly go by Kip."

She squinted at him. "You looked older in the dark, Kip from Florida. Same way I looked younger."

"You looked beautiful," he told her. "You look beautiful right now."

"You can dial back the bullshit. Our fluids have mingled."

"I've never been with someone like you before," he heard himself saying.

"Someone like me?"

"Someone famous."

She turned the red plate back and forth on her lap. Whole weather patterns passed across her features.

"What am I supposed to do with that," she said finally.

"You don't have to do anything. You're beautiful, that's all."

"I'd like you to stop talking."

She shut her eyes and lay back down. He couldn't shake the impression that she was holding still so he could study her. The upturned nose, the graded cheeks. Lips that looked as though they took effort to close. He looked for seams, suture marks, evidence of choices made. Her face resisted his attempts to deconstruct it.

All at once her eyes snapped open. "What did you mean when you said I was famous?" she said slowly. "Famous for what?"

His heart sank. "Vanessa—"

"Famous for my poise before the camera? Famous for my low-key sense of style? Famous for taking the Donkey King's cock up my ass?"

"I think I should go."

"No! Please stay, handsome stranger. I'm begging you. Stay here and undress me with your eyes."

He tried to stand and nothing happened. He'd been magically stricken. Vanessa sat up silently, almost mechanically, like a vampire in some campy midnight movie.

"Are you looking to see how they made me so perfect? Best of luck, little man. I wasn't some rush job. They did me top-dollar. You'd have to stick me in an MRI machine."

He forced himself to take a breath. "I don't understand why you're so angry."

"You can put that in the jar with all the other shit that you don't understand."

She turned to face the wall, as if he'd already gone, and Kip discovered he could move his legs again. He left the room and the apartment and the building in what felt like a single unbroken motion. There was no sign of Kthulu on the street outside, and it seemed somehow appropriate that it had been stolen—but it was just around the corner, parked at an absurd angle, taking up two entire spaces in the lot of an In-N-Out Burger. Such was Kip's disorientation that he found himself seriously entertaining the notion that someone had hotwired his car, driven it thirty feet, then changed their mind and wandered off on foot.

He was shivering all over as he pulled out into traffic, as though he'd spent the last twelve hours underwater. His chest started heaving as Kthulu took him up into the Hills, and he felt inexplicably carsick. It took him most of the drive back to Hollywood to figure out the reason.

He'd been sure that his first time would be with Kira.

5

Kip found a job that same week at a silk-screening shop on West Sunset,
printing band logos and tour dates onto black long-sleeved T-shirts. Always black, always long-sleeved, always metal. The only variety lay in
the logos. The owner was a barrel-chested troll with a salt-and-pepper
mullet who stopped talking only to crack a new Heineken or light a
fresh Kool. His given name was Jackie Lee Slaughter, or so he insisted
("more like Slaughterberg," said Leslie), and he was even more of a sidewalk philosopher than Z was himself. It made Kip nostalgic to listen to
him. It was inevitable that they'd become friends—mandatory, in fact.
The only other option was to quit.

Jackie's pet obsession was the idea of a schism—what he referred to
as the "expulsion from paradise"—by which metal had split into two
rival sects: the Cult of Dionysus and the Cult of Set. Every band since
Black Sabbath, he insisted, existed on one side or the other of this mystical divide. The traditional heavy metal of the seventies, he liked to
say—spitting and raving at whoever happened to be within earshot—
was like a chemical solution of unstable elements that finally, inevitably, on the cusp of the eighties, became supersaturated and began to
crystallize. He actually talked this way, with a borderline-creepy lack of
self-awareness, like some community college professor in disgrace.

The Dionysian acts, according to Jackie, worshipped at the altar of sex, drugs, and melody; among the Cult of Set—the devotees of chaos—violence and rhythm reigned supreme. You could tell which team any given band played for, simply and infallibly, by counting the number of women at their shows. Van Halen, Faster Pussycat, Ratt, W.A.S.P., Poison, Whitesnake, Twisted Sister, the Crüe—Dionysians all. Slayer, Death Angel, Deicide, Megadeth, Anthrax—team chaos, as their names made abundantly clear. Los Angeles had long been in the sweaty grip of Dionysus, god of quaaludes and jug wine and music to fuck to; but a sea change was coming. *The barbarians are at the gates*, Slaughter would holler at anyone who'd listen, raising his arms like some cut-rate desert prophet. *And they ain't wearing spandex.*

In spite of Jackie's doomsday prophecy, or possibly even because of it, Leslie doubled down on glam. He dragged Kip out to see London at the Roxy, Skid Row at Gazzarri's, even Quiet Riot—of all hideous experiences—at some crumbling, piss-soaked stadium in the Valley. Sometimes Jackie tagged along, in the interest (as he put it) of empirical research; Kip went for reasons unclear even to himself. He never asked where they were headed in advance, and Leslie never told him. Which was how it came to pass, on an otherwise unremarkable Tuesday in September, that he found himself watching Dusty Sinclair, the man Kira was currently not-being-from-Florida with, attempting to tie a paisley scarf around a mic stand on the main stage at the Whisky.

"Textbook Dionysian setup," Jackie announced, in the ear-piercing whisper that he always used in clubs. "You'll never see Tom Araya tying hankies to his mic."

"Get me out of here," Kip mumbled.

"Also, nota bene: the abundance of females." He squeezed Kip's arm and made a low-pitched clucking sound. "Credit where credit is due, actually. There's some premium-quality scrunt at this gig."

"I need to talk to Leslie. Where's Leslie?"

"Where do *you* think Leslie is?"

Kip shook his head woodenly. "Percy," he said.

"They went to the can—which means Blackwood must be holding. We won't be seeing Leslie for a while."

"Holding—?"

"When two dudes go into the bathroom together at the Whisky, Norvald, they ain't in there putting on makeup. Not if they lock the door."

It crossed Kip's mind dimly, in the midst of his confusion, that not even Jackie knew Leslie liked boys.

"What's with the face, kid? You look—I don't know what, exactly. Kind of constipated."

"Get me *out* of here," Kip repeated. But he stayed where he was, fascinated in spite of himself. The room was barely at half capacity: it was pay-to-play night at the Whisky, your standard wannabe showcase, and the band was setting up its own gear. Dusty, the picture of unearned self-confidence, called out something to the soundman, then shaded his eyes and looked straight down at Kip. He flashed him a thumbs-up, which made no sense at all. The drummer and the guitar player were hanging a banner—chrome-style lettering across a fork of hot pink lightning, impressively airbrushed onto what looked like a plastic shower curtain. Above the name, even more beautifully detailed, was the head of a stag with a green neon crucifix between its antlers. Kip didn't look around for Kira—he'd be seeing her soon enough. She was the band's manager now, according to Leslie. Whatever that meant.

"Changed their name again, looks like," said Jackie.

"I noticed that."

"What does it say, though? The banner, I mean. I'm kind of near-sighted."

Kip let out the breath he'd been holding. "It says 'Marijuana.'"

"Whoa."

Kip didn't reply.

"The worst name of all time," Jackie said thoughtfully. "Or the *best* name of all time. I can't decide."

"I could help you with that."

Just then Kira pushed past them, her kohl-rimmed eyes fixed fiercely on the stage. Her hair was elaborate now, layered and feathered and platinum-white, and her freckled cheeks were slashed with bars of war-paint. She struck Kip as intentionally disguised. The possibility occurred to him—watching her conferring in urgent undertones with Dusty, who'd never looked more solemn—that the goal of everything she'd done since leaving Florida had been to disfigure herself: to look into the mirror and see no one that she knew. The bitterness he felt then almost choked him. He saw with awful clarity that Kira's quest was endless, that she would never stop struggling to feel more alive, to break out of her skin—to demand more of the universe than it saw fit to give. The best he ever could have hoped for was to paddle in her wake.

The man of the hour was shading his eyes from the houselights and biting his lip, visibly struggling to follow what Kira was saying. Even now Kip couldn't bring himself to hate him. Kira let go of Dusty's sleeve and he rose to his full six-foot-plus and gestured to the drummer, who turned and yanked the rumpled banner straight. Kip was trying not to look at it. The symbol in the background, of the stag and glowing crucifix, was the one he'd seen on Kira's father's truck.

"What does marijuana have to do with Jägermeister?" muttered Jackie. "Confusing."

"Did you say something?"

"Jägermeister. Saint Eustace."

"I can't help you with that one. I'm leaving."

"So leave, then."

"I'm gone."

But he stopped after just a few steps. He hadn't been this close to Kira in forever.

She stood with her back to him, alone in the uncrowded lee of the stage, trying to fill the empty space around her by sheer force of will: a wedding-cake-haired silhouette against the dimming houselights, tense and determined, no different from the countless other so-called band moms cluttering the Strip. This half-full Tuesday gig was life or death to her. She wanted it so badly and it wasn't going to happen. Dusty couldn't give her what she hoped for, beautiful and well dressed and obliging though he was. Her new life would fail her. She'd picked the wrong band.

Kip was making his way toward her when Blackwood hit the first chord—a warbling high-pitched complaint, like the opening squeal of a tantrum—and Dusty grabbed the paisley scarf and jerked the mic stand sideways.

"West Hollywood, California, USA, Planet Earth—we are . . . Marijuana. Approach the throne, bitches!"

To Kip's considerable surprise, assorted bitches of both sexes did approach—enough to screen Kira temporarily from view. Blackwood hit a second chord and leaned suggestively toward Dusty's mic.

"This first tune is entitled 'Bad Trip.' What's it about, Mr. Sinclair?"

Dusty whipped his hair sideways and held up a fist. "It's about doing what you want to do, saying what you want to say, and being exactly who you want to be."

Jackie found Kip on the curb outside the venue when it was over, clutching his knees and humming to himself. He approached with circumspection.

"Norvald no likey?"

"Leave me alone, Jackie."

"I'm curious to hear your take on what we both just witnessed. I'm guessing that you might have some opinions."

That was all the prodding Kip required. His sat up and his mouth fell open and the words shot out like water from a hose. The immortal Randy Rhoads, lead axeman for Ozzy, had once described playing guitar onstage as something beyond his control—some supernatural power speaking through him, some alien entity, using his body and his brain as a transmitter—and suddenly, raving like a maniac at Jackie Lee Slaughter, Kip understood exactly what he meant. He'd never felt so articulate in his life. He felt borderline infallible. Long before his rabid little rant was done, Kip had made a pivotal discovery: He might never be able to hate Dusty Sinclair—not fully, not deeply. But he was excellent at hating Dusty's band.

"Wow," Jackie mumbled. "Okay."

"You asked."

Jackie was looking at him strangely. "I asked," he said. "That's true. And you obliged."

"I have—feelings, I guess you'd say."

"Strong feelings."

"You know that division of yours? The two sides in metal?"

"Ecstasy and chaos. Dionysus and Set."

"I think I've figured out which side I'm on."

Jackie patted him fondly on the shoulder. "Was there ever any doubt?"

They were heading toward the Rainbow, but Kip had no intention of running into Kira again, so they went into a FatBurger at Hammond and Sunset and sat behind its plate-glass window staring out at nothing. Jackie was buying, which wasn't like Jackie. Something had him keyed up.

"Listen, Norvald. You know me as the shirt guy. The guy who makes shirts."

"I don't care to comment."

"Shirts punch my meal ticket. There's a *sick* profit margin in shirts. You'd be pissed off. Disgusted."

"That's why you're the shirt guy."

"Hear me out. Shirts are the nut of my operation at this point—no question about it. But I tell you this in confidence: they're a means to an end only. I think of the shirts as phase one, and phase two is impending. Bear with me a minute. The Hair of the Serpent."

"Sorry, Jackie. You've lost me."

Jackie pushed someone's dirty plate to one side and leaned forward on his elbows, raising his voice like a tourist trying to make himself understood in a foreign bazaar: "*The Hair of the Serpent.*"

"Serpents don't have hair. They're snakes."

Jackie shot him a sly smile. "This is literature, Norvald. There's a thing known as poetic license. Maybe you guys don't have that down in Florida."

"I'm even more lost now. I can't see the hand in front of my face."

"Phase two of the operation. A publishing venture. Are you hearing my words? *Metal Blade* meets *Metal Meltdown* meets *Metal Maniacs* meets *Metal Curse*. Album reviews and gig reviews and pictures of Strip kittens wearing my shirts. That's what lets me write it off as a deduction."

Kip looked at him closely. "You're starting a zine?"

"Glossy paper. Five-color printing. A pull-out poster maybe."

"And you want me to—what? Write for it?"

"You already are, Kipper. All you gotta do is type up that batshit monologue you hit me with."

"I don't have a typewriter."

"Not an issue. There's one at the office. I might get a burger. You hungry at all?"

Kip squinted out at the foot traffic, coaxing his eyes into focus, head still buzzing from some mind-altering cocktail of exhilaration and disgust. A middle-aged man in buckskin chaps, a leather cowboy hat, and a tight white T-shirt sauntered slowly by. Printed in iron-on decal lettering across the front of the shirt was ROCK & ROLL COWBOYS / LOVE TO PARTY / FUCK / & EAT PUSSY. He looked perfectly at home on a street otherwise populated by people a third of his age. He noticed Kip watching him, doffed his hat courteously, then continued on his merry way.

"I don't know, Jackie," Kip said finally. "I might not be your guy."

Jackie looked at him with genuine concern. "What are you doing out here, Norvald? I'm feeling the need to ask. What made you drive that shitwagon of yours all the way across the continent?"

"I'm just saying—"

"You came for the curly fries, maybe? The opportunities in silk-screening?"

The rock & roll cowboy was leering at a troupe of wide-eyed suburbanites now, Valley girls barely in their teens, sticking his tongue out obscenely and waggling his paunch. Kip tried to visualize the series of missteps that separated himself, at his current coordinates in time and space, from the freakshow on the far side of the glass. It was frighteningly easy to do.

"Does it pay?"

Jackie understood him instantly. "Fifty bucks a review."

Kip set down his Coke. "Are you serious?"

"I told you before, Kipper. Business is good."

"I think I'll go ahead and have that burger."

They'd just started eating when Leslie went by. He was weaving up the sidewalk like a street performer doing an impression of a drunk, right hand shading his eyes from nonexistent sunshine. The foot traffic parted for him as if for a celebrity. Blood was running down his shirt-front and his chin.

"Christ almighty," Jackie stammered. "Are you seeing what I'm—"

Kip was already running. He caught up with Leslie on the far side of Hammond—he was talking to himself under his breath, daubing at his lips with the hem of his shirt, and at first he didn't answer to his name. In the glow of the streetlamps his hair seemed to glitter. When he turned his head Kip saw that it was peppered with pea-sized shards of automotive glass.

"Everybody wears lipstick and nobody's gay. You said that to me, Norvald. Don't think I don't remember."

"Slow down just a second. Let's find somewhere to sit."

Leslie shook his head and made a noise in his throat, garbled and wet, that Kip could barely stand to listen to.

"Come on, Z. Sit down."

"I don't want to sit down."

"Okay."

"I want to keep going."

"We can walk all the way to Burbank if you want."

That did something to Leslie. He shoved Kip away and sped up again, listing clumsily to one side like a sailor with an artificial leg.

"I'm sorry, Z. If you could just—"

"Don't call me that, Norvald. Don't call me that ever."

He made it almost three more blocks before his strength gave out. By dumb luck they were a few steps from a bus stop, one with an actual bench, and the people waiting there scattered when they saw what was coming. Jackie had caught up at some point, and the three of them sat there for a while, grateful for the reprieve. Leslie's shaking died down as he told them what had happened.

"Fucking Percy," Jackie muttered. "I just lent him fifty bucks."

"Shut up, Jackie."

"It was my fault," said Leslie. "I touched him."

Kip leaned his head back and stared up into the light-polluted sky. He felt clearheaded, even clairvoyant, able to foresee exactly what Leslie was going to say before each word emerged. It was the same sensation he'd had sitting on the porch with Kira's father—an awareness of passing beyond restraint, beyond ordinary fear, into a place of violence.

"Stop saying this is your fault, Z. I don't like to hear you say that."

"I'm an idiot. I knew he didn't want me." He took hold of Kip's forearm and dug in his nails. "But I couldn't not touch him. You understand, don't you? He's the most beautiful human being in the world."

Jackie gave a sort of cough. "You don't need to hear my take on that, probably, but in my personal opinion—"

"Could you guys wait here a minute?" Kip said, in what he'd intended as a reassuring tone. "I think I forgot something."

Jackie frowned at him. "Where?"

"Back at the club."

"Are you nuts? This kid is *damaged*, man. I think his jaw is broken."

"I'll be back before you know it."

"Bullshit," Jackie said angrily, hailing a cab. "You're coming with us."

Leslie seemed to fall asleep on the way to the ER, or whatever passes for sleep in someone injured that badly, and Jackie invested his considerable reserves of social energy into convincing the driver not to kick them to the curb. The ride was endless, unendurable, but the homicidal calm that Kip was feeling never left him. They waited for forty-five minutes in a shadowless room under a sign that said INTAKE before two balding men in matching green pajamas appeared and spirited Leslie away. Jackie stuck around for a while, grumbling and pacing, then went home with Kip's blessing. It was important to be alone now. He needed to keep very still until he came back to himself.

An hour later he was on his way to Burbank.

6

The lights were still on when Kip got to the Palace, just as he'd foreseen,
and a kid he didn't recognize lay passed out on the lawn. He took the
front steps in a single fluid motion, almost dancing, and slipped into
the house without a sound. The turntable was spinning in the living
room but there was no one there to hear it. No one was in the TV room
either, or in the hallway, or in the bathroom. He was sweating but his
hands were dry and cool. The impatience in him would have settled for
anyone—Percy, Dusty, even the drummer whose name he could never
remember. The thought crossed his mind yet again, more insistently
now, that he ought to be concerned about the state that he was in. But
he wasn't concerned. He knew exactly where he was and why.

He forced himself to stop in the hallway and count down from a
hundred. It took him forever. The curtain had already lowered: white as
snow on a television screen, luminous and rustling, brilliant enough to
bring tears to his eyes. When it lifted he found himself in the kitchen,
pulling drawers open at random and shaking their contents out onto
the floor. The noise was enormous. He watched the goings-on with interest from the back of his own skull.

"Kip?"

That thin voice surprised him. He stopped and turned toward her,
still gripping the last thing his fingers had closed on: the pitcher to an

old electric blender. The moment was not without a certain comedy. He noticed, in a far-off way, that seeing Kira didn't disconcert him. She lacked definition. She was wearing an oversized L.A. Guns shirt and her hair stood up wildly, especially in back. He didn't ask why.

"Leslie's in the hospital," he told her.

"In the hospital? What happened?"

"Fuck you." His voice sounded carefree.

"It's four in the goddamn morning, Kip. I come down here, you're pulling stuff out of drawers—"

"I'm not here to talk to you. Go back upstairs and tell them."

"Tell them what?" She came cautiously toward him, wide-awake now. "Did Leslie and Percy get into a fight? Is that what you're trying to tell me?"

"Go upstairs," he repeated, feeling suddenly tired.

"For Christ's sake, stop making all that noise. If anyone hears—"

"Where were you when it happened? Were you out in the van? Did you watch?"

She darted forward on the balls of her bare feet and gripped his sleeve. "I don't know if you're wasted or what, but you've got to leave, Kip—right now. Right away. Will you do that for me?"

Some small part of him shifted. She was right, of course. Right as always. It was time for him to go.

"Tell me why you're here," he said. "Why you want to be a part of this. Tell me that and I'll leave."

"I'm not—" she said, then seemed to change her mind. "Don't ask me that."

"I'd like to hear it, Kira."

"Dusty's not pretending to be something he's not," she said after a moment, sounding oddly short of breath. "He's not *faking* it, Kip. He's not pretending to be Satan's personal trainer, like all those shitheads back in Venice. He's not interested in seeming brutal, or evil, or even especially tough. He's past all that. He's interested—"

"I'm listening."

"He's interested in love."

"In love?" Kip repeated. The light seemed to flicker. "His band—the band you *manage*—closes every set with a song called 'Ride Her Till She Bleeds.'"

He could see that he'd hurt her. "What would you happen to know about the subject, Kip Norvald? How much experience do you have?"

He said nothing to that.

"For your information, seeing as how we're on the topic, *both* Dusty and Percy—"

"Percy put Leslie's face through the windshield of a Buick LeSabre," Kip said. "Tommy Fulham was there, and Ty Patterson, and that ugly little roadie with the kinky orange hair. They took turns kicking Leslie in the head and in the dick when he was lying on the asphalt. Where were you, Kira?"

A subtle twitch ran through her. She mumbled something he could barely hear.

"What was that?"

She took a step backward. "I was in the club. I must have been. With Dusty."

"Dusty showed up right at the end. He watched it happen for a while, until he got bored, then told everybody to get in the van. Before he drove off he blew Leslie a kiss."

She said a word then, very quietly, that might have been *okay*. She was looking past him out into the yard. He knew her well enough to see that she believed him.

"Kira."

She seemed not to hear.

"I'll go, Kira. I'll leave right now. I'll go if you come with me."

She shook her head.

"I want to tell you something else. It isn't only Leslie. Something's happening to me."

"What do you mean?"

"It's this thing that comes and—I don't know. It turns me into something. As soon as I saw Leslie with his face all bashed in—"

"So *this* is weird," came a voice.

Dusty was standing where Kira had been a few seconds before, his blond hair fetchingly tousled, wearing nothing but a pair of paisley briefs. Even now, obviously pissed off by what he was seeing, he looked somehow endearing. The anonymous drummer drifted in from the hallway. Kira turned slowly toward them.

"Dusty," she said. "It's all right. It's just Kip."

"*Quesadilla*, babe?"

"Go on back to bed. I'll be up in a minute."

"No," Kip heard himself say.

"Huh?"

"I want to talk to you."

Dusty seemed to see him clearly for the first time ever. He raised his golden eyebrows. "Then you better get talking."

"You two fixing breakfast?" said the drummer. "I'll take flapjacks and sausage."

"Shut up, Charlie," said Kira.

"Who's going to shut me up, cunt? Your little boyfriend over there?"

Kip was still watching Dusty. He looked as though he'd arrived at some sort of decision. "Chill out, Charlie. Let's be sociable."

The drummer's grin widened. "I'm feeling sociable as hell."

"This chicken-neck isn't anybody's boyfriend." Dusty was grinning now too. "He hangs with that faggot."

"Is that right?" the drummer asked Kip.

"That's right."

"Then I guess you came here to apologize," he said, coming up to the counter. "For your special friend, I mean. On account of him sticking his hand down our bass player's pants."

"Something like that," said Kip.

Kira was with Dusty now, smiling up at him and nuzzling his neck. The drummer stepped around the counter with his arms loose at his sides. His full name had come to Kip out of nowhere: Charlie "Boilermaker" Crews. There was something catlike in the way he held himself.

"We're going to let you walk out of here, Norvald," came Dusty's disembodied voice. "Seeing as how you and my lady used to hang."

"The fuck we are," said the drummer.

"I want to talk to you," Kip repeated.

"Run along," said Dusty. "Now. Don't make me say it twice."

Kip turned his head to answer but no one was there. He was floating in space, white and shimmering and humid, like the coastal fog they'd gone through taking Leslie to the hospital. He shook his head to clear his vision. All he saw now was the drummer. He was close enough to smell his aftershave.

"I don't *want* this little boy to run along." The drummer took Kip's cheek and pinched it. "I want this little boy to—"

From somewhere below and behind him Kip brought his right hand upward in a wide and lazy arc until it made contact with the drummer's jaw. As it passed across his features the house seemed to tilt. Kip heard something like music: a downward progression, percussive and fractured, like a chandelier being dragged behind a truck. He tried to understand what he was hearing. It seemed somehow important. But he was distracted by the pitcher's handle spinning on the floor.

"Ambulance," a voice was saying. "Ambulance. Police."

"What?" Kip said. "What was that?"

The words came out clumsily, effortfully, as though he'd had a stroke. He was not in the house now. He was sitting in Kthulu and the engine was on, sputtering and hacking, steaming in the glare of someone's headlights. He was looking up at Kira through the open window on the driver's side. He asked her again but she paid no attention. She was checking to make sure that his seat belt was buckled. Her face was pale and it appeared that she'd been talking for some time.

"Get in," he said. The words came out correctly. He let the steering wheel loose and examined his hands. They were still cool and dry.

"Hurry up, Kira. Get in. It's time to go."

She went back into the house without a word.

7

Kip's review of the Marijuana gig came out in the inaugural issue of *Hair of the Serpent*, which appeared without warning, as if by necromancy, in a handful of record stores and consignment shops and tattoo parlors in West Hollywood and Santa Monica and Venice Beach—and even, if the rumors could be believed, out in the Valley—on the same day that Leslie got the screws taken out of his jaw. A lot of people, it turned out, owed Jackie Lee Slaughter a favor.

The inside of that first issue looked as if it had been cranked out on somebody's old dot-matrix printer, but the cover was exactly what Jackie had promised: glossy top-dollar card stock sporting an airbrushed illustration, in eye-stabbing color, of naked Siamese twins reclining in the arms of a colossal purple goat with human hands. The masthead font was a brazen ripoff of a logo that Kip himself had designed, less than three weeks before, for a thrash band from Ventura called the Slugfuckers. He'd expected to feel a modest flutter the first time he saw his name in print—a twinge of satisfaction, hopefully—but the rush of pride that hit him made him physically drunk. He walked the Strip all morning, catching sight of the cover through random shop windows, grinning like an escapee from the funny farm in Fresno. How ridiculous that something so trivial could upend his whole sense of his place in the world.

He had three copies with him, that same afternoon, when he went to bring Leslie home from L.A. General. He found him in the waiting area, a little gray in the face but otherwise the picture of health, fidgeting and muttering to himself as if he'd been waiting there for hours. They'd only just released him, but that was Leslie, especially now—always wanting to move, to get on to the next place, in case somebody had him in their crosshairs.

"Took you long enough," he said, still slurring slightly.

"Didn't you tell me four thirty?"

"Early discharge." Leslie winced as he got to his feet. "Sounds kind of disgusting when you say it out loud."

"An early discharge, said the wise man, is better than no discharge at all."

"Speaking of which," said Leslie, attempting a leer. It looked painful. "Where is she?"

"She hates hospitals, Leslie. You know that."

"Sure. Okay." The look in Leslie's eyes was hard to read. "What's that tucked in your armpit?"

"Oh—this? Nothing really. Just Jackie's new zine."

"His *zine*?" Leslie stopped a few feet from the sliding glass doors. "The one with the weird name? *The Horn of the Monkey*?"

"*Hair of the Serpent*," Kip said, stifling his annoyance. "I can show you in the car."

"Show me now."

Kip passed him one of the copies reluctantly, bracing himself for abuse—but Leslie gave every indication of being impressed. When he reached the reviews page ("Serpent's Eggs"), he let out an actual whistle.

"And there you are, Charles Norvald Dickens. Black on white. You're a part of it now."

"A part of what?" Kip said, uneasy again.

"The discourse. The debate. The public record."

"It's a review of a gig, Z. A *pay-to-play* gig."

"Shut up and let me read."

He was still having trouble focusing his eyes—an aftereffect of his concussion—so Kip ended up reading it to him. It was all he could do to make Leslie wait until they'd gotten to the car.

The legendary Sunset Strip, as the *Serpent*'s bright young readers don't need to be told, is flush with bands fighting the good fight: the struggle to force someone—anyone, really—to acknowledge their rock 'n' roll greatness. That's why they came here, after all, from Boise or Phoenix or Buffalo or Atlanta or Des Moines: there's no other reason to relocate to this glorified suburb tricked by mass narcissistic personality disorder into believing that it's actually a city. Hollywood is America's hair trap: a Vegas slots-hall version of what passes—at least at the tail end of a coke binge—for popular culture. But try telling that to your buck-toothed second cousin from St. Louis, the one who's always thought she ought to be in pictures.

And while you're at it, tell it to four pie-eyed young men named Tommy Fulham, Charlie "Boilermaker" Crews, Percy Blackwood, and Dusty Sinclair.

Most nights of the week, you'll find the main stage at the Roxy and Gazzarri's and the Whisky A Go Go decorated with chemically emboldened young men in AquaNet and Lycra and zebra-print scarves, every one of them on the bullet train to stardom. How can they be so sure, you ask? Weren't you paying attention at the beginning of this screed? They're going to make it because they're HERE, onstage at the Roxy, and they're onstage at the Roxy BECAUSE THEY'RE GOING TO MAKE IT. Shut up and sit down. Let the girls to the front. These boys are already filling clubs, stadiums, arenas—just at a slightly different set of coordinates in the space-time continuum. They have a glitter cannon too, and glitter cannons are expensive. You don't invest in one of those, you dunderheads, if you haven't "made it" at some point in the foreseeable future. Any further questions?

Now—the band would really appreciate it if you'd let those ladies through.

Marijuana—formerly WhiteOut, formerly Rubber Tiger, formerly Krakow—were the presumptive superstars on offer on a recent Tuesday night at the Whisky, fabled incubator of Van Halen, Mötley Crüe, Ratt, W.A.S.P., the Stooges, and the Doors. We here at *Serpent* HQ (some of whom will actually admit to having been there) are pretty sure we heard both Ozzy and David Lee Roth turning over in their graves during the gig, which is all the more impressive because neither one is dead. Marijuana's rhythm section made your humble correspondent imagine a pair of bonobos playing Blue Öyster Cult covers in the living room of a ranch house somewhere out in the Valley, while a kid who's just run away from his babysitter hangs out in the kitchen, doing his best to keep time on a plastic salad strainer. The singer's voice, it must be said, had a gravelly hoarseness—presumably from begging the audience to stop pelting him with dog biscuits and rotten fruit at the last open-mic night he was forced to depart from in tears.

And those, cherished reader, were the highlights.

By the first limping chorus of the opening tune, we understood why this band changes its name so often—they're the Sunset Strip equivalent of a

```
witness-protection program. Whatever Fulham, Crews,
Blackwood, and Sinclair were peddling that night,
it wasn't heavy metal. We're not even sure it quali-
fies as heavy wood.
```

Leslie chewed on his lip for a while once Kip had finished. "Wow," he said eventually.

"'Wow' in what sense, exactly?"

Leslie shrugged.

"Wow, I can't believe someone actually printed this garbage? Wow, I've never been so amused and entertained?"

"I don't know where to start."

"Jesus."

"You don't have to hit every sentence out of the park, first of all."

"That makes sense. I can handle that."

"All right, then."

"What else?"

Leslie let out a breath. "I really think you might have killed that band."

Satisfaction flooded Kip's cerebral cortex. "That was pretty much the plan."

"I can't take issue with your argument, either. You were balanced and fair." He cleared his throat. "Congratulations, Chanticleer. I think you've found your calling."

Kip tried not to blush. "You'd have done better."

"Bullshit."

"To tell you the truth, Z—"

"Please don't call me that."

"—I wrote this the way I thought *you* might write it. I basically pretended to be you."

Leslie nodded for a moment, neither flattered nor surprised. Then he smiled for the first time since Kip had found him in the waiting room.

"Disagree," he said cheerfully. "This is your racket, not mine. And anyway—I'm out."

Kip stared at him. "What are you talking about? Are you leaving L.A.?"

"No such plan at this time. I'm just quitting the scene."

Kip actually laughed with relief. "It's about damn time, Leslie. The interesting shit is happening *miles* from the Strip. Jackie's been turning me on to these venues in the Valley, like the Reseda Country Club, and this warehouse in Burbank called the Puppet Ranch—"

"Thrash joints," said Leslie morosely.

"Exactly."

"Sorry, Norvald. Not for me. That's basically just shit with onions."

"Excuse me?"

"Same crap, different condiments. It's like putting onions on a piece of—"

"Don't ever say that again." Kip shook his head. "You're wrong, anyway. Glam and thrash have about as much in common as—I don't know. Things with nothing in common."

"I'm done with the scene, Kip. The records, the shows, the fanzines, the tape trading. All of it." He tossed *Hair of the Serpent* onto the back seat. "I'm retiring from metal."

Kip started the car and U-turned into traffic. The outrage he felt did his driving no favors. Leslie didn't seem to notice.

"Metal is your *life*, Leslie."

"Not anymore. Things happened to me, Norvald. On the tectonic level."

"On the what?"

"Tectonic changes," Leslie murmured. "Continental drift."

"I have no idea who I'm talking to here. It's not Leslie Z—that's all I know."

"You're right about that."

"Then who the fuck is it?"

Leslie drew himself up with all the dignity he could muster. "It's Leslie Aaron Vogler."

Kip forced himself to drive an entire city block before he answered. He was on the verge of tears. Leslie gazed dreamily out at the street.

"What are you going to do now? Can you answer me that? Are you going to quit smoking weed and get a buzz cut and start buying your pants at the Gap? Are you going to start listening to the fucking Pet Shop Boys?"

"I'll tell you something, Norvald." Leslie closed his eyes and ran a thumb along his swollen jaw. "I'll listen to pretty much any band that doesn't want me dead."

8

Half an hour later they arrived at the apartment—the one with the view of the 405 that Leslie still, against all probability, shared with Kira—to find her waiting for them with a three-course home-cooked dinner. Hush puppies and meat loaf and baked beans and ice cream for dessert: she'd made only soft things, things that Leslie could chew. It must have taken her hours. She was asking forgiveness, petitioning him for clemency, that much was clear; but the new Leslie—the post-Percy, post-metal Leslie—was even harder to read than the previous model. He ate without comment. Kip detected no trace of resentment in his expression, or anger, or even regret. He looked lost in a daydream. The half smile on his face gave Kip the chills.

Leslie wasn't the only one going through changes. Sometime in the six weeks since the worst night of their lives, Kira had cut the cord with Dusty Sinclair permanently—or so she claimed—and her hair looked like a peroxided rat's nest again, not a waterfall at a cheap Italian restaurant. A backpack full of spandex leggings and animal-print tops and assorted beauty paraphernalia that she'd been keeping at the Palace was in the bathroom now, slightly too close to the toilet; and there were moments, in the course of that tense, stilted dinner, when Kip allowed himself to wonder whether she might have left that bag out deliberately, for him to take note of—because he'd also sensed a change, subtle but potentially momentous, in Kira's attitude toward him.

"Sit down, boys," she said abruptly. "I've got news."

"We're sitting already," said Leslie. It was the first time he'd spoken since the food had been served.

"Sit down harder."

"I'm not sure how much more news I can handle," Kip muttered. "Are you going new wave on me too?"

"Not today, Satan." Kira rarely beamed—she *never* beamed—but she was beaming at them now. "I got promoted to shift manager at the Rainbow. First raise I've ever gotten in my life."

Kip raised his beer. "That's fucking awesome, Kira. Mazel tov."

"I can even hire people if I want."

Kip smiled at her politely. Eventually he realized that he'd been asked a question.

"I can't work at the Rainbow," Leslie said flatly. "I'm out of the scene."

She didn't ask him what the hell that meant—she was still treading lightly. She bobbed her head for a while, as if waiting for more, then looked past him at Kip.

"I'd love to, Kira. You know I would. But I've got a job already."

"What, at the print shop? That's barely a job."

"At the *Serpent*," he said, trying not to sound smug. "Jackie's putting me on writing full-time."

That brought Leslie to life. "I *told* you, Norvald of the North! The call of destiny!"

"Wow, Kip," Kira said, after the slightest perceptible pause. "When did you find out?"

"Jackie told me last week."

"Last *week*?" The reproach in her voice was unmistakable. "When were you planning on letting me know?"

Kip kept his head down and reached for the beans. Meeting her eyes seemed risky. It was the first time in months that she'd acknowledged any kind of bond between them.

"What's the latest on Crews?" he said, if only to say something.

"What do you care?"

"Jackie heard he might press charges."

"He's not pressing charges," said Leslie.

Kira raised her eyebrows. "And you know that how?"

"He's not pressing charges," Leslie repeated, looking past her at Kip. "Because I'm not pressing charges. Our lawyers traded wampum."

The table fell silent. A helicopter passed overhead—traffic cops, most likely—low enough to rattle the windows. Someone's car alarm went off.

"You have a lawyer?" Kip said finally. "Since when?"

"My parents do." He took a dainty bite of meat loaf. "They want me to come home. Already sent me a ticket."

"Come home and do what, exactly?" said Kira, her voice hard and thin. Going home was her doomsday scenario. Leslie took another bite.

"My best guess?" he said eventually. "The graveyard shift at Perkins."

She gave a choked laugh. Kip watched Leslie ignore her. He didn't see the humor in it, personally. He could picture Leslie working the night shift all too well.

After dinner they set up the secondhand turntable Kira had bought to celebrate her promotion and put on Metallica's . . . And Justice for All, which had dropped not long before. Opinions diverged. Kira decreed that they'd sold out at last; Leslie, after an initial show of reluctance to discuss metal at all, admitted to being impressed by certain riffs, but was put off by the absence of bass in the mix; Kip made no attempt to hide the fact that he was blown away. This music was as angry as anything coming out of Florida, and almost as heavy—but what set it apart from Deicide, or Repulsion, or even a thrash band like Slayer was the righteous focus of the album's lyrics. Metallica had written about real life before—speed and aggression weren't the only things they'd lifted from punk—but practically every song on Justice had a definite target: corruption, pollution, child abuse, war. This was anger with ideology behind it. Kip could already see entire sentences of the review he'd write for *Serpent*, and the satisfaction it would give him to see it in print. The last track on side two—a dirge-in-ballad's-clothing called "One"—lit up corners of his brain he'd never known existed.

"One" was narrated by a hospitalized soldier, a land-mine casualty, lying deaf and blind and limbless in some devastated country. It was possibly the most hopeless song that Kip had ever heard. The soldier had been burned clean of any vestige of patriotism or pride—all that remained for him was agony, and a wild, almost sexual longing for death. But lurid as these details were, what made the song so crushing was its simple realism. No sorcery, no demons, no slasher-flick clichés. Men like that maimed soldier existed. There was no need to invent them.

"*Hold my breath as I wish for death*," Kip mumbled when it was over.

"Uh-huh," said Leslie.

"That's the fucking *chorus*."

"Yeah."

"Listen to that squeaky-clean production," said Kira. "That's not what war sounds like."

Kip rolled his eyes. "Did we just listen to the same record?"

"You can *hear* that it's bullshit. Those boys have never been in any kind of combat. They're copping a pose."

"That's not even an argument." He shook his head in genuine disgust. "You're just trying to score points with Leslie."

She glared at him. "And why would I do that?"

"You know why."

The room went as hushed as a midwestern Sunday dinner. Even Leslie seemed to notice. Kip couldn't stop himself.

"I get what you're saying, Kira. No one in the band has actually been blown up by a land mine. They're definitely not as legit as WhiteOut— the musical force behind such hard-hitting numbers as 'Open Up and Say Please' and 'Tell Me Your Name on Your Way out the Door.'"

She pushed her chair back slowly from the table. "At least Dusty writes about things he knows something about. He might be a pig, or a moron, or even a racist—"

"Hold up now," said Leslie.

"—but in his own dumbfuck way he's one hundred percent real. 'Love on the Sly' is a true song. Dusty *lived* that. Smoking crack and playing G-D-C over and over and banging some cross-eyed drunk bitch from the Valley. That song is a memoir. You can't imagine *half* the shit that Dusty's done."

"I guess I'll have to take your word on that."

"I guess you fucking will."

Kip passed a hand slowly over his face, stalling for time, trying to understand how things had gone south so fast. "Are you hearing this, Z?"

"Don't call me that," said Leslie. He smiled tightly at Kira. "So it doesn't matter to you if Dusty's a racist?"

"That's not what I said."

"I just want to understand you. It doesn't matter if he hates faggots, or Mexicans, or his mother—or even you, Kira—as long as he means what he says? That excuses it all?"

Kira looked back and forth between them, hard-eyed and pale, then snatched up a red leather jacket with flames on its sleeves from the floor. It was too big for her, Kip noticed, and too small for Leslie. She was still trying to get it on as the apartment door closed behind her. He tried not to ask himself where she was headed.

"Whose jacket is that?"

"Did you say something?" said Leslie.

"That jacket. The red one. I don't think I've seen it before."

Leslie didn't answer. They stared at the half-eaten meal for a while. Poison's new single, "Every Rose Has Its Thorn," came up through the floor in unctuous slabs of overprocessed sound. It appeared to be playing on some kind of loop. Somebody was going through a breakup.

"Can you believe that shit?" Kip got out finally. "Dusty Sinclair not fake? That idiot has got to be one of the biggest posers I've ever—"

"I love you, Norvald," Leslie said. "But you're a chump."

9

After that Kira took up the old protocol, always happening to be out when Kip dropped by. He ran through all the most likely explanations and scenarios, gauging how each one sat in his gut and his brain, and finally went with having caused her serious offense. He found out which nights she was working at the Rainbow—Leslie refused to tell him—and went to see her early on a Tuesday, when business was slow.

When he stepped into the maraschino-colored twilight of the so-called Kandy Lounge, however, the person behind the bar turned out to be a pudgier, uglier version of Mötörhead's frontman, Lemmy Kilmister, complete with dyed black sideburns and an enormous fleshy mole on his left cheek. He regarded Kip with poker-faced indifference. No one else was in the room.

"Is Kira around?"

"Kira who?"

"Come on, dude."

"Come on, *Lemmy*."

Kip looked hard at him, momentarily destabilized. "You're not Lemmy," he said finally.

"Suit yourself," said the man, moving off down the bar.

Kip sat down on a bar stool and watched the man work. Kilmister was at least six feet tall, probably more, and usually decked out in vintage SS gear. But the bartender had clearly made a study of the genuine article at close quarters—which would have been easy enough, since everyone on the Strip knew that the video poker machine at the end of the bar was the place Lemmy wanted to die. The light grew redder and more womblike the longer Kip waited. At some point the simulacrum drifted back in his direction.

"You drink or you leave. This ain't a coffee shop."

"Kira Carson."

"Nice to meet you, Kira. Drink or leave."

"Just let her know I'm here, man. I walked all the way from Silver Lake on my prosthetic leg."

"Explain to me why she should give a shit."

"We grew up together. I'm her cousin, Ray Carson."

"Is that right. Where was this?"

"Venice, Florida. Ponceville."

"Get your story straight, cousin."

"Just tell her."

The bartender leaned forward. "What school did she go to?"

"She was homeschooled. Not that it's any of your business."

He slopped pints for a long and empty interval. "Later," he said.

"Excuse me?"

"Shifts got switched. Kira's on graveyard." He smiled to himself. "You might not recognize her, though. She's changed a lot."

Kip came back just before midnight and found Kira there, exactly as advertised, pouring Cuervo shots for a group of suntanned men in pleated slacks who looked as though their taste in music ran to easy listening. He'd been in L.A. almost a full year by then, long enough to be able to classify them by genus, if not by species: salarymen for some label or other, probably Warner Brothers, whose offices were a few blocks down the street. No one was flirting with Kira, for once—most likely because she was wearing glued-on muttonchops and a Civil War infantryman's cap and an enormous latex wart on her left cheek. She moved with the same exaggerated, leg-dragging shuffle as the other fake Lemmy. Her most consummate disappearing act yet.

"Mister Kilmister, I presume."

She hesitated less than a second. "Kip! Jesus Christ—Dennis had me freaked out that one of my *real* cousins had tracked me down somehow."

"That explains the disguise."

She laughed. "Today's Lemmy's birthday. We're just waiting for him to show."

"Isn't he usually here at happy hour?"

"Rain or shine, when he's in town." She smoothed down her sideburns. "We're kind of worried that he might be dead."

Before Kip could reply she was off down the bar, pulling pints for three kids dressed in black satin tunics with the puppyish glow of a freshly signed act. Sure enough, they sat down with the Cuervo drinkers, who turned out to be A&R reps for Warner/Reprise. Kip watched them celebrating, unable to dredge up even the faintest twinge of envy. He'd covered enough bands by then to know that this little party at the Rainbow was likely to be the high point of their musical career.

"Konkordium," Kira told him when she came back, though he hadn't asked. "They play thrash, but on period instruments."

"Period instruments?"

"Harpsichords. Lutes. Stuff like that." She adjusted her wig. "What are you having?"

"I'll take a Jack and Coke tonight. In Lemmy's loving memory."

"Excellent choice. We happen to have those pre-mixed."

He sat quietly until she'd fixed his drink. "I'm sorry, Kira."

"No Kira here, friend."

"Could you pass along a message, Mr. Kilmister? I'm trying to apologize."

She gave him a sidelong glance, touched the brim of her cap, then went to pull a pint of Guinness for a man with bleach-damaged hair who resembled a seasick Vince Neil.

"What for?" she said when she came back again.

For some reason he found himself hedging. "That's not Vince Neil, is it? From Mötley?"

"I can neither confirm nor deny."

"He looks shorter in real life. And greener."

"You're kind of dicking me around here, Kip."

He took a gulp of his Jack and Coke and looked at her. The unblinking gray eyes. The freckles along her forehead where the dimpled scar began—the one that turned red when she got angry or excited. It occurred to him now, as he tried to get his thoughts in order, that the scar he'd given Charlie Crews would look about the same.

"I'm listening," said Kira.

"I want to apologize for what I said at Leslie's dinner. And for what I did to Crews. And for what an asshole I've been since . . ." His voice trailed away.

"Since when?"

"Since you decided to become a different person."

He'd thought that might set her off again—he was sure that it would—but instead she pulled the fake wart off her cheek, examined it closely, and set it on the bar beside his glass.

"Dusty would never have apologized for any of that."

"Then I guess I should apologize for not being Dusty."

That of all things brought a smile to her lips. "No, you shouldn't, Kip Norvald." Her scar seemed to change color, to darken very subtly, but in that syrupy light it was hard to be sure. She topped off his drink and moved back down the bar.

Sometime after his fifth refill Kip got down from his stool—gingerly, so as not to break anything—and made his way to the little two-stall bathroom on the Rainbow's second floor. The stairs were steeper than he remembered, and darker, and something was blocking the bathroom door from the inside.

He worked himself in sideways, an inch at a time, sucking his gut in like a swimsuit model. The bathroom was barely any brighter than the stairwell, and he'd had six Jack and Cokes, maybe seven—which was why it took him longer than it might otherwise have to recognize the man lying curled on the floor in a puddle of vomit and blood.

"Do you know if Lemmy's dead yet?" he asked Kira once he'd made it back downstairs.

She narrowed her eyes at him. "Why are you asking?"

"I think Vince Neil might be on his way to join him."

By the time Kira had found someone to sub for her—the Lemmy impersonator from that afternoon, who apparently lived on the premises—and they'd gotten upstairs with a first-aid kit and towels, a line of pissed-off drunks extended halfway down the stairs. Kira ignored them. She was skinnier than Kip had ever seen her, borderline gaunt, and she slipped into the bathroom with ease. Something thumped hard against the far side of the door—a boot? a head?—and it opened just enough to let him in. He found Kira squatting by the urinal with a towel in her lap, cradling Neil's blood-spattered head between her knees. The tableau put him in mind of a postcard his grandmother kept on her fridge: the Savior tended to by Mary Magdalene. Kira was saying something that he couldn't quite make out.

"What's that?"

"I said come over here and help me sit him up. I'm not sure what's wrong with him. He can't really talk."

"He can't really sing, either."

"Will you get over here?"

Between the two of them they managed to haul Neil's lifeless-seeming body to the corner stall and up onto a toilet. Kip was covered in blood and vomit himself by then, and god knew what else, but Kira remained magically pristine. He'd never seen her so professional, so effortlessly in command—she moved with the grim economy of a veteran EMT. She dug a pair of scissors out of the first-aid kit and cut the soiled wifebeater away from Neil's sweaty torso and wadded it up and tossed it in the trash. She wiped his face clean—insofar as that was possible—but left his hair exactly as it was. A childlike smile was creeping across Neil's features now, unnerving to behold.

"Kira," he whispered.

"Right here, scumbag."

"Kira, baby. Is that you?"

"The one and only. I'm taking a hundred bucks out of your wallet."

"Take it, honey. Everything I got. It's fucken yours."

"I'd like an apology, too."

But by then he'd lapsed back into gibberish. She dug a money clip out of his jeans—a thick wad of hundreds—and chose two of the less disgusting bills, pocketing one and passing the other to Kip.

"I'll be back in five minutes. See if you can keep him from flushing himself down the toilet."

Kip and *Hit Parader* magazine's hottest vocalist (male) 1985–86 spent the next fifteen minutes in stupefied silence, broken only by whoever happened to be attending to his or her necessities in the neighboring stall. Kip was just sober enough to appreciate the improbability of his situation. Leslie would want to hear what had gone down exactly, to the smallest detail—and what he, Christopher Chanticleer Norvald, had done with the once-in-a-lifetime chance that he'd been given.

Delicately and slowly, with as much dignity as the stall's cramped quarters would permit, Kip bent down until his mouth was at the level of Neil's ear. His hair smelled of gin, menthol smoke, and what might have been vanilla extract. He looked to be asleep.

"Vince. Wake up, Vince. This is your conscience speaking."

"Kira?"

"This is an important message. You suck, Vince. Your band sucks. Mötley Crüe is an embarrassment to yourself and to your family. You spend more time on your bangs than you do on your songs."

Neil sighed softly in answer.

"Glam is dead, Vince. No more blowjobs for you. No more cocaine facials. Are you listening? No more drinks on the house. Nod your head if you can hear me."

Someone banged on the door. The bowed head seemed to bob.

"I'm glad you understand me, Vince. Because a storm is coming."

Then suddenly Kira was back, pulling Kip up to make room for an older man, maybe forty, with buzzed hair and a look of stoic suffering. He moved past Kip as if he were a bathroom fixture, his sad eyes fixed unwaveringly on Neil. Kip felt a passing urge to punch him in the kidney.

"Vince Neil Wharton," the man said, taking Neil by the hair. "Vince Neil Wharton, we are opening our eyes." He jerked the head back so hard that it made Kip's eye's water. "We are opening our eyes and answering Richard's questions."

"Richard." Neil let out a giggle. "Go *away*."

"We blew it, Vince. We goofed. We dropped the ball. We fucked the monkey."

"I was just—"

"Here's what's happening now. We're getting up, Vince. We're getting up and buttoning our jeans and thanking this young lady for not putting in a call to the *Enquirer* and making herself a quick ten thousand dollars."

That seemed to hit the mark. "Thanks, baby," Neil mumbled in Kira's direction.

"Don't mention it."

The man with the buzz cut gave one final yank on Neil's hair, apparently for emphasis, then steered him with practiced efficiency out the door. He winked at Kira as he passed her. He was wearing a red leather jacket with flames on the sleeves.

"Interesting jacket," Kip said once the door had swung shut.

"That's just Richard," said Kira, mopping under the sink. "He's management."

"Management," Kip repeated. "Okay."

"This is going to take a while, Kip. Maybe now's not the best time to talk."

"I want to see you," Kip told her. "Not just here at the Rainbow. I don't care what the terms are. It's crazy for us not to see each other."

She dropped the mop and spun around and stared into his face. She was close enough that he could see the dark brown roots along her hairline. The scar had gone scarlet. He braced for the worst.

"What are you up to tomorrow?"

"Excuse me?"

She made a fist and rapped three times against his forehead. "Tomorrow, Norvald. As in Wednesday. Are you free?"

"Pretty much, yeah." He crossed his arms and pinched himself as hard as he could through the fabric of his shirt. "I'm supposed to pull something together about the new Judas Priest full-length."

"*Ram It Down.*"

"That's the one." He realized he was blushing. "It's for *Circus*, believe it or not. Four hundred words by midnight."

"So what do you think?"

"About the record? It's dogshit."

She laughed. "There's a burger place on La Cienega I've been wanting to try. They make *tempura* burgers, whatever that means."

"Tempura burgers. Sounds crunchy."

"If you think you can swing it."

He willed himself to nod. "The review shouldn't take long. I'm just going to write *Judas Priest does it again* a hundred times in a row."

"I'm glad we're friends again, Chanticleer. I missed you a lot."

Sixteen contradictory emotions made the circuit of Kip's brain. "Okay," he managed to murmur. His face prickled strangely.

"That's all I get? *Okay?*"

"Jesus, Kira. You know that I'm—"

Just then the door swung open and a man wearing Wayfarers and a purple leather top hat staggered in. Slash impersonators were legion that year, outnumbering even the Nikki Sixx lookalikes, but the resemblance in this case was downright spooky. He had Slash's corkscrew curls, his nose ring, even his trademark leather chaps with buckles down the seams. The illusion was perfect. Then he opened his mouth.

"I'm a cowboy," the man informed them, in a lisping screech that sounded vaguely French. He took in a deep breath and began to sing:

"*I've had seven fuzzy navels, and I'm still standing tall. I've seen a hundred faces, bitches, AND I'VE ROCKED THEM ALL!*"

10

For a while the good old days were back again. On the tectonic level, as Leslie would say, certain shifts were ongoing—but on the surface all was comfortable and calm. The changes were imperceptible, hidden just out of sight, like seawater eating away at a pier.

Kira kept a bar stool free for Kip whenever she worked the Rainbow— the last one on the left, right by the taps—and they chatted for hours about trivial things, whatever happened to be rattling around in their brains, the way they'd always used to do in Venice. It was clear to him now that she'd rounded some corner. She wasn't afraid of the past anymore, or of her family, or of herself; and she wasn't trying to keep him at a distance.

Little by little, no matter how hard he tried to smother it, hope began to kindle in Kip's blasted heart again.

One day he found himself talking about his mother: spontaneously, impulsively, before he'd fully grasped what he was saying. He told Kira about the deadening succession of nondescript towns, Bucksville, Greenville, Wellborn, Suwanee, Atico, Athena, Mexico Beach; the motor parks, the public restrooms, the community clinics; the mildew-and-Lysol smell of rooms you have to pay for by the week. He told her about testifying against his father in a Fort Myers courthouse the week he turned fourteen years old. No one knew about that, not even Leslie. He told her about the last time he'd laid eyes on his mother, in Gainesville three

years back—how he'd snuck into her boyfriend's house through a bedroom window, cutting a hole in the bug screen with an X-Acto knife,
and finally found her hiding in the bathtub. How she'd followed him
half-naked through that ruined bungalow, bleeding from the gums and
begging him to tell her who he was.

When he'd finished Kira studied him in silence. He tried to look
casual.

"I'm glad you told me all this," she said quietly. "It means that you
trust me."

"Sure," Kip answered hoarsely. He clung tightly to the bar.

"I guess I'm just wondering why." She corrected herself. "Why *now*,
I mean."

"I shouldn't have told you."

"Shut up. It's just—" She hesitated again. "It would have been good
to know all this a year ago, you know?"

He was about to ask her what she meant—to ask her about sixteen
questions, more or less at the same time—when a man in a hot pink
bandanna gave a whistle and she flounced off down the bar. The face
Kira put on for certain regulars brought Kip genuine amusement, even
satisfaction of a kind. It also made him very slightly ill.

"I don't like it when they whistle at you," he felt compelled to say
when she'd come back. "You have a name."

"You don't think I actually *tell* it to these bottom-feeders, do you?"
she said, blowing Pink Bandanna a kiss over her shoulder. "That gentle-
man thinks my name is Kandy Rainbow."

"I guess it's none of my business."

"You guessed right." She put on her Kira Carson face again. "We were
talking about your mother."

Kip's mother was on his mind for a definite reason: a letter had just
arrived at Oona's house in Venice, asking for money as always, post-
marked Ojai, California. She was close, in other words—too close for his
psychic comfort. That made perfect sense to Kira.

"My sympathies, Norvald. Half the reason we came out here was to
get left the hell alone."

"Two-thirds of the reason."

She reached across the bar and pinched his cheek. "Another dose?"

"Please, nurse. I'd consider it a kindness."

She topped off his mug and took a sip before she put it in his hands. He gave her a compliment, half-joking, half-sincere, on her gracious bedside manner, and she curtsied in thanks. What Kip had neglected to mention was that every so often, usually while watching her flirting for tips, he caught himself thinking about how his mother had spent half her life in darkened rooms exactly like the Kandy Lounge, pining away for some trainwreck—some shocking lost cause—while plotting her escape from another. There was a warning in that, both for him and for Kira. He'd seen firsthand what a life of longing gets you.

Kira had her own concerns that winter, most of which were somehow tangled up with Leslie. He hadn't forgiven her for what had happened at the Whisky, not completely, but it was more than just that. He wasn't wearing his black leather jacket with the polished chrome studs anymore, or his zebra-print shawl, or his bullet belt, or any of his forty-seven highly collectible tour shirts with their necks slashed in the trademark Vogler style. He was walking around in the only thing he owned with zero metal connotations: a shapeless gray hoodie, sweat-stained and filthy, with CAMP CEDAR PINES printed across the back in puffy yellow letters. He was losing weight and keeping human interaction to a minimum and coming and going at inscrutable hours. That past Monday, she told Kip, the LAPD had brought him home at 5:45 in the morning, though he hadn't been drunk, as far as anyone could tell, and hadn't broken any laws. According to the cops he'd just seemed lost.

"You know Leslie," Kip said cheerfully, in a voice that even he found unconvincing. "His ways are not for us mere mortals—"

"Fuck that, Norvald. He's using."

"Using what?"

She took his glass and slopped it. "There's only one thing I know makes you spend all day sitting on a dirty mattress staring at the floor."

He blinked at her for a long moment, buying time, pretending that he didn't understand. He needed things to be okay a few weeks longer. A couple of days at least.

"You're not going to say anything?"

He glanced toward the exit. "Where do you think he keeps his works?"

"Not in the house, I'm pretty sure. I searched his room." She shrugged. "Probably wherever he goes off to."

Kip sat back and dug his fists into his eyes. Even just another hour. Was that so much to ask?

"Then I guess we've got to find out where that is."

"Funny," she said. "You're a comedian now."

"How's that?"

"I'd do a lot of things for Leslie, but I am *not* going on a smack crawl to every goddamn dealer in West Hollywood. That's the kind of shit that gets a person—"

"I'll do it."

"What?"

"I'll do it," he repeated. "I'll figure it out."

She stared at him as he put a twenty on the bar and stood to go. The changes were out in the open again—a fault line was opening under Kip's feet. He had to keep ahead of it somehow.

Leslie bought his heroin from a man named Gustavo Beniste, who was forty-six years old and had a daughter in med school at UCLA. Beniste lived in a two-room apartment a few blocks from the La Brea tar pits, above a sign advertising Luscious Taste Jeans & Fabric Imports, the front for his modest narcotics enterprise. He was scrawny and gregarious and seemed to subsist exclusively on Diet Dr Pepper and cocaine. He agreed to cut Leslie off without a murmur of objection.

"He'll just cop somewhere else, though, if you want to know the truth," Beniste said, his voice regretful as a social worker's. "They sell heroin at the Baby Gap these days."

Kip hadn't needed to stake out Leslie's apartment to track down his connection, or do any detective work to speak of, because Beniste turned out to be a friend of Jackie Slaughter's. They'd met back in college—had briefly been roommates, in fact—and Beniste still hooked him up occasionally with muscle relaxants and weed. "I wasn't the matchmaker, though," Jackie insisted. "Everybody goes to Ricky. If I was a betting man, which I'm not, my money would have to be on Percy Blackwood."

"No way," Kip answered, doing his best to keep his rage in check. "No fucking way. Leslie would never go to Percy's dealer."

"Why not?"

"It would compromise his sense of self-respect."

"You've never been addicted to anything," Jackie told him with a mournful little grin. "I get it."

"How the hell would you know?"

"Because you mention self-respect," he said. "That's how I know."

For six weeks Beniste's prediction seemed off by a mile. He'd been true to his word, turning off the tap right away, and Leslie's tantrums and anxiety attacks were proof enough of his withdrawal. Leslie never seemed to suspect Kip's involvement, or even Kira's; he was grateful, he confessed to them, that the universe had somehow intervened. He could have scored elsewhere, obviously, but he didn't. He seemed to view the pain of kicking heroin as something he deserved.

Day by day the Z of bygone days began to reemerge. By the end of the month he was laughing again, and doing little things around the house, and voicing no objection when Kip put on songs he used to like. He bought himself new clothes—mostly from a Banana Republic on Wilshire, which Kira struggled to be okay with—and enrolled in cooking classes at a community college in West Hollywood. Anyone who knew him at all could sense his mortal embarrassment at the trouble he'd caused: his entire sense of self, painstakingly constructed under combat conditions in the most hostile of environments, was founded on the principle of absolute control. Addiction was therefore the worst of all sins—the only sin, it sometimes seemed to Kip, that Leslie's moral code had any use for.

It was Kira's idea to throw a party to celebrate the six-week anniversary of Leslie's final trip to Luscious Taste. It would double as a housewarming for Kip's new apartment: a dingy one-bedroom at the corner of Cahuenga and Fountain, financed by Jackie as a bridge loan against future earnings by the magazine. The plan was for a mellow get-together—just the guest of honor, one or two friends from his cooking class, Kip, Kira, Jackie, and a handful of rigorously vetted acquaintances from the days when he still wore mascara. To everyone's amazement Leslie didn't try to stop her.

The party was a bust, which broke Kip's heart a little. The effort Kira had put into that night was hard to overlook, from the lasagna she'd baked to the snapshots of a grinning, healthy Leslie stuck to the fridge—not to mention the banner she'd painted, artful and meticulous as ever, that read WHY DO YOU THINK THEY CALL IT DOPE in bleeding silver letters. She'd hung it across the arch that separated the living room from the kitchen, low enough that Leslie had to duck each time he went to get a beer.

The night felt off from the start. It was obvious that the banner embarrassed Leslie and that the party embarrassed him more, the way everything seemed to embarrass him lately: Kip could almost see him grinding his teeth behind his tight-lipped smile. The people from cooking class—a middle-aged Armenian man and a Mexican girl with braces, who looked as though she might still be in junior high—were duly freaked out by the overall vibe. Leslie sat on the living room couch for exactly one hour, answering everybody's questions in a courteous voice that didn't sound remotely like him, then excused himself and drifted toward the bedroom. Kip sat on a milk crate full of records and watched him go, feeling absolutely useless. He'd never seen Kira so anxious, so bewildered in the face of her inability to influence events. She barely knew the people she'd invited—she'd lost most of her friends, such as they were, the moment she walked out on Dusty.

The party might have died a merciful death there and then if not for Jackie, who'd never met a captive audience he didn't like.

"Don't confuse death metal with *black* metal, friend," he was barking at someone in a Def Leppard shirt. "You've been in Hollywood so long that your ears are clogged with bongwater and hair spray and cum. The future of the art form is being dredged up from the bottom of the sea as we speak, and not along the Gulf Coast, either—no offense, Norvald. The music I'm talking about could never have come out of swamp country. It's a product of the coldest, darkest places on the planetary map. This is crazy shit—*terrifying* shit—and it's being put out by children. Sixteen, seventeen years old. These kids are too young to think in terms of cause and effect, you understand me? They mean what they say when they sing about death. They're not copping an attitude out in those woods. This is the next wave of metal, no question about that— but metal is just the beginning. It's a *death* cult, you follow? These kids want to be *Vikings*. Playing in a band is just something to pass the time until they die in battle."

Something made Kip glance at Kira. She'd stopped short halfway to the kitchen and stood listening to Jackie, arms cradling a stack of dirty plates. She looked saddened by what she was hearing, personally affected, as though she'd found out someone dear to her was dead. But there was impatience in her eyes as well. Impatience or excitement.

"I thought black metal was—I don't know. English bands from five years back," she said. "Venom and so on."

Questions of this kind were what Jackie lived for. "Not even close," he said. "The music I'm talking about, this Scandinavian shit, makes Venom sound like KC and the Sunshine Band." He reached into the leopard-print tote he always carried with him and pulled out a small stack of vinyl, handing Kip the topmost LP. "I'm guessing that you haven't heard this yet."

Kip took the record with an odd twinge of reluctance. *Deathcrush*, by someone called Mayhem. "Can't say I have."

"Mind if I put it on?"

Kip shrugged. "This party's skunked anyway. I'm pretty sure Leslie's asleep."

Jackie said nothing to that—the intricacies of Kip's secondhand Panasonic demanded his full concentration. The vinyl of the LP was not so much black as mud-colored, so flimsy that it looked almost homemade. The needle met the lead groove with a noise like tearing plastic. The sound quality was atrocious. It began with a sustained note of feedback, perhaps accidental, held for so long that nothing more seemed to be coming— then three down-tuned chords on a guitar, the classic *diabolus in musica* tritone, cut through apparently at random by what sounded like some sort of table saw. The vocals when they came had a strangely incidental quality, swelling and ebbing, sometimes male-sounding, sometimes female. By the time the song was over Kip was too depressed to move.

"*This* is the future?" he shouted to Jackie.

"Believe it, pilgrim."

"It sounds like it was recorded on someone's answering machine, and mixed by—I don't know what." He thought for a moment. "A child."

"I don't think there was any mixing involved, to be honest."

"Turn it *off*," said Kira, as near as Kip could make out. Something had upset her. The few people left in the room looked either bored or badly frightened. The kid in the Def Leppard shirt seemed ready to burst into tears.

"I didn't say I *liked* it," Jackie answered. Kip was reading lips by that point. Somehow, though the volume knob was still where it had been for the last record—*Highway to Hell* by AC/DC—no one could understand what anyone was saying. Kira and Jackie were screaming at each other now, to all appearances fighting for real. Jackie took Kira by the wrist and Kira slapped him. No one else seemed to notice. Kip was crossing the room to stop them when a movement just behind them caught his eye.

Leslie was standing in the little stucco archway that led to the kitchen, the top of his head brushing the plasterwork, mumbling and laughing. He seemed to be saying "Florida" over and over, though it could also have been "horrible," for all that Kip could tell, or possibly "forever." He came into the room uncertainly, taking faltering steps, as though he'd aged a hundred years in half an hour. His eyes fell closed completely as he sat down on the floor. He was flat on his back by the time Kira reached him. His face had gone expressionless and slack.

"He's dying," Kip said, but of course no one heard him. The music was still forcing itself like hard-packed winter snow into his ears. Then the music was gone and he was crouched next to Kira and Jackie was pulling ten-pound sacks of ice out of the freezer. Leslie's eyes when Kira pushed them open had no pupils at all: they were the eyes of an insect, unblinking and flat. The music was over but it felt as if the music was still playing. Leslie's lips went blue, then purplish gray, then a color Kip had never seen before.

Jackie took the bags of ice into the bathroom and turned the shower on full and dumped the bags out one by one into the tub. Everyone else had crowded in behind him. A girl Kip didn't know was standing up against the sink, in everybody's way, saying Leslie's name over and over. The kid in the Def Leppard shirt stood next to her doing absolutely nothing. Kip and Kira pulled off Leslie's shoes and hoisted him into the bathtub, clothes and all. Leslie didn't seem to notice. Kira was slapping him across the face hard, as hard as she could, and Kip reached out to stop her but Jackie hissed at him to let her be. The bathtub was taking forever to fill. It seemed to be leaking. Suddenly the buzzer rang and two women in their twenties appeared, carrying a collapsible stretcher between them, exactly like the EMTs who'd come for Harley Boy after his accident out in the Grids. Kip had no idea where they'd come from. He stepped back with his hands in the air, as if he were being arrested, and watched them go about their silent business. They were the same EMTs, he decided. Not similar but the same. It was the only explanation that made sense to him.

When it was over he let himself sink down onto the sofa and Kira came and took his hand and held it. The police had shown up eventually, too late to do any good—they'd acted as if it was their sixteenth OD call of the night, which it probably was. Their sole contribution, as far as Kip could tell, had been to keep Leslie's friends out of the ambulance. They hadn't even found the heroin.

Now everyone but Kira was gone and he was starting to come back down to earth, or up from whatever hole he'd fallen into, staring at a flattened pack of menthols on the floor between his feet. Salem Ultra Lights. He didn't know anybody who smoked Salems. They could have been left by the cooking class kids, or by the paramedics, or even by one of the cops. He felt no anger at being kept out of the ambulance, no moral indignation, no anxiety. What he felt was a kind of horrified relief.

He let his eyes close and leaned back until his head touched the dry-wall behind him. It made a hollow sound, a sad little thump, as walls in cheap apartments had done all his life. Kira was with him, he could feel her and hear her, but he kept his eyes shut. He was trying to remember. What exactly had the revelation been—the one that had come to him on that long-ago afternoon in Leslie's bedroom, sitting alone on the floor, staring up at the ceiling, listening in slack-jawed amazement to Death?

That everything wasn't going to be all right. Not now and not ever.

He was beginning to understand how small he was, how inad-equate, how irrelevant to the workings of the world. The days when Leslie Vogler had looked out for him—when the simple fact of Leslie's existence had somehow seemed a promise of safe passage—were so far gone that he could barely recollect them. At some point, without his noticing, their roles had been reversed. All he seemed to do now was to look out for Leslie: to pick him up from the hospital, from the pave-ment, from the floor. To try to protect him. To fail.

Kira shifted her body and took in a breath. She was going to say something. Panic shot through him, icy and unexpected, laced with an almost sickening resentment. They'd failed so spectacularly, all three of them. The distance between the lives they'd pictured for themselves in some preposterous Technicolor California and what they'd actually found was as vast as the country they'd driven across in Kthulu. But the reason for their failure had never been California itself, or the city of Los Angeles, or even the Strip with all of its corruptions. They themselves were the reason. Their selfishness, their immaturity, their weakness. They were hicks from Central Florida and that fact would never change. Kira had been right to cut and run, as much as it had hurt; but no escape was possible. The lives each of them had, right there and then, were all they'd ever have. At last his eyes were open.

He felt Kira beside him. His stomach was cramping. Whether he was angry at her or at Leslie or at his own stupidity and helplessness made little difference now.

"Kip—"

He found her thigh and gripped it. "I don't want to talk."

"All right." He felt her leg stiffen. "That hurts."

His grip tightened. He could see that it surprised her. She could have slipped free but she sat there unmoving.

"I've been unfair," she said. "I've been unfair to you."

She waited for him to speak, to ask what she meant, but he gave no reply. The violence in him made it difficult to focus. He wondered whether what she said was true.

"That hurts," she said again, in a voice that didn't match what she was saying.

"Tell me why."

She knew what he meant right away. "I tried to, Kip. That night at Xanadu—do you remember? When you pulled that stupid stunt. I tried to tell you then."

Her eyes were near enough to his that he could see them start to water. With pain or with its opposite. "I wouldn't blame you if you *did*," she said, as if in answer to some unspoken threat. He took her by the wrist and brought her closer.

"Tell me in a way that I can understand."

"I always treated Leslie better. Always put him above you. Even though you loved me and he didn't." She laughed. "Leslie doesn't need me for anything. Most days he doesn't even *see* me. That helps—" She shook her head. "I guess you could say it helps me to relax."

"Relax," he repeated.

She said nothing.

"So you treated him better."

"I'll tell you something, Kip. I'm scared of you. Not like some people are—in the opposite way. I don't get frightened when you lose your shit. When you do that I'm fine." She put her free hand over his, over the fingers that held her. "It's the rest of the time that's the problem. Things aren't always real for me—I've told you. And what you want from me makes it worse. It just makes everything go dead."

"I don't understand you."

"It's hard to explain. Everything flattens out." She pushed his fingertips into the soft skin on the inside of her wrist. "You want to know what's real for me?"

He gave a nod.

"What's real for me is this."

She drew back and hit him with the flat of her hand. The pain of it shocked him. His eyes and mouth were open but he couldn't make a sound. Anger was what she wanted from him now. The knowledge wrung tears from him and those tears in turn brought the blood to Kira's face and made her breath go shallow. She wanted this and he would give her what she wanted.

He took her by the hair. Her eyes were shining and triumphant. She studied him intently as his anger tried to choke him. He'd never seen this side of her but other men had seen it. He stood and wound her hair around his fist and pulled her down the hallway. It seemed to him that she was laughing. He felt nothing any longer. He was closer to the White Room than he'd ever been by choice. A veil had closed around him and its light consumed all sound and form and color. He never would have ventured there for any other soul.

Late that night he opened his eyes onto the familiar half dark of his room to find her sitting up beside him. When she spoke his name he realized that she'd been saying it over and over, running her fingers along his forearm, gently coaxing him awake.

"I came so close to fucking this up, Kip. I *did* fuck it up. I need you to forgive me."

He found himself smiling. "I'm pretty sure we're past all that."

"I've figured out when I fell for you. The exact place and time." She took his hand and kissed it. "Do you want to know when?"

He said that he did.

"You probably think it was when you roundhoused Crews at the Palace, or when you pulled some other macho horseshit, or maybe just now, when we—" She hesitated. "When we did what we did. But that's not when it was."

He was wide-awake now. "When was it?"

"No guesses?"

"That night at the Fountain?"

"I don't think it counts if you're tripping your balls off, Norvald. We were both in love with everything that night."

"I'm hoping this isn't some kind of trick question."

She shook her head.

"Tell me."

"We were sitting onstage at that roller rink in Sarasota, the Stardust, listening to Cannibal Corpse. You had your bony teenage ass on the boards and your back against somebody's cabinet—the bass player's, I think. You were so fucking *gone*. Like a religious conversion. Nothing else existed for you then. Not even me."

She paused there a moment and stared into space. He watched her remembering.

"You'd only been growing your hair out for a few months, so it was sticking up every which way, especially in back. Just this preppy-looking kid in some awful pastel polo shirt with his eyes rolling back in his head. You looked strung out on something. I was so full of envy. I just wanted to grab that stupid hair of yours and pull." She laughed to herself. "But you were beautiful sitting there with your arms around your knees. There was *light* coming off of you, I swear. You were glowing. I spent that whole set just watching, staring at you staring at the band, and you never once noticed. You were lost to the world. It came to me right then, in a voice I could actually hear. I'm in love with this boy."

"Then why didn't you—"

"I've been lying here, like this, for I don't know how long—an hour maybe." She took in a breath. "I've been thinking about that night and how hard it hit me. The fucking awe you felt listening to the music, those five goons in sweatpants—I've never believed in anything half as much. It scared me, if you want to know the truth. I felt like a ghost, watching you. I felt like I'd just found out that I'd died."

He tried to speak but she stopped him. "None of that matters now. That's what I'm trying to tell you."

"Of course not."

"I've been trying so hard, ever since we came out here, to make up some new person to be—something that would at least feel halfway real. I don't have to tell you. You've seen all the haircuts." She looked up at the ceiling. "But I'll never get out of this skin. I've learned that much. I'd have to fucking set myself on fire."

"Kira—"

"You get what I'm saying, don't you?" She studied his face. "Don't bother answering. Of course you do."

She held out a hand and he took it.

"It feels fine to be here. It feels peaceful. That summer-night feeling. If this was the country there'd be fucking crickets." She went quiet for a moment. "What I've figured out, after all this time, is basically just—there's no one I can tell this to but you. You and Leslie. Even the idea of trying to explain it to anybody else makes me want to throw up." She pressed herself against him. "I can bullshit myself but I can't bullshit you. Because you know me, Kip. You *know* me. So you have to understand."

11

Kira never went back to the apartment with the view of the 405. Kip drove over one day in Kthulu to pick up her clothes while she was working at the Rainbow, ten days after Leslie's overdose, and that was it. The place already felt abandoned. Other than a shoebox full of demos there was nothing there that anyone would miss.

There were moments, in the course of those first weeks, when the ease of it all made him question his sanity. She borrowed his keys on day five, slipped them out of the breast pocket of his jacket without even asking, and had dupes made in a hardware store on her walk home from work. No agonizing, no weighing of options. It was all so straightforward, so self-understood. Suddenly Kira was his.

He'd have liked to hear Leslie's take—he was dying to hear it—but Leslie was gone. Showing an initiative no one on earth could have predicted, the Voglers had touched down at LAX within twenty-four hours of the OD, dressed as if for a funeral, and had taken their son back to Florida as soon as his doctors had cleared him for travel. Under normal circumstances Kip might have protested, even somehow tried to intervene—but those first delirious, sleep-deprived days with Kira were so wonderfully murky that the weight of Leslie's leaving didn't register for weeks. Kip had visited the hospital only once, the afternoon after the party: it had been a tense forty minutes, full of false starts and mis-understandings, and he'd felt grateful when the time had come to leave.

He'd arrived at L.A. General to find Leslie propped up in bed with a tray in his lap, gray in the face but undeniably alive, watching *Unsolved Mysteries* on the ceiling TV. That episode's theme, as far as Kip could figure out, was girls going missing in swamps. Leslie lay there like a sultan in a pair of silk pajamas, slightly dazed from the sedation, slurping applesauce through a candy-colored straw. He looked downright cozy. Kip couldn't decide whether to congratulate him on his recovery or kick him in the teeth.

"Where's Kira?"

"At the Rainbow."

"Fair enough," said Leslie. "She's working?"

"You want the truth? She's too pissed off to come."

"Fair enough," Leslie repeated.

They watched the show for a while. Lots of footage of trailers and flat-bottom boats.

"I keep expecting to see the Furberold kid," said Leslie. "I keep ex-pecting to see Ponceville and the Grids."

"Me too."

"Jackie says you're going to a shrink now. A therapist. For that road rage you've got."

Kip kept his eyes on the TV. "I'm pretty sure they don't call it that unless it happens in a car."

"So you do not deny."

"I don't see the point in talking about this."

"You might be surprised to know that I approve of psychotherapy."

Kip thought it over. "That does surprise me, actually."

"Just make sure they don't get rid of it completely. The road rage, I mean. It's probably the coolest thing about you."

When *Unsolved Mysteries* ended Leslie yawned and changed the chan-nel to the news. The student protests in China looked to be heating up again, and attempts to make even the slightest dent in the giant oil spill in Alaska were failing miserably—but it wasn't until CBS showed footage of the first-ever McDonald's in the Soviet Union that Kip started paying attention. Lines were forming daily along Ovchinnikovskaya Embankment, Connie Chung reported, though the grand opening wasn't until the Fourth of July. Russians were gathering there, she explained, to experience free enterprise in action. The way she said it made Kip's skin crawl. He glanced out of the corner of his eye at Leslie—a purely reflexive reaction—to get a sense of his take. Leslie was picking his nose and staring out the window.

"It's hard to imagine a Commie sitting down in his fur hat and eating a big old greasy Quarter Pounder," Kip heard himself say.

"Huh?"

"Russia. Moscow. First-ever McDonald's."

Leslie shrugged.

"You have no opinion about this? None at all?"

"There was a Mickey D's in the food court of the American pavilion at the '64 World's Fair in Copenhagen," Leslie said after the slightest perceptible pause. "Nikita Khrushchev sent KGB agents in plainclothes to bring him twelve boxes of chicken McNuggets. His dipping sauce of choice was honey-mustard."

Something on the far side of the window caught Leslie's attention. Kip stared at the back of his head for what felt like an hour.

"You're full of shit. McNuggets weren't even *invented* in '64."

"Have it your own ignorant way, Chanticleer."

Kip gritted his teeth. "Here's another question for you. I'd appreciate an answer."

"I can't keep you from asking. I'm zip-corded to this bed, basically."

Kip looked around for the remote but couldn't find it. He got to his feet and unplugged the TV.

"Here we go," said Leslie.

"What the fuck crawled up your ass and died there?"

"That's a pretty insensitive way of formulating the question, all things considered."

Kip came right up to where Leslie's head lay on the oversized hospital pillow. "All right, Leslie," he said. "No more questions."

"Norvald—"

"I'm talking now. You shut your mouth and listen."

Leslie shut his mouth. He wasn't yawning anymore, or talking smart, or gazing smugly out the dirty window. He was lying motionless in his hideous beeping plastic bed with his spidery fingers clenched around the railings. Kip took a certain satisfaction in the sight.

"We've been in L.A. for nineteen months—that's more than a year and a half, Leslie—and I've spent most of it changing your diapers. There's always some problem, some crisis, and it's always up to me and Kira to make it okay. First it was money, then a place to live, then Percy— then it was *heroin*, for fuck's sake, which has got to be the dumbest, most predictable shit I can think of. And now—" He shook his head for a slow count of ten, opening and closing his fists. "Now I don't know what the fucking issue is, to tell you the truth. Except that you don't seem to care about anything—not a single damn thing. Not me, not Kira, not your haircut, not music, not anything else you used to care about. Nothing. Zero. Not even yourself."

He paused there, expecting some scathing rebuttal. Leslie watched him in silence.

"No comment? Really? Then I'll tell you my theory. You're a rich kid—a pampered little rich kid, plain and simple, who's never had to beg for pocket change, or shoplift groceries, or hold down a crap job, or watch his parents beat each other up over the phone bill." He sucked in a breath. "You use people, Leslie. You've always looked down on Kira and me, always thought you were God's gift, always made us feel like trash. At first I told myself it was because you really were smarter—then because your record collection was bigger, then because you were trying to protect yourself somehow. But I finally get it. It's none of those things. It's because your parents drive a fucking Volvo."

Kip braced himself against the contoured plastic headboard. He'd managed to stop himself before he started shouting but only just barely.

He'd said things already that he couldn't take back. Leslie was sitting bolt upright, eyes open wide, with a look on his face that could have signified anything from amazement to disgust.

"All right," Kip said. "Go ahead, Z. Put me in my place."

But Leslie just sat there, staring at Kip as though he couldn't quite place him.

"Say something," Kip murmured. "Stand up for yourself."

"Nate and Rachel are coming."

Kip hesitated. "Nate and Rachel?"

"I'm talking about my legal guardians. The Voglers."

"They're actually coming out here?"

"It's not all that hard, Kip. They got on a plane."

"Sure. I'm just—" He felt his face reddening. "I'm impressed, I guess. Good parents."

"Good parents," Leslie repeated. He spoke the words deliberately, gently, almost like an incantation. "That doesn't quite cut it."

"You lost me."

"The Voglers are exalted human beings."

"Right," Kip said, if only to say something. "They always seemed like nice people."

"I love them."

"Right," Kip said again. Leslie lay swaddled in his blankets now, eyes half-open, taking deep and steady breaths. He seemed to be imagining the Voglers coming down from Heaven on a moonbeam.

"So what's their agenda?" Kip said finally.

"They have no agenda."

"You know what I mean. Are they still trying to lure you back to the land of the walking dead?"

"*This* is the land of the walking dead," Leslie answered.

"Come on, Z. You've got plenty of reasons for staying."

"Name one."

"Well—those classes you're taking, for starters. And your apartment. You like your apartment."

"Don't patronize me, Norvald. Don't do it."

"You can't go back," Kip blurted out. "We left scorched earth behind us."

"That's ridiculous."

"I'm quoting you, Leslie. That's a direct fucking quote."

Leslie shook his head. "Sounds like vintage Chanticleer to me. *Hair of the Serpent*, issue seven, volume five."

Kip was starting to feel lightheaded. "So what's the plan, Leslie? Move back in with the parents? Get yourself some braces and enroll at Venice High?"

Leslie's look darkened. "You think I need braces?"

"Don't do this, Leslie. Don't do this to me."

"They'll be here any minute."

"I'm sorry about what I said before. All that rich-kid stuff. I was angry about—"

"You and Kira."

Kip stopped short. "What about us?"

"Something tells me you're fucking. Just a feeling I have."

He found himself coughing to hide his confusion. His gut impulse was to deny everything, to make up some story, as though sex with Kira weren't the thing he'd wanted most in all the world.

"I get it," said Leslie. "No comment at this time."

"Hold on. You can't turn this around—"

"Last night," Leslie said. He was looking past Kip now, past the TV set, toward the door that led out into the hallway. "After I got brought here. That's when it must have happened. Am I right?"

Kip stared down at the floor.

"I'll bet Kira likes your road rage. I'll bet it tickles her in all her special places."

"Don't say it like that. It sounds bad when you say it like that."

"Come on, Kip. You're all set now. You got what you wanted."

"Don't do this."

"You wanted it so badly. It was hard for me to watch."

"I'm warning you—"

"Listen to me, Norvald. I say this to you out of friendship. There are things about Kira that you need to know."

Just then, with perfect sitcom timing, the Voglers appeared. They didn't knock, or push the door open, or otherwise call attention to their presence: they simply materialized. They gave no visible acknowledgment of their son on the bed, or of the undeniable oddness of the situation. Their attention was focused entirely on Kip.

"Mr. Norvald," Rachel Vogler said. She might have been making an observation for her husband's benefit—she seemed not to be addressing Kip at all, though her small green eyes drilled into him. He stepped back from the bed.

"Hello, Mrs. Vogler. I wish we were meeting under different circumstances."

"We don't blame you," Nathaniel Vogler said. His voice was musical and dark. Kip couldn't remember ever having heard him speak before.

"I'm glad to hear that, Mr. Vogler. The truth is, I don't—"

"We blame the other one," Rachel Vogler said.

"The other one?"

"That's right."

"I'm not sure I understand."

"Of course you understand." Her body seemed to twitch. "The Carson girl."

"Hey, Rachel," Leslie said softly. "Hey, Nate."

They went to him then—Mrs. Vogler on the right side of the bed, Mr. Vogler on the left—and from then on Kip was only in the way. He lingered a few minutes longer, fascinated by that strange, bloodless family reunion: no physical contact, no terms of endearment. Just a lukewarm bath of certainty and calm.

Something like a vision came to him as he loitered there unnoticed within arm's reach of the bed. He seemed to see the remainder of Leslie's life playing out in time-lapse on the screen of the ceiling TV: the red bedroom in Venice, painted eggshell-white now, its closet full of oxford shirts and chinos. Leslie at thirty, a harmless, solitary eccentric, cooking elaborate meals for his parents to enjoy. An office job in Sarasota or in Tampa. He could see it all so clearly. It was a good enough life—beautiful, even, in its self-effacing way. Solitude and service. A devoted caregiver. It made Kip want to gouge out his own eyes.

"I'll be going," he said. Neither of the Voglers looked up. This was yet another experience he'd never had before with Leslie: the sense of having overstayed his welcome.

"See you, Norvald."

"I'll swing by tomorrow, all right? Sometime after four."

"We'll expect you," said Rachel. But when Kip came back the next day they were gone.

12

Time seemed to accelerate after Kira moved in. Months went by in a blur.
They were drinking too much, and they got high most nights, but it
wasn't just that. The transitions were rushed. The most important weeks
of Kip's life flickered past in a series of jump cuts, fitful and tricky to
follow, like a dream sequence in some pretentious student film.

A few days into May—he could never remember the date, thinking
back, though he had reason to remember—Kira took him to a Celtic
Frost gig at a place called Fender's Ballroom down in Long Beach. She
insisted on paying, in spite of the fact that she wasn't a Frost fan, and
he took care to show his gratitude. She'd been absentminded lately, lost
in her own private narrative, and when Kira went quiet it was because
she was taking stock, evaluating, visualizing avenues not taken. She was
never not a flight risk, but some weeks the odds were higher. He knew
her well enough by then to brace for heavy weather.

But there was nothing distant about Kira that particular afternoon.
She was affectionate and cheerful—almost giddy—and dressed to the
nines in a dog-collar choker, a secondhand tartan skirt from the kind of
prep school she could never have afforded, and eye shadow that looked
airbrushed straight across her eyes, like Daryl Hannah in that movie
about killer sex robots with Harrison Ford. She seemed to think that
they were celebrating something.

It was a matinee show—no alcohol, all ages—so the action was in the parking lot outside. They took Kthulu, which gave every indication of being on its last legs, to Kira's favorite burger joint on the west side—a place called the Apple Pan, where nothing, not even the waiters, had been replaced since roughly 1964—then got to the venue early and wandered the lot, taking in the whole menagerie.

It did not disappoint. A woman dressed as a nurse from some seventies stag film, complete with stethoscope and red crosses taped over her nipples. A man with no eyebrows, in a British barrister's curly white wig, sipping from a beaker of what Kip could only hope was fake blood. A redheaded girl, maybe fourteen years old, eyes huge and dilated, looking frightened and lost. The rock & roll cowboy, in stained buckskin chaps, wearing a homemade muscle shirt that read PROUD OWNER OF A BONER-FIED 9" COCK. Tattoos of the comedy and tragedy masks, the Van Halen symbol, the Pontiac logo, dollar signs, pentagrams, Chinese dragons, the grim reaper, the POW/MIA insignia. Barbed wire and razor wire and concertina wire. Eddie, the Iron Maiden mascot. Daffy Duck. Every imaginable variation on the classic flaming skull, including one that looked—maybe intentionally, maybe not—like an early eighties Danny DeVito. A middle-aged woman who could only have been somebody's mom, in a cardigan and a Tipper Gore updo, drinking wine from a half-gallon bottle and smoking a joint. The inevitable guy with the boa constrictor. The obvious dealers, making long, lazy loops through the crowd. Everyone else looking as if they'd lived their entire lives in anticipation of whatever bullshit nonevent was going to happen next.

"Kira Carson!"

The man walking toward them was clean-cut and suntanned and had no business at a show by Celtic Frost. He should have seemed out of place, incongruous, and therefore at a social disadvantage—but that wasn't how he seemed at all. Apparently he was right where he belonged.

"Kira freaking Carson. You look *bonkers*."

"Harper," she mumbled. "Okay." Suddenly she looked sleep-deprived and frail.

"What are you doing here? I almost wouldn't've recognized—"

"This is Kip," she said, straightening out of her slump. "We're actually here to see the band."

Harper arched one strawberry-blond eyebrow at this piece of news. "Sure thing, Carson. Whatever you say."

"Me and Kip live together these days."

Harper nodded blankly. "As in—"

"As in we split the rent and have sex with each other," Kip cut in. "That sort of thing."

"Want some black beauties, honey?" Harper said, still looking only at Kira. "Friends-and-family discount. In fond memory of."

No one spoke for a moment. Kip could feel his fists clenching. It had been months since the last time. He'd started to miss it.

"There were some kids looking for bennies over there," Kira said, pointing past Harper at a gaggle of underage drunks. "You walked right past them, Harper. Must be losing your touch."

He nodded at her, more amused than ever. "Still got that same number?"

She made a point of not answering, of catching Kip's eye and smiling, but by then Harper had moved on anyway. Los Angeles was full of people like him—men in their twenties, mostly aspiring actors, who glided around on invisible cushions of beauty and health. They had what the city valued most, and they sensed it on a neurochemical level, as a warm and steady buzzing in their tiny lizard brains. Kip and Kira watched him work the crowd.

"That's the best-looking dealer I've ever seen in my life."

"He comes into the Rainbow," Kira murmured. "Not often. Just sometimes."

"Lucky you."

"Do me a favor, Kip. Would you do me one favor? Don't get on my dick about this."

These days, Kira had said. Me and Kip live together *these days*. She might have been talking about having to wear a retainer.

"What do you want from me, Kira? A trophy for fucking?"

She gave no sign of having heard him. She started walking again, making an elaborate show of interest in the bootlegs a group of hard-eyed men were selling out of the back of a Datsun. She found a handful of demos by Mayhem, the band Jackie Slaughter had been raving about the night of Leslie's overdose; she studied them carefully, taking her time about it, for all the world as if she were alone. The men gave her the Mayhem tapes for nothing. She didn't even have to ask. Two stoned teenagers passed them—a boy and a girl with identical mullets, holding hands and smirking at each other. So much energy went into not acting like an asshole whenever he was on the scene with Kira. He was always bracing for the worst: the next shock, the next humiliation, the next life-or-death challenge. He had never been anyone's boyfriend before. Was it like this for everyone? How did they stand it?

The tone had been set for the rest of the show. Each new banger they bumped into was someone Kira knew well, from the Rainbow or the Palace or god knows where else, and the lust in every pair of eyes was unmistakable. None of them seemed to care that Kira wasn't as conventionally pretty as your standard Valley bunny on the Strip—she had that spooky legitimacy, that one-boot-in-the-grave aura, and it hit them like a dose of horny goat weed. Kip spent most of the next hour at the door of the White Room, mentally testing its handle, waiting for one of them to try to touch her.

The show itself was hardly better. Celtic Frost, fabled progenitors of one of metal's most perverse and hopeless strains, now seemed—to the general bewilderment of the capacity crowd—to have rebranded themselves as Switzerland's answer to Faster Pussycat. The legendary Tom Warrior stumbled around the stage in some kind of kimono, barely awake, his hair teased up into a brittle brown meringue. The spectacle struck Kip as symbolic in the most depressing way. Glam had followed him into his post-Sunset life, along with the rest of his problems, like a wad of black bubblegum stuck to his heel.

On South Figueroa, almost exactly halfway home, Kthulu decided to give up the ghost. Kip had never understood much about cars—he could barely drive stick—but he knew a death rattle when he heard one. He was pretty sure the engine block was dragging on the street.

"Pull over," said Kira.

"I think we can make it."

"You want to go out in a blaze of glory, is that it? Or are you just trying to piss me off?"

"We can make it."

The inevitable happened in front of a doughnut shop at the corner of Figueroa and West El Segundo. The customers gawked at them through its greasy plate-glass window, visibly irritated by the noise, holding their half-eaten maple crullers and Boston creams in that dainty two-fingered way that always made Kip think of British matrons. He shut his eyes and counted down from ten and tried to forget where he was: this nightmarish megasuburb with its doughnut shops and full-service gas stations and temples consecrated to Coca-Cola and deep-fat fryers and flavorless pucks of ground beef. It made him feel as dead inside as Kira claimed to be. Maybe Leslie had been right to go back home.

Kira volunteered to go to the pay phone on the corner—as much to get away from him, he suspected, as for any other reason—and he watched her on the line with AAA. Her face was barely recognizable as she spoke into the receiver: the face of a functional, reasoning, rent-paying adult. *Me and Kip live together these days.* He forced himself to look away, back through the window of the shop, where the only person smiling was a chubby kid in pigtails with a cruller in each hand. He was not in the proper frame of mind to watch a bunch of total strangers eating doughnuts. He tilted the rearview to look back down Figueroa.

A woman was strolling up the street, dreamy and unhurried, stopping every now and again to shade her eyes and look toward the Hollywood Hills. He watched her idly at first. She was dressed as if for a period piece set in the fifties: cat's-eye sunglasses, a cream-colored pantsuit, a silk babushka holding back her hair. She looked the way someone in witness protection might look, Kip thought—someone on the run from the mob in a low-budget thriller. But the way she held herself was beautiful.

Kira was still on the phone, reading somebody the riot act, gripping the receiver in her right hand and making karate-chopping motions with her left. He allowed himself to wonder, as he watched her through the windshield, who the poor sap on the other end might be.

The woman in the rearview was close enough now that he could read her expression: the sheepish smile of someone new to California— someone who'd only just realized that they'd escaped, however briefly, from the ruins of their past. Leslie had smiled like that once, and so had Kira; and so, presumably, had Kip himself. Maybe that was why the woman seemed familiar.

She passed Kthulu without seeing him and moved deliberately along the window of the shop, touching it lightly with her fingers, as though the people on the other side were monkeys at the zoo. The girl with the pigtails took an oversized bite of her cruller, glad for the attention, and the woman turned toward her and blew her a kiss. Kip suddenly felt like a child at the movies, left alone at a drive-in, abandoned by his parents in the family sedan. All he saw now was the woman. He felt weighted down, immobilized, transfixed by melancholy. He was struggling for breath. He was seeing her for the first time but she was someone that he knew.

A few steps past the pay phone she paused one last time to gaze up at the Hills, posing for imagined paparazzi—and in that instant, as if a lever had been thrown, the answer came to him.

Kira must have caught sight of his face through the windshield, because the first thing she said when she got back in was, "What the hell is wrong now?"

Kip braced his arms against the dashboard. Apparently he could move and breathe again.

"I swear to god, Kip, if you can't even answer—"

"That woman who passed you a few minutes back. With the scarf and the glasses."

"Who—the Grace Kelly impersonator? What about her?"

"I think that was my mother."

She stared at him. His face had started itching.

"You *think* so?" she said finally.

He nodded.

"That's—" She shifted on the seat. "Jesus. So did you say something to her, or—"

"I understand what you mean now," he murmured.

"About what?"

"About not being able to tell when things are real."

"I'll be honest with you, Kip. You want me to be honest? You're freaking me out."

He turned the key in the ignition out of simple force of habit, his head hot and empty, and the noise brought him back to himself right away. It sounded like a head-on collision played backward. Kira yanked his arm away and killed the engine.

"Yes or no. Was it her?"

He didn't know how to answer. His ears were still ringing. He managed to nod.

"Go after her, then. This car's fucked anyway. I can wait for the tow."

"Don't do that," he said.

"What?"

He looked at her. "Don't tell me what to do."

He'd thought that might set her off again—he'd expected it to—but instead she ran her fingers through his hair. She seemed less angry than mournful. She was probably imagining her own mother, that voiceless, faceless phantom, gliding forlornly up South Figueroa.

"What do we do now?"

Her question seemed to refer to more than his mother or Kthulu or the fight they'd had outside the show. It seemed to refer to everything there was. Her attempt at a smile was heartbreaking to see.

"Nothing," Kip answered. "I'd like to do nothing."

"Okay," she said, taking his hand. "We'll do nothing."

Tentatively, cautiously, he let himself remember where they were. The doughnut shop, the pay phone, the Hollywood Hills. He let it convince him. The hallucination—or delusion, or whatever it had been—was a memory now. He leaned back stiffly in the seat and told her he was sorry.

"I'm sorry too, Kip. Today's been—I don't know what."

"Not what you hoped for."

"I'll tell you something," she said. "I wouldn't mind a doughnut."

"Me too," he said. "I'm all right now. I'm good."

"Of course you are. Let's get out of this death trap before it explodes."

13

A week went by, then a month, then almost half a year. Things with Kira got better. Her new position at the Rainbow kept her busy—busier than her paychecks justified—which turned out to be a godsend. Doubt crept in when she had time to mull things over.

Kip was forever on the alert, forever watchful. It got to the point where he could sense approaching trouble on the surface of his skin. To keep himself sane, he decided to try the work cure himself: he took every job he could find, from photocopied fanzines all the way up to the glossies. He was still extruding product for *Hair of the Serpent* at a steady drip, but now he also wrote for *Metal Maniacs* and *Hit Parader* and *Kerrang!* and *Kentucky Fried Afterbirth* and *Circus* and *The Grimoire of Exalted Deeds*. Work led to exposure, which led to more work: every metal rag in the English-speaking world, to quote Jackie Slaughter, was "desperate for intelligible content." He wrote for *Decibel* and *Gear Gods* and *Metal Meltdown* and *Terrorizer*. He wrote for *Zero Tolerance* and *Noisecreep* and *Madhouse* and *The Devil's Bodkin*. He wrote for a mimeographed quarterly out of Baton Rouge whose editor-in-chief answered only to "Narzdglach" and insisted that everything he published—even the record reviews—be composed in Middle English. Half the time Kip wrote for nothing. He couldn't rewire his brain, it turned out, but he could push it to the point where it stopped fixating on Kira. All he had to do was make himself so tired that he couldn't spell his name.

He spent his rare hours of down time cruising Central Los Angeles in Jackie's Dodge Dart, making lefts and rights at random, in the irrational hope of encountering the ghost again. The plan was to confront her, to make her see reason. His mother had no business sashaying up South Figueroa in cat's-eye sunglasses like the winner of some existential sweepstakes. She was free to spread misery across the rest of the country—the rest of the planet, for all Kip cared—but L.A. was his. The thought of her there, going blithely about her sordid life in the city he'd chosen, indifferent to his presence, never failed to make his throat go tight with rage.

Kip's anger had a sell-by date, however, and by summer he'd long since abandoned his search. The fever dream had broken abruptly, from one day to the next; apparently he didn't need it anymore. He wasn't relaxed, not exactly, not yet, but he was finding his footing. Things with Kira had been uneventful long enough that his anxiety had gone underground, like a grizzly in winter, to wait for the scent of fresh blood on the air.

He went to Jackie's basement print shop five days a week, whether he was working on anything for *H.O.T.S.* or not; if Kira was around when he got home, they went record shopping or had sex or ordered a pizza. The barometer he'd painstakingly developed for her mental weather hadn't risen or fallen in any significant way since early spring; even the sex had taken on a brutal sameness. What turned her on didn't come naturally to him, he'd long since made his peace with that—but he liked to think he'd grown into his role. He'd gotten comfortable in his improbable new life, in other words, which occasionally made him feel like a character in the opening montage of one of Leslie's beloved slasher flicks: the carefree stoner, victim number one, driving a minivan full of co-eds to a cabin on the shore of Hatchet Lake.

It was with something like relief, then, that he opened his apartment door one October evening to find Kira cross-legged on the kitchen floor with her back against the stove, staring down at a postcard—VENICE, FLORIDA: SHARK TOOTH CAPITAL OF THE WORLD—as though she'd just been sent a ransom note. He set down the groceries he was carrying and asked her what was wrong.

"It's Leslie."

The grizzly was back in an instant. He was sitting on the floor himself now, propped against Kira's left shoulder, shaking his head as if to keep awake. Of course it was Leslie. The two of them had opted, in their cozy self-absorption, to imagine that limping back to Florida with his tail between his legs would somehow be the end of Leslie's story. But there had never been more than one possible ending. It was simply a question of when.

"Tell me," he said, reaching for the postcard. Kira brought it to her chest and shook her head. He didn't force the issue.

"Kira."

No answer.

"What was it this time?" he heard himself croak. "Was it junk?"

Her expression was blanker now, harder to read. She took a long moment to answer. "Oh, Kip."

"Just tell me. Is he dead?"

"He's coming back," she said. "He wants to stay with us."

Kip had already opened his mouth to speak, to comfort her, to rise to the occasion. Now he stared at her absurdly. But she didn't seem to see him.

"I need you to explain," he said.

"I know."

"I'm kind of getting competing signals here. They're not matching up. 'Cognitive dissonance,' I think is the term."

She bobbed her head. "I don't want this," she said.

"Okay. That's fine. What don't you want?"

She looked up at him now. "I don't want Leslie here."

He patted her knee reflexively, trying to slow things down, to recover his balance. "Leslie's not the easiest roommate," he murmured. "I hear you."

"I don't want him in Los Angeles at all."

"Right." He took back his hand. "I'm still sort of getting this cognitive—"

"Something happened, Kip." She shook her head. "Between me and Leslie. A month or so after the Whisky."

"Right," he repeated. The room went green, then bluish white, as though a flashbulb had gone off. A sudden jab of color like a pinprick. When his vision cleared he found himself slumped against the fridge with Kira close beside him. Why were they both still sitting on the floor?

"Hold on. I can't seem to—"

"You look bad," she said, leaning forward without touching him. A terrible gentleness had crept into her voice. "You're looking bad, Kip. Do you want to lie down?"

"You're not talking about what I think you're talking about. I'm pretty sure we can both agree that Leslie isn't—" He stopped himself. "That Leslie isn't the kind of person who would ever want to—"

"He came home one night, maybe four in the morning, and knocked on the door of my room. I was happy to see him. We hadn't said more than three words to each other in weeks, Kip—you know how it was. Things had been shit between us ever since the Whisky. It was so goddamn painful. I thought they might get back to normal when he started school, or when he met some new people, or when he got himself clean. But none of that seemed to matter." She took in a breath. "I was desperate by then. You know I was. So when I saw the look on his face—the *interest* there—I just felt so excited. It was going to be like Florida again."

"Slow down for a second."

"We weren't together, Kip. You and me, I mean—not then. Remember that."

"Kira—"

"Leslie came in and sat on the bed and I sat down next to him and pretty soon I realized it wasn't going to be like Florida at all. I was just as surprised then as you are right now. He used to say that he appreciated the ladies, whatever that means, but it amazed me just the same. It really amazed me. I thought I could always tell exactly what any boy wanted." She shook her head again. "You usually aren't so hard to figure out."

Kip pressed his palms against the grooved linoleum. He'd never looked at it so closely before. It buckled slightly where it passed under the stove. Kira couldn't seem to stop talking.

"Not with him, though. I had no idea. He said he'd been with girls before—he even mentioned someone I knew from Ponceville—but it didn't seem that way. Not that it mattered. I'd have done anything to make up for what happened with Percy. I'm not going to lie to you, Kip. I'd have eaten glass just to get him to look at me like a normal human being. I'd have fucked anybody he asked me to. Just to know he wouldn't look at me and see the parking lot behind the Whisky with those assholes standing over him. Standing over him and laughing. And me and Dusty watching from the van."

He flinched at that as though she'd slapped him. "You were there," he said, bringing a hand up to his face. "Right there in the van. Of course you were."

She gave no sign of having heard him. "When it was over we just stayed there on the bed. It didn't seem like anything horrible had just happened. It seemed fine, to be honest. I felt okay about it. Then he said the weirdest thing."

Kip looked up at the ceiling. The ceiling was awful.

"He said, 'You can tell Kip if you want.' Those were his exact words."

Kip pulled himself up and rested his cheek against the imitation-marble countertop. It felt good against his skin. An LP sleeve lay nearby: a pentagram in one corner, an indecipherable band name, a picture of some snowbound northern forest.

"I just had no idea what Leslie meant by that. Whether he wanted me to tell you for some evil reason, some rivalry thing, or if he was saying that you wouldn't mind—that it was beautiful, that it was for the best, that we all loved each other. But I knew that it wasn't for the best. Of course I did. That's what I meant the night we got together, after they took Leslie away. Do you remember? I said I'd been unfair—"

Her voice was an ambient drone to him now, static at the low end of the dial. If it had been anyone but Leslie. He looked down at her mutely, fists pressed to his sides, as uncertain as she must have been about what would happen next. Then his body gave a twitch—a sharp involuntary shudder—and guided him out into the color-corrected California night.

14

On November 14, 1990, two days after Kip turned twenty, his mother was found dead in a Rodeway Motor Inn on the outskirts of San Bernardino. She'd checked into the motel in the company of a man—a man who was long gone by the time her body was discovered—but the coroner's report listed her death simply as "accidental/pending." No search for the "male companion" had as yet been undertaken.

Kip learned all this from Oona, who called him as soon as she was notified, filling him in on the details with a raw-voiced dignity he couldn't help but envy. She asked him if he would see to the arrangements locally and he promised that he would. She didn't ask how he was feeling: she assumed he'd been preparing for precisely this day for the better part of a decade, as she herself had been, and of course she was right. But he was shocked just the same by the absence of emotion—not on her part so much as on his. It made him feel sociopathic. His mother had died facedown on an unmade twin bed, wearing nothing but a recently purchased light gray oxford shirt and a yellow espadrille on her left foot. Violence, Oona informed him, was "not indicated." The coroner had determined that the deceased had spent her final twenty-four hours injecting pharmaceutical-grade methedrine and freebasing cocaine.

"She was coming to see you," Oona told him before she hung up. "That was the idea, at least. That's why she headed out to California."

Kip took his time answering. "That's bullshit."

"I know." He heard her light a Camel, take a deep, emphatic drag, then stub it out again. "I'm not sure why I said that, to be honest."

"It's okay, Oona. I love you."

"You too, Kipper. Take care of yourself."

That phone call, brief and unsentimental though it was, brought a violent end to what Kip had taken to calling his "lost weekend," though the only thing it had in common with John Lennon's notorious six-month bender was that some of it happened in Hollywood. Maybe Kira had been getting shitfaced and having bathroom sex with random strangers; for his part, Kip had spent his days writing lackluster copy and watching TV. He was starting to feel the passage of time on a cellular level—to actually experience its relentless forward motion as a physical sensation. It didn't feel good. The only person he saw with any regularity anymore was Jackie Slaughter, and a microdose of Jackie went a powerful long way.

It ended up being Vanessa Bordeaux, of all people, who drove him to the interment ceremony. They'd been meeting up since October, at Kip's instigation—but only occasionally, and only for coffee. Vanessa was going to Chapman College now, over the hills in Orange County, double-majoring in political science and something called Cold War Exit Studies; she wore loose-fitting tracksuits these days, and orthopedic shoes—not unlike Oona, in fact—and seemed genuinely at home in her new life. Between mini-lectures on the Tiananmen Square massacre or the Solidarność movement in Poland, she sipped her cortado—always a double shot, pulled short, with two-percent milk—and listened to Kip's one-note aria of heartbreak. It was therapeutic for her, apparently, to extend him sympathy.

"How are you feeling?" she asked him that November afternoon, once the bleak little farce of a ceremony was over. They were sitting in a Coffee Bean and Tea Leaf in West Hollywood, just around the corner from the Whisky.

"Good. I feel good," Kip said shakily. "It's weird that you're here."

She gave him a thin smile. "It *is* kind of weird."

"I wasn't sure who else to call, if you want to know the truth. I've already asked Jackie for so much—"

"Kip," she said softly. "You look sort of sick."

"I am. I feel sick. Thank you so much for coming."

"Let's get you some water."

"Water. Sure."

"You could have tried that girl of yours." She waved to a barista. "Lord knows she owes you."

"Which girl?"

"Was there ever more than one?"

Kip stared down into his little mug of lukewarm Swedish roast. It actually felt good to be talking about Kira. For once it was the less depressing option.

"We've seen each other, you know. A few times."

"Oh, I know."

"There's no big drama there, is what I'm trying to say. Not anymore."

"You didn't call her, though," Vanessa said, handing him a tiny paper cup of water.

He shrugged.

"You can't still be pissed off that she fucked your friend."

"*Our* friend."

"And the difference is?"

"You don't understand. Me and Kira and Leslie—" He searched for the right words. "It's just always been crazy. Every day some new crisis. Things got to the point where I needed—I don't know what, exactly. A blank slate, I guess."

"And how has that been working out?"

"It's been a rough day, Vanessa. Maybe now's not the time—"

"You'll have to do something drastic," she said, getting up from the table. "Something ballsy. 'No half-steppin',' to quote Big Daddy Kane."

"I don't know who that is."

"It's hip-hop, Kip. The actual sound of the present. You need to let some air into your coffin."

"Where the hell are you going?"

She kissed him on the forehead. "Buy her a big bag of drugs. She likes drugs, doesn't she? Of course she does. She works at the Rainbow."

Kip stared up at her with something close to awe. "That's the worst advice I've ever gotten in my life."

15

Three months after walking out on Kira—and a few weeks shy of what would have been their one-year anniversary—Kip stepped into the sticky brown gloom of the Kandy Lounge with a folded manila envelope in a pocket of his coat. The Rainbow was no longer friendly territory, not exactly, and he entered with a light and stealthy tread. Sometimes Kira was happy to see him, sometimes she wasn't. It depended on how their last conversation had ended, how sentimental she was feeling, and who else might be sitting at the bar.

He hung back just inside the door, giving his senses time to adjust. The man he still thought of as Fat Lemmy lumbered past with a milk crate of empty simple-syrup bottles, acknowledging his presence with a grunt. Kip and Kira had been seeing more of each other lately, even sleeping together now and then, when the stars somehow miraculously aligned; but he couldn't shake the feeling that he'd come to the wrong bar. These days he felt like a tourist whenever he visited the Strip.

An hour or so later, however, toward the fuzzy end of happy hour, Kip felt like the opposite of a tourist, whatever that was. Kira was in a nostalgic mood, the place was almost empty, and he was a man on a mission. A suicide mission, possibly. The envelope lay brightly on the polished wooden bar.

Eventually she noticed. "What's that you've got there?"

"An envelope," he said, affecting an air of worldly nonchalance.

"That was going to be my first guess."

"An envelope containing certain tickets."

"Christopher Chanticleer Norvald, international man of mystery." But he could tell she was intrigued. "Tickets to a show?"

"Might could be."

"Now you're just talking like a hillbilly." She reached for the envelope and he made no move to stop her. "*I'm* the trailer trash part of this outfit, remember." She held it up to the light like a counterfeit bill. "Who we going to see?"

"Mercyful Fate."

He hadn't miscalculated. Kira had always slipped *Don't Break the Oath* into Kthulu's cassette player on their rides home from Tampa—the Fate were the only band he'd never heard her accuse of "phoning it in." She cocked her head at him now, arching an eyebrow ironically, but he wasn't fooled.

"I hadn't heard anything about the Fate coming to town."

"They aren't coming to town."

"Road trip?" she murmured. "I wouldn't mind that, actually. I've been wanting to get out of L.A. for ages."

"I know."

"Okay. But are you sure Jackie won't be needing—"

"We won't be able to use Jackie's car."

"Maybe I can talk to someone."

"There's no point."

Her eyes clouded. "Why not?"

"Last time I checked, there was an ocean between here and Amsterdam."

The way her face and even her posture changed made all the months of scrimping and hustling worthwhile. It could have gone either way—he'd known that from the start. It could have seemed desperate. Instead he'd amazed her. He willed himself to fix the moment clearly in his mind.

"What are you talking about?" she said at last. She sounded short of breath.

"I'm talking about Europe, Kira. Amsterdam and Copenhagen and Berlin. What you always used to say you wanted." He hesitated. "Not Norway, though. Norway's too expensive."

"I was kidding about Norway. I don't really want to go there."

He smiled at her. "Here's hoping you weren't kidding about Paris."

Tears of astonishment shone in her eyes. She reached across the bar and grabbed him by the hair and kissed him. "Just don't tell me where you got the money from."

"I won't."

"Not from *Horns of the Rattlesnake* or whatever it's called—I know that much."

"Blood and sperm donations, mostly. Heaven knows how many little Kips I've fathered."

"Lucky ladies." She was still trying to get her head around it.

"You okay?"

"I never thought I'd get to fucking *Gainesville*, never mind California. But Amsterdam—Berlin . . ." Her voice trailed away.

"They're open tickets," he told her. "I know you might have some trouble getting the time—"

"When do we leave?"

For once he knew exactly what to say. "Ten days from now."

"Hey, Dennis!" she shouted to Fat Lemmy, who was wiping down the tabletops with bleach. "I'm going to Paris in an airplane."

"And I'm going to Bakersfield in a colostomy bag," Fat Lemmy said without a moment's hesitation.

16

In what Kip tried hard not to interpret as an omen for the rest of their grand tour—which had cost him every cent he had, and as much again borrowed from Jackie—he and Kira arrived at the Zondaar Bar in Amsterdam's red-light district on their first night in Europe to find a dark and shuttered club. According to a handwritten note in the window, Mercyful Fate's frontman, King Diamond, was regrettably down with the *griep*.

"No way," Kip muttered. "No way this is happening."

"*C'est la vie*," said Kira, curiously unfazed.

He squinted at her. "*C'est la vie?*"

"I'm practicing my French."

They drifted more or less aimlessly through the district with their coats pulled up against the sleet, dutifully stopping to admire each canal they went over, committing to the role of awestruck tourists. It didn't take much effort. They'd never been out of the country before, never experienced jet lag—never even seen snow, except on the far side of some salt flats in Nevada. When the sleet turned to actual flakes Kip caught sight of Kira a few steps behind him, revolving in the dusk like a bedraggled wind-up toy, biting her lip to keep from looking too ridiculously happy. She didn't seem to mind that they weren't seeing her all-time favorite band. She didn't mind anything. The rest of the world, including Kip, might never have existed.

He looked on in silence, a casual observer, aware that the moment was important without knowing why. It was the strangest sensation— almost as if he were already past what he was seeing, looking back on it from years into the future. Something significant was happening, any fool could see that. But it was happening only to Kira.

"I always thought that I would *hate* the cold," she said. "Remember that?"

"I remember."

"It turns out that I don't, Kip. Not at all."

They went into the first bar they came across where the women had clothes on and found themselves in the company of twelve or thirteen disappointed metalheads, most of them already shitfaced. A tiny redheaded man in a Mötörhead jacket was expounding on the state of the thrash scene in his homeland of Denmark, and everyone else was listening attentively, most likely because he was buying. The bartender had a second pair of eyes tattooed above the ones that he'd been born with. He seemed hospitable enough.

"Drinks for you," declared the bartender.

"I'll take a Corona in a bottle," Kip told him.

"No Corona fuck you," said the bartender in the same friendly tone.

"Heineken," said Kira. "Yes? Two Heinekens, please."

They downed their beers in record time, then ordered shots, then had the same again. Kira kept getting giddier. The red-haired man was holding forth, in English, on a topic that Kip couldn't quite puzzle out—something about a religious sect composed entirely of children that was multiplying in secret, hidden away in the forest, waiting on some cryptic sign to take over the world. Eventually it emerged that he was talking about a band—a group of bands, in fact, who lived in the middle of nowhere and painted their faces the way King Diamond did. One of these groups, it turned out, was none other than Mayhem. The redhead's voice had gone shrill. He seemed to be upset.

"In closing, their music is sounding like shit—the brain in their heads is not doing its work. Even *Diamond* is saying to stop with the paint. The monstrous paint is only for the King."

"You're from Denmark?" Kira surprised Kip by asking. "That's where the Fate is from, right?"

The redhead acknowledged proudly that he was, in fact, from that noble peninsula between Germany and Sweden that had nurtured the talents of both Mercyful Fate, the greatest metal band on earth, and its mutton-chopped and pompadoured lead singer.

"You *look* like him, too!" said a plump German girl who was sitting in the lap of a gargantuan skinhead. She seemed to mean it as a compliment, and the redhead took it as such. He ordered yet another round, which was gratefully accepted by everyone but the skinhead, who sat glaring at the little Dane with what appeared to be a look of injured pride. When the girl in his lap drank to the health of both King Diamond and their generous host, he gave an evil-sounding grunt and poured his pint onto the floor.

"I propose a toast to all our brothers and sisters who drove ten hours through a snowstorm to get to this show, and now have to sit around in crap bars like this one, drinking lukewarm Dutch horse piss," the skinhead announced. His English, Kip noted, was shockingly good. "All because a bunch of Danish cunts couldn't be bothered to leave their bullshit country."

The redhead set his beer down with great care, as if he were balancing it on the head of a pin. "The Vikings came from Denmark," he said, giving the German girl a wink. "The original *berserkers*. But today we are a happy country—the most happy in the world. Why don't you come over here and let me show you why?"

The skinhead rose to his full height now. His girlfriend slid off his lap and onto the stool he'd occupied without ever touching the floor, like a circus trick. Kip pictured them rehearsing it at home.

"Outside," said the bartender.

The two men ignored him. The little Dane, who truly resembled a twelve-year-old Viking, climbed onto the bar and arched his back, arms out like a Mexican cliff-diver. Everyone but the skinhead got out of the way.

"Stop this, somebody," the girl said comfortably, but it was obvious that she wanted nothing stopped. Kip touched Kira on the elbow and they headed for the exit. The Dane was about to launch himself at the German, who held his own arms outstretched as if to catch him, when the bartender cut his legs out from under him with what looked to be some sort of hockey stick. A collective whoop of appreciation went up as Kira reached the door and yanked it open. The sound of breaking glass and chanting chased them out into the street.

Snow was falling densely now—in cotton-candy clusters, like some high school Christmas pageant—and Kira was in the thick of it, spotlit by a flickering streetlamp, impossibly lovely, turning in circles with her black mouth hanging open. Lost to all the world again, but most of all to him.

"I feel *different*," she said when she finally stopped spinning, gripping the lamppost with both hands to steady herself. "Do you?"

"Mostly what I feel is wasted."

"Let's never go back, Kip. You want that too, don't you? Let's *never* go back."

He'd booked a cheap room around the corner from the venue, for practical reasons, but he had no sense anymore of where the venue was. Kira was delighted to take over. There was a knife-edge to her happiness now, a manic single-mindedness. The dead-eyed streetwalkers and panhandlers around them brought her nothing but amusement. The farther she traveled from her father's house, apparently, the less the world oppressed her. Kip was trailing in her wake again—he should have felt the same, all things considered. What he felt instead was fear.

From that point the night lost definition. In no way could he account for the fact that he'd gotten so drunk. In time the hotel simply rose up before them. Their room was the size of a crushed can of beer but the bed was enormous. Kira was kneeling on the mattress now, her face so close to his that she looked like a stranger, saying something in a savage voice that made no sense at all. Her mood had tipped sideways. He pressed his eyes shut and the scene changed again. They were kissing each other in a foreign country. He could touch the ceiling easily. She was standing above him, wearing an inside-out Mercyful Fate shirt, fists raised and eyes shining like someone in the front row at a show. He could see what she wanted. She drew back and slapped him so hard that he stumbled. He reached for the wall and she hit him again.

"Kira—"

"Make it real." She hit him again with the heel of her palm. "Make it real, god damn you. You're not even trying."

He didn't want to go to the White Room, not even for her. Tears ran into his mouth.

"Kira, please."

She was the one who was crying. He touched her face and felt the grief behind it. She spat at him and knocked his hand away. He gripped her shoulder and pushed her, with the last of his strength, so that she fell out of the bed onto the floor. She cursed him for a coward. She was crying for his weakness and for all the times he'd failed her. And she was right to cry. He understood that now. He couldn't make things real for her. He could only make things dead.

17

Copenhagen was worse.

They spent one dismal night there, two shell-shocked Americans, meandering through the old town in search of a bar or a restaurant or even a face that they could make some basic sense of. The entire city struck Kip as a monument to his lack of education. He knew nothing about Denmark and neither did Kira. They were both pretending not to remember how the night before had ended. Something irreversible had happened and he didn't understand it. He felt numb with foreboding. He didn't understand it but he knew that it was real.

They had to do something. A dreadlocked old man in a harborside tavern told them about a neighborhood founded by anarchists, a district of the city where the police had no authority and people lived rent-free and took drugs and fucked in broad daylight, but they couldn't seem to get there. They got drunk instead. Sunset found them on the Gothersgade, Kira stumbling and catching herself over and over, Kip shouting at her retreating back that she was going to leave him. They checked out early that same morning and caught the first train to Berlin.

The sky above the Baltic Sea was a garish blue, clashing with the mud-green water, but by the time they reached Berlin the clouds had lowered like a hood. Kira lay asleep with her head in Kip's lap, as though nothing had changed between them, and she didn't seem to hear him when he smoothed the hair back from her face and told her they'd arrived. Berlin-Spandau Station was the end of the line, and no one disturbed them as he sat very still, extending the moment as long as he could, cradling her head between his knees and staring blankly up the aisle. There was no violence in her now that he could feel—no panic, no despair. The train smelled of disinfectant and fried onions but Kip didn't mind. He'd have given ten years of his life to stay right where he was.

They spent that first afternoon walking the Wall—in part because Kip's guidebook recommended it, but mostly because it was free. He'd burned through half his traveler's checks already, which baffled him, because so far they'd done almost nothing but drink. He took the initiative that day, eager to experience something like the weight of history—something bigger than the two of them—and Kira went along without a murmur. The collapse of the Soviet bloc was so recent that east and west Berlin still felt like different planets. The city was a film set, artificial and suspect, to Kip just as much as to Kira. They had made a resolution to drink coffee instead of beer that day, which turned out to make next to no difference. It was warmer than in Copenhagen but somehow it felt colder. All told they spent eleven hours out of doors, working their way across Berlin from north to south, without once catching sight of the sun. Kip would never have thought a city so immense could seem so desolate.

He woke late the next morning—though for once there'd been no hangover to sleep off—and sat up in bed to find a scribbled note from Kira, telling him she'd gone to the shabby little anarchist café on the corner. He felt no urge to go and find her. He opened the bathroom window to let in some air, squinted down into the soot-encrusted shaftway for a while, then crawled back under the sheets and shut his eyes. He opened them an hour later to the sound of Kira whistling AC/DC in the shower. He lay quietly and listened. Something must have made her happy while he'd been in bed asleep.

The source of Kira's excitement was a woman she'd just met at the café: a Viennese girl with a mohawk who went either by Justice or Sophie, depending on factors unknown. But all that really mattered was that Justice/Sophie had invited them to a party that night, in an honest-to-god squat—a former carburetor factory in Kreuzberg, less than fifteen blocks away. She'd written the address down in ballpoint pen on Kira's inner wrist.

The factory turned out to be smaller and quainter than Kip had imagined: a three-story building a century old, with high gothic windows and intricate brickwork. They arrived at ten sharp, desperate to get someone or something between them, and found no sign whatsoever of a party. The main stairwell was lit by bare pink bulbs, like in the red-light district back in Amsterdam, and plastered from floor to ceiling with photocopied flyers for exotic-sounding bands. It looked as though the place might be some sort of music venue. Kip tried to find someone to ask, but the handful of people they encountered floated past them like chain-smoking ghosts.

They never did track down Justice/Sophie, but they forgot all about her soon enough. On their way back downstairs Kira stopped without warning and let out a laugh. She was looking at a flyer.

"No fucking way, Norvald."

"What is it?"

She stepped away so he could see it for himself.

"That can't be true. When?"

She shook her head. "The day after tomorrow."

He'd been right about the building. The club was in the basement. Its name, if it had one, was nowhere on the flyer—just the address, the date, the cover charge, and the logos of the bands.

> **TRAUER (GER)**
> **DRAUGR (NOR)**
> **CANNIBAL CORPSE (US)**

Kip spoke first. "Obviously we have to go to this."

"Isn't that the day we leave for Paris?"

"I can change the tickets."

"Remember that show in Sarasota, at the skating rink? Remember that weird little roadie? Remember sitting right up on the stage?"

"Of course I remember."

"There's a reason this is happening, Kip."

"I was thinking that too."

She frowned at the flyer. "Draugr," she said.

"Never heard of them."

"Don't lie to me. You write about metal for money. You've heard of every bullshit band on earth."

"Not this bullshit band."

She gave a happy sigh and passed her arm through his. "Then I reckon we'll *both* learn something on this trip."

The club was called Saferoom, it turned out, and it had its own entrance at the back of the factory: a pair of fire doors leading down into a vaulted brickwork cellar. The doors were flanked by two enormous bouncers, one of whom appeared to be wearing an actual spiked helmet from World War I, but no one asked them for money. The crowd inside had nothing in common with the halfhearted stoner anarchists they'd seen in the building a few days before—and they didn't look like Cannibal Corpse fans, either. They were keyed up and twitchy and dressed to the gills. They wore tight black biker jackets and bullet belts and bondage boots with seven-inch platform heels. Some of them were wearing what looked to be cassocks. They stared at Kip and Kira openly, aggressively, as if it were obvious they'd come to the wrong gig. He caught snatches of languages other than German, even something that sounded like Latin, but not a single word of English. It put him on edge. He hadn't felt so examined—so judged and dissected—since the Death show at the youth center a hundred years before.

Kira took his hand at one point, but not because she needed reassurance. She was weak with excitement. She was fantasizing about starting over, about unmaking herself again, more completely this time—he was sure of it now. He could feel it in the way she gripped his palm.

"Can you feel it, Kip?"

"I'm not sure what you mean."

"This place—I can't explain it. It's real." She bobbed her head. "You've got to *feel* that."

"We're going to get our asses kicked. That's most of what I'm feeling."

"You're right," she said happily, pulling him closer. "*Anything* could happen here."

Not even the color-by-numbers metal of the first act on the bill was enough to take the edge off Kira's high. Trauer turned out to be four foppish glammers in what looked to be Elizabethan powdered wigs, whose entire performance consisted of a twelve-part mini-opera about being invited to a really awesome party. With the exception of a handful of whatever the German equivalent of Hell's Angels was—who were obviously friends or roadies—they were barely tolerated by the crowd. Kira led Kip straight to the geometric center of the room, its acoustical sweet spot, and stood pressed up against him for the entire set. By the time it became clear that the party the bewigged Germans were screaming about was actually nuclear war, it had begun to seem conceivable to Kip that everything was going to be all right. Someone passed him a joint. Kira brought her mouth to his ear and whispered that the singer reminded her of Ray, her hillbilly cousin, who was now assistant floor manager at a Home Depot in Gainesville. Kip dragged on the joint contentedly and told her he agreed. He felt sleepy and nostalgic. He hadn't thought of Harley Boy in ages.

Afterward they wandered lazily through the crowd—which was thickening around them by the minute—and ended up at a row of merch tables underneath the stairs. Kira didn't want to talk. She was less giddy now, more abstracted. The merchandise was professionally arrayed along the wall: neat stacks of Trauer shirts, black and long-sleeved and heavy, with mountains of Cannibal Corpse CDs and EUROPEAN BLOODBATH '91 shirts and posters beside them, as gory and cartoonish as ever. Copies of the new LP looked to be selling briskly. He picked one up to show Kira, curious to hear what she thought of the cover. But Kira had already moved on.

She was down at the last table, shoulders hunched in concentration, leafing through some sort of xeroxed pamphlet. Only now did he notice that there was no merchandise for the Norwegian act—no CDs, no vinyl, not even a demo. Just a tidy little pile of stapled pages. It made him uneasy for reasons he couldn't explain. A small sheaf of paper. No one else around. He came up behind Kira and saw that the page she was reading was covered in Celtic or Norse script of some kind, accompanied by a drawing, clumsy and hard to decipher, of a girl in peasant clothing being eaten by a wolf.

"Jesus," Kip said. A feeling like remorse washed over him. The girl lay spread-eagled in a snowdrift in what looked to be a forest, her skirt torn up the middle. The crudeness of the drawing made it all the more obscene. The wolf stood hunched over the girl the way Kira herself stood over the table, dripping black blood from its jaws onto her belly.

"I agree," said Kira. But she meant something different. On the back of the pamphlet a few sentences in English had been written out by hand:

THERE IS NO GROUP NAMED DRAUGR. THERE IS COLD AND WIND AND THERE IS NO MORE LIGHT. THE WOLF PRESIDES ABOVE THE CHILD. THE CHILD SUFFERS AND THE WOLF SUFFERS. THE SUFFERING THEY SHARE BECOMES A CEREMONY. THE SUFFERING THEY SHARE BECOMES A WEDDING. THE SUFFERING THEY SHARE BECOMES A PASSAGE. INTO WINTER. INTO DARKNESS. INTO TRUTH.

FEAR IS NAMELESS. NIGHT IS NAMELESS. DEATH IS NAMELESS. WORSHIP HIM.

"I'm beginning to understand why they don't sell any T-shirts," Kip murmured.

"This is so bizarre," said Kira. "Like a religion or something. A secret society."

"Sounds like your standard *Lord of the Rings* crap to me."

"You used to love those books. You told me so."

"I read them as novels, Kira, not nonfiction. You don't see me running around in chainmail and a fucking battle-axe."

She took in a deep breath and held it. "Maybe that's the problem," she said.

"The problem with me?"

"With everybody."

"You're high."

"We're always trying to make life feel *real*—to make it louder and brighter, more crazy, more like how we think reality is supposed to be—"

"You're talking about yourself now. Only yourself."

"—but maybe the answer is to pick some random fairy tale, some stupid fantasy, and take it as seriously as you possibly can. Go down so deep that everything just flips. Reality turns flat and gray. The fantasy gets bright."

He nodded for what felt like a minute or more. "I don't like this."

"Oh, Kip," she told him gently. "You don't have to." The resignation in her voice scared him worse than any drawing ever could.

"What is it?" he hissed. "What is it now, Kira? Am I disappointing you again?"

The lights dropped before she could answer. She took his arm, but only to step past him. Then the room exploded into sound.

The chord that rang out was familiar enough—an overdriven minor triad—but what stood his hair on end was how it felt. Distorted guitar had always had a certain temperature to him: it had always, no matter how vicious the music, been a sound he understood in terms of heat. Embedded in that warmth—hidden inside it—lived a cryptic form of life-affirming power. Deicide and Death and Morbid Angel played their riffs to raise the dead, not to inter them. That was the nature of the exchange, the secret truth of the transaction, however bleak the songs might sound to virgin ears. Rage and violence and pain instead of nothingness.

This chord was cold. It was thin as a wire, serrated and glasslike, with no low end at all that he could hear. It hit him like a sandstorm in some freezing northern desert. Claustrophobia overtook him in the darkness. A hundred mouths were shrieking in the impossible coldness of that single ringing chord. But when it ended he heard nothing but the seething of the amps.

He could never say, in the years afterward, how long that spell of glacial silence lasted. When it was broken, it was broken by voices—but not by singing, or by speaking, or by any sound of human provenance at all. The voices sprang up at a distance, at the limits of hearing, and found their way slowly together. A call heard through the forest, across wind-blasted steppes, over pack ice in winter. Kip had never heard it before, not that he could remember, but he recognized that plaintive chorus instantly. It was the howling of a pack of wolves converging on a kill.

As the lights came up he made out human outlines. He felt what he'd felt at his very first show—that what he was seeing and hearing should have been preposterous. Why wasn't it preposterous? He saw their faces now and what they'd done to them. He'd expected something theatrical, kabuki-like; these men looked as though they'd smeared their skin with animal fat and ashes. It was impossible to pinpoint their eyes through the paint, much less where they were looking, but he felt their eyes on him. On him and on Kira.

The freezing chord rang out again and the bank of lights kept rising. In place of leather and chains and bullet belts the men on stage were dressed in simple black. Against his will their faces held him spellbound. He saw what Kira was seeing now, he realized, and he felt what she was feeling. The same defenselessness, the same disgust. The same attraction. He understood her better in that instant than he ever had before. He closed his eyes and became her. It felt good to escape from his body. It felt somehow sexual. By the time the drumming started he'd forgotten where he was.

⚡

"What was *that*?" someone stammered, which was how he realized the set was over. The voice of a man—an American, he thought, though he no longer had much faith in his own judgment. He'd been listening with his eyes shut, clutching Kira's hand in his, following the blond child in the peasant dress as she stumbled through the woods. The snow up to her ankles, to her kneecaps, to her hips. The black wolf slavering behind her. He took in a breath to tell Kira what he'd seen but she was already in motion, working her way with quiet purpose through the crowd. There was no need to chase after her. He knew where she was going.

He found her under the stairs, at the little merch table, and this time she was talking to a man. There was always a man. This one was gaunt and stoop-shouldered with long straight black hair. His face was unremarkable, forgettable, but Kip already knew he'd remember it the rest of his life. The man had been saying something to Kira: something solemn and momentous. Something private. He shut his mouth as soon as Kip came into earshot.

"Who's this?" Kip said, louder than he'd intended. He was practically shouting. He slung an arm around Kira's shoulder and flashed the man his most all-American grin. "Who are you, friend? Are you a wolf? Are you a vampire? Do you suck the blood of helpless little girls?"

"Shut up, Kip," said Kira.

"You may find these interesting," the man said to her, as though Kip had never been born. "I'm thinking you will." He sounded as if he'd learned his English from old Boris Karloff movies. He passed her a book of some kind and she took it, frowning very slightly. Kip looked back over his shoulder at the bright and empty stage. He felt desperately homesick. The man said something else to Kira, a few murmured syllables, then gave a kind of curtsy and moved off into the crowd.

"Life of the party," Kip said cheerfully. "A real buttercup."

"They'll be on soon," Kira said, leading him away from the table. "The Corpse, I mean. Let's try to get up front."

"What was that little book he gave you? A guide to home embalming?"

She didn't answer.

"Kira."

She made an exaggerated show of stopping and turning to face him.

Her attempt to conceal her excitement made her seem about fifteen. Her arms were crossed and her lips were pressed together so tightly that they all but disappeared. She stared at him impassively. A low-end roar was building. It was happening at last.

"I've had enough, Kira. I'm done. I'm going home."

That wrung a laugh from her. "You're joking."

"I'm going."

"What about the Corpse?"

"Fuck the Corpse."

She looked genuinely confused. "But they're about to—"

"What was he whispering to you about?"

"Kip—"

"Did he want to eat your brains, Kira? Is that what he asked you? And did you say 'yes please'?"

"I can't deal with this anymore." She shook her head. "Everywhere we go. It's just sad."

"Can't deal with what? Can't deal with what?"

"How much of that joint did you smoke, for Christ's sake? You sound like a skipping CD."

"That doesn't matter," he heard himself answer. "My thoughts are clear as crystal. My eyes are fucking open. I can see into the future."

She shook her head a second time and he lunged at her and caught her by the shirt. She looked straight through him now, squinting a little, as though he were a mist that was about to burn away.

"Tell me you're leaving me, Kira. Just say the words. That's all you have to do."

He was forcing something, choking the life out of something, murdering something that might otherwise have taken weeks or months to die. It was finally over. He'd done it out of desperation, out of insecurity, out of weakness. But for the first time in a year his hands were free.

The roar seemed to falter. The houselights were dimming. What she said next was overridden by the buzzing in his brain.

"What was that?"

"All right, Kip," she said. "All right. I'm going to leave you."

He took a step backward then and stood before her with his arms half raised, awkward and unsteady, like a cowboy who's been beaten to the draw. She looked calm again, not disgusted anymore—but also as if she expected him to kill her. He gave her what he hoped was a reassuring smile and she nodded and took him gently by the wrist. Her mouth was forming words again.

"I can't hear you," he shouted.

"Come on, Norvald. They've already cut the lights."

She headed for the stage and pulled him after. They were having an adventure. He could admire her again objectively, as if from a distance, as if decades had gone by. Kira Beth Carson. He remembered her at the Death show on the last day of his childhood: chipped green nails, long-sleeved Iron Maiden tour shirt, hair the dull metallic red that cheap black dye turns in the Florida sun. Acid-wash jeans with a hole in one knee. A white leather choker. Kira in the mosh pit, standing absolutely still. Zit-faced bangers all around her being raptured up to heaven.

A light somewhere had started strobing. Kira said something that sounded like "Venice." He closed his eyes and let her guide him. He knew what was coming. He didn't regret it. The crowd was already shrieking, triggered purely by instinct, and he raised his arms and threw the devil horns with all the rest. Kira was to the left of him, craning her small body upward, angling for a better line of sight. The crush was the law now. The tide swept them forward, foreseeable as always, relentless as always. He lost sight of Kira and found her again. The tide rose between them. He watched her receding. He was clawing his way toward her when the realization hit him. She was nowhere he could follow. She was out of range already. She was gone.

1

One year later Kip was applying the first of three coats of wax to his Honda Accord, which he'd only just bought, when a pair of vaguely midwestern-looking men in suits struck up a conversation with him about his vehicle.

Both of the men used that word—*vehicle*—which on any other day might have given Kip pause; but this was a sunny Christmas Eve, unseasonably warm even for Los Angeles, and he was crushing on his car too hard to pay them much attention. He decided they were Mormons. They watched him working for a while.

The older of the two, who reminded Kip of the movie star Matthew Modine, commented that you didn't see too many vehicles of that particular shade of eggplant on the road these days. It seemed to be intended as a compliment.

"Eggplant?" said Kip, shaking his head. "This isn't eggplant."

"No? What is it?"

"Aubergine."

"I stand corrected." The man smiled at him. "Means the same thing, though, unless I'm much mistaken."

"I'm pretty sure that eggplant's not a color."

The younger man agreed with Kip. "Anyhow, I guess I'd have to say—if anybody asked me—that what I'm looking at here is more of a maroon."

"Beautiful shade, whatever the name," the older man said. He glanced up the street. "You seem to know a thing or two about cars."

"I don't even know how to put on this wax."

"My mistake."

"You guys live in the neighborhood?"

"Don't I wish. I'm from Bakersfield. Just in town for the day."

"I'm from back east," the younger man said. "Baltimore."

They seemed to expect Kip to say something further. He got to his feet.

"Can I do something for you gentlemen?"

"Are you Christopher Norvald, the journalist?"

It was the older man who'd spoken. He didn't look as much like Matthew Modine as Kip had first thought. At close quarters he looked more like William H. Macy. Kip set his rag down on the Honda's hood.

"I don't know if I'd say 'journalist.' I write record reviews."

"Extremely pleased to meet you, sir."

"What's this about?"

"You're not in any sort of trouble, Mr. Norvald. None at all. Might we ask for a few minutes of your time?"

"Telling me I'm not in trouble makes me think that I'm in trouble."

"Not at all."

"Would you mind stating your business?"

"We'd be happy to," said the older man before his associate could answer. "I'm Agent Robert Calkins, of the Federal Bureau of Investigation. I'm here today as a liaison."

"A liaison," Kip repeated.

"Yes, sir. This is Special Agent Mothersbaugh."

"Special agent of what?" Kip asked, hearing his voice start to rise.

"Special Agent Patrick Mothersbaugh," the younger man said, taking what looked like some kind of leather passport holder out of the inside pocket of his blazer. "First off, I'd like to apologize for the imposition."

"You haven't imposed on me yet." By now Kip was contending with an overpowering urge to take off running down the middle of the street. "Is that some sort of badge?"

"My identification," said Agent Mothersbaugh, extending it respectfully. "Would you like to see Detective Calkins's, as well?"

Kip didn't answer, not right away, because he was staring down at the document in his hands in disbelief. Below an unflattering photograph of Mothersbaugh were printed his name, the words DISTRICT OF COLUMBIA *FULL*, and a column of numbers and letters that barely registered. Below that, accompanied by a crimp-edged gold seal, the words INTERNATL POLICE/INTERPOL were printed in blue sans-serif lettering. Kip closed the little wallet, which looked brand-new, and handed it back.

"I knew it. You guys always tell someone they're not in trouble when they're in major fucking trouble. I don't even—"

"Could we get out of this sun, Mr. Norvald?" Calkins said. "Unless you'd prefer not to speak in front of your dependents?"

"Dependents?" Kip mumbled. "No dependents. It's just me."

He started walking up the steps to his apartment and the cops, or whatever the hell they were, fell in noiselessly behind him. He felt as if he'd already been arrested.

"Nice place," said Detective Calkins, once they'd gotten themselves situated in Kip's decrepit living room. His tone made it clear that he'd said those same words virtually every day of his professional life. Mothersbaugh sat ramrod straight on the boxy little sofa, fingers drumming lightly on his well-pressed khaki slacks. He'd seemed diffident before, even mildly depressed, but his spirits were improving. They were getting to the part that he enjoyed.

"How long have you resided here, Mr. Norvald?"

"Is this the bit where you ask me questions you already know the answers to, to see if I screw up?"

"Mr. Norvald—"

"I told you five minutes ago to state your business. I don't have to say another fucking word."

To his considerable surprise they looked uneasy. Calkins apologized again for the imposition, glancing at Mothersbaugh, who cleared his throat self-consciously. Kip was starting to think they were new to the job.

"You're absolutely right, Mr. Norvald. It's of no importance how long you've resided here."

"All right, then."

"But you're being overly modest, I think, when you describe yourself as a writer of record reviews. I just read your profile of Alice in Chains in *SPIN*—I especially enjoyed the part where you're crossing Oklahoma on that tour bus. You boys must have had quite a time."

So there it was. Kip almost felt relieved. He'd done more than a few bumps of cocaine with certain individuals on that bus, and had actually scored them a dime bag in Oklahoma City when the opportunity had presented itself by chance. Possession of cocaine was not a felony, as far as he knew—but possession with intent to distribute almost certainly was. He tried and failed to remember, if he'd ever actually known, how many grams constituted intent to distribute. He cursed himself, not for the first time, for a professional kisser of leather-clad asses.

Mothersbaugh was still talking. "I liked the part where Layne Staley shared his thoughts on the importance of early Christian mysticism in his songwriting. The Dead Sea scrolls. The Gnostic Gospels."

"Layne's the spiritual type," Kip told him.

"I went out and bought the record, actually. The new one."

"My condolences."

Mothersbaugh smiled. "I'm more of an old-schooler, myself. Venom. Obituary. Cannibal Corpse."

The folding chair seemed to wobble. Kip was beginning to suspect that the men on his sofa were part of an elaborate hoax perpetrated by a couple of guys he knew at the L.A. offices of *Revolver* magazine. The more he thought about it, the more sense it made. Andy and Carlos were known for their pranks.

"Obituary," he said. "The Tandy brothers. Florida's best and brightest."

"So brutal," Mothersbaugh said primly. "So *uncompromising*."

"No argument there."

"You're from Florida yourself, aren't you?" said Calkins.

Kip attempted to read his expression. "That's right."

"Is that where you met Kira Beth Carson?"

Immediately his stomach started clenching. He gripped the seat of his chair to keep from falling over.

"Mr. Norvald?"

"I don't—" he said, then caught himself.

"You don't what, Mr. Norvald?"

"I don't think I can help you."

Calkins sat heavily forward. "Clean slate, Mr. Norvald. Full disclosure. Agent Mothersbaugh and myself are here to ask for any information you might have regarding Miss Carson, with whom we understand you had—a friendship?"

Kip bowed his head.

"A *friendship* from the fall of 1987 to the winter of 1991, at which time you traveled in her company to Holland, Denmark, and Germany. Miss Carson is currently a person of interest, both to Interpol and to the authorities in the Scandinavian nation of Norway. As I've already stated—"

"Norway," Kip murmured.

"That's correct, sir." He paused. "We realize this may be a lot to take in."

"I want to know what she's done."

Mothersbaugh and Calkins squinted at him, then at each other, as though he'd asked them something difficult to answer.

"First of all," said Mothersbaugh, "she's disappeared."

"That's not a crime."

"No, it isn't."

"And it can't be a missing persons case, anyway. She's twenty—" Kip shook his head to stop the ringing in his ears. "It's the end of December. That means she just turned twenty-three."

"There's no age limit in missing persons cases, Mr. Norvald."

"Someone has to be searching for her, though, don't they? Who is it?" He looked from one of their placid chalk-white faces to the other. "Her father?"

"The father is deceased," said Calkins. "Are you not in contact with the Carson family?"

"You know that I'm not."

Calkins shrugged.

"What has she done?"

It was Mothersbaugh's turn now. He took a deep breath.

"Our first record of Miss Carson's movements—after you parted ways with her on January the eleventh—is from the seventeenth of that same month. On that date she crossed the border into Denmark, using her own passport, then the borders of both Sweden and Norway in the same twenty-four-hour period. She was traveling as a passenger in a gray Volkswagen Vanagon, license EV11868, registered to one Per Ivar Lund, twenty-seven years old, of Kristiansand, Norway."

Kip kept his face blank.

"Are you now, or have you ever been, in contact with Per Ivar Lund?"

"I can't do this right now."

"You'll be doing us a service, Mr. Norvald. You'll be doing Miss Carson a service."

"Fuck you."

"I'll repeat the question, if you don't mind. Have you ever been in contact with Per Ivar Lund?"

Mothersbaugh waited comfortably, equably, until Kip shook his head.

"Thank you." Mothersbaugh pursed his lips. "After crossing into Norway, Miss Carson's movements become harder to track. Did you hear from her during this time?"

Kip shook his head again.

"She attempted to cash a check made out in your name at the Stat-Bank in Oslo on the fifteenth of May. A check for forty U.S. dollars. Were you aware of this?"

"You know the answer already. She cashed it."

Mothersbaugh gestured to Calkins, who passed him a folder.

"It's unclear to us, from that point forward, how Miss Carson supported herself. She used no credit cards, made no bank withdrawals, applied for no employment, and appealed to no family members or friends for assistance, as far as we've been able to determine." He frowned down at the folder. "This makes it all but impossible, as I'm sure you can appreciate, to establish her whereabouts with any degree of certainty. But we're confident that she remained in Norway for the remainder of that summer. And we know for a fact that she was there the following September, because we have footage of Miss Carson from the closed-circuit surveillance system of a sporting goods establishment in the city of Bergen. The footage was recorded at four eighteen on the morning of the nineteenth of that month."

No, said a small voice, as clearly as if Kip had spoken aloud. Calkins and Mothersbaugh gave no reaction.

"From that point forward, Miss Carson became—as I've said—a person of interest to Norwegian law enforcement. Specifically, Mr. Norvald, she became a material witness and a suspect in a series of cases involving destruction of private property, which is a felony-grade offense in Norway, as well as in the theft of thirteen thousand kroner worth of firearms and munitions. What brought her to the attention of Interpol, however, was less the felonies *per se* than the persons with whom she appears to be involved. These associates, of which Per Ivar Lund was one, are wanted in connection with a broad array of criminal offenses, both domestically and across international borders." He opened the folder. "I'll read the list of charges, if I may."

Kira, no.

"Destruction of private property, damage to public property, burglary, theft, arson, statutory rape, assault with intent to cause grievous bodily harm, assault with intent to kill, and two counts of murder in the second degree." He looked dourly at Calkins. "A further and parallel investigation has been opened, just in the past week, into allegations of human trafficking."

"Human trafficking?" A sound came out of Kip that might have been a laugh. "You guys are just making shit up at this point."

"The investigation I mention has a bearing on the case of Miss Carson herself, Mr. Norvald."

"What?"

Calkins sat forward now, stern but sympathetic, more actor-like than ever. "We're exploring the possibility that your friend may not be associating with this group of individuals, as it stands at present, of her own volition."

"Go ahead and tell me what that means."

"This is a group with a tight-knit, quasi-religious system of values and personal behavior," Mothersbaugh cut in. "In the States they'd be referred to as a cult."

"A cult?"

"There's a chance," continued Calkins, "that Miss Carson might not have elected to associate with these individuals—"

"We're exploring the possibility that she was taken."

The sound of someone trying to start a lawn mower carried in through the window. It started and stalled, started and stalled, over and over again.

"Taken?" Kip said finally.

"That's correct, Mr. Norvald."

"Excuse me," he said, getting up from the chair.

The bathroom was at the back of the apartment, just past the windowless cubby Kip slept in, and it smelled of cigarettes and standing water and the aftershave of some phantom former tenant. He sat on the edge of the toilet and let his forehead come to rest against the sink. He tried to imagine Kira doing something—anything at all—against her will. Tears stood in his eyes, making the bathroom light shudder, but whether they were tears of pity or anger or panic he couldn't possibly have said. Kira wanted by the police—by Interpol. He couldn't get his head around it. A year of unbroken silence and now this. Kira breaking into gun shops on the far side of the world.

He came back to find Calkins and Mothersbaugh exactly as they'd been when he'd left—the same postures, the same facial expressions, everything. How often they must have found themselves in shabby living rooms like this one, waiting patiently for the luckless relative or lover to recover his composure. It didn't matter whether or not they'd heard him sobbing in the bathroom. They knew perfectly well what he'd been doing.

"I'll tell you anything I can," he said.

"That's fine, Mr. Norvald. Our thanks in advance."

"What about the man—Lund, was that his name? Have you gone and talked to him?"

"Mr. Lund was discovered on the fifth of this month, burned to death in his vehicle. Coroner ruled it a suicide."

Kip had to restrain himself from bolting for the bathroom again. "Right," he said eventually, as though someone had asked him a question.

"We're currently collaborating with a joint national and provincial investigation on the ground," said Mothersbaugh. "The Norwegians have primary jurisdiction, obviously."

"I don't know what that means."

"We're doing our best," said Calkins. "Unfortunately, the previously mentioned individuals are proving difficult to find."

"You haven't mentioned any individuals."

"I won't lie to you, Mr. Norvald," said Mothersbaugh. "At the moment it's pretty rough going."

"You've got nothing. Is that what you're saying?"

"How are the attacks of rage, Mr. Norvald?"

"Excuse me?"

Calkins and Mothersbaugh exchanged one of their glances. "Let's just make sure we have this right," said Calkins. He brought a pocket notepad out of his blazer and flipped it crisply open. "*Periodic short-interval bouts of reflexive aggression, distinguished by a dissociative fugue state and active tendency to violence.* That's not our assessment, obviously. We retrieved it from your records."

He stared at them. "My records from ten years ago."

"This is strictly procedural, you understand. It's mandated."

"I'm in therapy."

"So am I," Mothersbaugh put in amiably.

"I don't have them anymore, is what I mean. The attacks. Whatever you want to call them. Not for going on two years." He took a step forward. "A year and ten months."

"Fair enough, Mr. Norvald."

No one spoke for a time. Kip was still on his feet. He couldn't decide what to do with himself.

"Have a seat, Mr. Norvald. This may take us a while."

"Longer than thirty minutes, I'm guessing."

Calkins bobbed his handsome graying head. "Unfortunately so."

"Am I allowed to ask you how you got my name?"

"We started in Florida—first Ponceville, then Venice. We talked to everyone we could."

"You didn't talk to Oona."

"Pardon?"

"My grandmother. I'd know."

"Mrs. Cartwright declined to help us in this matter."

Kip found himself grinning. "Oona's never had much love for law enforcement."

Mothersbaugh seemed not to hear. He was getting out his recording equipment—which included a stereo mic, for some reason—and Kip sat down and watched him. It was unexpectedly soothing. For the first time in years he found himself thinking about Florida by choice. The South Venice Youth Center. The shuffleboard courts down on Commerce. Caspersen Beach and garage sales and all-ages shows and racist cops and bonfires out at the Grids. He tried to remember his day-to-day life, to feel the emotions he'd suffered under so excruciatingly at age seventeen; nothing came. The handful of memories he dredged up were snapshots at best—pictures without depth, without color, warped by the weather and bleached by the sun. He'd dedicated the past three years to paving that life over.

"It was Leslie Vogler, wasn't it."

Mothersbaugh looked up from his equipment. "Come again, Mr. Norvald?"

"Leslie Vogler. Son of Nathan and Rachel. Fifty-seven Madrugada Drive."

Mothersbaugh set down the two-pronged mic stand he'd been fidgeting with and rubbed his eyes. At the center of the coffee table, just past his recorder, stood a hand-blown glass bong in Rastafarian colors. He nudged it aside and went back to his work.

"Give me an answer before you turn your machine on," Kip said. "Or I'm done."

Mothersbaugh regarded him blankly for a moment, then checked in with Calkins, who sat resolutely staring out the window.

"At the present time," he said deliberately, "we can neither confirm nor deny."

2

Kip touched down at Tampa International at three p.m. on the sixteenth
of January, picked up his rental a half hour later, and was southbound
on I-75 by a quarter to four. The ease of his homecoming put him on
edge. One of those low-flying winter rainstorms was rolling in from the
Gulf, a sky-high wall of cloud the same angry gray as the ocean; the
country to one side of the highway was in sunshine and the other was
in shadow. He'd forgotten how stunning the sky in Florida could be. In
their laughably stilted phone conversation, Leslie had cautioned him
to brace himself for changes, even shocks, but so far everything looked
just the same. He could easily have convinced himself that he'd never
gone away.

He made it past Gibsonton and Apollo Beach without feeling much.
Sarasota's sprawl touched Tampa's now, he registered in passing, and the
field where he'd picked magic mushrooms with Kira was the parking
lot of a brand-new Cracker Barrel. Leslie had told him that you could
drink alcohol in public in Venice these days, and that they'd closed off
the main access road to the Grids—due to flooding, ostensibly, though
everyone knew what the real reason was. Kip wondered where kids had
their near-death experiences now.

A glimpse of the Stardust Lanes marquee out the passenger-side window brought him out of his reverie. Leslie had suggested that they meet

at the Perkins on State Street, which he'd taken as a sentimental gesture; the thought of the reunion made Kip jittery in a vaguely pleasant way. Not long after Kira's disappearing act they'd begun a correspondence— bashful and halting at first, but more open and sincere as time went on—most of which consisted of Leslie filling him in on the details of his glamorous new life.

Leslie's decision not to come back to L.A. had been less a consequence of Kira's cold shoulder, apparently, than of a remarkable business opportunity that had come his way, via none other than Ray Carson, who'd moved on from his position at Home Depot to manage a small chain of boutique hotels. These days Leslie's life was a pageant of corporate wellness retreats and bright-eyed young interns and company cars. He was sober and fit and lived on his own in a newly built condo complex over on Venice Island, where Barnum & Bailey's winter quarters had once been. Kip read Leslie's semi-regular updates with genuine amusement, even the occasional twinge of envy. He'd been trying to coax him out to the West Coast for months.

The rain hit Kip hard on the outskirts of town, coming down all at once in that Florida way, as though a bomb hatch had dropped open in the clouds. He pulled the car over and waited it out. A few minutes later he found himself parked with one wheel up on the curb at the corner of Harbor and Baynard, within beer-can-lobbing distance of the youth center, which was now, as far as he could tell, one of those weird little stores that sell supplements to bodybuilders and women with calcium deficiencies. Three sparrow-like ladies with aubergine beehives came out at that moment, so delicate and graceful that they seemed not to touch the earth, and he felt his first real shiver of nostalgia.

He drove past the Voglers' house, then past Oona's, slumping down in his seat like the world's most incompetent private detective, and made it to the Perkins by ten after six. He found Leslie sitting in the last booth on the left, frowning intently at the tabletop, tracing circuit-board-like patterns with his finger in a pile of NutraSweet. Kip had never known him to do anything like that before—it seemed like something from the movie *Close Encounters*—but a lot about Leslie was different. So much was different, in fact, that Kip hung back for a moment, keeping well out of sight, arranging his features carefully into an expression of good cheer.

Leslie greeted him politely, almost formally, and gestured to the seat across from him, as though the corner booth at Perkins were his private conference room. By that point Kip knew with absolute certainty that everything Leslie had told him in his letters was a lie.

"You're different," he stammered. The words just came out.

"I think the term you're looking for is *fat*."

"It's not that," said Kip, which was partially true. While it was undeniable that he'd put on a shocking amount of weight—sixty pounds at least, which Kip would never have imagined was physically possible for someone with Leslie's metabolism—the rest of him was just as disconcerting. The threadbare polo shirt, the sweat-stained yachting bracelet, the hideous pleated knee-length madras shorts. The workplace-appropriate haircut. The nails that needed trimming. He looked both carefully assembled and suicidally unkempt.

"All right, kids. The geek is sleepy. Kindly step back from the glass."

"You're right," said Kip. "I'm sorry."

"I told you to brace yourself."

"You did."

"You weren't supposed to come back here, Norvald. You were supposed to stay on the other damn side of the country. I thought we had a deal."

That was as close as Leslie came to an acknowledgment of the grotesqueness of the situation. Kip mumbled an apology. Somehow he felt ashamed.

"It's not only me," said Leslie. "Look at you. You've changed at least as much."

"I have? In what way?"

"Do you really have to ask?" He yawned into his fist. "You've gotten cooler."

It wasn't intended as praise. They sat there staring at the little heap of artificial sweetener until someone finally came to take their order.

"I'll take the French dip sandwich and a chocolate malt," Kip said heartily, like somebody's dad on a TV show. "I love the French dip here. What about you, Z?"

"No one calls me that now." Leslie bit his lip in concentration. "Neither of those things, obviously."

"Obviously why?"

"I'm pre-prediabetic."

Kip held tightly to the built-in table, genuinely shaken. "Jesus. I had no idea."

"I told you there'd been changes."

"I'm not—I guess I'm not sure what to say. I'm so sorry."

Leslie asked the waitress for a chicken Caesar bread bowl, hold the croutons, with extra Thousand Island dressing on the side.

"There's sugar in Thousand Island," Kip couldn't stop himself from saying. "A ton of sugar."

"That's between me and my nutritionist."

"Of course." Kip nodded. "What does pre-prediabetic mean, exactly?"

Leslie regarded him coldly. "It means what it sounds like."

"Who's your nutritionist?"

"Rachel Vogler."

"Your mom?"

"My mom," Leslie said. "And my nutritionist."

It went on like that until the food arrived. Kip was reduced to asking boilerplate questions. Leslie was working as a paralegal for a trust and estate lawyer in Grove City, if he could be believed, and taking continuing education classes up in Tampa. Yes, he still lived at the Voglers'. No, he didn't do the cooking. Each new question put him more on the defensive.

Then, about half an hour in—just as Kip was reaching the end of his emotional endurance—Leslie reached across the table and took a long, gurgling sip of his chocolate malt. Things were shaky enough that it felt like a breakthrough.

"Oona always said the malts here have a secret ingredient."

"Corn syrup."

"How are you, Leslie? How are you really? I mean, other than—"

"Other than what, exactly?"

"I'm asking how you're doing, damn it. Whether you're okay. That's all I'm asking here."

Leslie set the malt down, carefully and precisely, at the center of the table. "I guess you must reckon us Florida crackers don't understand about subtext."

"You're not a cracker, Leslie."

"Because I'm not white enough, you mean?"

"Because you're not poor enough. Not even close. I hate to disappoint you."

Leslie stared straight past him for a while, off into the misty middle distance, as though working out some complex calculation in his head. Kip thought back on all the other times Leslie had preferred to pretend that he didn't exist. The sky was clearing now, just in time for the sunset, and a dark-haired woman was sweeping rainwater off the handicapped access ramp. Kip felt a sudden urge to join her.

"You look depressed, Norvald. Does real life depress you?"

Kip didn't answer.

"I wrote Percy a letter, too," Leslie said, smiling out at the woman. "In case you're looking for something to chuckle about."

"Leslie—"

"Piece of shit never wrote back, of course. You have my permission to laugh."

Only now did Kip appreciate how much time had gone by. The physical change in Leslie should have driven it home, but that still seemed surreal. It took the mention of Percy Blackwood to give the past two years their appropriate weight.

"Percy died, Leslie. Six months ago."

He watched the news hit. For the briefest of instants Leslie lost his composure—he pressed both hands to his face and kept them there, like a little boy trying to vanish. When the hands came down the mask was back in place.

"What was it?" he said evenly. "A car crash? Some kind of OD?"

"I'm not sure."

"Don't lie to me, Norvald."

"I heard he had AIDS."

Leslie gave no reaction. "And you found that fitting. The price for his sins."

"I'm trying to understand why you're pissed off at me," Kip said, his voice starting to quaver. "I'm trying to understand how that's even fucking possible."

"You're the one who sounds angry." Leslie held up his hands. "But at least I know why."

The light seemed to stutter, as though some pickup in the lot outside were flashing its brights, and the noises from the other tables fell away. It was obvious to Kip what Leslie was saying, the implication was clear, but still he had to overcome his disbelief. He counted down from ten before he spoke.

"Maybe you're wrong, Z. Maybe you don't have a clue about why I'm angry, or why I'm sitting here, or why I was ever friends with you at all." He leaned across the table. "That's the problem with narcissistic personality disorder. Other people don't exist for you—not as living things, with actual emotions—so you can never figure any of us out. We're like zombies in a shooter game to you. There's only two things you can do with us. You can blow our brains out or you can run away."

"Whoever your therapist is, Norvald, you're not paying them enough." Leslie smiled down at his fingertips. "The old Kip would have put his fist through something."

"The better question, though," Kip said, ignoring him, "is whether you can understand yourself. Do you have reasons for the idiotic crap you pull? I'm asking sincerely, believe it or not. Why did you work so hard to get between me and Kira? Why did you disappear without saying I'm sorry or thank you or fuck off or anything else? And how is it that—after years of putting up with your bullshit, after bailing you out of one disaster after another—when I finally fly across the country to see you, the best friend you'll ever have in your self-centered little life, you act like it's a fucking imposition?"

Leslie sat back now, slowly and heavily. "The big questions."

Kip said nothing.

"I had sex with your girlfriend. Speaking of idiotic."

"I know all about that. Kira said she had to draw you a diagram."

Leslie shot him a look of worldly irony, one of his all-time best—then averted his eyes in an odd, nervous way, tracing the contours of the maze on the tabletop. He opened his mouth to speak, then reconsidered. The light had gone strange again, the clouds lit from inside, and Kip realized another storm was coming. The woman with the broom was standing motionless, an arm's length from the window, looking straight up at the copper-colored sky.

"You were a part of it," Leslie said, almost too faintly to hear. "A big part. That's the best I can explain it."

"What is that supposed to mean? A part of what?"

"A part of everything that went to hell."

"Don't talk down to me, Z. That's not even an answer."

"You're right, Kip. I'm sorry."

No more irony now. Leslie was looking straight at him.

"What's done is done," Kip said eventually, gesturing to the waitress for the check. "I didn't come here for some kind of friendship audit."

Leslie laid both his hands flat on the table. "It's a funny thing in a way, fucking up like I did. I can't compare it to any other kind of feeling. You're down in this—in this sort of *crevasse*, if that's the right word, where it's really hard to see. It gets tighter and tighter. And the only way that you can go is down."

Kip took his time answering. "I guess I should have tried harder to get down there with you."

"You *were* down there with me." Leslie was still watching him, his thin mouth gone crooked. "Just you, Kip. No one else."

Kip managed to nod. "Just me," he repeated.

The woman was smoking a cigarette now, drawing the smoke in deeply and keeping it in, holding her right palm out to check for rain. Kip felt tears in his eyes. Whatever else might have changed, Leslie hadn't lost his talent for pulling the rug out from under him. He tried not to blink.

"I wanted to be with you, Leslie," he mumbled. "You didn't always make it easy."

"Thanks for saying that, Kip. I mean it. You're lying, but I appreciate the gesture."

"Jesus Christ. I just *said*—"

"What exactly did our friends in law enforcement tell you?"

Kip sipped his malt slowly. He needed a moment.

"About Kira, you mean?"

"That's why we're both here, isn't it?"

Kip set his mug aside—Perkins still used real glass—and weighed the pros and cons of every answer he could think of.

"Sure," he said finally. "That's why we're both here."

The grin Leslie chose to give him now was open and unguarded. "At long last, a straightforward answer. Kipper Norvald's all growed up."

"I was thinking we could, you know, pool our resources—"

"Let's hit it, then. Pump the accelerator. I haven't got all day."

"What does that even mean?"

"I've got places to be."

"Leslie—it's six thirty-five on a Tuesday. In *Venice*."

"So I couldn't possibly have anything else going on? Is that what you're saying?"

"What I'm saying is we haven't seen each other in almost two years—"

"Two years and six days."

"—and someone we both care about is being hunted by Interpol. Fucking *Interpol*, Leslie."

"I asked what they told you. I'm not the one wasting time here."

Kip stared hard at Leslie. He'd gone back to tracing patterns on the tabletop.

"Okay. I was visited by two agents: Calkins and Mothersbaugh. They came to Venice first, I know that much. They talked to you."

Leslie shrugged.

"According to Mothersbaugh, the group they're after has ties of some kind to the metal scene in Oslo—they overlap somehow—

but it's not the same thing as the actual bands. No one knows the connection."

"Go on."

"They know who plays in the bands, more or less, but pretty much everyone uses made-up names, and Mothersbaugh told me they're not sure how many of these kids—a lot of them are still in their teens—are part of the other, secret thing. They don't even have a definite sense of what they're dealing with. It's weird as shit, Z. In an hour's conversation they called it a cult and a gang and a political movement. Calkins even compared it to a terrorist cell." Kip shook his head. "I'm guessing that's because they've been stockpiling weapons."

"Because of that," said Leslie. "And also because of the burnings."

"I'm not sure what you mean."

"The arson," he said matter-of-factly. "The putting-to-the-torch."

"The what?"

"Churches mostly. A post office somewhere."

"Calkins mentioned arson, but he never—"

"Shut up for a second." Leslie brushed the sweetener off the table with a look of mild distaste, as though it had been left there by some previous customer. "We're talking about a group of people who believe that Christianity is a foreign religion—an eastern, Semitic faith—forced onto the Norse countries by European invaders back in the Dark Ages."

Kip blinked at him. "The Dark Ages. Okay."

"Norway's earliest Christian churches were built on heathen mounds and stone circles—pagan places of worship—to humiliate the locals, basically. To take away their faith. These people Kira's running around robbing gun shops with consider themselves *Vikings*. This isn't a joke to them, or a pose, or some kind of elaborate role-playing game. They want to knock their country back a thousand years."

"By torching some churches? Doesn't that seem—"

"What?"

"I don't know. A bit naïve?"

"You're right, Kip. My mistake. Interpol is probably overreacting."

"Fuck you." Kip took hold of the bridge of his nose, just past the septum, and pinched it as hard as he could.

"Norvald, what are you doing?"

"I'm trying to get my head around this thing."

"Take all the time you need, brother. It's just another Tuesday night in Venice."

"I thought they were Satanists. Something like that."

Leslie spread his arms wide. "What is Satan but the ancient adversary of the Christ?"

"You got all this from Mothersbaugh? Seriously?"

"That and more, if you can believe it. He was surprisingly chatty. He's a metalhead himself—or claims to be."

"He fed me the same line."

"We come in all guises, Norvald. All colors and creeds."

Kip pinched the bridge of his nose again. "No way you got all this from Mothersbaugh."

"There's a record store in Oslo that doubles as a crash pad. They hold their meetings in the basement."

"Meetings?"

"Orgies, blood rituals, drum circles—whatever Nazis do on weekends. The address is 56A Schweigaards Gate. Half an hour's walk from the center of town."

"So why hasn't anybody been arrested yet?"

"I wondered the same thing. My guess is that they're waiting for something major to go down. And there are problems with the local police—a jurisdiction issue. A pissing contest, basically. The vibe I'm getting is that everything's on hold."

Kip sat there dumbfounded. "I still don't understand how you know all this."

Leslie looked sly again. "I have my ways and methods." He reached across the table and drank what was left of the malt.

"That's it? That's all you're going to tell me?"

"There's a map of Oslo at the Tampa public library. It's from '86, but I'm assuming that the layout hasn't changed. This is Norway we're talking about."

"That explains the address, maybe. I don't see how you figured out the rest."

"The rest of what?"

"Whatever you just called it—their belief system." Kip groped for the appropriate term. "Their ideology."

Leslie let out a sigh of profound satisfaction. He'd been waiting to be asked that very question.

"I suppose you could say I made use of my contacts in the field."

"You've lost me again."

His grin slowly widened. "Remember Chris Rozz? The kid with the car full of garbage?"

"Of course I remember."

"He works at MetalHaven—that tape shop we used to go to in the Sarasota mall. They sell vinyl now, and picture discs. Most of it was special order, obviously. But he got me what I needed."

"What could a shop in the Sarasota mall—"

"Use your powers of deduction. Flex your pointy head a little. Take a guess."

"Maybe you could just tell me."

"It's simple, Kip. I listened to their records."

3

Two days later Kip found himself sitting in his grandmother's kitchen, watching her chain-smoking Camels and reading the Sarasota County police blotter, for all the world as if the past three years had never come and gone. Forty-eight hours was too long to be in Venice, at least for him—all the old fears and superstitions were bubbling up like swamp gas. But it felt good to smell that smoke, and to see Oona's face, and to listen to her talk about the blotter.

"Here's a forty-year-old female, Port Charlotte resident, booked for grand theft automotive. They caught her because she left her dentures in the vehicle. Her *dentures*, Christopher."

"You'd think she might have noticed they were missing."

"These people don't eat. They live on conspiracy theories and crystal." She sighed. "The state police found her hiding in a dishwasher in a mobile home outside of Murdock. Her ponytail was sticking out of the machine."

"It says all that in the blotter?"

She shook her head impatiently. "I saw it on the news."

"Oh."

"Goddamned crystal—pardon my language. Turns your brain into cheese grits."

It was quiet in the bungalow—that sepulchral Venice quiet—and Kip could hear the cigarette paper crackling every time she took a drag. She studied the blotter with a learned air.

"I see a news item like that," she said softly, "I get to understanding why you left the state."

"We've got idiots in California, too."

"Maybe so, Christopher. Maybe so. But they've probably still got their teeth."

"I was happy here in Venice," he heard himself saying. "I liked living with you."

"I know you did, sweetheart. We had us a time."

He took one of her yellow-fingered hands and marveled, as always, at the smoothness of its palm. "I had to go where the work was, Oona. You know that."

"You had to go where the girl was."

The resentment in her voice took him completely by surprise. He stood up carefully and went and got a beer out of the fridge. It still gave him a childish thrill to do that in his grandmother's house. She sat watching him across the mint-green counter.

"I guess I can't argue with that," he said as he sat down.

She let out a thin jet of cream-colored smoke. "I'd say it was none of my business," she said. "If you weren't about to do it all again."

Kip picked up the notebook he'd bought that morning at the dusty old drugstore on Ponce de Léon—an old-fashioned composition book, the kind he'd always used in school, with the marbled black cover and round-cornered pages. Next to it on the countertop lay the records he'd picked up that morning from Leslie: *Blood Fire Death* by Bathory, *A Blaze in the Northern Sky* by Darkthrone, *Deathcrush* by Mayhem, and a graphite-colored LP, without a title or a band name or text of any kind, on whose cover a girl in peasant clothing was being eaten by a wolf.

He'd been up half the night with Leslie, playing the first three over and over on the beautiful old turntable in the Voglers' sunken parlor, subjecting the lyrics to critical exegesis as they'd used to do with records by bands they adored. By an hour after midnight the suspicion and the awkwardness had burned away and they had been themselves again. He hadn't caught so much as a glimpse of either Rachel or Nate—when he'd asked about them, Leslie had explained that he'd poisoned them and stuffed their bodies underneath the porch. It was as close to the old days as Kip could have wished for. But he'd left before they'd put the nameless record on.

"So what's your plan?" said Oona.

"Plan?"

"I'm assuming you have one." She stopped in mid-drag. "Tell me that you have one, Christopher."

Kip arranged the LPs in a row across the counter. "I've already told you. We go there and get her."

"If she wants to be got."

"That's right."

Oona stubbed out her Camel and stared at him. He did his best to stare back.

"And what if she doesn't? Is there a plan B?"

"Let's talk about something else."

She nodded to herself. "I didn't think so."

"Let's just have a nice day, Oona. Don't try to talk me out of this."

"I stopped trying to talk anybody out of anything around the time that you were born."

"So you always say."

"I've got to ask you, though, sweetheart. Have you thought about what it means—" She gestured over her shoulder, out through the picture window, in the general direction of the Voglers'. "Have you considered what it means to take him with you? To that place? To those people? A young man like that?"

He didn't need to ask her what she meant. "It was Leslie's idea to come. He insisted on it, actually. He knows what he's doing."

"That's not what I asked you."

He turned his beer back and forth on the counter. "I've thought about it."

"And you're going to do it anyway."

"I need him, Oona. I need his knowledge and—I just need him, that's all. He's kind of my ace in the hole."

"Your ace in the hole," she repeated. "That boy. Leslie Vogler."

"That's right."

"Some people would say that's a pretty good argument for catching the next plane back to California."

Kip said nothing to that. He picked up the unnamed LP and brought it over to the window.

"You still have that little turntable somewhere?"

"Not to play that trash on, Christopher. I keep a Christian home."

"Please, sweetheart."

She tapped out a fresh Camel. "Wait till I'm at my bridge game. I'm gone in an hour."

As soon as his grandmother had left he went to her bedroom to look for the antediluvian Sears Roebuck turntable that she used on rare occasions to play her Fabian and Frankie Valli singles. It was cracked along the bottom and its platter wobbled slightly as it spun, causing subtle fluctuations in the speed, but he wasn't listening for pleasure. The room had the smell he remembered—lavender and ancient wool and something like boiled sugar—but he was no better able to puzzle out its mysteries now than he'd been at seventeen. He closed the door behind him and pulled the turntable out from under the bed and put the record on.

It began as the show in Berlin had begun—the cold, ringing chord, the heavy interval of silence, the choir of howling voices drawing faintly through the trees. This time the voices sounded less like wolves and more like human beings. How he could be so certain that the setting was a forest—how he could sense the trees without hearing them—was more than he could say. But he felt them so clearly. Tree-shaped holes in the music. They did something to him. He was back in the blackness of that underground club, in the closeness, in the suffocating calm. He was in the woods again and he was in the crowd. He searched the room for Kira. He saw her stepping out into the snow.

The second side was nothing like the first. No howling, no distortion, no music at all. It sounded like a primitive field recording, made in an age when the ability to capture sound was still new to the world. A lone man's voice speaking. Faint murmurs and sighs from the listeners. Unnamable night sounds. A bonfire hissing. The wind in the trees.

The voice began gently. It was like no voice that Kip had ever heard. It was the voice of a grown man, an elder, not some kid in a band. Deliberate and mournful and dry as old leaves. He seemed to be telling some manner of fable. Kip knew the sound of Norwegian only from a handful of tracks Leslie had played him, but even so he could tell that the dialect was a strange one, if in fact it was Norwegian at all. Often the speaker lapsed into silence—if not for the barely audible rustlings of the forest and the fire, Kip might have thought that the needle had lifted. But always the voice returned, without preamble or warning, slightly louder and more urgent than before.

By midway through the recording the man's voice had strengthened to the point that it seemed to be addressing a sizable audience, perhaps a congregation. It was strident now, righteous—the words it spoke were the words of a sermon, or a divination, or possibly a statement at a trial. The forest noises had been swallowed by the buzzing of the crowd. An order of some kind was given. The wind fell away and the buzzing stopped dead and in the sudden lull Kip seemed to hear the sobbing of a child. He sensed the presence of many listeners, a great assembly, keeping absolutely still. Something was about to happen. He heard nothing any longer but the turntable's quiet humming and the crackling of the needle and the hopeless high-pitched keening of that pale small voice alone.

4

He awoke in a dark room surrounded by strangers. Something terrible had happened. The air was unnaturally dry and he was strapped into his seat. He licked his cracked lips and took a deep, deliberate breath, doing his best not to panic. He was starting to remember. He was high above the ocean. A woman in a turquoise suit came toward him and he asked her for water. By the time she came back, steering a rattling cart of bottles up the aisle, he'd regained some sense of where he was and why.

Carefully he took in his surroundings. The cabin hummed and rattled in the artificial dusk. Someone two or three rows ahead was drinking coffee. Leslie was in the window seat, curled up sideways with his thin mouth hanging open. Kip looked him over systematically, taking advantage of the opportunity, still trying to reconcile this strange new Leslie with the one he'd known before. He was wearing sharply pressed chinos, argyle socks, and boating shoes with curling leather tassels. His aftershave smelled like the blue liquid barbers keep their scissors in.

"I need you to understand something," Leslie had told him six days earlier, toward the end of that awful dinner at the Perkins. "It's important to me, before this avalanche gets rolling, that we get one thing crystal clear."

"Absolutely, Z. Anything you need."

"Don't call me that."

They settled their bill and stepped outside into the twilight. The rain was just starting. Leslie came to a stop between two parked cars, shaking his head as if disgusted with himself. Kip prepared for the worst.

"If I do come along on this death trip of yours—and I'm not saying I will—it won't be because I love Kira."

"I hear you, man. Whatever the reason—"

"I'll be going because I love you."

A truck passed with its brights on. "I know," Kip said absurdly. Nothing else came to him.

"*I love you too, Leslie,*" said Leslie. "*Thank you for sharing. I appreciate your honesty and strength.*"

"I love you too, Leslie," Kip echoed. "You know that."

"And?"

"And—the rest of what you said."

Leslie, to Kip's astonishment, had seemed content with that.

"Last time I saw you, you wanted to tell me something, Leslie," he'd said then, stepping back under the awning. "Something about Kira. Something I didn't know."

"Shit, man." Leslie's whole posture changed. "I'm pretty sure you learned it for yourself."

"Pretend that I didn't."

"You're going to make me say it? Really?"

Kip didn't answer.

"I was going to tell you—" He passed a hand across his face and started over. "That she's too fucked up, Kip. That things happened to her. Worse things than we knew. That you were going about it all wrong with that simpering, aw-shucks attitude of yours—all that puppy-dog devotion. I was going to tell you that she reads tenderness as weakness. That she hates her own guts. That the harder you try with a person like that—a person with that pathology, you understand?—the deeper you're digging your own fucking grave."

"Oh," Kip had said quietly. "That."

"I told you so, damn it. You knew it already."

Kip had nodded for a second or two, slumped mutely back against the picture window, watching the raindrops hissing on the blacktop. Then he'd stood up straight again.

"I disagree."

"Are you shitting me, Norvald? Even after everything that's happened?"

"Kira doesn't hate herself. Not anymore."

"Then why—"

"That's why we've got to go there, Leslie. To find out why. That's how we get her back."

The cabin lights were brought up and a pleasant Nordic voice announced that they were starting their descent. Kip reached past Leslie and raised the sunshade on a burning silver cloudscape that looked as solid as a cliff. It was late in the morning, and at that altitude the light was overpowering—but he couldn't imagine it breaking through those continents of mist to reach the ground below. It was hard to believe that any ground existed.

They came out over Oslo, grayscaled and oddly depthless through the polarizing glass, and everything that met his eye was foreign to his sight. The fractured white coastline. The monochrome dullness. Nowhere was the sky above them brighter than the earth. The plane seemed to be moving dangerously slowly, barely faster than a man could walk—it was a mystery to him why they didn't fall. Cloud engulfed them again. All he saw were the winglights. When he felt the shock of touchdown he was sure they'd hit the sea.

The shining modern terminal confused him even further. It looked less like an airport than some lavish public spa. Lacquered floors and recessed lighting. Effortless transitions. Leslie was in high spirits, alert and well rested, taking note of each new detail with a cackle of delight. Kip felt hidden in the wake of Leslie's exuberant otherness, the next best thing to invisible, the way he'd often felt at Venice High. The fact that Leslie was attempting to disguise himself as a middle-aged office manager made very little difference. No one else in that whole terminal was black.

"Everything's in English," Leslie whispered. "Are you sure we're not in Scotland?"

"I'm not, actually."

"I miss Venice already."

"No, you don't."

Leslie sighed and squinted off into the distance. "I'm getting a wintery vibe from this country."

"You catch on fast."

"I'm thinking I should maybe not have worn my boat shoes."

They progressed through passport control and baggage claim and customs with supernatural efficiency. Once again things were moving too fast for Kip's liking. They were in the taxi line already and snow was coming down and Leslie was hugging himself against the shocking cold. His shoes flapped loudly as he stamped his feet for warmth. Kip glanced down at the worn-out Chuck Taylors on his own feet, their heels smooth as cue balls. He might as well have been barefoot.

"Can we even afford a taxi here?"

"You tell me, Norvald. This trip is on you—remember?"

"I remember."

"Good boy. Think of it as your karmic debt for not wasting your life."

"You haven't wasted your life, Leslie."

"A joke." Leslie smiled down strangely at the curb. "A simple jest."

"When we get back from this thing, no matter how it plays out—if you ever wanted to come out west again—"

"You'd offer me a pull-out couch? A second chance at happiness?"

"Call it whatever you want."

"Duly noted, Francis of Assisi. Here's our cab."

The driver started for downtown Oslo without asking them where they were headed. His beard was straw-colored, wavy and matted, like the fur of a golden retriever. It wasn't hard to imagine him at the bow of a dragon-prowed longboat, possibly holding an axe.

"You *can* afford this, right?" Leslie said under his breath. "All of this, I mean."

"I said I could. Let's change the subject."

"Fine by me."

They rode in silence past snowbound fields and densely wooded suburbs. Kip saw red barns in the distance that could have been in Wisconsin. The road was wet with runoff. The amount of snow to every side confounded him completely.

"Winter," Leslie said. "Actual winter. Not that California bullshit."

"Or that Florida bullshit."

"So what's the plan, Norvald? What happens now?"

"For Christ's sake, Leslie. We've talked this through a dozen times already."

"Remind me what we said."

"We find out where Kira is. We go there. We get her. The end."

Leslie asked no further questions. He just sat there.

"Don't look at me like that. I've run through the scenarios in my head, Z. All sorts of scenarios."

"Me too. They all turn out messy."

They were passing rows of close-set houses now and the occasional supermarket and modernist apartment block. Kip kept catching himself forgetting it was daytime. Leslie was propping his eyelids open with his thumbs.

"We've got the address," Kip said. "The address of the shop. That's where we'll start."

"That's where we'll start," said Leslie.

"Right."

"Start how, exactly?"

Kip blinked at him. "Today is Thursday—"

"Today is Friday, Kip. We just got off an overnight flight."

"Even better. The shop should be open. We go tonight and find out what they know."

"Find out what they know," Leslie murmured. He sounded like someone talking in his sleep.

"Will you stop repeating everything I say?"

"I'm making sure I've got this right, that's all. The plan is to go—you and me—to the shop that an agent of Interpol says is the front for a paramilitary cell—"

"He used that word? *Paramilitary*?"

"—and just walk in, two boneheads from West Central Florida, and ask if anyone has Kira locked up in their basement?"

"Of course not."

"Well! That's sure a load off my shoulders."

"What I'm thinking is, we check the place out—buy some bootlegs or something—" He stopped himself. "Why are you making that face?"

"I keep getting this feeling."

"A *feeling*. Okay." Kip willed himself to stay calm. "What kind of a feeling?"

"That you're looking at me and seeing some completely different person."

"I genuinely have no idea—"

"I'm Black, Norvald. I'm a fat nerdy pimply depressive Black bastard. And just because I haven't gotten laid since Judas Priest put out a decent record doesn't mean that I've stopped being gay."

Kip bit his lip for a moment. "I want you to tell me what you're pissed off about, Leslie. I really do. But also I want to ignore you."

"How could I be pissed off about anything? I'm enjoying an all-expenses-paid vacation to the Land of the Fjords. I'm looking forward to sampling the local cuisine and learning how to say 'suck my dick' in Norwegian." Leslie settled down into the seat and closed his eyes. "Which is why I'm in no hurry to be dead."

They found a room in a backpackers' hostel half a block from Karl Johans Gate and went straight back out to buy some clothes to keep themselves from freezing. The weather had turned ugly and the snowmelt on the cobblestones had hardened into ice: within three steps of the entrance Kip was sitting in the street. Leslie helped him up and he took another step, tentative as a toddler, then went down even harder than before. The pedestrian zone was crowded with midday shoppers and he fully expected them to laugh at him, the whole city of Oslo in one thundering chorus—but the city of Oslo remained unamused. He considered the possibility that no one laughed in Norway.

They went into the first outdoor outfitters they came across, Leslie's boat shoes squeaking sharply on the polished cedar floor, and bought themselves matching black wool hats and quilted winter gloves. The freckle-faced salesgirl was the first kindly soul they'd encountered since leaving the airport. Her name was Living—that was what Kip thought he heard, at least—and she helped them to pick out heavy cable-knit sweaters and Thinsulate parkas and hiking boots and moisture-wicking socks. She made no comment about Kip's dripping sneakers, or his mud-spattered shirtfront, or even his limp; after twenty minutes in the glow of her attention he'd almost forgotten where he was and why. But it all came rushing back to him when he looked at the receipt.

"I must not be doing the math right."

"I give you a discount," said the salesgirl. "Very welcome!"

"Is this in dollars?" he said helplessly.

"Don't make a scene, Norvald."

"Fuck you, Z. This is half a month's rent."

"There is some question?" said Living.

"Damn right there's a question."

"Your waffles," said Leslie.

Her eyes widened. "Again, please?"

"They're a delicacy here, am I right? The Norsk waffle cake?"

"The *kakevafler*!" she tittered. "I should tell you a place?"

"What I want you to tell me—" Kip began, but no one was listening. Leslie was already blowing the salesgirl a kiss and ushering him out into the cold.

The waffles were in fact otherworldly, surreal, filled with sweet nut-brown cheese and clotted cream and tiny blood-red berries Kip had never seen before. They tasted like sunlight. Leslie ordered for them both—a first round, then a second, then a third—and made a big deal out of picking up the negligible bill. Jet lag hit them not long after and they staggered woozily back to their cramped little room. It had been designed for four people, with two sets of bunk beds arranged in an L, but the other bunks were empty. The whole hostel seemed empty. They'd barely gotten out of their new boots before they fell asleep.

When Kip opened his eyes three full hours had passed but the ashen sky outside looked just the same. His shirt was damp with sweat, and his entire right side ached, but he felt wonderfully clearheaded and alert. Leslie lay twisted on top of his sheets with a peaceful half smile on his lips. Kip watched him awhile, getting more and more restless, trying to decide whether to interrupt his dream. Finally he got up and changed into clean clothes and pulled on the obscenely overpriced sweater he'd just bought and left a note saying he'd be back before nightfall, if night even existed in Norway. It was hard to imagine that steady dismal daylight ever changing.

The walk from the hostel to Schweigaards Gate took him less than half an hour. The shop was supposedly in a bad part of town—according to Leslie, at least—but Kip found himself hard-pressed to tell the difference. Street after street of apartment houses from the turn of the century, their upper stories pastel shades of rose or blue or ivory, the ground floors tidy and subdued. The uniformity amazed him. It was hard to imagine anything indecent happening in those houses, let alone criminal. The people he passed looked hardworking and sober. He was beginning to feel like a fool.

A half block shy of 56A he stopped and took the measure of the building. A color that might once have been yellow on the upper floors; undistinguished gray below. No sign and no awning. The windows blacked out from inside. He'd seen porn shops on the Strip that called more attention to themselves. He walked past without slowing, hiding his face in the hood of his parka, then crossed the street and doubled slowly back. He was acting like a hoodlum on a cop show. Luckily no one else was on the street.

For the next forty minutes he waited in an entryway directly across from the shop, doing a sad little shuffle to keep himself warm, and in all that time no one went in or out. He was no good at this. His teeth were chattering like a wind-up skeleton's and he knew he had to move. His choices, as far as he understood them, were either to cross the street or catch the next flight home.

On closer inspection the door of 56A looked to have been reinforced from the inside. The doorbell had been painted over and the handle didn't turn. He stood very still for a blank span of time, right palm flat against the doorframe, listening for any sound of life. He stared at the ancient bell as if it might betray some secret. Then his sight moved slowly leftward to a plastic mailbox fastened to the wall.

The box held three letters. He turned them over one by one, forcing himself to be deliberate and thorough, attempting to read their contents with his fingers. The first was a bill, that much was clear, or possibly a disconnection notice. The name in the little plastic window read AARSETH, ØYSTEIN. One of the two agents—he couldn't remember which one—had mentioned that name. He folded the bill in half and stuffed it in his pocket.

The handwriting on the remaining two was nearly identical—he saw that at once—though the envelopes could not have been more different. The first was eggshell blue, heavy and stiff and ostentatious, the sort of paper wedding notices are sent in. The sender's address had been painstakingly redacted, first with a pencil and then with a black felt-tip marker. The letter was addressed not to Aarseth but to what Kip took to be the name of the shop: Euronymous.

"Euronymous," Kip said under his breath. Somehow he'd expected something fiercer. He wondered what the word meant in Norwegian.

The other envelope was spattered with ink and taped shut at both ends. It looked to have been used and reused many times. It held more than a letter: something thick and oddly angled. A set of keys, Kip decided. He shook it and listened. It bore no postage or return address.

A city bus passed, sending coffee-colored slush onto the pavement, and in that instant something fell against the far side of the door. Kip staggered backward, coming close to falling over, flapping his arms wildly like some panicked flightless bird. He'd been careless and stupid. He caught sight of furtive movement behind the nearest blacked-out window, a stooped and hooded figure—then recognized his own silhouette reflected. He turned and walked down Schweigaards Gate without a glance behind him.

Leslie was awake when he got back, propped up on both of their pillows, eating the last remaining *kakevaffel* with little coos of joy. Apart from his bare feet he was fully dressed for winter, parka and scarf and skiing cap and all.

"Cheese on a waffle," he said dreamily. "*Lingonberries.* Who knew?"

"I was planning to eat that."

"Sorry, partner. This is research."

Kip kept quiet and waited.

"I give up already. Where have you been?"

He set the letters on the edge of Leslie's bunk. Leslie sat up, still chewing, then put the waffle absentmindedly aside. His eyes had gone moon-shaped. "No fucking way."

"I checked the door first, to be safe."

"*To be safe,*" Leslie murmured. "That cracks me right up."

"It's all right. No one saw me."

"How the hell would you know?"

"Go ahead, Agent Vogler. Open them. You've got top-secret clearance."

Leslie wedged the door shut with the room's only chair and arranged the letters in a row across the floor between the bunks. His first idea was to steam them open—by borrowing an iron from the management, if possible—but in the end he slit them open with the nail file from his personal grooming kit. They saved the hand-delivered envelope for last.

The bill was for water, a quarterly statement, and told them only that the premises had been in steady use for the past three months.

Kip regretted having taken it, regretted losing his head, but he kept his apprehension to himself. Before opening the blue letter—before even picking it up again—Leslie found his quilted gloves and pulled them on.

"What are you doing that for?"

"Just a precaution."

"You can't leave fingerprints on paper."

Leslie shot him a look. "Kip Norvald, forensic scientist. Of course you can."

"Anyway—we're not giving these back." Kip held his breath for a moment. "Are we giving these back?"

"I'll tell you something," Leslie said slowly. "I want no physical contact with these people."

Kip sat back on his heels and watched him as he worked two fingers into the cut he'd made and extracted a sheet of loosely folded paper. Its outer side was covered in chickenscratch, dense and indecipherable—letters from some unknown alphabet. Runes, Kip decided. At the bottom he saw a word he recognized.

"*Euronymous*," he mumbled. "I think that's the shop."

Leslie stopped what he was doing. "Excuse me?"

"You're looking at me like I just said something crazy."

"It's a stage name, Norvald. An alias. It's right on the back of the *Deathcrush* EP—the one we listened to a hundred times in Venice. Euronymous and Aarseth are one and the same."

Kip frowned down at the letter. "I guess I missed that somehow."

"I thought we weren't putzing around here, Kip. I thought this was more than a sightseeing visit. I thought we both agreed to do our homework."

"We did. Definitely."

"The shop is called Helvete. Which means 'hell' in Norwegian."

"Helvete," Kip echoed. "Okay."

"You know what I'm starting to feel like? Like I'm in 'Nam, up to my eyeballs in the proverbial shit, with somebody who thinks 'Vietcong' is a colorful local name for peanut curry."

"In no way is that a reasonable comparison."

"Do your homework."

"I will. Absolutely."

Leslie heaved a sigh and flipped the paper over. At the top of the page, all in caps, was a passage in English:

THEY AQUIRED SUPERHUMAN FORCE. NO KNYFE COULD CUT THEM. NO FIRE BURN THEM. A CLUB ALONE CAN SLOW THEM BY THE BREKING OF THER BONES.

  THEY COME NAKED AND SHINING WITH PAINT ON THER FACES AND WOLF SKENS ABOUT THEM. FIRE IN EYESOCKETS. THEY GRYND THER TEETH AND FROTHING AT THE LIPS. THEY BITE AT THER SHIELD RIMS. THEY CHEW ON THE PIECES. THEY RIDE INTO BATTLE. THEY ARE BLEEDING AND SHRIKING AND HOWLING AS WOLVES

"Fuck."

"Quoting someone," said Leslie. "That's why it's in English."

Kip sank down onto the edge of his bunk. "A how-to manual, sounds like."

Leslie handed him the letter. "Viking shit."

"That's supposed to make me feel better?"

"It's make-believe, Norvald. Fantasy stuff. Think about all the mumbo-jumbo Trey Azagthoth used to talk. Glen Benton burning a cross into his forehead."

"Trey Azagthoth never robbed a gun shop. Glen Benton isn't wanted by Interpol."

"As far as we know."

"As far as we know," Kip repeated. "Okay."

Oddly enough, it did make him feel better to think of the scene back at home with all of its grandstanding. The lyrics of your average Deicide song were freakier than the contents of that letter. He turned it back over and looked at the runes.

"I kind of wish that we could read Norwegian."

Leslie was watching him. "We can still go home, Norvald. Remember that. We can get on an airplane whenever we want."

"Open the next one."

"The next one's all yours."

He reached down and picked up the last of the envelopes. Because of the weight at one end and the cheapness of the paper it hung drooping in his fingers like a dirty piece of cloth. Suddenly he was in no rush to know what was inside.

Leslie leaned closer. "Give it here if you don't want it."

"I'm thinking maybe it's keys." He slid the contents circumspectly out onto his palm. Something wrapped in a kerchief. A collection of objects, hard but not metallic. Clicking faintly together.

"Not keys," said Leslie.

Kip shook his head.

They sat staring wordlessly down at the bundle. Linen with a silk border. Embroidered initials in one corner. *EVF.*

A commotion started up in the hallway—actual tourists, from the sound of them. Leslie went to the door and set his back against it. That struck Kip as a bit melodramatic, even for Leslie. To spare them both further embarrassment he unfolded the linen and shook the objects out onto his hand.

They bite at their shield rims. They chew on the pieces.

Bright in his palm lay a small pile of teeth. Clean and white as new ivory. A few stray flecks of gold.

"Give them here, Kip. It's all right. I've got gloves."

Leslie took them from him gently and went back to the door and listened with his ear against the wood. When the sounds had died down he knelt again between the bunks and motioned for Kip to join him. They smoothed out the kerchief and arranged the teeth by size in an attempt to guess how many mouths they had come from. Kip had trouble deciding. A few of the molars were subtly yellowed at their crowns but that could have meant anything. Leslie moved them around like chess pieces, sucking his lower lip in concentration. Eventually he said something under his breath.

"What was that?"

"They're not all from one person."

"How can you tell?"

"I can't tell. I'm guessing. Some look older than the rest."

Kip was having trouble speaking. "Gold fillings," he got out finally.

"Just on three of them. That's not what this is about."

"Don't be an asshole. We don't have a clue."

Leslie didn't seem to hear him. "We can rule some things out," he was saying. "We can pare down our hypotheses and all that. Like Occam."

"Like who?"

"Occam, stupid. Occam's razor."

Kip almost burst out laughing. "You're just tossing words around."

"This isn't someone disposing of evidence, either. You wouldn't do it this way. You wouldn't trust the postal service."

"Hand-delivered," Kip said.

"What?"

"This one was hand-delivered. No return address. No postage."

Leslie squinted at the envelope. The noise in the hall had started up again. He began to sweep the teeth into his hand.

"Stop," said Kip.

"What for?"

Kip didn't answer. As if in a dream he took the smallest of the teeth between his fingers. A smooth pale incisor. He carried it to the window to make absolutely sure.

"You want to tell me what the fuck is going on?"

Kip set it on the windowsill and stepped out of the light. When Leslie finally spoke again Kip knew he'd seen it too.

"Okay now," Leslie stammered. "It's okay now. It's okay now. It's okay."

At the center of the incisor, exactly halfway up its face, was a shallow indentation where a gem had once been set.

5

They got up late the next morning and spent the few remaining hours of daylight at a crucifix-shaped building constructed to house the hulls of several thousand-year-old ships. Leslie had decided to play tourist, apparently, as if nothing out of the ordinary had happened the night before, and Kip was more than willing to oblige. He felt desensitized, adrift in his own body, as if his guidewires had been cut. Leslie, on the other hand—as far as Kip could tell—was happier than ever. Everything he saw seemed to enchant him.

"These were *grave* ships, Norvald. They found them buried in the ground, upright and fully loaded, as if they were still sailing. How wicked is that?"

"Pretty wicked."

"Here's the stuff that was buried with them," Leslie said, steering him by the elbow toward a row of glass vitrines. "These swords and spears and helmets were for the dead warriors to use." He peered at a yellow index card glued neatly to the wall. "The shields too. Everything. For use in battle on the other side."

"It's cold in here, Leslie."

"Remember what we agreed on? We're doing our homework." He shook his head in mock annoyance. "These could be your fucking ancestors, Norvald of the North. Your grandparents' grandparents' grandparents.'"

Kip didn't bother to answer.

"It says here that this amulet is supposed to be Thor's hammer," Leslie went on, already at the next display. "And this crazy grinning monkey face is Odin." He let out a chuckle. "I always thought Thor's hammer was invented by some hack at Marvel Comics."

Kip didn't answer. He was looking at the whittled face of Odin. It looked nothing like the wise old man he'd always seen in books. This was a leering one-eyed demon face, baring its teeth and sticking out its tongue.

"*Odin is the embodiment of every form of frenzy,*" Leslie read to him. "*From the bloodlust of the naked berserkers, who dedicated themselves to his glory, to erotic and poetic madness alike.*"

"That doesn't sound much like Marvel."

"*In the Ynglinga saga it is stated: At times Odin will call up dead men out of the ground, or sit down under those who have been hanged. On this account he is referred to as Prince of the Anonymous, the Corpse Father, Lord of the Hanged. War and sacrifice are his dominions—*"

By then Kip barely heard him. He was staring past the totem at a row of shields hung on a nearby wall: the wood stained black, the braces gone, the edges cracked and splintered. He didn't need to read the card to guess what sort of men had used them. In the wood he saw the marks that the berserkers' teeth had made.

On their way back to the hostel they stopped to get dinner. Leslie had asked someone at the Vikingskipshuset for recommendations—the apple-cheeked matron who ran the gift shop—and she'd suggested a traditional Nordic restaurant just east of downtown. He had put forth the argument, as they sat together at the back of an otherwise-empty municipal OsloBuss, that it might be to their advantage to find out how

Vikings ate. He was putting on even more of a show of high spirits than he'd done at the museum, laying it on thick for some disembodied audience, but Kip had begun to sense the fear behind his jolly tourist act. Somehow the knowledge helped him to relax.

"Supposedly this place serves *lapskaus*," Leslie said. "I'm guessing that you don't know what that is."

"You win a nickel."

"It's traditional Norwegian stew. You take beef and brown it and add it to stock. The Norsemen used to eat it on their ships."

"I'll be honest with you, Z. I'm not that hungry."

"We're not here on some goddamn weight-loss program, Norvald. You're going to need all the muscle mass you can build up."

They were crossing a bridge now, over a winding, narrow side arm of the bay. Kip looked down into the blackly gleaming water. "I hope not," he said.

He turned back to find Leslie grinning like a madman. "Jesus, Norvald. I can't believe I never made this connection before."

"What is it now?"

"That thing that used to freak people out about you. You know the thing."

"I'm not sure I—"

"Come on, Kip. That fucked up way you sometimes get. Those fits."

"That fucked up way I *used* to get, you mean."

"Your family's Norwegian. Didn't you tell me that?"

"Just on my father's side."

"On your father's side. Right." Leslie brought his fists to his temples and stuck out his thumbs.

"What's that supposed to be?"

"Viking horns, motherfucker. It's in your damn *genes*."

"I thought you said you'd done your homework. Horns were actually never—"

"Christopher Chanticleer Norvald," Leslie said dreamily. "Part-time berserker."

By blind chance the restaurant turned out to be one Kip had passed on his walk to Schweigaards Gate the day before. It was candlelit and tasteful and crowded with Norwegians in expensive-looking clothes. The hostess found it amusing that they wanted a table. Kip tried not to visualize getting the check.

"This must be what celebrities feel like," Leslie said once they'd been wedged into a corner. People were staring at them openly. He winked at some girls at the bar, who broke into scandalized giggles. "I feel like a taller, less talented Prince."

"I'm pretty sure Prince doesn't wear pleated chinos."

"This is a *feeling* I'm talking about. A state of inner being."

The stew when it came was mud-colored and savory, surprisingly subtle, with caramelized leeks and potatoes in a broth of thickened mead. Kip wasn't sure what mead was made of, exactly, but he hadn't felt so unconcerned in days. They ordered pints of bitter golden beer and sipped them slowly.

"Now we're talkin'," said Leslie.

"This is our plan, is it? Beef stew and beer?"

"Got a better one?"

Kip stared down into his pint. "That letter," he said.

Leslie ignored him.

"We need to find someone who speaks Norwegian."

"By a stroke of luck we find ourselves in Norway."

"Let's get it translated, then. Let's do it tonight."

"What's the rush?"

"No rush at all. Sorry to bother you. Enjoy your soup."

"My *lapskaus*."

"You think she's dead, don't you."

Leslie took a long pull of his beer and speared a chunk of beef with his fork and cut it into tidy little segments. "What happens if I say yes, Norvald? Do we go home? Do you ditch me with the check? Do you jam that butter knife into my eye?"

"I want to know what's in that letter."

"You already know what's in it. Wizards. Werewolves. Creatures of the night." Leslie directed his attention toward his *lapskaus*. The urge to slap him across his pompous face was all but overwhelming.

"You're scared of what we'll find out," Kip said finally.

Leslie didn't deny it. He was staring at the bar.

"Is that a cop?"

Kip followed Leslie's line of sight. "That guy sitting alone? The one with the mustache?"

Leslie nodded. "He's reading a paper. Trying not to look obvious."

"He looks incredibly obvious. He looks like an extra on *NYPD Blue*."

"Does that mean you think he's a cop, or that you think he isn't?"

"We haven't done anything, Leslie. We went to a museum. We're drinking a beer."

"He keeps looking at me."

"He probably thinks you're Prince."

Two pints later they were on the street again. It seemed too cold for snow but snow was falling. The man with the mustache had stayed where he was, and Kip was tempted to go right back in and join him. It felt like midnight on the far side of the moon.

"What time is it?"

"No idea."

"Nine, I'm guessing. Maybe not even that."

"What does it matter?"

"She isn't dead, Leslie."

Leslie's eyes were dull and far away. He took a long time answering.

"What if she is?"

Kip was already walking. "If she is that doesn't change a fucking thing."

"I admire your can-do attitude, Captain America. I'm sure you'll go far. But right now you're going in the wrong direction."

Kip turned up the collar of his parka against the wind and sped up slightly. It took Leslie more than half a block to grasp where they were going.

"Jesus, Kip—not now. Not like this. You must be suicidal."

"Just drunk."

"Hold on a second, will you? Don't do this. Slow down, for Christ's sake—let's just talk this through."

"You've been talking all day."

"First of all, no way is that shop open. Not this late. Secondly, we can't just go and ring the goddamn bell. We need some kind of—"

The wind was strong enough that Kip could hear it in the streetcar wires. Leslie had drawn even with him and was waving a gloved hand in his face, as if checking to see whether he'd gone blind.

"I can't go in there with you. Listen to me. You know that, don't you?"

"I know it."

They were at Schweigaards Gate already. At some point the chill had left him. His eyes were watering and his body felt electric.

"All right, you fucking lunatic. I'll wait out here as long as I can stand it. But that's not very long. I'm a son of the South."

Kip nodded distractedly.

"Are you hearing me, asshole? As soon as my bits start to tingle I'm catching a taxi."

Kip almost laughed. "We can't afford a taxi."

The windows of 56A were even blacker than they'd been by daylight and its door looked massive in the blowing dark. He went to the mailbox first, opening it gingerly, though no one could have heard him for the wind. Of course it was empty. He stared down into it stupidly, aware of the fact that he was stalling for time, hoping to cobble together some sort of cover story. Nothing came to him that didn't sound preposterous. But the truth was preposterous. The truth defied all belief. He counted down from ten and turned the handle of the door and watched it open in a kind of numb amazement.

For the space of a few seconds he believed himself alone. A larger room than he'd expected. Black walls, curling carpets, maplike waterstains across the ceiling. Posters and picture discs on narrow wooden shelves. Venom and Slayer and Mercyful Fate. Exotic-looking knives and throwing stars, the kind you'd see in an army surplus store back in the States. CDs stacked at random on the floor. If he'd been told in that moment that the shop was run by children he'd have had no cause to doubt it. He caught sight of a man behind the counter as the front door rattled closed.

"Hey," he said awkwardly, raising a hand.

The man had been reading some sort of catalog and he folded down a page to mark his place. His straight black hair was carefully brushed and fell far past his sloping shoulders. There was something delicate about his features, something androgynous and mild. He was nothing like the flame-haired Norseman Kip had been expecting.

"*Hei,*" the man answered, reaching under the counter.

Kip took in a breath to speak but stopped himself. As yet he could have been anyone, Norwegian or foreigner, friend or enemy, victim or accomplice. It was the moment before the first riff drops, when everything is possible.

"*Nej?*" said the man, bringing up a rusted pressed-tin box and prizing its lid open with his thumb. "*Hva vil du?*"

"English," Kip answered, unable to move. "Can we talk in English?"

The man's expression shifted. "You can tell me what you want."

"I'm not sure." Kip took a half step toward the counter. The man looked him up and down for a moment, then made what might have been a gesture of indifference. "Picture discs," he said flatly. "Tour shirts. Demos. Long players."

Kip ran his eyes methodically over the shelves. Death Angel. Deicide. Entombed. Sepultura. Nowhere did he see the albums he and Leslie had listened to so carefully in Venice. He tried to make sense of their absence. The man began cutting clippings from the catalog with an enormous pair of scissors that he'd taken from the tin. They looked like something used for shearing sheep.

"This is all mainstream shit," Kip said finally.

The man raised his head. "Again, please?"

"These records. These posters. If I wanted a VHS tape of *Powerslave Live* I could have stayed back home in Florida."

Now the man was looking at him closely. He might have been slightly nearsighted. He set the catalog aside and came around the counter. He was both shorter and more powerfully built than Kip had realized.

"Name," said the man, so softly that Kip barely understood him.

"Dusty Sinclair."

"Doosty," the man repeated.

"Close enough."

He didn't offer his own in return and Kip didn't ask. He brought the scissors thoughtfully to his lips. "We have traded tapes, Doosty? We have—" He searched for the word. "We have *corresponded*?"

Kip shook his head.

"No," the man murmured, seemingly to himself. "I would know this."

A night bus passed outside. The man sniffed the air strangely.

"I just got to Oslo," Kip said. "I was told if I came here—"

"You're exactly right, Doosty." The man took a step closer. "This is the mainstream shit."

"I heard you had real music here. Norwegian music."

"Who tells you?"

Kip hesitated. "Excuse me?"

"The music we have here. Who tells you?"

Through the blacked-out windowpanes he could hear the wind rising. His thoughts went to Leslie. He hoped he was gone.

"Per Ivar Lund."

He'd spoken the name impulsively, as soon it came to him, with no thought of the implications. He didn't know the implications. It hung in the air a moment, an almost visible thing, giving off a faint hum. Then it pulled back into the darkness like a ghost.

"Per," said the man. "Per is done."

"Done with what?"

"He finished his life in Kristiansand. One month ago." The man turned one of his palms slowly upward—the same all-purpose gesture as before. "He suicided."

Kip felt his head bobbing. "He always seemed weak."

The man went so utterly still, so unmoving and catlike, that Kip braced himself for some sudden act of violence. His eyes were on Kip but he seemed not to see him. He seemed to be listening to something in the street outside.

"Come tomorrow," he said. "I'll have the record then."

Only later, when Kip was already stumbling home through the wet wind along Schweigaards Gate, did it occur to him that he'd mentioned no record by name.

6

Back at the hostel Kip found Leslie eating Norwegian chocolate bars and licorice in his bunk. Crumpled scraps of silver wrapper lay around him on the mattress. He sat up and watched Kip unlacing his boots.

"That didn't take long. I've only been here for one Firkløver and a half. Highly recommended, by the way."

"I saw him, Leslie. We talked about music."

"You saw who?"

"Euronymous. Aarseth."

"Describe him."

"Small but ripped. Black stringy hair. There was no one else in there. It had to be him."

Leslie set aside the bar he'd been eating and licked his lips clean. The sight of it made Kip slightly queasy.

"All right, Norvald. Tell me everything that happened."

Kip's courage had left him on the long walk home. As he recounted the events of the past hour he could feel his teeth chattering. He was talking too quickly. Leslie had taken out a notebook and begun to jot things down.

"Did he seem at all suspicious?"

"*Suspicious* doesn't even do him justice." Kip tried to slow down.

"He's so goddamn creepy. He's got this weird way of talking—all stilted and fake. Like he learned English from watching *Conan the Barbarian*."

Leslie stopped writing.

"What's wrong?"

"I don't know about this, Norvald."

"It's under control."

"Those aren't the vibrations I'm getting. I see you. You're freaked."

Kip shook his head mechanically. "I'm locked in, Z. I'm right on target."

"Sooner or later you're going to say the wrong thing to them, you know. It's guaranteed to happen."

"I could use a little encouragement right now, to be honest. Some moral support."

"Huh?"

"I kind of hoped you'd be excited for me."

"*Excited* for you?"

"We're making progress. Things are happening. That's all I'm trying to say." He nodded to himself. "We're getting closer."

"Closer to what?"

A sound carried in from the hall—the squeaking of a rolling suitcase—and both of them fell silent as they listened to it pass. Business was picking up, apparently. Leslie lay back in his bunk.

"Tell me you're enjoying this, Norvald. Tell me that and I'm on the first flight back to Tampa."

The next morning Kip woke up alone in the room. He saw for the first time how joyless it was. No carpet on the plain pine floor, no pictures on the walls. Nothing but the standing lamp and the folding chair and the window with the flat gray light behind it. He climbed down from his bunk, still in yesterday's clothes, and went out to look for Leslie. He felt as if he hadn't slept at all.

He found him in what passed for the lobby, sprawled over not one but two vinyl beanbags, scribbling in his little notebook. The shaggy-headed teen at the front desk was bobbing his head to a nonexistent beat and reading something with total attention—a UK metal zine called *Kerrang!*, as chance would have it, that Kip occasionally wrote for. His most recent contribution had been an interview with Def Leppard's one-armed drummer, whose name escaped him at the moment, about practical jokes the band played while on tour. The distance between that conversation and the one he intended to have that same night with Øystein Aarseth made him momentarily giddy. It suddenly hit him how little he knew.

"Did you happen to notice what our bellhop is reading?" he said, taking a seat across from Leslie.

"Hampus."

"Excuse me?"

"His name is Hampus Olander. He moved here seven months ago from Stockholm."

"Okay. Did you see what he's reading?"

"Every second kid in this country is a metalhead, Norvald. If we'd come here three or four years ago—back when I still gave a shit—I'd have thought we'd died and gone to banger heaven."

"Maybe we have."

Leslie put aside his pen. "That might just be the single dumbest thing you've ever said to me."

"I'm serious. I can see why Kira came here."

"I don't want to talk about Kira."

"She always wanted the stakes to be higher, didn't she? Life and death, she used to say. And *everything* is life and death for these kids. No middle ground. No compromise."

"He talks to one of them for fifteen minutes and—bingo! He's an expert."

"Everyone else is a sellout. Everyone else is weak. Aarseth even hates the records that he sells in his own shop."

"And that gets you all hot and bothered."

"What? Not at all. But for Kira—"

"Exactly. At last you see the light. I'm glad you've come around."

Kip was on his guard at once. "Come around to what?"

"Kira wasn't 'taken,' Kip. No one 'took' anybody. That girl came here, with those people, because she wanted to. Because it turned her on. You just said as much yourself."

Kip stared at him. "I'm going to have to defer to the professionals on this one. They were very clear, at least to me, that they're not ruling out the possibility—"

"The *professionals*." Leslie made a face.

"Don't start doing that again. Don't start repeating—"

"He never came here, you know. Mothersbaugh. He never even came to Norway."

"Shut up, Z. There's no way you could know that."

"They're preparing a preliminary assessment, he told me. Those were his exact words. A cost appraisal, basically. To figure out if it's even worth their time."

"You're talking out of your ass right now. One hundred percent just talking—"

"What am I doing here, Kip?"

"Excuse me?"

"I'm asking you in all sincerity. I'd like to hear your take."

Kip looked around at the depressing little lobby. "I need some coffee before we do this. Is there a machine?"

Leslie didn't answer. The look in his eyes was more frightening than anything Kip had seen the night before. He'd come to some sort of decision.

"All right. You said it yourself, Z. I'm out of my depth here. I'm a hack from California who's spent the last two and a half years writing about music I have zero interest in. Exactly the kind of radio-friendly crap these people hate." He glanced at Hampus the bellhop and lowered his voice. "I need your knowledge—I admit it. I need your understanding. It makes no difference how long you've been quote-unquote *retired* from the scene. You have the gift."

Leslie let his eyes close. "I don't understand the first thing about these batshit sons of bitches. Nothing you couldn't get off the back of an LP."

"You can tell me what's bullshit," Kip said, feeling himself start to panic. "You can tell me what's true. You can keep me from making some stupid mistake."

Leslie nodded. "Or we can take those letters straight to Interpol and tell them what we know."

Kip could feel his face twitching. "We don't know anything yet. You just said so yourself."

"We've got a bag of teeth. A bag of *teeth*, Norvald. That's physical evidence."

"You're contradicting yourself, do you realize that? You basically just told me the police are amateurs."

"And what does that make us?"

"You're scared," Kip said. "That's fine. I understand."

"I'll tell you something for free. If you're not scared, boy, you're fucked. Next time it's *your* teeth in that mailbox."

Kip held up a hand. "Let me just say what I think. Can I do that? These kids aren't capable of—whatever it is we think is happening. Breaking into a gun shop, maybe. Even setting some buildings on fire. But not the rest. Not what happened to Kira."

"What are you talking about?"

"I don't think it's *them*, Leslie. There's somebody else."

"Who?"

He hesitated. "The voice on that record. The one giving that speech—or sermon, or whatever it is—in the woods."

Leslie chose not to dignify that with an answer. They sat glaring at each other now with their heads slightly bowed, their bent knees almost touching, like exhausted commuters on an evening train. Hampus grunted softly in the background, still reading *Kerrang!*, still paying them no attention whatsoever. Kip's beanbag squeaked grotesquely as he eased his body forward.

"If you want to leave just tell me. I can go and change the ticket. But I'm staying till I find her."

"You think that hillbilly bitch would do the same for me, Norvald? Or for anyone else on this planet, you included? I'm sitting here, watching you, shaking my head. That girl is either in an unmarked grave somewhere or she's a goddamn Nazi."

Kip waited until he was sure Leslie had nothing else to say.

"It doesn't matter what Kira would do."

"I'm shaking my head at this. Just sitting here literally shaking my head."

"We loved each other," Kip said quietly. "All of us. Not just me and Kira."

"Keep me the fuck out of this equation."

"I can't do that, Leslie. I'm sorry."

"She left you, Kip. She walked right out. She dumped you on your ass."

"We don't know that for sure."

"Jesus Christ, man. She predicted it a hundred times. Before you even got together. She just knew."

A humming started up somewhere—the far side of the wall, perhaps, or underneath the floor. Kip got to his feet.

"I tell you what I think."

"Go ahead."

"You don't stop loving someone. Ever. It's a permanent condition."

"Kira didn't see it that way."

He was the one shaking his head now—some animal reflex. "You can want to be away from someone. You can want to be away from them forever. After Kira left I felt that way myself."

"Then explain to me—"

"But loving someone is a fact. That's how I see it. It's a mutation to your basic way of thinking. And the way that I think—the way I understand the world—comes down to you and me and Kira. It's that simple, Leslie. For better or for worse. That's how it's going to be until I die."

The humming fell away. He'd never seen Leslie look so gray-faced and brittle, sunk down in that hideous purple beanbag like some lost king on a throne. So regretful and wise. So aghast at man's folly. Leslie gazed down in perfect sadness at the notebook in his lap. Eventually he worked himself upright.

"We need to talk about Satan."

Kip heard himself laugh. "Satan. Yes. Absolutely."

"Go get something to write on."

7

That afternoon the shop was full of people. Most of them looked like approximations of Aarseth—dyed-black hair in various stages of discoloration, combat boots and biker jackets, band shirts with cutoff sleeves and completely illegible logos—but some were so young that they still just looked like kids. They were drinking beer and striking disaffected poses, staring off into the middle distance, attempting to be invisible and conspicuous at once. It reminded Kip of Venice. He wondered how many of them had known Kira.

Discreetly he worked his way into the crowd. Smoke hung thick in the air and a riff shook the floor: a cascading bandsaw tritone he was sure he'd heard before. No one looked at him twice. No one was looking at anyone. People's lips were moving and from this he judged that they were having conversations but he might as well have been watching closed-circuit TV. He was seeing a video of himself—grainy security footage—conducting highly sophisticated surveillance operations behind enemy lines. He was looking for Aarseth or hiding from Aarseth; it was hard to say which. He was casing the joint. He was trying to avoid being beaten to death with a bottle of lager.

At some point he found himself with his back against the counter and he ducked underneath it and rummaged through the cluttered plywood shelves below the register. Dozens of unopened utility statements.

The little tin box where Aarseth kept his coins and scissors. A small stack of catalogs for sporting goods and a German guide to large-bore hunting rifles. A cheaply printed pamphlet, in Cyrillic, full of leering Jewish caricatures. A book in English detailing the Armenian genocide. A beginner's guide to calisthenics. On the lowest shelf, next to three neatly rolled joints, a Polaroid of a head of long blond hair, gender unknown, streaked with clotted blood and chips of splintered bone.

"True Norwegian black metal," a voice above him shouted.

He jerked back in surprise, expecting Aarseth—but in Aarseth's place he saw a stocky girl with frizzled orange hair. She stared down at him coldly.

"I've heard this song before," he said, if only to say something.

The girl didn't answer.

"Do you know who it is?"

"Hva vil du?"

"This record. This album. You'll have to speak English."

"Burzum," the girl said. She spoke the word slowly and with great precision, like a magic spell.

"I like it," he told her. She seemed not to hear him.

"I like it," he repeated. "Do you speak any English?"

She nodded.

"Do you know Øystein Aarseth? Euronymous? I'm trying to—"

Her bleary eyes went wide. "Your death is here."

He'd been reading her lips—a skill he'd honed in half a decade's worth of talk in crowded clubs—and it was possible, even likely, that he'd misunderstood. She might have been speaking Norwegian, or Swedish, or some secret language of her own invention.

"I'm not sure I heard that right. Who did you say is here?"

"Komme." She leaned over the counter and caught the sleeve of his parka and guided him up. She was drunk but in no way flirtatious. She had an air about her of someone fulfilling an onerous duty. She watched him slip under the counter and took hold of him again and propelled him toward the back room of the shop.

The music went shrill as they moved through the crowd, working itself into hysterics, the high end inscribing itself across his inner ear like a tack across a blackboard. They passed through a doorway, then another, then a tattered velvet curtain. A cast-iron staircase came up out of nowhere. The girl went down into the dark and Kip went stumbling after. All his bluster had left him. He was following a drunken groupie down into some kind of crypt.

At the bottom of the stairs, in a room almost completely filled with crates and shipping boxes, she was waiting for him with three men in corpse paint holding gleaming silver knives. Even in that low light Kip knew one of them was Aarseth.

"Our American," said Aarseth. He gave no sign of surprise. The men beside him scowled at Kip out of their blackened eye sockets, neither moving nor speaking, then went back to whatever they were doing with the knives. They held them loosely by the blade, hefting them in their open palms, less like killers than discriminating shoppers. Unreality broke over him again. He looked at these men with their faces crudely and childishly painted and thought of the Polaroid he'd seen upstairs and could draw no plausible connection between them. The girl gestured at him and hissed something softly into Aarseth's ear. Aarseth ignored her. He had eyes only for Kip.

"Per Ivar's friend Dusty."

"You said to come back."

"I said this." Aarseth smiled. "And you did what I say."

What light there was bled weakly through the gaps between the crates. Aarseth was dressed in the same clothes as the night before, as far as Kip could tell, with the addition of the corpse paint and enormous steel-tipped boots. Something hung from his wrist that Kip couldn't make out—a dark wooden object, lopsided and heavy. The others had turned away now but the blades of the knives held the light. Blades as long as his forearm and perfectly straight. Eventually he saw that they were bayonets.

"You like weapons," said Aarseth.

"I like music better."

Aarseth was still smiling. "Of course! You are here for the music."

"You said you'd have a record for me."

"There are no record shops in America?"

"Not like this one."

The answer clearly pleased him. "Yes," he said. "Not like this one."

The girl said something angrily in Norwegian and retreated up the staircase. Aarseth's face remained unchanged. Kip focused on his breathing.

"What did she say?"

Aarseth was a long time answering. "She says you are a counterfeit."

"I don't get it. A counterfeit what?"

"An actor." Aarseth made a curious clutching motion in the dark, as if trying to catch a nonexistent fly. "A liar."

"She wanted to fuck me."

"Of course. She is a whore."

Aarseth leaned toward him now, observing his reaction. He was waiting for something. Some confirmation. Some tell.

"I don't take it personally," Kip found himself mumbling. "I'm probably the first American she's ever seen up close."

Aarseth shook his head comfortably. "You are not her first American."

The words were out before he could check them. "I actually had a friend come through town—one year back, maybe less. I wonder if she ever showed up here."

"A friend," Aarseth repeated. "Like Per Ivar Lund."

"Nothing like him."

"Ah." His eyes seemed to brighten. "Not weak."

"A girl from America. From California." Kip pushed the hair back from his forehead. "She had a scar here."

"I see—an American girl." His voice was unchanged but his expression had clouded. "And this is the reason you came."

"You know why I came. You said you'd have a record—"

"The girl from Berlin?" Aarseth said languidly. "Magnus Haugan's bitch?"

The air seized in Kip's throat. It occurred to him then that Aarseth's voice never varied, never betrayed the least emotion, no matter what he happened to be saying. If it was an act of some kind it was a consummate act. The fey psychopath. The object he held was a turned length of wood, like the leg of a table, with nails driven through its head to make a mace.

"This girl," Kip got out finally. "She had that kind of scar?"

Aarseth touched a finger lightly to his own forehead. "Why should I say?"

"Cut the shit. Did you meet her or didn't you?"

Aarseth clapped his hands lightly and the men with the knives spun around as if they'd heard a shot. The iron railing dug into Kip's shoulders as they crowded around him. Some new element was in play. Some form of brinksmanship. He was pushing his luck to its outermost limit. Aarseth lifted his weapon with a stately dignity and brought it down against the hollow of Kip's chest.

"Your friend Lund," he said softly. "Your friend who is dead."

"I don't care about Lund."

Aarseth nodded. "How well did you know him, I wonder."

"I keep telling you—"

"Lund was interested in Haugan's bitch as well."

"I don't understand."

Again he made his strange and sphinxlike gesture. "He had her and lost her. He was hoping to—*recover* her. Would this be the word?"

"Recover her from where?"

"Lund was thinking he could do this. Without grievance. Without harm." Aarseth went quiet for a moment. "You say your friend was weak. You are mistaken. He died as a man."

Kip took his tongue between his teeth and bit down hard to keep from answering. He was thinking of the only time he'd seen Lund, in that basement club in Kreuzberg: a stoop-shouldered man with a humorless face. Lund who had since burned to death in his car. One of the men stood behind him now, just out of his field of vision, close enough that Kip could smell his breath. It stank sweetly of lager. At some point Aarseth's eyes had fallen closed.

"I answered to your question, Per Ivar's friend Dusty. Now answer to mine."

A hand closed on Kip's collar. It felt almost gentle. He waited but Aarseth said nothing.

"What do you want to know?"

His dark eyes came open. "You meet the devil in the forest."

"That's not a question."

"You meet the devil in the forest," Aarseth repeated, his voice inflectionless as ever. "How do you greet him?"

The man to Aarseth's left had started giggling. It was unsettling to watch someone in corpse paint doing that. The question was a riddle. A trap of some kind. Kip could feel himself faltering. He tried to remember what Leslie had taught him.

"There isn't any devil in the forest."

"What do you say?"

"I create my own good. I create my own evil." He braced himself against the railing. "'Satan' is just a Christian word. It's what they call free will."

For a bright suspended instant no one spoke. The men stared at him. They were going to spit in his face. They were going to buy him a beer. They were going to take their bayonets and skin him like a lamb.

Finally Aarseth heaved a sigh. "I thought you were police."

"No one's perfect," said Kip.

Someone called down from upstairs. Aarseth spoke calmly to the men and they wrapped the bayonets in oilcloth and packed them away in the nearest of the crates and screwed the top shut and went swiftly up the stairs in single file. He himself stayed as he was, neither moving nor blinking. He was waiting for something. He looked almost wistful.

"The Count," he said at last. "The Count can tell."

Kip wasn't sure he'd heard correctly. "The Count of what?"

In place of a reply Aarseth gestured deeper into the cellar, past the boxes and crates, toward a passageway that Kip had failed to notice. Reflected light shone palely at its turning.

"All right, then," Kip heard himself mutter.

"All *right*, then," Aarseth echoed. He gave Kip two thumbs-up, flashing his teeth, then turned and started slowly up the staircase. At the sixth or seventh step he paused.

"I'll tell you one thing else, Per Ivar's friend."

"What is it?"

"There is a devil in the forest. I have met him."

8

The passage was long and damp and lined with chicken-wire cages locked with combination padlocks, the kind high school kids put on their lockers. Kip fully expected them to contain Japanese katanas or semiautomatic rifles or heaps of human bones but most were empty, and the few that weren't were packed haphazardly with boxes of cassettes and piles of shirts and crates of shrink-wrapped vinyl. He made out the titles of records by Burzum and Darkthrone and Aarseth's own band, Mayhem, and a scattering of other releases by Helvete's tiny label. None of them were of interest to him now.

A few steps from the turning he hung back and listened. The music that had been so punishing upstairs was now a distant keening in a minor key. He wavered there, unsure what to do next, shifting from one foot to the other in the clammy dark. He seemed to have burned through his last reserves of both stupidity and courage. Things were moving too quickly. For the first time since he'd come downstairs he had a chance to think.

"Hvem er det?"

A man's voice, thin but confident. Kip took a half step forward.

"Hvem her det nå? Øystein?"

"No," he answered, willing himself to step around the corner.

He found himself on the threshold of a filthy room with walls of yellowed plaster. A cot, a high-backed armchair, a candelabrum in the corner. The words BLACK METAL crudely painted in block script above the armchair. In the middle of the room a crowbar and an open packing crate. Above the crate a handsome man with blond hair past his shoulders.

Before Kip had managed to make sense of what he was seeing the man was coming toward him with the crowbar in his hands.

"Hvem er du?"

"English, please. Do you speak English?"

The man stopped short and gave a low curse of surprise. But his English when he answered was ready and fluid—much better than Aarseth's. He stood leaning on the crowbar like a dandy on a cane.

"If you're looking for the toilet then you've missed it, I'm afraid."

"Can I come in?"

"That depends."

Kip held up his hands and took a tentative step forward. "Are you the Count?"

"Are you a cop?"

"That's the second time someone's made that joke tonight."

The man smiled. "It's the parka you're wearing. Something about it just screams 'law enforcement.'"

Kip kept his eyes on the crowbar. "Were you going to hit me with that?"

"Who are you, friend? Some new disciple of the horse's ass upstairs?"

Kip hesitated. "Euronymous, you mean?"

"That answers my question. No one calls him that but the members of his fan club."

"I couldn't give two shits about Euronymous."

The man looked him over. "It's not easy to get in the great Øystein's good graces. He has a weakness for Americans, it's true—but I'm curious, I confess. You'll have to tell me how you managed it."

"What makes you think I did?"

"You're here, first of all. Down here, in the throne room." The man's grin widened. "And you've still got your teeth."

It was intended as a joke, it must have been, but the cellar floor tipped under Kip regardless. He thought of the battered filthy envelope, of the threadbare linen handkerchief so carefully folded. For all he knew this man himself had sent it.

"Øystein sends you to me," he said quietly, apparently to himself. "What is he playing at?"

"Euronymous—Øystein—says you might know someone—"

"Time is passing, friend. Come in or fuck off."

The man turned the crate over and offered it to him with a courtly flourish. He was dressed in what looked to be an actual priest's cassock, minus the collar, cinched at the waist with a studded leather cummerbund. His hair was as lovingly maintained as Aarseth's, as carefully brushed and arranged, but there was nothing androgynous about him. His pale eyes shone with interest. On the metal cot behind him lay a military duffel and a heavy butane lighter and an expensive-looking pair of field binoculars. He might have been packing for a backwoods camping trip. He sat down and waited for Kip to address him.

"Do you live here?" Kip asked him.

"Hell no, friend. I'm from Bergen. This place is a sewer."

"Are you actually a count?"

He laughed. "No one uses their Christian name here. 'The Count' is something I play at, that's all. For when I make my music."

Something stirred in Kip's brain. "Burzum," he said.

"Gesundheit."

"You're Count Grishnackh, aren't you. That's your music they're playing upstairs."

Again the man studied him. "I'm amazed Øystein let you down here. Truly."

"It surprises me too, to be honest."

"He must see something in you." Grishnackh nodded to himself. "Or he's doing this to fuck with me somehow."

"I wouldn't know about that."

"In any case, I accept Øystein's challenge. You can tell him that from me."

Kip said nothing.

"Now, then. What's your made-up name, friend?"

"Dusty."

"You're a stranger here, Dusty. This isn't your place." He took up the binoculars and stared at Kip through them. "But you don't seem afraid."

Kip shrugged his shoulders.

"That must mean you're off. Slightly mentally ill. Maybe that's what Øystein likes about you."

"Or maybe he's planning to kill me," Kip said without thinking.

"What! Øystein Aarseth? All the great Euronymous does is talk. He's nothing but a—" Grishnackh thought for a moment. "A *hype man*. Is that what your Africans call it?"

"My what?"

"Your *Africans*. Your rappers. The man who jumps around before the show."

He felt himself nodding.

"I suppose 'gatekeeper' is the better term. This is how Øystein thinks of himself. As the gatekeeper." Grishnackh heaved a sigh. "But what's beyond the gate, Dusty—*that* is past his understanding."

"If you say so."

"What a strange way of talking! I just *did* say so." He sat back on the cot. "But you—you may be different." He brought his hands together in a vaguely prayer-like gesture. "Are you different?"

"I'm just a kid who likes metal."

"Bullshit, Dusty. Most people—most Norwegians—would run from this place. And here you are." Grishnackh shook his head. "Like some tough guy. Some fucking Charles Norris."

"Chuck Norris, I think you mean."

"You're in trouble just for coming here, you know. You could get yourself deported, Dusty. Even sent to prison."

"I've been there before," Kip said calmly.

That got Grishnackh's attention. "To prison?"

"Let's talk about Øystein."

Grishnackh was sitting up straight now. "I'll tell you about Øystein.

He's not even a genuine Norseman. He's a Laplander—a Sami. He's worse than a Jew."

Kip didn't answer.

"Has he talked to you about the devil yet?"

"About ten minutes ago."

"You see? He's still stuck up to his neck in Christianity. This weakens a person, like worms in the brain." He held up a finger. "When you abandon Christ—truly abandon him—Satan falls away as well."

"I guess that stands to reason."

"What exactly did he tell you? About the devil, I mean."

"He said that he'd met him."

Grishnackh cursed in Norwegian and snatched at Kip's sleeve. "Now let *me* tell you something. Øystein Aarseth is a coward. He needs to name things, you see, so as not to fear them—to categorize them, itemize them, like a tax accountant. I've been in those woods myself, the ones he talks about, and I've never seen Satan. I've never seen God, either. But I see the darkness that creeps up over my house."

His mouth snapped shut then with a wooden-sounding click, like the jaws of a marionette. His lips were working strangely and his eyes were wide and starting. He seemed almost to have forgotten Kip was there.

"Count?"

Grishnackh gave a slight nod.

"I'm looking for someone. An American girl. Aarseth told me you knew her."

"What did I just tell you about Aarseth?"

"That he believes things he shouldn't."

"That he *speaks* things he shouldn't," said Grishnackh. "That he gives names to what is rightfully left nameless."

"Nameless?" Kip took in a breath. "Please tell me what that means."

"You may be Øystein's new American, Dusty, but that doesn't make you mine."

"Hold on," Kip stammered. "Hold on a second. If you could just—"

"Run along, friend. Good luck finding your bitch."

9

Over the next seven weeks Kip spent as much time at 56A as Leslie would allow. Aarseth's unpredictable hours mystified him at first, and he'd often find Helvete locked and dark when he arrived; eventually, however, once he'd become accepted by the Circle, he knew in advance when the door would be open. It took time to put his new friends' suspicions to rest—the steady parade of tiny cuts, the petty humiliations, reminded him of starting over at an unfamiliar school—but that, after all, was something life had well prepared him for. And also he had Leslie.

It was plain to see that Euronymous and the Count were bitter rivals, and it didn't take Leslie long to realize that Kip's status as a foreigner, and especially as an American, could be leveraged to his strategic benefit. He belonged to no faction, he carried no baggage, and therefore he was free to choose a side. Soon enough, if he played his cards right, the two camps would start competing for his favor. "These are *kids*, Norvald. Don't forget that. It makes them dangerous—no question about it. But it also makes them dumb."

They were fighting over him within the month.

That first night at Helvete, after his talk with the Count, Kip had found Aarseth sitting in a metal folding chair at the top of the stairs, visibly drunk, the corpse paint smudged around his mouth and hairline. He'd clearly been waiting, with mounting impatience, for Kip to emerge from the throne room. He started in on Grishnackh right away.

"*Nektet*," slurred Aarseth. "Rejected."

"What?"

"I should have cautioned you, Per Ivar's friend. The Count is not so welcoming as I."

"I'd have to disagree," said Kip. "The Count was very helpful."

"Helpful?" Aarseth scoffed. "And how?"

"The first thing he did was explain about you."

He watched the words land. Leslie would have enjoyed it. Aarseth gave a kind of groan and took him by the elbow. "My turn now," he hissed. "Grishnackh is—*false*, you understand? False prophet. A liar. He wants to be where I am, Dusty—right here in my place." He sucked in a breath. "But you know this."

"I'm a stranger here," said Kip. "I don't know anything."

Aarseth studied him then, his painted mouth hanging open. "I understand this," he said finally. "Do you understand this, Dusty?"

"I don't know what you mean."

"It would be good for you—for an American, a stranger here in Norway—to have a friend."

"You're right."

"Of course I am." Aarseth's masklike face arranged itself into what might have been a grin. "And this is why you have to choose."

"The Circle" was what they called themselves, at least when Aarseth was around; but infighting was so bitter, and consensus so fleeting, that soon the name—at least to Kip—had come to seem a kind of inside joke. Leslie was right about how insecure they were. He was right about everything. The idea that a few dozen paranoid depressives with impulse-control issues could pose any serious threat to the fabric of Scandinavian society was hard for Kip to credit as he sat listening to two teenagers argue over whose drummer was faster, or whose worldview was bleaker, or whether or not the Nazi High Command was hiding under the Ross Ice Shelf in the Antarctic, monitoring surface life in SS airships that humanity mistook for UFOs.

Behind these theatrics of late adolescence, however, Kip caught occasional glimpses of something else, something furtive—a presence that revealed itself only in flickers, like the violence half concealed by Grishnackh's smile. Events were alluded to in unguarded moments; passing references were made, then instantly suppressed. There were details that Euronymous kept from the Count, and things the Count knew that Euronymous wanted nothing to do with, for reasons Kip had yet to understand. They were jealous of each other, that much couldn't have been clearer—envious, suspicious, covetous of each other's influence over the Circle—but there were matters, evidently, that both agreed should not be spoken of.

Each day he grew more certain. There was something underneath.

Back at the hostel, no matter the hour, Leslie would demand a full debriefing. They had moved into cheaper quarters by then, by generous arrangement with Hampus the bellhop; he and Leslie went out drinking most nights, sometimes to the occasional gig. Hampus had nothing but contempt for black metal—he called it "devil's penis envy music"—but he was a gold mine of intelligence about the local scene. Death metal still reigned supreme, he insisted: Swedish bands like Entombed and Dissection drew crowds that the face-painted posers who hung out in Aarseth's shabby little shop could only dream of. The Helvete scene was negligible, insignificant, and it was going to stay that way. Besides, he sometimes added quietly, everybody knew the shop was just a front.

Kip, meanwhile, was packing and unpacking stock in Helvete's basement, going on beer runs, doing everything but ringing up the sales. Even those members of the Circle who distrusted him, and there were more than a few, were getting used to having him around. True to Leslie's predictions, his foreignness—even, to some degree, his ignorance of the language—lent him a special status, both privileged and powerless, something between a visiting dignitary and a mascot. More and more of the regulars began to seek his company, even as they laughed at him for his mainstream metal views. The rules—and there were many rules—did not apply to him. He wondered whether it had been that way for Kira.

The struggle between Aarseth and Grishnackh was for nothing less than control of the Circle, and from what Kip could tell the stakes were absolute. The Count framed the conflict as talk versus action: Euronymous preached armed insurrection against what he called "daylight society," and especially against the Church of Norway, but his words were empty fantasy. He was unwilling—or unable—to cut his ties to the church he railed against.

The problem, Grishnackh argued, was that Øystein Aarseth was afraid to die.

"Listen closely now, Dusty," he told Kip one night in the throne room. "The entire Christian concept of 'right and wrong' must be rejected. The so-called *evil* that the Church of Norway fears, and that our laws supposedly protect us from, is the name that they have given to the power that came *before*: the gods our people worshipped and the forces that they served. The forces of nature, in other words. What our forefathers called the Aesir. And the Aesir are still here, Dusty. All around us. Even in this corrupt and filthy city."

"Filthy?" Kip answered. "I've got to say, compared to where I'm from—"

"I've said all this to Øystein, of course, but he chooses not to listen. I've shown him the Aesir's traces. He's seen them himself—in the woods, in the snow. But he failed to free his Sami mind from its conditioning. You understand? He wanted to see the goat-faced man they teach in Sunday school. And so, of course, he saw him."

Kip hesitated, trying to read Grishnackh's expression. "Sunday school here sounds pretty different from the States," he said.

"I'm not interested in making jokes now, Dusty. These are words to live or die by."

"All right."

"The priests came here a thousand years ago, clinging like women to the skirts of the Judeo-Christian armies, and built their dainty wooden churches over our most sacred sites. But I'll tell you a secret. Those sites are not destroyed, Dusty. They have only been hidden. The gods are still there—whispering."

Kip said nothing to that.

"I see the fire in your eyes, Dusty. I know that you hear me. But men like our friend Euronymous—much as it pains me to say it—move through this world with wax from votive candles plugging up their ears."

Euronymous's rebuttal, that same afternoon, was concise and to the point. "Watch out for Grishnackh and his Viking shit."

Slowly but surely, over the days and weeks, Kip began to find his footing in the Circle. It was a question of balance, as with any other form of espionage. Grishnackh was more volatile, and therefore the more clear and present danger; but Aarseth was much harder to predict. Every so often, Kip would glance up from a conversation to discover him watching from a distance, unmoving and silent, the smile on his face impossible to make sense of. With Grishnackh, on the other hand, Kip always knew why. He used his smile as cover for his anger.

The moment he'd been working toward came suddenly, two days shy of the fifth week. He was alone with the Count in the throne room, packing Burzum CDs into brown paper mailers, when suddenly Grishnackh took him by the shoulder.

"And how are things with Crazy Dusty? Does he still not care a damn?"

"Not much."

"I happen to be asking for a reason."

Kip put down the box he'd been holding. "I'm listening."

"I'm sure you've seen the bag that I keep packed. The military duffel."

"I figured it was for a camping trip."

"A camping trip, friend? In the middle of winter?"

"What else?"

Grishnackh closed his eyes. "Things are too—*open* here, Dusty. Too undisciplined. I came here on business. My business is done."

"But this is where the Circle is."

"Exactly."

"You've lost me."

"I don't intend to sit around in this moldy basement talking about revolution until we get ourselves arrested. I'm going back to the Atlantic coast, to Bergen, where my people are. We have churches there too. Some of the most beautiful in Norway."

Kip shrugged and said nothing. Keeping his mouth shut, he'd learned, was the best way to get Grishnackh talking.

"We have a saying in this country. I think you might like it. A man ought to set foot in a church exactly three times in his life." Grishnackh held up three fingers. "And the third time should be in a box."

"That's funny."

"I was too young to resist on the first two occasions, but I plan on making my third visit count. And the box that *I'll* be bringing, Dusty, is a box of fucking matches."

"Aarseth says the time isn't right for—"

"Fuck Aarseth." Grishnackh punched him lightly in the shoulder. "You're more than just a talker. Am I wrong in thinking this? You told me once that you'd spent time in prison."

Every possible answer to this question made the circuit of Kip's skull.

"You're right," he said. "I did."

"Then picture this with me. A bonfire where the ancient fires were set. Both an act of worship, brother, and an act of war. A symbol that even the most degenerate can understand—a small flame, no greater than a candle, feeding on the timbers of a Christian house of God."

Kip felt suddenly light-headed. All the waiting had been worth it. He had only to accept.

Grishnackh's voice dropped to a whisper. "You also said that the blood of this race flows in your own veins. Were you lying to me?"

"I wasn't lying," he heard himself answer.

"Of course you weren't. And that's why you must come."

Kip kept his face impassive.

"What makes you hesitate, Dusty? Is it the Circle? You have no respect for Øystein Aarseth, that much is plain. In any case, he can't hold back the tide. He knows that he's—what's the saying in English?"

"Over the hill," Kip said softly.

"Exactly. That's *exactly* what he is."

"All right, Grishnackh. I'll go."

Grishnackh gave a reedy laugh and clapped his hands together. "Crazy Dusty! I never doubted it. Now, the first thing you must do—"

"I'll go on one condition."

His eyes darkened at once. "A *condition*. And what might that be?"

"I want an answer to my question."

He raised his eyebrows. "But you haven't asked me any!"

Kip watched him. For a moment he seemed not to understand.

"The girl," he said.

Kip nodded.

A look that might almost have been regret passed over Grishnackh's boyish face. When he spoke again his voice was greatly changed.

"Dusty," he said.

"I'm listening."

"You should never ask a thing unless you want to know the answer."

Kip was on his feet already, pulling on his gloves and parka. Grishnackh shook his head and cursed under his breath.

"Hold on, Dusty. Hold on one damn minute."

"I'm tired of this."

"Haugan took her. I told you."

"I don't know what that means."

"You'll be pleased to know that Haugan is in Bergen. You could see him tomorrow."

"Tell me about him."

"I'll tell you *this*, Dusty." Grishnackh cleared his throat strangely. "Magnus Haugan is the smallest of your worries."

Kip stood poised in the doorway, suspended there mutely, waiting for him to go on. But he didn't go on. He sat on the cot with his mouth tightly closed.

"You can take me to Haugan? You know where he lives?"

"We are going to meet him."

"When?"

"We leave Oslo at midday tomorrow."

"I'll be there."

"Of *course* you will!" Grishnackh was his jaunty self again, leaping up from the cot and shaking Kip's hand with mock formality. "That pleases me greatly. But I have a condition as well."

"What is it?"

"If we're going to break the law together, Dusty, we really ought to know each other's names." He kept Kip's hand in both of his. "Our true names."

Kip felt his arm stiffen. "I'm not sure what you mean."

"Surely 'Dusty' is an invention?"

Kip thought hard for a moment. "I already told you it was. My given name is Christopher."

"What a happenstance! My parents named me Kristian." Grishnackh laughed again. "For obvious reasons, I changed it."

"To what?"

"My legal name now is Varg. This is what you will call me."

"Varg," Kip repeated. The sound hung strangely in the room.

"An old word, brother Christopher. Very old. A way of saying wolf."

"Wolf," Kip said. "Okay."

"It suits me, don't you think?"

"Sure." Kip took back his hand. "I should probably head—"

"She was here, Christopher."

"What?"

"That girlfriend of yours. She stayed here, in this room. With her good friend Magnus Haugan."

Kip kept his voice steady. "You're sure about that?"

Grishnackh bowed and reached for something on the floor behind the cot. "She left this bag. Or Magnus did. I haven't looked inside."

"A bag," Kip said hoarsely. "Okay."

Grishnackh pressed a dark bundle into Kip's hands: a small canvas backpack, gray and water-stained and slightly damp. "A gift," he said, and stepped out of the room.

Kip sat on the cot with the pack in his lap, listening to Grishnackh's steps receding down the passage. Even once they were gone he forced himself to wait for a slow count of ten, the way Oona had taught him long ago, to pacify his nerves.

Inside the pack he found two pairs of plain black socks and a half-eaten package of *goro* cookies and a band shirt that he recognized immediately as Kira's: MERCYFUL FATE U.S. CANADA 1989. Below that, a thin stack of pages torn from a palm-sized spiral notebook. He arranged them in a row across the mattress.

> *I listened to music to make me alive. To make the *world* alive I mean to say or at least to make it real. I had a problem with that. With believing in things. Everything felt unreal to me & nothing ever mattered. ~~Not even myself~~ my own self least of all.*

> *There was never any music in my house when I grew up. Not even shit music. Mostly it was just quiet. My mother would sometimes stay shut up for weeks & weeks. It was a dead place but not the way Your house is dead Corpse Father. Not the kind of dead that ~~erases you~~ Per and Magnus talk about. My fathers house was just a flat gray place where bad things sometimes happened. ~~They happened in silence mostly. I don't know if You'll understand me when I~~*

*Ive started this & torn it up a dozen times at least. When can I just *see* You*

Magnus tells me Im stupid. That of course You understand. Of course You know. He tells me that You know us like a rider knows his horses. Like a hunter knows his deer. But the longer I go without seeing You the more mixed up I get. The more ~~desperate or~~ doubtful. How could You understand my childhood when You never were a child?

I know what Youll tell me. The past is dead skin. You might even be angry at this letter. But its for me Corpse Father not for anyone else. I need to get this straight before I burn away to ashes.

When music finally hit me it was too much. It was painful. Like the color got switched on in a TV set I'd always thought was black & white. I felt too alive & things were too real & it was too beautiful it made me go crazy. I thought that I could be like everybody. Not as good as them maybe but just as alive. I bought my first records & went to my first shows & felt actual love & was loved. I really did Corpse Father. I did and I was. Whenever I got that ~~sickness~~ that doubtful feeling the music could kill it. If it was ~~powerful~~ extreme enough it could. I thought I ~~recognized myself~~ forgave myself ~~and I was not insane~~ and that if I saw my reflection in ~~the expression on the face of~~ the eyes of the boy that I loved, just a regular kid, that must mean I was real. It was beautiful & bright & painful & that pain could only be a proof of something. It was proof that I existed.

I kept myself believing that for almost two whole years.

Then I stopped. Music was still everything, the weight & the colors, the ~~ladder rock~~ branch I held on to. I couldn't imagine ~~a day or~~ an hour without it. But it changed me Corpse Father. I did terrible things. ~~I degraded myself.~~ I fooled my friends & lied to them & fucked people I felt nothing for at all. Men with no goddamn clue how to touch me. Girls

I didnt even want to know. Thats when I understood musics actual power Corpse Father. When it made me do the things I didnt want. ~~When it made me do violence against myself.~~ My friends were still true friends to me & they cared about & helped me. & the whole time they were helping me I wanted just to die.

But now You exist & I know You exist. I can hardly believe it. It was music that ~~gave me~~ brought me to You and I never will regret it. I know about Your house Corpse Father. Where you gather the names. Where you cook them & eat them. I offer you mine.

10

"I'm questioning what I'm hearing here, Norvald. Am I really hearing this? Absolutely not. No fucking way."

"This is a good thing, Z. A major thing. I know he trusts me now."

"You know diddly shit. We'll see how smug you're feeling when they turn you into jerky."

"If they wanted me dead they'd have killed me already. They wouldn't put me on a train for seven hours."

Leslie stared at him. "Why the hell would Grishnackh even *want* you along? Have you asked yourself that?"

Kip hesitated. "He thinks I've done time."

"What?"

"For aggravated assault. And for arson."

Leslie raised his eyes to heaven. "And why the holy fuck would he think that?"

"I know what I'm doing. I promise. Try to have a little faith."

"I like the sound of that, actually. *Try to have a little faith.* I can say it while I'm sprinkling your ashes in the fjord."

"This was always the plan, Z. From the very beginning."

"To set churches on fire?"

"Whatever it takes."

"You know what I think? I think you *enjoy* this. I think it gets your dick hard. It's not even about Kira anymore."

Kip took a deep breath. "One more time. Kira was with a man named Haugan. Magnus Haugan. Varg says he's in Bergen. I'm going to meet him."

"Let's just say—for giggles, as a kind of thought experiment—that your new boyfriend comes through. What happens then?" Leslie took the kerchief from the nightstand and opened it. "You're going to ask this Magnus Haugan, as one man of the world to another, what happened to the girl who fits this tooth?"

"That's exactly what I'm going to do."

"Excellent. Thanks for the input. I was just double-checking." Leslie's oversized head was bobbing around like one of those plastic dogs people put on their dashboards. "And what if he tells you that he chopped her up and made her into *julepølse*?"

"Something tells me I don't want to know what that is."

"You promised me, Norvald. We had an agreement. Informed choices. Strategic thinking. No Rambo maneuvers. You gullible son of a bitch. That was the *deal*."

Kip brought both his hands up to cover his face. Leslie's fear was creeping into him and that was unacceptable. There could be no fear from now on. No doubt. No hesitation. For the first time he regretted not having made the trip alone.

"Don't do this to me, Leslie. Not today."

"I can't deal with this. I can't deal with this."

"Is there something you're not telling me?"

Leslie turned to face the wall. "You're going the same way Kira went. Always toward the bigger kick. The more batshit-crazy thrill."

"You're right. That's how we find her."

"That's how we get *murdered*, Norvald. End of story. Fade to black."

Kip smiled at him. "I always liked that song."

"'Fade to Black'?" Leslie made a gagging sound into his shirtsleeve. "It's a *ballad*."

"A ballad that happens to appear on *Ride the Lightning*. Which happens to be the fourth-best record of all time."

Leslie didn't answer right away. "The sixth-best record," he said finally.

"I'll see your six and raise you two."

"Don't try to distract me."

"I'm doing this, Leslie. I'm going to Bergen."

"Listen to me, Norvald. You can't—"

"I can't what?"

He shook his head. "Just don't do anything illegal."

"Or what? I'll get arrested?"

Leslie kept his mouth shut. He seemed to have fallen asleep. Kip pulled back the covers and lowered his feet to the floor.

"What did you do, Leslie?"

"Nothing."

"You're lying."

"I talked to the cops."

The room went cold and still and airless. In half a decade of friendship, much of it spent attempting to make sense of the things that Leslie said and did, Kip had never been more stupefied.

"Help me understand this," he said slowly.

"How many new and entertaining ways do I have to find to say it? They're going to kill you, Norvald. You're a sacrificial lamb. That's the one and only reason that they've let you this far in. Grishnackh's pissing in the Kool-Aid and you're drinking it like pop."

To his own amazement Kip felt very calm. It was Leslie who was shouting.

"Okay," he said. "Just tell me what you told them."

"Everything I know. You're fucking welcome."

Kip braced himself against the wall and tried to organize his thoughts. He felt Leslie's eyes on him. He bent forward, keeping his movements deliberate, and pulled his boots out from under the bed.

"They're watching Helvete?"

"What the hell do you think?"

"I'm going through with it, Leslie."

Leslie just lay there. "I don't know you anymore. I swear to god."

Kip worked his feet into the boots and tied them carefully and went to the nightstand. He set down a folded stack of bills and picked up the kerchief.

"You kept some things to yourself," he said. "You kept the teeth."

Leslie didn't answer.

"Did you tell them anything, Leslie? Did you even go to them at all?"

"You just wait. You wait and see."

"Here's the money for the room. Thanks for your help."

11

Helvete the next day was packed with hangers-on—some by blind chance, some because they'd heard rumors of Grishnackh's departure, some because they'd caught the scent of trouble in the air. There were people in the shop that Kip had never seen before. He could only assume he was under surveillance. It made no difference now.

He'd spent the night in the throne room, sleeping fitfully on the creaking sweat-stained cot, waking time and again in that perfect inky blackness in an ecstasy of fear. In spite of his foreboding, or perhaps because of it, he felt nearer to Kira than he'd been in years. He sensed her beside him in that formless nowhere-place. At one point he sat up with a cry of sadness from a dream of ruined gray sepulchres to find her leaning against him, close and warm and undeniable, running her nail-bitten fingers gently through his hair.

Now it was noon of that last day and Grishnackh was sitting next to him on the ancient beer-stained sofa in the front room of the shop, visibly struggling to hide his excitement, whispering with a goateed man in a leather coat who barely seemed alive. They were leaving on the Bergensbanen at four, according to Grishnackh, and people passed the couch like supplicants in a slow and constant stream. He paid them no attention whatsoever. The light of mania was in his small pale eyes. Only the man in the leather coat was real to him.

Euronymous for his part maintained a princely distance, feigning bored indifference, holding court behind the counter as on any other day. He recommended albums and rang up purchases and held forth on the matchlessness of Venom and the worthlessness of thrash. It was Grishnackh's day and hour and he couldn't help but know it. The rules of engagement were changing forever. Kip settled back into the cushions, silently counting down the minutes, doing his best to savor Aarseth's secret misery. It made for a decent way to pass the time.

The man in the trench coat went by the name of Samoth and played in a band called Emperor that was said to be depressing beyond words. He fixed Kip in a baleful stare as Grishnackh introduced them. One of the few details he was willing to reveal about himself was that he came from Telemark, a rural part of the country known primarily for its fish. His English was terrible. It was clear from the start that he was performing for the Count, and that he viewed Kip as a rival, quite possibly a threat. He carried something just inside his coat that he caressed absentmindedly whenever he spoke. At one point he turned in his chair and made a gesture to Euronymous that looked like the sign of the cross but might simply have been an elaborate wave. Then he asked Kip what he planned to say to the devil when he met him in the woods.

"I'll tell him, 'Samoth misses you. He says you never call.'"

The look on Samoth's face when Grishnackh laughed made the whole trip to Norway worthwhile. He lurched to his feet in a fury, his right hand jammed inside his coat like Napoleon posing for a portrait; the Count reached out quickly and pulled him back down. A flurry of Norwegian ensued that Kip didn't bother trying to decipher. For a minute or two all was right with the world.

He was resting comfortably with his eyes lightly closed when the shop door clattered open and he felt the whole room change. All conversation stopped. Someone to his right, possibly Samoth, muttered a curse. He opened his eyes and took in all their dumbstruck faces. It could only mean the shop was being raided.

"*God ettermiddag, alle sammen.*"

He was up before the voice had finished speaking. Samoth was on his feet and so was Grishnackh. Leslie Vogler was the only point of movement, neatly attired in his forest-green parka and pinstriped oxford shirt and chinos, threading his way through the stunned crowd as if through a petrified forest.

"You all speak English? Of course you do. This is Norway. Excellent school system here. Democratic socialism at its finest." His voice shook only slightly. He was directly in front of Aarseth now, resting his elbows lightly on the counter. So far no one else had moved at all.

"Are you Euronymous, Prince of Death? I bet you are. You've got that Renaissance-fair-weed-dealer kind of vibe."

"You want what," Aarseth answered, his own voice as inflectionless as ever. He was in charge again, the gatekeeper, the center of the Circle.

"Who, me? I'm just looking for some good-time metal music." Leslie produced a crinkled scrap of paper and passed it to Aarseth. "You sell music here, don't you?"

Aarseth squinted at the paper while the whole room held its breath. "Mayhem," he said finally, loudly enough for everyone to hear. "*Deathcrush*."

"For a friend," said Leslie affably. "I actually think it's dogshit."

By this point even Aarseth's mouth was hanging open. The fact of Leslie in that place was so incongruous that it verged on the obscene. Everything around him hung suspended, immobile, like objects in a resin paperweight. He stood up straight and turned to face the room.

"I'm a stranger to this fine country of yours—as some of you deep thinkers have probably guessed—and I have questions about your basic way of life. This quote-unquote *black* metal, for starters. As far as I can figure out—and I consider myself a connoisseur—you're just a bunch of bony fish-faced crackers who can't tell a power chord from a bucket of *lutefisk*, and whose only decent riffs were ripped off from the first Bathory LP. I'm hoping someone here might be able to tell me—"

He was grinning in anticipation of his next punch line when Samoth pulled a small black snub-nosed revolver from his coat and raised it in a single practiced motion to the back of Leslie's skull. Leslie gave

what sounded like a sigh of satisfaction. His face was inexplicably serene. Samoth's heavy-lidded eyes were wide as saucers now, as though
the weapon in his hands astounded him. He looked as if he'd already
pulled the trigger.

"Apologies," Leslie said, more softly now. "I might have been off the
mark about the *lutefisk*. What I actually meant to say was—"

Kip was fully in motion when Samoth's face turned toward him with
its teeth bared in a rictus of surprise. Had Kip's reasoning mind been in
charge of his body it would never have guided him across that room
with such surefootedness and grace. The old brutality moved through
him. It employed him as its vessel. He took part only as a witness as he
pivoted past Samoth and drove his right fist into Leslie's cheek with all
the strength he had.

A firecracker went off or something much like it and an angry hiss
slid out through Samoth's teeth. Kip watched Leslie go down as the
black room went white. Three careful years undone in half a second.
The familiar dreamlike stillness. Someone shouting in Norwegian. Leslie
stumbling toward the door with blood cascading down his shirt. His
own voice spitting insults at that hunched retreating form.

Four hours later Kip was sitting with his face against the window of a
six-seat compartment on the dinner train to Bergen. His hand was swaddled in an ice pack but the pain was still electric. He'd thrown up once
already and would soon be sick again. He took a breath and clenched
his teeth and worked his hand free of its bandage. The middle two fingers had been braced and taped together. He had no clear recollection
of when or how this had been done.

"You should have used the heel of your hand, Christopher. The heel,
not the fist. Or a bottle. Or the butt of our friend's gun."

He turned his head and forced his eyes to focus. The look on Grishnackh's face might easily have been mistaken for affection. The same
could not be said for Samoth.

"Maybe I went a little overboard."

"Overboard, Christopher? Like a sailor on a boat?"

"It means I did too much. More than I should have."

Grishnackh slapped his knee. "I say you did! You would have killed him if we let you. What was it made you so angry, do you think? That he was an American or that he was a Black?"

Kip shook his head. "I should have just let Sam here pull the trigger."

"Even Samoth knows better, I think, than to shoot a man in daylight in a place of public business." Grishnackh heaved a sigh. "He's not a crazy shit like you are, Christopher. He's not an *Ulfhedinn*."

"Then why is he here?"

Samoth muttered something in Norwegian.

"What says our boy?"

Grishnackh waved a hand. "He expresses concern for the state of your fingers."

"Then why not say it in English?"

"Be patient with him, Christopher. His English is small."

Samoth repeated the same words as before, grinding the heel of his palm against his thigh for emphasis. The Count nodded indulgently.

"Never smite on the jaw, he says. The fleshy portions only. This is fundamental."

"That's all?"

"Not quite." Grishnackh smiled. "He also says you look like a policeman."

"I'm happy to tell him what he looks like. All he needs to do is ask."

Kip pulled up the hood of his parka and repositioned the ice pack and directed his attention to the far side of the glass. They were in the woods already, dark and dense and uniform, so different from the spare and sunlit pinewoods of the Gulf. Here and there between the snow-clad firs a flash of open country. Houses fastened to hillsides. The sky like a hull. He tried to get a sense of the position of the sun, of how much daylight might be left, but the sun was less a thing than an idea. He closed his eyes and slept. When he opened them the ground outside was brighter than the sky.

"Rise up, brothers!" Grishnackh said merrily, coming in from the aisle with four sweating bottles of lemon-lime soda.

"I'd rather have a Hansa."

"What! Beer?" The Count looked scandalized. "I never touch the stuff."

"Who's the fourth one for?"

"Odin, of course!" said Grishnackh, setting down the sodas with a flourish. Samoth took his gloomily and drank without a word.

"Am I sensing resentments? We stop this right now." Grishnackh clinked his bottle with Samoth's. *"Stopp tullet ditt."*

"La oss drepe ham snart."

"There!" announced Grishnackh. "Our comrade-in-arms says: *Let's start being friends.*"

"He's got an interesting way of expressing himself."

Grishnackh pursed his lips. "Yes. Your berserking at Helvete may have made him slightly shy."

"He doesn't seem shy."

"Remember, Christopher—we Norwegians don't like speaking so much, even with each other." He held his bottle aloft. "Now drink. We get to Bergen in one hour."

As they came out of the mountains the cloud cover lifted and the moon lit up the forest like a silver-oxide print. Grishnackh was muttering to himself and switching seats every few minutes and fussing with the EQ of his Walkman. The train passed over gorges and deep fissured inlets and graceful hanging cataracts of ice. Between tunnels Kip caught his first glimpse of the city. It was smaller and prettier than he'd expected. Samoth was openly priming his pistol.

"I'm feeling happy," Grishnackh said. "And also full of hope."

"I'm not sure that the Circle would approve."

"Don't be an idiot, Christopher. We're not in Aarseth's basement any longer. We're allowed to have ourselves a bit of fun."

"Sam here has a funny way of showing it."

The Count switched seats yet again, from Samoth's side of the compartment to Kip's. "He's just as excited as we are," he whispered. "He's never had the chance before to fire his revolver."

Kip looked at the gun. "You said we were coming here to start some fires."

"You weren't listening, brother. I said we were coming here to start a war."

Already the woods had been replaced by malls and clustered tracts of housing. It happened so abruptly in that country. The city looked larger and more brilliant than it had from above. It looked prosperous and supervised and safe.

"What happens when we get to town?"

"Ah, Christopher! That would be telling."

"Talk to me about Haugan."

Grishnackh shot a glance at Samoth. "All this fuss about old Haugan. You disappoint me, brother."

"I'll be honest with you, brother. I can live with that."

Samoth let out a grunt that seemed intended to express either disbelief or disapproval but in fact expressed nothing. Grishnackh managed to look both resigned and impatient. He gave a slight shrug.

"You'll meet Haugan. I told you."

"Where?"

His expression changed subtly. "He works in a bar. We can visit him after."

"I want to know the bar's name."

"Are you bargaining now, Christopher? What will you do to us—to Samoth and myself—if we don't prefer to bargain?"

"I intend to keep my word to you," Kip said evenly, looking back and forth between them. "I'd thought, as a Norseman, you could be counted on to keep yours."

"Just do your part," said Grishnackh, bringing his army duffel down from the rack above the seats. "Do it without flinching, Crazy Dusty. I will honor our arrangement."

"What arrangement?" grumbled Samoth. "Is this *drittsekk* getting money?"

"Shhh," hissed Grishnackh. "Quiet now."

They'd reached the station and were rolling up the platform. Kip saw no one but a woman in a kind of six-wheeled golf cart and two middle-aged men wearing jackets emblazoned with the flag of Norway. One of them waved to someone farther up the train.

"There's hardly anybody out there."

"Those two," said Grishnackh.

"*Those* two? The ones in the jackets?"

Grishnackh nodded. "I know them."

Kip peered out through the glass, attempting to arrive at some guess as to whether the men were station security or police officers or members of some Norwegian offshoot of the Aryan Brotherhood. They looked more like maintenance workers. Grishnackh had already started up the aisle toward the next car, looking for a group of passengers to hide behind. Samoth seemed to have vanished in a puff of smoke.

"Do you still see them, Christopher?"

Grishnackh had made it to the end of the car and stood with his back against the partition between the luggage racks and the restroom. The hydraulic door slid open and a few somnambulistic tourists dragged identical black rollers up the aisle. There were more people on the platform now—maybe two or three dozen. The men in the jackets were nowhere in sight.

"You owe these guys money or something?"

"Listen closely, Christopher. My bag is on the seat behind you. I want you to take it and walk up the platform and past the shops and out to the main concourse. Leave through the south exit. Wait for me outside."

"Outside where?"

"Go, damn you."

"What about my pack?"

"Give it to me. I'll need something to carry."

Kip kept him in suspense for one drawn-out breath, relishing his anxiety, then dropped his pack and pulled the duffel toward him. It was bafflingly heavy.

"What the hell is in this thing? A nuclear warhead?"

"Just take it and go."

Kip picked up the duffel with both hands, cradling it like an infant, and staggered out onto the platform. He felt observed, perhaps followed, and made sure not to hurry. The concourse was so deserted that if he hadn't seen the city through the Bergensbanen's windows he might have questioned its existence. The only people in the pretty neoclassical foyer were a scattering of drunks of the kind you might find in any railroad station on the planet and a man in a loose-fitting tracksuit holding a bundle of what looked to be evangelical pamphlets. He gave no reaction as Kip shambled past him. He seemed to be communing with invisible confederates. The Aesir, Kip decided.

Grishnackh and Samoth were sitting at a bus stop less than a stone's throw from the entrance. It struck Kip as an odd choice of rendezvous point, inexplicably risky, until he realized they were actually waiting for the bus. The Count's mood had improved again. He flashed Kip a playful thumbs-up.

"What the fuck is in here?" Kip said, lowering the duffel to the curb at Grishnackh's feet.

"You seem to be having second notions, Christopher. Are you having second notions?"

"Let's just get this done."

Grishnackh turned to Samoth with a look of sly amusement. They'd been discussing him in his absence. He found himself thinking, as he watched them leering at each other, of something he'd said the night before to Leslie. *If they wanted me dead they'd have killed me already.* It rang out in his memory like a bell.

"*Ulvetid,*" Samoth said quietly. He pronounced the word with an odd sort of care, as though it were unfamiliar even to him. Grishnackh looked thoughtful. Eventually he nodded.

"*Ulvetid?*" Kip repeated. "What is that?"

His question pleased them both. Grishnackh arched his back and glanced behind him at the station to make sure they were alone. "*Ulv* time," he said. "Berserker time. The hour of the wolf."

Samoth rummaged briefly through his pack and brought out a sandwich bag of crinkled yellow plastic. When it caught the light Kip saw that it was packed with dried apricots speckled with mildew. He persisted in this misapprehension until he was holding half a dozen in his hand and Samoth and Grishnackh were chewing their own portions with gleeful half-disgusted faces. He found himself transported irresistibly back to the pasture at Mile 25, to the wet steaming dark, to the rain and the sawgrass and Kira. The water running down her straight black hair into the mud. That pasture long paved over and forgotten. He closed his hand around the caps and slipped them into a pocket of his parka.

"You still seem impatient, Christopher."

Kip looked up and saw that Grishnackh's eyes were closed. "That's not the word I'd use," he said.

"Tell me how I can help you."

"I like to know where I'm headed when I'm doing something that can get me thrown in jail."

"But you *know* where we're headed. I've explained it already. We're going to the woods to light a fire."

"You mind if I ask why we're taking the bus?"

"This is Norway," said Samoth. "Excellent public transport."

It was the first and last joke Kip would ever hear him make.

They rode the bus for only a handful of stops before getting off at a well-tended park with a pagoda at its center that was magically free of ice and snow. The urge to bolt into the dark came over him but he managed to keep still until it passed. No more than five minutes later they boarded a streetcar that was empty save for a man in his sixties who might easily have passed for Grishnackh's father. He sported a week's worth of sparse blond beard and his belly hung out of the bottom of his sweater and he stank of alcohol and roasted meat. He watched the three of them stow their bags and take their seats, dragging two nicotine-stained fingers through his beard. He mumbled something in Norwegian and leaned to one side and spat onto the floor.

"What did that man just say?"

Grishnackh didn't seem to hear. He and Samoth were conversing again in self-important whispers. Kip repeated his question.

"Nothing of importance. It's amusing, really."

"What is?"

Grishnackh smiled to himself. "He called us the devil's shield maidens."

"I don't know what that means."

"You surprise me, Christopher. A shield maiden is a Norse fighting woman. One who takes up arms and rides to battle with her brothers. Many range forth with Odin himself, the One-Eyed One, on those nights when the Wild Hunt descends on the country."

Kip frowned. "So by referring to us as the devil's shield maidens—"

"He is calling us homosexuals."

"Okay."

"But what troubles me more, Christopher, is that this man has seen us."

"I don't think you need to worry about that. He's too loaded to remember us in the morning."

Grishnackh blinked at him. "Again you misunderstand. Samoth and myself have drawn certain runes on our bodies. We should now be invisible to the naked eye."

They were passing through the innermost belt of suburbs and the buildings looked like country houses set too close together. The larger ones reminded Kip of barns. He saw no one on the streets or on the platforms. It struck him as very likely that theirs was the last streetcar of the night and he found himself wondering how the hell they were going to get back to the city. The need to ask this question built in him slowly, like the urge to yawn or cough or scream in terror, and had just grown irresistible when Samoth and Grishnackh stood up without warning.

Samoth whispered something to the old drunk as he passed him, some-thing amicable and gentle, and at the next stop the man lurched to his feet and stepped down ahead of them onto the platform. To Kip's considerable surprise he stood waiting there shyly, wavering from one foot to the other with a bashful toothy grin. They watched the streetcar roll out of sight around the nearest bend, leaning slightly to one side, all four of them, like characters in some hackneyed buddy comedy. When it was gone they walked together up the platform and through a nearly lightless underpass and out into a copse of tall blue firs. It felt like being in the middle of the forest. At the first of a series of rough-cut stone steps the man turned to Samoth and asked him a question.

"What's he saying?"

"He wants to know where we're going," said Grishnackh. "He wants to know whether we told him the truth."

"About what?"

"About having vodka."

"We have vodka?"

Grishnackh spoke softly to Samoth, shook his head as if to clear it, then brought his boot against the old drunk's back and pushed. The man let out what could almost have been a shout of joy and hit the lowest of the steps with his right shoulder. The buddy-movie feeling only intensified as Kip watched Grishnackh and Samoth prancing and cavorting around the drunk's body, prodding his backside almost dain-tily with the toes of their boots before starting to kick. The man jerked and spasmed with each blow he took, making muted, unconvincing noises. Kira would have found the scene implausible and trite. Grish-nackh paused for breath after a half-dozen kicks but Samoth kept at it, smiling and nodding at Kip as he worked. The Count stood a few paces off now, spinning slowly in place with his blond head thrown back. Kip hadn't witnessed so much carefree levity since touching down in Oslo. He gritted his teeth and bowed his head and gave the man a few symbolic kicks himself.

They left the drunk slumped in the gravel and followed a paved road uphill through a neighborhood of painted clapboard houses. Late though the hour was they passed a group of schoolchildren, ten years at the oldest, lobbing snowballs at one another over a row of ragged hedges. Grishnackh and Samoth ignored them completely. Samoth was carrying himself strangely now, walking flat-footedly and working his jaws as he went, as though in conversation with himself or with some unseen third companion. Grishnackh seemed uncommonly alert, wide-awake and full of energy, all but goose-stepping up the middle of the street. When Kip caught up with him he noticed that his face was damp with sweat.

"Sammy seems to be having some trouble. Maybe we should slow down."

"He's not having any trouble. Just the opposite."

"What's that supposed to mean?"

"The amanita, Christopher. The toadstool. He's going through the changes."

"This seems like a strange time to want to get high."

"Little Dusty from Florida. You don't belong here."

"No argument there."

"We eat as the Ulfhednar ate. No bladed weapons could cut them. No fire could blacken their skin. When the *berserkergang* came over them they knew not pain nor fear."

"The Ulfhednar," Kip said slowly. His pronunciation was awful.

"Exactly, Christopher."

"Did they go around beating up drunks in the woods?"

"Anyone," said Grishnackh, wiping his lips with the back of his hand. "Anyone foolish enough to get in their way." He gave Kip a wink. "In the heat of battle, it is said, they cut down friend as willingly as foe."

Kip was still trying to come up with an answer when Grishnackh cut left without warning and scrambled up an embankment into a wooded hillside park. They were still within the city, or at least in settled country, but the trees grew thickly enough that within ten steps all sight and sound of human habitation fell away. They felt their way upward along a switchbacking trail, orienting themselves in the darkness by the snow skirting the trunks and by the firmness of the ground beneath their feet. Samoth was stammering curses at the sky and Kip was glad to hear them. As long as he was arguing with ghosts he wasn't playing with the gun.

"There!" said Grishnackh.

It took Kip a long moment to see what he was seeing. A shape through the trees, dimly lit from below, like a stage set or the scene of some disaster. Kip could only imagine that the structure was illuminated for the benefit of passing hikers but there was no one there to see it. No one but the three of them and Samoth's angry spirits.

Grishnackh called something out in Norwegian—some manner of command or entreaty—but Samoth didn't answer. He came to a stumbling halt and sat down cross-legged on the ground and dug his fists into his eyes. The pistol lay obscurely on the frozen ground beside him. Kip went to him and crouched just out of arm's reach, watching him as he retched and gasped and shuddered, thinking about mushrooms and *berserkergang* and what Grishnackh had told him. He reached for the pistol but some force stayed his hand. Superstition or cowardice. He left Samoth to the mercy of his visions and continued up the path.

The church floated above him, dragon-spired and knife-gabled, more a witch's tower out of a fable than a site of Christian worship. He came out of the trees into the churchyard, breathless from his climb and from the strangeness of that place. The god glorified under that serpent-scaled roof was not the one that Oona spent her Sundays with in Venice.

"Here," Grishnackh hissed. He stood bent to half his height in the improbably tiny doorway with his duffel lying in the snow behind him. The frame was beaten iron but the door itself was wood, gleaming coldly in the floodlights, its slats and its braces gone glossy with age. Grishnackh was panting like a mastiff. He was trying to pick the lock with a loop of wire and a ballpoint pen.

"That doesn't seem to be working, Varg."

"Get over here and hold this thing steady, damn it. I didn't come all this way—"

He was still in mid-sentence when Kip stepped to the door and brought the heel of his boot against the ancient wood and kicked. The door shot open as though sundered by Mjölnir itself and Grishnackh fell headlong into the blackness. A few seconds later his flashlight came on and in its glow Kip could see that his pupils were huge as an owl's. He licked the sweat from his lips and reached for the duffel and dragged it inside.

"Take this torch, Christopher. I can't see what I'm doing."

"You've had that thing this whole time? What were you saving it for?"

"I can't *hear* myself when you talk." Grishnackh brought out two paper bundles and unwrapped them with loving care, like votive offerings. The devices they contained were cylindrical and slick with something that smelled like motor oil along their soldered bases. He attached two powder dipped fuses no longer than a finger while Kip looked nervously about him in the feeble yellow light. The ceiling of the church was lower than he'd expected and black with soot from candles put out centuries before his grandparents were born. He tried to picture that dark unwelcoming space filled with families at prayer but some part of him refused. It was easier to imagine it full of grizzly bears, or witches, or even the Aesir. It was easier to imagine it on fire.

"Christopher."

"I'm right here, Varg."

"Take this and keep your mouth shut and do what I do."

Kip eased the cylinder gradually out of Grishnackh's trembling arms. It felt heavier in that moment than the whole duffel had been. Grishnackh seemed at a loss after handing it over, crouching low with his eyes open wide and a hand at his ear, as though listening to something moving underneath the chapel floor. Then he shook himself the way a dog might and picked up the second of the bombs and carried it to the chancel with its polished effigy of the Christ no larger than a doll and propped it matter-of-factly against the wooden steps. As Kip came toward him up the nave he took hold of the effigy's legs in an absentminded way and spoke his own name solemnly and snapped the figure free.

"That will be all, Christopher. Set yours down where you're standing. You have my permission to leave."

"I'm not going anywhere."

Grishnackh brought out the heavy brass lighter Kip had first seen in the throne room. "Crazy Dusty," he said fondly. "You're about to make me cry."

"I need the name of Haugan's bar."

Grishnackh thumbed the lighter's silver wheel and blinked into the flame. The expression on his face was one of adolescent wonder.

"Did you hear what I said? I need the name—"

"Best to start running, Dusty."

By the time he'd compelled his reluctant body into motion the first of the fuses was more than half gone. The beam of the little flashlight danced playfully among the rafters as he stumbled up the aisle. The shockwave caught him at the door and threw him out into the snow and he lay there gasping for breath and waiting on the second blast but nothing came. He uncovered his ears and listened. Somewhere someone was singing. He rolled over and looked up at the stars and tried to make some sense of what had happened.

After what seemed like half the night he got to his feet and limped back to the door and looked in. The chapel was thick with smoke but otherwise he saw no trace of fire. He found Grishnackh flat on his back in the middle of the floor, flapping his arms and legs in slow motion, as though trying to make an angel on the burnished wooden boards.

"Beautiful," Grishnackh whispered in English. "Beautiful. Beautiful. *Nydelig ild.*"

"What are you talking about?"

"It's burning, Dusty. Can't you see it burning?"

Kip took him by the legs and dragged him out into the snow. It took some doing. Tears were running freely down his wet and twitching face.

"So beautiful. So beautiful."

It was colder in the churchyard now than it had been before. Kip stood over Grishnackh for a time, watching as his features ran through every conceivable human emotion. He looked over his shoulder. Still no sign of fire. He bent to one side and took up a fistful of snow and ground it slowly and methodically into Grishnackh's face and hair.

"*Gå bort, drittsekk—Gå veg fra—*"

"I'm going, Varg. I'll be gone soon. But first you're going to tell me."

"*Hvem er du?* Who is speaking?"

"We were going to a bar after this. You said that on the train we took today. Oslo to Bergen. Look at me, Varg. You remember that train."

"I know who it is! It's Dusty from America. I can't talk to you because everything's on fire."

"You're on fire too, Varg."

"I am! Yes! Can you see it? Isn't it the most beautiful—"

"I'm going to cover you with snow and put the fire out."

The Count's voice changed in an instant. "Please do not do that, Dusty."

"Tell me the name."

"Of course I will. What name is it you want?"

"The name of the bar."

"It's back in the old town." Grishnackh let out a groan. "One of those horrible Irish pubs that are taking over the world. The Bergen Arms."

"Tell me how I'll recognize Haugan."

"Get out of my way, Dusty. I can't see the fire."

"You're right. It's a beautiful fire. A perfect fire. You really ought to see it."

Grishnackh cursed in Norwegian. For the first time he seemed almost frightened. "Let me back up, Dusty. Let me look."

"Haugan. How will I know him."

"Idiot! He works there."

"I need to know what he looks like."

"So you can ask about the girl? You can ask me instead." Grishnackh's eyelashes fluttered. "He gave her to Nameless. The Corpse Father took her."

For a moment Kip said nothing. "Tell me what that means."

"He took her. He ate her. He burned her away."

"Who is Nameless?"

"Don't worry. You'll meet him."

"Listen to me carefully, Varg. I need you—"

"You *need* me! I like this." His owl-dark eyes had rolled back in their sockets. "But I don't need you at all. I'm looking through you, in fact— looking into the future. And I don't see you there."

Kip left him in the snow reaching like a mystic or an infant toward the silent empty church. His lips formed noises like Samoth's, unintelligible and frantic, meant for confederates Kip had no interest in meeting. Other than these gibberings no sound was to be heard in all that starry blackness as he made his way across the churchyard and down the slope toward where he guessed the road might be. No shouting, no sirens. That vast and roofless quiet might have cowed him in another place, an earlier hour, a different state of being. Now all he thought and sensed and feared had narrowed to a single point of light.

12

Sometime later he was standing on a cobbled street in the old town look-ing through a leaded glass window at a man pulling pints in a bar. The man had on what looked to be some sort of mackintosh and his long red hair was neatly tucked behind his ears. The honeyed glow of the bar was the only light to speak of and Kip stood squarely in the middle of the street and waited. By his reckoning it was past two o'clock in the morning. He had no idea when last call might be in this city, or anywhere else in the country of Norway, but the question was of no consequence. It was just a way to occupy his mind.

Within the hour the last of the patrons had settled up and left, whispering to one another as they passed him, and he watched as the man counted out for the night and ran a dishrag along the top of the bar and treated himself to a whiskey without once glancing out at the street. Kip stayed just as he was. The proud and prosperous city that surrounded him seemed diffuse and insubstantial. Real was only the bar, and the window, and the man in the mackintosh sipping his drink. He felt no apprehension or excitement. He didn't even feel the cold.

He crossed the street unhurriedly and sat on a stoop while the man locked the door of the bar at its top and its bottom and lit a cigarette and started walking. He followed him down to the brightly lit harbor. A few streets from the water the man fumbled with a ring of keys and let himself into a nondescript modern building and Kip caught the door just before it swung shut. The man was a dozen steps ahead, crossing the immaculate lobby with slow, dragging steps, like someone overcome by grief. He never looked behind him. At the door of his apartment he struggled with the keys again, cursing under his breath, but it was only when he'd gotten it open and stood gripping the doorframe that Kip realized how blind drunk Haugan was.

"*Jeg skal sove*," Haugan mumbled.

"Magnus Haugan?"

He reared back and regarded Kip out of sullen bloodshot eyes. Eventually he nodded. "*Jeg skal sove*," he repeated.

Kip leaned to one side to look past him. A cluttered dirty entryway. The neglected-looking kitchen of a man who lived alone. "*Jeg snakker ikke Norsk*," he said. "Do you speak English?"

"*Faen ta deg*," hissed Haugan, shaking his head. "*Faen ta deg*. Go away."

"I have a few questions—"

"Fuck you and your questions."

He took Haugan by the collar and threw him headlong into the apartment with no conscious sense of effort. Everything he did now had a clear and simple purpose. Haugan flew gracelessly forward with his thick arms outstretched and hit the tile floor of the kitchen and lay there facedown like a dead man. Kip had expected him to cry out in surprise or in pain, to fight back or insult him or break down in tears, but Haugan did none of these things. After perhaps half a minute he emitted a long-suffering sigh and raised himself onto all fours. There was a resignation to his movements now. An acceptance of his lot.

"Am I letting you up, Mr. Haugan? Are we trying again?"

Haugan stayed as he was, with his head lolling forward and his fists against the tiles. He appeared to be weighing his options.

"I wouldn't have thought that was such a hard question."

"*Faen ta deg, fjott.*"

"I'm looking for a woman. An American. You met her through Per Ivar Lund."

"Kira," said Haugan.

"Kira Carson. That's right."

He let out a yawn. "Six days."

"I don't follow."

"Six days ago you would have found her. Right here in this kitchen. Now I think maybe you come a little late."

He was raising his head to say something else as Kip brought the heel of his boot down on Haugan's left fist. It took Haugan a full second to grasp what was happening and he made to jerk his arm away but even as he did so the knuckles cracked one after another *pop pop pop* like kernels of corn in a skillet. He let out a single thin warbling cry and went still. The fist lay pulped and defeated-looking against the cheap yellow tiles but even so Kip had to restrain himself from stomping it to jelly. He hadn't been able to see Haugan's face when he'd spoken Kira's name but the sound of his voice had been more than enough. The arrogance behind it. The cold satisfaction.

He caught his breath for a moment, waiting for his hands to stop trembling, then went to the refrigerator and took out a half-empty bottle of Hansa Pilsner and emptied it onto Haugan's ashen face. The noise that came out of him as he struggled awake was like something a farm animal might make. A confused and plaintive bleating. Kip waited until Haugan's eyes had fully opened before taking out the linen handkerchief he'd found so many weeks before and unfolding it and bringing its contents down to where Haugan could see them.

"A little late, Magnus? A little late for what?"

Haugan moved his lips soundlessly.

"I didn't quite catch that."

"I gave her to someone."

"You gave her to Nameless."

Haugan looked up at him with genuine surprise. "Then you know already."

"I'm going to ask you a favor. Pretend I know nothing."

Haugan curled into a ball and started retching. He'd seemed young from a distance but now he looked older. When his fit had subsided he coughed one final time into his sleeve and asked for water.

"Water later," Kip said. "Talking first."

Haugan looked at him, then gave a nod, as though the terms were only fair.

"She wanted to see him. He never comes seeking. He keeps to the woods."

"The woods," Kip repeated.

"That's right."

"Where in the woods?"

"I brought her to him. To his house. He called and she came."

"Tell me why."

He closed his eyes. "Her reason was no different from any of the others'. No different from mine."

"What reason?"

"She was tired." Haugan seemed to shiver slightly. "In the head, you understand me? She was ready to be gone."

Kip watched as he tried to sit up, wheezing quietly from the effort. His face had gone the color of old snow.

"So I was right." Kip stared down into his palm. "This tooth is hers."

"Nothing is hers," Haugan said. "Not now."

In the silence that fell Kip could make out muffled footfalls from the floor above and the clatter of a passing streetcar and the melancholy humming of the fridge. The sound had always soothed him. He nodded to himself for what seemed a great while, not quite looking at Haugan, not quite looking away.

"You'll take me to him," he said finally. "I don't care what you're afraid of."

Haugan actually laughed. "Of course I can take you. Nameless welcomes all seekers."

"That's big of him," Kip said. "Now get on your feet."

13

Haugan drove his decrepit Volkswagen hatchback up into the hills with Kip sitting behind him like a passenger in a taxi, watching his reflection in the rearview, resting a bone-handled filleting knife from the kitchen in the gap between the headrest and the seat. Both of them knew he wasn't going to use it—not in a car doing 80 km per hour—but the knife was important. It was part of the ritual they were acting out together.

In no time at all they were driving through forest so primeval that they might have been traveling backward in time. Kip had been worried that Haugan might not be able to manage the stick shift with his damaged hand but he drove well enough. He seemed so sober now that Kip found himself wondering, as the lights of the city receded, whether his earlier show of drunkenness had been some kind of act. No other explanation came to him. He struggled to keep awake, once even dropped the knife altogether, but Haugan paid no attention. He seemed to have forgotten anyone else was in the car.

"How much farther?"

"Not very."

"Tell me about this place. It's some sort of a compound?"

Haugan was a long time answering. "A house."

"What kind of a house."

"I told you already."

"Go ahead and get cute with me, fucker. I'll cut off your ears."

Haugan said nothing. The knife brushed his cheek as they entered a curve but he seemed not to notice. Perhaps a minute passed before he spoke.

"We're going to the house where Nameless is."

"Him and who else?"

"I can't say."

Kip sucked in a breath. "So help me, if you think that I won't—"

"I can't say," repeated Haugan. "Because I've never been inside."

"Why the hell not?"

Haugan shifted into second as the road before them steepened. "Because I'm afraid."

Kip looked hard at the face in the mirror. He'd been prepared for almost any other answer. "I don't understand," he said.

"Of course not."

"Who is this person to you, Magnus? Why go to him if you're so scared?"

Haugan didn't answer.

"You think of him as a prophet, is that it? Some kind of a savior?"

"Spoken like a true Christian," Haugan said primly.

"Enlighten me."

When Haugan spoke again it was clear that he was repeating words that someone else had uttered. He pronounced them measuredly, in a kind of singsong, like a divinity student reciting from scripture.

"There is a war. A war for those who hear the whisper. Those who hear will come to me and leave their names behind. Their names and the lives that pertained to those names. They will walk the earth in righteousness and robe themselves in fire. As for the rest—the churchgoers, the moralists, the coloniz- ers, the Semites—they will be as the trees in the forest."

Kip felt something inside himself twist. "And you're one of the spe- cial ones, are you, Magnus? High and mighty? Robed in fire?"

"I know what I am," Haugan said softly.

"You're a cult leader's pimp. You're a fucking procurer."

The face in the rearview seemed almost to smile. "And soon I won't even be that."

Kip sat hunched in the back seat, wide-awake now, white-knuckling the knife and breathing hard. Haugan shifted into first. Snow was starting to fall.

"What about all the others?"

"Which others?"

"The trees in the forest. What happens to them?"

Haugan looked surprised by the question. "They do what trees do."

"What is that?"

"Feed the fire."

Soon after that he pulled the hatchback over alongside the concrete abutment of a railroad viaduct and killed the engine. The road was narrow and shoulderless and Kip realized with a faint twinge of panic that he had no memory of having left the highway. Haugan put the keys on the dash and stepped out into the snowfall and set off down a logging trail without a glance behind him. He moved efficiently, impatiently, barely using his flashlight. Kip came stumbling after.

"Slow down, Magnus. I'm not done asking questions."

"Then ask," Haugan said without slowing.

"The first I ever heard of Nameless was at a merch table at a metal show in Berlin. The same show where Kira met Per Ivar Lund. A stack of shitty little pamphlets where the records should have been."

"Is this a question?"

"Hold on." Kip stood still for a moment with his hands on his knees. "Stop walking."

"You are tired," said Haugan.

"Why metal?" He tried to think clearly. "Why music at all?"

"He speaks to the young in the speech of the young."

"Give me a straight fucking answer."

"Nameless himself is the absence of music. The end of all music. The end of all longing. The peace that comes after."

"Bullshit."

Haugan watched him and waited.

"You're forgetting that I know Kira Carson. Better than you, Magnus. Better than anyone. The Kira I know would never buy the New Age crap you're selling. She'd jump off a bridge first."

Haugan nodded. "Now perhaps you understand."

The trail was carpeted in copper-colored needles and it jackknifed sharply downward before climbing again to follow a frozen creekbed up into a hanging valley. The sky to the east was beginning to pale when Haugan turned onto a footpath that Kip never would have noticed on his own. He led them up a steep and tapering gully, moving deliberately now, then past a series of snowbound ponds and a stand of the most massive firs that Kip had ever seen. The path was barely wider than a deer track and so faint that Haugan himself had to backtrack more than once. It took all of Kip's attention not to fall too far behind.

"Go now," Haugan said abruptly.

"What?"

He'd stopped where the path passed between two young birches, slender and moon-colored against the conifers above. "You go on."

"So you can double back and ditch me? Not a chance."

Haugan met his eyes for the first time since they'd left the logging trail. In the gathering light of morning he looked startlingly old.

"*Vi har ankommet,*" he said.

"What does that mean?"

"*Vi har ankommet,*" he repeated. "We are here."

Kip looked past him through the birches then and saw it plain as day. An unpainted clapboard cottage, old but not ancient, set into a spade-shaped clearing like a stone into a brooch. A stovepipe jutting slantwise where a tree had cracked the chimney. Shuttered windows with no light behind them. Spruce boughs resting on the gables. A half-open screen door, askew in its frame, like the door of Oona's bungalow in Venice. That detail alone made the scene believable to him. Otherwise he would have thought it the persistence of some dream.

"I want you out in front," he said. "Keep in front where I can see you."

Haugan stepped lightly off the path and shook his head.

"Shake your head at me again, brother. I'll split you from your asshole to the dimple in your chin."

"You are trying to frighten me." The look on Haugan's face was one
of pity. "You need to know something. I came here to stay."

Kip's mouth opened and shut. He and Haugan stood unmoving
within arm's reach of each other as the antediluvian forest groaned
around them in the cold. He smelled woodsmoke but saw no evidence
of fire. The light had gone strange. They were less than thirty paces from
the house.

"Something's wrong here," he murmured.

Haugan smiled at him sadly. Even as he stood there with the silent
house behind him he appeared to be receding very slowly out of view.
Kip looked on as if spellbound, as if stricken, seeing his breath pull
smoothly up into the windless winter sky. The urge to turn and run was
irresistible. The urge to run was irresistible but instead he was stepping
out into the newly fallen snow. He was crossing the little clearing toward the entrance of the house.

The front steps bowed under his weight as he climbed them—he
could feel the damp wood yielding—but they made no sound at all that
he could hear. The crooked door hung open to receive him. It had been
weatherproofed or varnished in some bygone age and a rag had been
stuffed through the hole where the handle had been. It swung noiselessly inward. Beyond it a wall of rancid air hung heavy as a caul.

He felt his way half-blindly over softly creaking floorboards as his
body grew accustomed to the closeness and the dark. He knew that he
should pause to recover his bearings but he had to keep in motion. Motion was a form of sanctuary. The air was hot and humid and he found it
hard to breathe. It pressed itself against his skin. The air was stupefying.
It was important to keep moving so as not to fall asleep.

He lurched heavily forward, all stealth long abandoned, from one
low-ceilinged room to the next. The smell of old sweat and dry rot and
leather. A workbench. A bookcase. A gun rack mounted above a fire-
place long since mortared over. Some manner of wooden effigy propped
up in a highbacked chair. Beyond the chair a doorway led into a kind of

scullery. He stopped when he reached it. By a cookstove in the corner crouched the figure of what might have been a man.

"Ah!" said the figure.

The sound might have had some meaning in Norwegian or in the vernacular of that nowhere-place or it might have been a meaningless release of pent-up breath. The figure's eyes were fixed on his and they looked calm and wide-awake. Its slender long-nailed fingers clutched what appeared in that uncertain light to be two braided lengths of chestnut-colored hair. The firebox of the stove had been opened and its glow fell on the figure where it squatted naked as a newborn with its own lank hair snaking down in coal-black tangles to the stained and pitted floor. As Kip stood awestruck in the doorway it made the sound again and without taking its eyes away from him fed the braid in its right hand slowly and meticulously into the fire.

"*God dag til deg,*" Kip heard himself stammer. "*Jeg vet ikke—*"

"Little Magnus," said the figure. It fed the second handful in after the first.

"Excuse me? I don't—"

"Little Magnus brought you here."

The voice was dry as paper. Kip reached for the doorframe and gripped it. He managed to keep his own voice fairly steady.

"Magnus Haugan. That's right."

The figure bobbed its matted head. In no hurry to speak again. In no hurry to rise.

"Can I ask how you knew that?"

"I was seeing you through the window. Out with Little Magnus in the snow."

"Of course." Kip felt himself nodding. "The door was open, so I—"

"Do you know who I am?"

As Kip took in breath to speak it placed both of its splay-fingered hands flat against the floorboards and pushed itself upward, the gaunt white body seeming to assemble itself as it straightened, the thin beard catching the firelight, the pale limbs extending, uncurling, resolving themselves into the approximation of a human being. A dark-browed man in early middle age with pocked and sunken cheeks. His left eye scarred and glaucous and his right eye black as coal. When he spoke again his voice was deeper and his English more precise.

"You are American. From the United States."

"Yes."

"You have been a long time coming here. A long travel. You'll have need of a drink."

He gestured toward a low square table all but hidden by a waist-high pile of cordwood. A kerosene lamp sat at its edge—a wire-handled camping lantern from the fifties or the sixties—and as Kip crossed that cramped and sweltering space the man tipped it to one side and held a disposable plastic lighter to its wick. Kip eased himself down onto a stool just as a second wave of vertigo broke over him. The heat was so intense that he'd begun to sweat through the state-of-the-art thermal undershirt he'd bought on his first day in Oslo. It seemed perfectly reasonable that the man across the table from him wore no clothes at all.

"I can offer you *akevitt*." The man took up a long-necked bottle and uncorked it. "Made here, in this same valley. From the sugars of the trees."

Kip managed to thank him. He watched the man pour the honey-colored liquor into a battered metal cup.

"I can offer you this small thing," the man said, extending the cup to him. "By way of thanks."

"Thanks?"

The man said nothing.

"For what?"

"For coming all this way."

"Are you saying—what are you saying, exactly? That makes it sound—"

"Yes?"

"Like you invited me. But that's not true. I didn't come because of you."

"Drink," said the man.

Kip took the cup carefully and tilted it back. The aquavit was raw and bitter.

"Good," said the man. "Now you may tell me why."

"A friend of mine was brought here. An American."

The man let out a long and measured breath. "Little Kira," he said finally.

"You know her?"

That face that seemed incapable of smiling now showed him its teeth. "I knew Kira. When she still went by that name."

"What name does she go by now?"

"Now?" said the man, working the cork back into the bottle. "She has no name now. But you knew this."

Kip clung with both hands to the little tin cup and said nothing. In that moment when anger was what he most needed, anger and the impunity it offered, the door to the White Room remained closed to him. Fear had always been the passkey, the catalyst, but as he sat in that dark narrow room with the man's terrible eyes crawling over him like flies on a cadaver even the fear he felt refused to do his bidding. There was suddenly too much of it and not enough of him.

"I want—"

"Yes. Tell me what you want."

"I want to know what happened to Kira. What you did to her."

"Strong talk," the man said. He put down the bottle. "Strong talk for an American lost in the woods. In another man's house. With barely enough breath in him to speak."

"You asked why I came," Kip croaked. "You asked and I told you."

"This you did." The man regarded him over the lantern's bell with something like affection. "But nothing I say in return will give you what you came for." He cocked his head in an oddly birdlike gesture. "If you know anything about this place, about me . . ." His voice trailed away. He pushed the hair back from his face, then adjusted the flame of the lantern, and by its glow Kip could see that the scar that had blinded his left eye ran up into his hairline. He pursed his lips and ran three hook-nailed fingers through his beard.

"You come here looking for your friend, as you say. Your friend once called Kira. And you imagine in your youth and righteous feeling that you are the first to have come here—the first to venture alone and defenseless into this country. Into this forest. But you are not the first. Many others have done so. They have come to this forest, to this house, to this room. They have sat at my table, these others who came. They have looked at me boldly and made their demands." He brought his palms together. "Tomorrow one will come, and the next day, and the next. And I will be here to receive them. Do you see?"

Kip stared down at the table. At his two hands with the empty cup between them.

"You're warning me off," he said.

The man shook his head regretfully. "I have no Kira for you."

"You can tell me what happened. That's all I'm asking. Tell me that one thing and I'll go home."

The man sat forward and rapped three times on the tabletop, resoundingly and sharply, like someone knocking at a door. "You want to bargain with me now. To strike a deal, as one might do with a devil. A devil in a fairy story." He took the cup out of Kip's hands and set it down beside the bottle. "But to bargain one must have something to exchange. Is this not so? And what you are offering is the gift of your departure." He looked away from Kip now, past the cordwood and the cookstove, into the twilit space beyond. "Do you understand me, friend? Your offer has no value."

Kip kept silent a moment. "Why is that?"

"Because you are already gone."

Some small sound made Kip glance over his shoulder. A second man stood just inside the doorway. It was the dull-eyed Norwegian he and Kira had met at the show in Berlin—the one whose picture he'd been shown by Mothersbaugh and Calkins, long ago and on the far side of the world. He heard himself saying the man's name aloud.

"Per Ivar was once," said Nameless.

The clothes Lund wore clung awkwardly to his body, as though he'd taken them from someone smaller, and the collar of his shirt was oddly creased. After a moment Kip realized it was a blouse. The man at the table made a fluttering gesture, some unspoken command, and Lund shambled forward like a golem and guided Kip upward. The stool he'd been sitting on fell to one side and he almost fell with it. His body felt leaden. He asked himself as he clutched at Lund's arm whether the aquavit could have been drugged or even poisoned but he knew that the man who had poured it had no need to do him harm. He'd been tested and found wanting. He'd shown himself to be a coward. He knew this and knew also that his failure was the only reason he was still alive.

Lund took him by the elbow and guided him out mutely through those reeking mildewed rooms. He put up no resistance. At the screen door Lund released him and stood gazing out at nothing as he faltered down the steps. The cold hit him like buckshot. It brought tears to his eyes and he sucked in a burning lungful and felt grateful for the shock. It was daylight now, or something close to daylight, but he saw no trace of Haugan. All was still.

He was halfway across the clearing before he looked back at the house. The shuttered windows. The weathered clapboard. The three inexplicably steep steps leading up to the door. He watched it a long time, ignoring his fear, attempting to get something clear in his mind. Then he came to his senses and made for the trees.

14

It took Kip the better part of the morning to find his way out to the road.
The car was exactly as Haugan had left it, unlocked with the keys in
plain sight on the dash, which would have astonished him if he'd had
any reserves of astonishment left. Instead he adjusted the mirror and
started the engine and drove down out of the hills and called Leslie
from the first pay phone he saw.

Hampus the bellhop answered on the second ring, courteous as
ever, but as soon as he realized who it was his voice went flat and hostile. It took four full minutes of groveling to convince him to put the
call through. Kip had never been happier to hear Leslie's world-weary
drawl.

"What."

"Leslie! Jesus Christ, man—I'm so sorry. You're all right? Nothing
broken?"

No answer. If not for the buzzing down the line he'd have thought
the connection was dead. He closed his eyes and did his utmost to be
patient.

"I know you're pissed off but please listen. I'm at a rest stop north of
Bergen and I'm running out of quarters. I don't have time—"

"No quarters."

"What?"

"This is Norway. The currency here is the krone."

"Will you just—I need you to shut up for a second. Can you do that? I'm trying to ask—"

"For my help?"

Kip cursed under his breath.

"I didn't quite catch that."

"Yes, Leslie. For your help. Of course for your help. Now if you could just—"

"I'll tell you what, Norvald. Whatever shitcake you've baked for yourself this time you can go ahead and eat it. Hampus says I shouldn't see you anymore."

He counted slowly down from ten. "*Hampus* says?"

"I'd be very careful about the next thing you say to me. Make sure it connects."

"All right."

"I'm listening."

"I found her."

The silence this time was so profound that not even the buzzing on the line could reassure him.

"Z?"

A faraway clicking. A faint play of voices. He had two ten-øre coins left.

"Don't fuck with me, Leslie. Not now. I don't think I could stand it."

The clicking again. "Norvald? Are you still there?"

"Fuck *yes* I'm still here. Are you coming?"

Twelve hours later he was standing on the Bergensbanen platform, the same one he'd lugged Grishnackh's duffel down the night before, watching the evening train from Oslo rolling in. It was crowded this time, full of weekenders and long-haul commuters, but Leslie was impossible to miss. His lips were badly swollen and his head was swathed in so much gauze that he looked like the survivor of an earthquake. Kip couldn't shake the suspicion, watching Leslie drag toward him, that the bandages were mostly for effect. But he felt gutted all the same.

"Norvald of the North."

"Leslie." Kip cleared his throat. "Thank you."

"Where is she?"

"An hour from here. There's a house in the woods." He hesitated. "I'm actually not sure I can do it justice."

"How many people are we talking?"

"Two that I saw. Maybe three. I'm not sure."

"It's good to be sure about this sort of thing, Kip. It's good to have the details very clear."

"I'll explain in the car."

They sat in Haugan's hatchback looking out at the foot traffic along Bryggen while Kip recounted everything as simply as he could. He tried to tell it soberly and plainly but a great deal of what he was saying sounded incredible even to him. When he reached the point in his narrative at which he stood watching the man known as Nameless stoking a fire with human hair he held his breath a moment, waiting for some kind of reaction, but Leslie just looked thoughtful. When he'd finished they stared through the windshield in silence. Neither of them mentioned Leslie's threat to call the cops.

"So let me get this straight. You never saw her."

"She's in there, Z. She's got to be."

"Her body, maybe."

"He wanted me gone. He couldn't get me out fast enough. I don't think I was in that house for more than fifteen minutes."

"Fifteen minutes? Really?"

"Maybe twenty." Kip passed a hand over his face. "I'm not a hundred percent on that."

"I'll add that to the list."

"What list?"

"The list of shit you're not a hundred percent on," Leslie said. He drummed the fingers of his right hand against the dashboard for a while, humming the first few bars of "Raining Blood" under his breath. Then he asked what Haugan's other keys were for.

In the hour they spent searching Haugan's apartment they found eighteen things that Leslie claimed were sure to come in handy. He worked from back to front, proceeding systematically, and appeared to be ticking items off a mental list. Kip just hung back and watched him. He gave every impression of having a plan.

The bathroom yielded a sealed first-aid kit, a thermos, a blanket with one metallic side for combatting hypothermia, two flashlights, and a roll of plumber's tape. In a closet off the hallway they found an internal-frame backpack and three knitted ski masks and a bowie knife with a nine-inch clip point blade. The fridge held nothing but beer and a half-full jar of some kind of colorless porridge that Leslie immediately ate. In an aluminum attaché case under Haugan's fastidiously made bed they found a flare gun and a dozen copper flares.

"That thing looks kind of heavy."

Leslie took it out and hefted it. "It's heavy as shit."

"Are we taking it?"

"Of course we're taking it," said Leslie, flashing Kip a ghastly blue-lipped grin. "What if we should find ourselves lost in the woods?"

By midnight they were back in the car and in less than an hour they were standing in the shadow of the viaduct. A train crossed above them, heavy and swaying, dropping ice onto the asphalt with a sound like beaten chimes. Leslie squinted at Kip doubtfully as he started down the trail.

"This is it?"

"This is it."

"Looks more like a place where people pull over to piss."

"Wait in the car if you want. I'll be back in six hours."

In place of an answer Leslie passed him on his spidery legs and loped into the woods. With the pack on his back and his round bandaged head he looked like an astronaut on some underfunded spacewalk. The beam of his flashlight gamboled crazily across the frozen ground.

"There's something I should tell you. I meant to do it at the station."

"Me too, Leslie. What happened at the shop—"

"I love you, Kip. I always have. Nothing's ever going to change that."

Kip hesitated. He couldn't see Leslie's face. "Sure," he heard himself murmur. That hadn't been what he'd meant to say at all.

"But this is it for me. I'm done after today."

"Done with what? With everything?"

For once Leslie seemed to have nothing to say.

"I've got to hand it to you, Z. You picked the worst possible moment to dump me."

"Just so you know." His voice was flat. "This here is our last go-round."

For three quarters of an hour they said almost nothing. More snow had fallen, obscuring the tracks Kip had made, and the going was even more laborious than it had been at dawn. By the time they'd reached the hanging valley the beams of their flashlights were starting to dim. They stopped and drank black tea from Haugan's thermos and chewed on some powdery muesli that Kip doled out sparingly from a crumpled paper bag. Leslie ate it with his eyes shut and his back against a tree.

"You all right?"

"Never better."

"That's not what I'm seeing."

"I guess this is getting real for me all of a sudden."

"Wait here. I'm serious. If I'm not back by sunup you can head to the car."

Leslie coughed quietly into his sleeve. "And then what?"

"Call down an air strike. Start a boy band. Run for president."

"Get a grip on yourself, Norvald. They'll never elect a Black man president."

Kip felt himself grinning. "Your ticket's still good. Back to Tampa, I mean. It's open-ended."

"You keep saying that." Leslie hummed to himself, quietly chewing his muesli, running the beam of his flashlight off into the woods.

"Weird," he said finally.

"What's weird?"

"This isn't where I thought my love of rock 'n' roll was going to take me."

"I was thinking the same thing."

The expression on Leslie's face as he met Kip's eyes was suddenly stripped of everything but tenderness. He leaned forward until their foreheads nearly met.

"I guess maybe we'll die here."

Kip looked down at the ground. "Maybe so."

A wind had come up, damp and fitful, and suddenly it was too cold not to move. Leslie swallowed and nodded and took up his pack.

"Where are you thinking they've got her?"

"In that house somewhere, that's all I know. Some other room. The attic."

"Remind me again why you're so sure."

"Something about what Nameless said."

"What did he say?"

"I don't know. I can't explain it. Maybe just the way he looked at me."

He'd thought Leslie might freak out or break into hysterical laughter but he took it serenely. "How much longer?"

"An hour the way we're going. Maybe a bit more."

"You still have that bag Grishnackh gave you? The berserker caps?"

"They're just a bunch of dried-up toadstools, Leslie."

"Let me see."

With a sense of foreboding Kip handed them over. Leslie's tired eyes brightened.

"Seems a pity to waste these."

"Put them away, Z. We're about to—"
"Fight fire with fire, motherfucker."

It was five in the morning when they turned onto the footpath, all but invisible now, and six before the house came into view. They knelt behind a fallen spruce at the edge of the clearing and covered themselves in Haugan's thermal blanket. After an hour they'd seen nothing. It was colder than it had been the night before, the sky through the branches resplendent with stars, and Kip could feel the heat of his body being sucked up into space. When the cold grew unbearable he pulled off the blanket and got to his feet. Leslie caught him quickly by the wrist.

"Not yet, Norvald."

"What are we waiting for?"

He looked pleased with himself. "You know what."

"I'll confess something to you. I don't have a clue."

"For those caps to kick in."

Kip slid back down and clenched his jaw to keep his teeth from chattering. Dawn was mustering to the southeast as he studied Leslie's face. No sweating, no flushed cheeks, no shortness of breath. Never in Kip's memory had he looked less like a berserker.

"How much longer are you figuring to—"

Leslie hushed him with a gesture. "Something's happening," he whispered.

First out the door was none other than Haugan, his right hand in a sling, his left holding what looked in that low light to be a club or a blackjack but might as easily have been the handle of a shovel. Lund was close on his heels, cadaverish as ever, and behind him came a girl with a shorn brown head who looked enough like Kira that Kip would have shouted her name if Leslie hadn't stopped him. When she stepped onto the snow she gave a bright squeal of panic or perhaps of delight that carried across the open ground as clearly as a bell. It wasn't Kira. For some reason Kip felt thankful.

The man known as Nameless appeared in that instant, as if her cry had invoked him, dressed in loose-fitting clothes and what looked from that distance to be a cape made from the tanned hide of a deer. He pulled the screen door shut behind him and came down the steps un-hurriedly and led the group along the clearing's edge and off into the trees. Kip turned slowly back to Leslie and allowed himself to breathe.

"Where do you think they're headed?"

"I'll tell you something, Norvald. I don't even want to guess."

Kip took a sip from the thermos. "They had pretty big packs on."

"I noticed that too."

"Which probably means we've got some time to work with."

"It might."

Kip looked back and forth between the treeline and the dark and si-lent house. A wisp of smoke rose blue and quavering from the stovepipe in the chimney. He sat back on his heels and waited. Far away an owl was calling. Leslie's breathing had gone shallow and his eyes had fallen closed.

"Not yet," he said again. "Not yet."

"It's time to go, Leslie."

Leslie shuddered and pressed his cheek against the rough bark of the spruce. He was starting to sweat. "This is not a good place, Norvald."

"And you needed to get high to figure that out?"

Leslie opened his eyes wide. A wind stirred the treetops. "All right, Kip," he murmured. "I'm ready."

"I'll be honest with you, Leslie. You don't look it."

"Just waiting on you."

They opened the pack and took out the ski masks and the bowie knife and a box of wooden matches. Leslie couldn't get his mask on over his bandages so Kip left his off too. He couldn't remember what they'd wanted them for. To give themselves false courage, he supposed. To ren-der themselves anonymous and therefore terrifying. His flashlight was dead so he rummaged in the bottom of the pack until he found the nub end of some sort of scented candle. As he did so the absurdity of what they were attempting broke over him and he spent a precious minute tamping down a premonition of impending doom. Eventually it ebbed and he closed the pack and stowed it under the spruce and hummed the opening riff of *Ride the Lightning* until he started to feel better. He was already on his feet when it dawned on him that something had gone badly wrong with Leslie. He didn't have to think too hard to guess what it might be.

"Jesus Christ. I don't believe this."

"I'll be along in a minute."

"We don't have a fucking minute."

"I just need to throw up."

Leslie rolled over with a sigh and pressed his face into the snow. Kip stared down at the spectacle playing itself out before him, making no effort to keep out of sight anymore, feeling the passage of each second like a small electric shock. He draped the blanket over Leslie's back and told him to keep quiet. Then he crossed the little clearing to the house.

The air inside was colder now but somehow no less stifling. He passed through the first of the low-ceilinged rooms, stopped a moment to listen, then lit his candle and went on into the next. The workbench, the bookcase, the slate mantelpiece. The dead man mummified and straightbacked in the corner. He moved forward lightly and kept his mind quiet. The house smelled of bedclothes. He heard nothing but the groaning of its timbers as they cooled.

He knew before he reached it that the last room would be empty. The blackened draw-hatch of the stove hung limply open and the lamp lay overturned against the wall. He stood in the doorway, watching the pre-dawn light push weakly through the single soot-streaked window, listening to the walls contract around him. Soon even what trace heat remained would dwindle away to nothing and the room fall into ruin. He righted the lamp and lit its wick and set it on the table. He held a palm to the window and felt the weather sucking softly at the glass. A sense of calm came over him. A sense of certainty. He understood that the house had been abandoned and that he had come too late.

Over the next hour he searched each room thoroughly, painstakingly, using the lantern until it was fully day. At some point he found himself back in the scullery, watching his breath condensing in the deepening cold, no wiser than he'd been when he began. He crossed the floor in his heavy winter boots and kicked the painted stool aside and pulled the bottle's cork and took a drink. He sat for a while on the low wooden table, still cradling the bottle, his mind chilled and blank. Time to see about Leslie. He was turning to leave when something caught at his heel. He bent stiffly over to see what it was.

A flat loop of canvas, no wider than a ribbon, sticking out between the floorboards where the little stool had been.

He pulled the table clear like someone rising out of an enchantment and by the time he'd gotten the trapdoor open the room felt as hot and airless as it had the night before. By the light of the lantern he saw four tarpapered steps descending into a crawl space barely wider than his shoulders. Even from where he stood he could tell that it ran past the end of the house. He lit the brass lighter he'd stolen from Grishnackh and went down the steps before he'd had the chance to think.

The height of the crawl space was less than a meter and he dropped the lighter twice as he compelled his body forward. He felt himself panting. He came to a corrugated livestock gate with a deadbolt that slid effortlessly open. Beyond the gate four more steps led down into a crudely excavated chamber with dark slanting walls that smelled sweetly of earth. A few thin rays of daylight cut into the blackness from hairline cracks along the ceiling and by their light he began to make out the contours of a mattress and a heap of rumpled bedding. It was too much for him suddenly and he sank to his knees. The ground beneath him was muddy and the air was dense with noises and with smells he had no name for. Among the bedding lay heaps of cast-off clothing carelessly arranged and as his eyes adjusted to the darkness some of them began to move.

He knelt there and watched them and felt the room tipping. He watched them take the form of human bodies. The smells he had no name for crept like smoke across the ceiling. He was not where he was.

He was not seeing what he was seeing. A low voice asked him in Norwegian what was going to happen now.

"Nothing. *Ingenting.*" He reached behind him for the deadbolt. *"Jeg ser—"*

A second voice came from close beside him, lisping and uncertain. "Kip?"

He fumbled for the lighter and held it out in front of him and saw an apparition rising with its hands pressed to the wall. Matted hair and blackened fingers. Dark mouth hanging strangely open. His own voice when he answered was no louder than a sigh.

"Kira," he said.

She came toward him with the earthen wall to guide her. So haltingly. So slowly. She still seemed not to see him. Her lips were opening and closing and he strained to catch the words.

"Kip for god's sake listen to me Kip for god's sake run away."

He took her in his arms until that awful lisping stopped. Her forehead dug into his chest below his collarbone and even as he told her she was safe tears came to his eyes and he knew that he was holding her so as not to see her face. Other bodies moved behind her and he saw them all too clearly. An old man and a young man and a woman cowering naked. Patterns had been cut into them and allowed to heal and then opened again and as the flickering light played over them he saw that they were runes. The boy clawed at the floor around him, jerking his head from side to side as if beset by flies. The old man made a shooing-away motion, insistent and angry, as though the gate and the steps were a nuisance to him. The fingers of both his hands had been sheared off at the knuckles and what remained looked like nothing so much as the flippers of some great cave-dwelling fish. Kip held tightly to Kira and shut out the rest. He was not where he was. He'd begun to unbutton his parka with the idea of draping it over her shoulders when the woman turned her scarred face toward the door and started shrieking.

"All right, Kira. All right now," he said faintly. "Time to go."

He took in a deep breath and looked at her face. Her jaw was badly bruised and swollen and her four front teeth were gone but he saw no sign that she'd been disfigured like the rest. He repeated that they had to go and asked if she could hear him. He told her to nod if she understood what he was saying and she didn't nod but he could see she'd understood. He guided her up the steps into the crawl space without looking at the people on the floor. The woman was still shrieking and it seemed to him as they moved with excruciating slowness through that suffocating burrow that he'd never heard a louder sound in all his life. It seemed to shake the crawl space and the house over their heads. It seemed to shake the floor above them but in fact the floor was shaking from the steps of running men.

"Please Kip please go Kip he's coming."

He gripped her by the shoulders and pushed past her to the hatch. He saw light in the scullery and a brief play of shadows as a boot came to rest on the topmost of the four tarpapered steps. Kira was begging him in her ravaged voice to leave her as he pulled the bowie knife from its sheath and brought it down in a wild erratic arc through the toe of the boot into the rotten wood beneath. Blood shot up the blade in a ludicrous soda-fountain gurgle and the knife slipped from his fingers as he tried to pull it free. He forced his way past Lund, who stood fixed grotesquely in place like a horse on a carousel, and got out just in time to see Haugan coming through the doorway with a double-barreled shotgun in the crook of his good arm. He reached out while Haugan was still pivoting and caught hold of the barrel and felt its recoil as the windowpane behind him disappeared. For an instant the blast drowned out even the shrieking. Haugan stood blinking down at the gun as if it might belong to someone else and Kip reared back with the last of his strength and drove his forehead into Haugan's face an inch below the eyes.

Haugan dropped like a dead man and Kip found himself holding the gun by its muzzle. He took it by the stock and broke it open. The ringing in his ears was deafening. Beyond the hole in the wall where the window had been the boughs of a spruce tree hung glittering in the morning light like cut-glass chandeliers. He felt at home in his fear now. He felt almost peaceful. Nothing mattered but Kira.

He was turning to call down to her when a bolt of ice passed through him and he crumpled to the floor. There was no pain but his arms and legs were useless. The room had gone quiet. Pain was coming but it hadn't found him yet. When at last he managed to roll onto his back he saw the gun in the hands of the shorn-headed girl and his first thought was that she had somehow shot him. It occurred to him to wonder dimly why he wasn't bleeding. Then a subtle movement caught his eye and he looked up to find Nameless high above him like an angel carved in wax.

The girl was shouting something as she levered the spent shells out of the shotgun but Nameless hushed her with a gesture. He was studying Kip closely. There was no anger in his expression but there was interest, curiosity, perhaps even surprise. He lowered himself into an elegant crouch, the rest of him preternaturally still, his pockmarked face a hand's width from Kip's own. Whatever he saw there seemed to gratify him. He took his tongue in his teeth and reached down languorously and pulled Kip's shirtfront open. With a curving birdlike fingernail he traced a figure there. He brought the weight of his torso down until the nail's point broke the skin.

Kip's mouth opened and something slipped into the air. Not a sound or a breath. Some small part of himself. Perhaps no more than an idea.

As if in answer a chemical light flooded the room and the whole house quaked and shivered in its glow. It amazed even Nameless. The girl raised the shotgun just as the light went strange again. Kip heard nothing at all but he felt the floor tremble. Nameless rose unwillingly, gesturing toward the shattered window, and as Kip watched him yelling at the girl the ringing slowly faded. He heard rustling under the floorboards and the girl's frightened curses and the sound of doors slamming or being forced open. He heard a high baleful whistling like something out of a war film and a voice that could only have been Leslie's yodeling obscenities behind it. It seemed to be coming from all sides at once. He pushed himself up onto his elbows just in time to witness Leslie dancing crazily past the hole where the window had been, his shirt unbuttoned and his pants around his ankles, waving the flare gun in drunken circles like a noisemaker on New Year's Eve. He fired again and missed the house completely. Then he was gone like a dream or a trick of the light and the scullery began to fill with smoke.

Nameless still loomed high above him staring out at the trees but now Kip's thoughts and fears were far away. The girl had vanished and he knew that she'd gone to kill Leslie. He shut his eyes and tried to move his feet inside his heavy boots but he felt nothing. He wondered how much time the girl would need. He was listening for the shot when Nameless reached a pale arm down to take him by the hair.

"*Espen,*" someone said or seemed to say.

Kip tipped his head back to see Kira there crying. She stood slumped to one side with the daylight behind her, her bare shoulders spasming, staring up at Nameless as though asking him for mercy. She looked younger in that gilded light than Kip had ever seen her. She looked like Kira Carson's long-lost child.

"Espen."

The kerosene lantern dangled from her left hand, dragging uselessly behind her, rattling across the pitted floor as she came forward. "Espen," she repeated. A man's name or some form of incantation. Her body was shaking and her swollen filthy face was slick with tears. The man to whom she'd spoken held his arms out to receive her. She whimpered and nodded. Her right foot turned inward. She stepped toward him almost shyly as her arm transcribed a hissing arc and robed the man in fire.

Kira didn't speak again until the house was far behind them. The day came up clear, as the night sky had promised, and for nearly an hour they could make out a column of bone-colored smoke suspended in the bright air like the spire of a church.

As soon as they'd gotten outside Kip had wrapped her in his parka and the silvered blanket and told her to wait for him at the treeline while he went to look for Leslie. She'd stood where he left her and watched the house burning. Ten minutes later a shot had rung out and he'd come racing back to find her sitting on the frozen ground, humming a Mercyful Fate riff to give herself courage, lacing up a pair of boots she'd gotten god knows where. Another shot carried to them then, no louder than a snapping twig. There was no need to tell her to hurry. The boots were too large and she had trouble at first, stumbling every few yards, but by the time they reached the first pond she was well ahead of him. The walking seemed to do her good. The sun had kept the tracks clear and he thanked the Aesir for their benevolence with every step he took.

At the second pond they found Leslie waiting for them, or for the girl with the shotgun, or for enemies that only he could see. His pants were in tatters and the right sleeve of his parka had been torn away and he lay flat on his back, oblivious to the wet snow, mumbling amicable curses at the sky. They sat him up and poured the last of the tea from Haugan's thermos down his throat and eventually prevailed on him to get up off the ground. Only when he stood did Kip see that his right hand was black with buckshot and the outermost two fingers had been blasted clear away.

The bleeding had lessened by then and Kip cleaned the wound ineptly and wrapped it in gauze from the first-aid kit and taped the whole mess straight to Leslie's chest, just below his collarbone, taking great care that the wounded hand be higher than his heart. He tried not to think beyond the steps required to get Leslie to the car.

"Look at me, Z. I'm talking to you. Look right here at me."

"I can see you in any direction, Norvald. You get what I'm saying? It doesn't matter where I turn my head."

"That's fine. Can you walk? Are you in too much pain?"

"Leslie Z is in pain. A whole shitload of pain. My point here is that I'm not Leslie Z."

"Lucky you," murmured Kira.

Kip glanced at her. Her eyes were restless and unfocused in her slack and soot-marked face. He turned back to Leslie.

"All right, whoever you are. I'm just letting you know that I'm taking my friend Leslie back to Bergen. You can come or you can stay. It's up to you."

Leslie shook his head reflectively, still staring at the sky.

"Might as well," he said at last.

They reached the car in two hours, greatly aided by the weather, and stowed Leslie gingerly in the back seat. He passed out within seconds. The Volkswagen started at once, as if it had just rolled off the assembly line, and the road lay clear and steaming in the sun.

"Kip?"

"It's all right."

"What's happening?"

"It's all right."

"Are you crying?"

He fully intended to give her an answer but he brought his forehead down against the steering wheel instead and let his arms go limp and shut his eyes. He heard or thought he heard her start to speak, then stop herself, then take a small quick breath to try again. But she didn't speak. She shifted her weight in the passenger seat and after what was almost certainly a very long time he felt her nail-bitten calloused fingers moving gently through his hair.

"We're not moving," said Leslie. "Norvald? Kira?"

"Right here."

"How come we're not moving?"

Kip sat upright again and put the car into gear and pulled out onto the roadway. Not a single car had passed them. Kira's fingers rested lightly on his nape.

"Forward motion. Forward motion."

"We're moving now," Kip told him. "Can't you feel it?"

Leslie muttered something unintelligible.

"Hang in there, Z. Lie back down. You're all right."

"I'll tell you kids something. You two shitkicking headbangers."

"We're listening," said Kira.

"I love this fucking country, man. I'm never going home."

VENICE 1996

Oona Alice Cartwright died in her sleep four years later, of congestive heart failure, and services were held in the "children's chapel" of her brand-new megachurch in downtown Venice. The chapel featured a rainbow-colored pulpit and towering bouquets of white nylon lilies and curlicues of glitter mixed into the epoxy of the floor. It wasn't much bigger than a suburban living room—but it was more than spacious enough to accommodate the handful of people Kip had seen fit to invite. He hadn't even let her church group know.

Kira was living in Port Charlotte, fifteen minutes away, so he was only mildly surprised to catch sight of her in the last pew on the left. What astonished him was Leslie. In classic Vogler style he sashayed in at the last possible instant, decked out in what he liked to call his "European look"—an ivory cashmere turtleneck, silver cigarette pants, snow-white buckskin loafers, and a blazer of some impossibly expensive-looking fabric louchely draped about his shoulders. The rest of the mourners might as well have been attired in paper bags.

Kip's eulogy went marginally better than he'd expected: he put the room to sleep, in other words, but at least he didn't blurt out anything idiotic or obscene. When he was halfway through he stole a glance at Kira. It always did him good to look at her.

She was wearing a pleated gray silk dress and two-inch heels, persuasive straight-world camouflage: he might have walked right past her in a crowd. These days her hair was a warm, weathered bronze, not unlike when he'd first seen her—only this time it had been colored by a professional, not dunked in cheap black drugstore dye that turned red in the sun. She looked healthy, at home in her own skin, beautiful in a strictly conventional sense. All these things made Kip happy. She was staring at something above or behind him—the faux-stained-glass window, most likely, on which a suntanned Saint George did battle with a pale and pudgy dragon—and doing her damnedest to keep a straight face. Leslie was standing directly behind her, restless as a grade schooler at morning assembly. He was stick-insect Leslie again, all kneecaps and elbows. Seeing the two of them together after so much time was like a drug experience. Kip was entering the home stretch and thanking god for it when he saw Kira reach casually over her shoulder, as though it were the most natural thing in the world, and take one of Leslie's hands in both of hers.

After the ghoulish reception in the church's Italianate foyer the three of them bought a twelve-pack at the BusyBee's and headed out to Caspersen Beach to catch what was left of the sunset. Kira had inherited her father's red Datsun four-by—the same one she'd painted the mural on back in high school—but its rickety plywood trailer had long since gone the way of the family dog-grooming business. Kip didn't ask her how she was making a living now and neither did Leslie. She seemed to prefer it that way.

"I was going to ask you about L.A.," she said. "But I'll be honest with you, Kip. I don't really want to know."

"L.A.'s always the same. You're not missing a thing."

"I'm not sure that's what the lady means," said Leslie. "Hard as it might be for certain overpaid hacks among us to believe." He gave Kira a wink.

"Someone *else* is doing all right for themselves, seems like," Kira said, looking Leslie up and down. "I'm not going to say who. I'm opting not to specify."

They were walking with their shoes off, shoulder to shoulder like a hair metal band at a photo shoot, along the curving spit of sand where they used to hunt for sharks' teeth and pass Kira's Walkman around and get high. Leslie was in the middle, taking his customary daddy-long-legs strides, and as usual Kip was struggling to keep up. He couldn't remember ever having seen such pride in Kira's eyes. On another day he might have felt resentful.

"The restaurant is kicking ass," Leslie said with standard Vogler modesty. "It's a kroner-printing factory, basically. We're officially the place to be seen."

"Of course you are."

"And just to be clear, what I mean by that is: the place to be seen spending way too much money on *kukevufler*."

Kira shook her head fondly.

"We're looking into opening a second location, if you can believe it. Maybe over in Bergen."

"Let's have a look at that hand," Kip said, catching him by the wrist. Leslie seemed not to mind. "Hampus calls it 'the claw.'"

"Looks pretty damn good, if you ask me. Considering how it looked when I left Oslo."

"Yet another miracle of socialized medicine," said Kira.

"Hampus says it's for the best." Leslie shrugged. "Two less fingers for me to chop off in the kitchen."

"Would you stop talking about Hampus all the time? It's getting boring."

"I couldn't agree more," said Kip. "I'm going into sugar shock."

"You all are just jealous," said Leslie. Then he caught himself. "Sorry—that's the jet lag talking. I didn't mean—"

"It's all right," said Kip, smiling past him at Kira. "We can take it."

"I'm kind of savoring this moment, actually," she said. "Go ahead and stay embarrassed for a while."

"Well, shit." Leslie shaded his eyes and looked off down the beach. "We're halfway to the point already. I remember this thing being longer."

"It was definitely longer."

"Maybe they shortened it. To make it easier on the cops."

"I'm pretty sure the cops have Jet Skis now."

A lazy silence fell. As far as Kip was concerned it could have lasted the rest of his life. They passed a blackened fire barrel, then an old man with a metal detector, then three teenagers sheltering from the wind in the lee of an overturned boat.

"I hope those kids are getting stoned," Leslie said to no one in particular. "I'll be downright disappointed if they aren't."

"You ought to be ashamed of yourself."

"You all had best be getting *flamed*," Leslie shouted. One of them flipped him off. He clutched his chest at that and faked a swoon.

"They've got nothing better to do," said Leslie. "Like us back in the day. It's enough to warm an old man's cockles."

"Let's keep your cockles out of this," said Kira.

At the end of the point they spread out a bedsheet and opened three cans of Miller High Life and Leslie stretched himself out like a hound and fell asleep. Kip and Kira sat cross-legged on either side of him, idly sipping their beers, staring out at the ocean like a pair of retirees. Which in a certain sense, Kip realized, they were.

"I was hoping you'd show," he said after a while. "A little nervous too, maybe. But mostly—you know. The other thing."

"Nervous about what?" She smiled at him. "That I'd still be as fucked up as last time?"

"You weren't fucked up last time. Cut yourself some slack, for Christ's sake. You were already a hundred times better."

She shrugged and said nothing.

"It's been a year, Kira. Almost a year."

"It's been eleven months."

He watched her. "I won't deny I've been wondering—"

"I'm doing better. You said so. Let's leave it right there."

Leslie grunted as if in agreement. The man with the metal detector wandered by, up to his kneecaps in the Gulf, sneaking glances at Kira. It was just like old times.

"It's good for you," Kip said suddenly.

"What is?"

"Being back in Venice. I wouldn't have believed it. But it's good."

"No fussing, Norvald. You promised."

"I'm making what normal folks call conversation. I'm not asking for specifics. I'm showing restraint."

A tide wind had come up, salt-smelling and damp. Kira tucked a lock of hair behind her ear, using just her ring finger, the way only she did it. Her makeup hid the scar along her hairline.

"I'm liking it about as much as I ever like anything."

"Bullshit," he said. "You're happy. I can tell."

She'd already turned to contradict him and he saw clearly when the change came over her. A relinquishing of something.

"It's true."

"What is?"

She smiled at him again. "That you can tell."

They said nothing else for a very long time. The big Gulf Coast sunset came garishly down. It always made Kip think of the lowering of a curtain: in a strip club, maybe, or in some kind of offshore casino. Kira glanced at him and took a swig of beer.

"Norvald," she said.

"Present."

"Remember when Ray half killed himself falling off the roof of Gunner Burton's Wagoneer? Remember when you ran off to get help?"

"Of course I remember."

She nodded to herself. "When you went and did that, I kind of— I don't know. Thought about you for the first time." She tipped back her High Life. "As a person, I mean."

"I guess that makes sense."

"You know what I thought?"

"Not a clue."

"I thought: Kip Norvald is still just a dumb goofy kid. But eventually— soon—he'll turn into a man." She took another swig. "The good kind. And I think I'd like to be there when that happens."

"You never told me that."

"That's part of why I feel all right today." She gave a shrug. "To know I wasn't wrong."

"That's the reason you're happy? You're serious?"

"Other things too, obviously. But that's one of them."

Kip took in a breath. "I said I wasn't going to ask for particulars—"

"Shut up, Kip."

He shut up. The sky just kept on getting pinker.

"Kira Carson?"

They both gave a start. One of the kids from the overturned boat stood behind them, ratty bangs and stoner eyes and sunburn, beaming down at them without a hint of shyness.

"I'm Skyler Davis's kid. That about makes us cousins."

"Jesus Christ."

"I live out the Tamiami, couple miles past the Shoney's—"

"State your business, Skyler Davis junior."

The kid squinted out at the waves. "Nothing. It's just, I've seen you around town—"

"If you're planning to propose," Kip told him, "you should probably get down on one knee."

"It's nothing like that," the kid said, squirming a little. He hesitated. "You drive that old pickup, don't you? That Datsun four-by?"

"Your point, son."

"Well, you've got that old pickup, and—" He glanced back up the beach. "You all got plans tonight?"

They stared up at the kid in disbelief—almost a kind of wonder. His long greasy hair and his acid-wash cutoffs and his tattered faded Morbid Angel T-shirt. ALTARS OF MADNESS TOUR US/CANADA 1987. Squinting with bloodshot sea-green eyes into the sun. The most beautiful sight that they had ever seen.

"I'm just spreading the word," the kid said with a grin. "There's a bonfire out at the Grids."

ACKNOWLEDGMENTS

Jin Auh, Charles Buchan, Eric Chinski, Susan Choi, Johnny Coffin, Kathy Daneman, Joanna Delgado Chiaberto, Matt Dojny, Dan Efram, Nathan Englander, Kelly Farber, Isaac Fitzgerald, Philip Gourevitch, William Hall, Barbara Wünschmann Henderson, Kirk Wallace Johnson, Kirsten Kearse, Alice Sola Kim, Kragen Lum, Larissa MacFarquhar, Giuliana Mayo, Hampus Öhman-Frölund, John Michael Osbourne, Gary Panter, Bernhard Robben, Mariel Roberts, Steve Salett, Leanne Shapton, Tara Sharma, Mona Simpson, Dave Stacey, Leslie Stein, Adrian Tomine, Thomas Überhoff, Kenneth Wachtel, Tara Westover, Elna Baker, Jared Whitham, Andrew Wylie.

A NOTE ABOUT THE AUTHOR

John Wray is the author of six critically acclaimed works of fiction, including *Godsend*, *The Lost Time Accidents*, and *Lowboy*. The recipient of a Whiting Award, a Guggenheim grant, and a Cullman Center Fellowship from the New York Public Library, he was named one of *Granta*'s Best of Young American Novelists in 2007. He lives in New York City.